Pink Wellies and Flat Caps

A romantic comedy by
Lynda Renham

Grateful thanks to Pearl and Michael, and the original Molly, for help with farming research, and to Michelle, for real life inspiration.

ISBN 978-0-9571372-4-0

second edition

Cover Illustration by Gracie Klumpp
www.gracieklumpp.com

Printed for Raucous Publishing in Great Britain by
SRP (Exeter)

Chapter One

Don't you just hate men's timing? Only a man could drop a bombshell on you while you're sitting in a fitting room with your tits hanging out. Not that I spend a great deal of time sitting in fitting rooms with my tits hanging out you understand. My friend Georgie had convinced me that if I am going to buy some new underwear then I really should have a proper bra fitting. It's not like I'm Dolly Parton or anything and I hasten to point out as such.

'Hidden Beauty is *the* place to go when buying a bra. They really know how to fit a woman,' she argues.

'But I really don't need a fitting,' I protest feebly.

'You can't just buy a bra off the peg,' she insists, dragging me into one of the most exclusive lingerie stores in London.
I assure her that I can and that, in fact, on an NHS salary it is all I can afford.

'You're marrying a well-paid advertising executive in a few weeks. Your breasts are important to him. He would want you to take good care of them,' she grins.
Important to him they may be, but in my experience Charlie has been more interested in getting bras off me than seeing me in them. I am also quite sure with his tight budgeting schemes he would, without doubt, balk at the prices in here. As it is he gets all agitated and red in the face if I leave the lights on in the flat. I glance at the tag and try to look nonchalant as I search for a price. Just about everything is printed on this tag, and in about fifty languages. Okay, a slight exaggeration, but how is it that they can get everything on this small piece of card except the price? Hidden Beauty has hidden prices it seems. This does not bode well for yours truly.

'Lovely isn't it?' whispers Georgie as she strokes the lace. 'I bought two of these last year and they were worth every penny.'

'How many pennies exactly?' I whisper, trying not to sound too panicky.

The Enya music in the background is doing nothing to calm my nerves. Between us, Charlie and I had just spent a small fortune on our forthcoming wedding. I really can't afford to be extravagant.

She laughs carelessly.

'About a hundred pounds each. Don't worry. Enjoy your day off.'

Don't worry, is she crazy? Georgie has no concept of money or more to the point, no concept of the lack of it. Georgie has a fantastic job as a fashion buyer for Harvey Nicholls where she is spectacularly overpaid and not in the least overworked. She always looks glamorous and toned. Two mornings she goes to the gym before work, and one evening to Pilates. With her sculptured bone structure and long thick black hair she could be mistaken for a model. Unfortunately, her (enviable) successful life also includes a prick of a boyfriend. That is if you can call him her 'boyfriend' seeing as he is someone else's husband (not enviable). But Georgie is mad about James and there seems little I can do to dissuade her. She is convinced that he will leave his wife any day now, and has thought this for the past year even though I keep telling her he never will. When she is not thinking about James she has her head in a crime novel. In stark contrast I am scandalously underpaid in what must be the most unglamorous job on the planet. I am the deputy practice manager at an NHS doctor's surgery. The truth is I am so shattered in the evenings that I can barely make it to the shower, let alone Pilates, and the only thing I do before work is hyperventilate. My stress levels are so high that I feel sure that just one session at the gym would be fatal. I would give myself a cardiac arrest just by releasing all my pent-up emotions. Even now I can feel the adrenalin rushing through my body, tinging my cheeks pink and brightening my eyes. However, I do have a lovely fiancé and a fairy-tale wedding booked. In just under a month I will be Mrs Charlie Marrow and I cannot wait.

'I can't pay a hundred pounds for a bra. I don't spend that much on my highlights,' I protest and make for the door but Georgie pulls me back to face the assistant who is rushing towards us swinging a tape measure.

After one look at me she grimaces and says,

'Well, already I can see you're wearing the wrong size bra. Just look at how you're hanging.'

Good heavens, what happened to *Good morning madam*? That works better for me than *look at how you're hanging*. I hope they don't greet men with that when they pop into their posh underwear shops. Mind you, a man might be flattered to be told how he is hanging. I'm Alice Lane by the way, thirty-two, living with my successful fiancé, soon to be married and therefore respectable by all accounts, but not hanging at all well apparently. Both Georgie and I look at my tits in a whole new light. Don't you just hate shop assistants who know it all? I've been wearing this bra for years. Is she telling me I have been hanging wrong all that time?

'She has a point,' says Georgie while looking critically at one breast and then the other. 'You're definitely hanging lopsided'.

What does she mean *I'm hanging lopsided*? Surely a bad-fitting bra wouldn't have me hanging lopsided. I feel an overwhelming urge to flee the shop but before I can, the assistant, who introduces herself as Justine, has pulled me into a fitting room. I grab Georgie for support.

'If you really want to focus on bra nirvana it is better to come in alone,' Justine says firmly.

Nirvana or no nirvana there is no way I am going in there alone with Justine, and I'm not sure how I can find any kind of nirvana if I'm going to bare my boobs. With Georgie's encouragement I remove my jumper to reveal the offending bra. Justine tuts knowingly and touches it reluctantly with her finger.

'It's quite saggy and very unsupportive,' she says grimacing.

I hope she is talking about the bra, and not my breast. I feel a desire to defend my saggy unsupportive brassiere but refrain.

'Turn around,' she orders.

I'm beginning to wonder if this is a bra shop or an army barracks. Blimey, she'll be strip-searching me next. I do as I'm told and come face to face with myself in the fitting room mirror. Good God, I actually do look a little lopsided. I'm convinced they do something to the mirrors in these rooms. I am glad to see that everything else looks acceptable and not in the least lopsided. My complexion is clear, glowing in fact, and considering I was dragged out by Georgie before I had time to put my face on I look okay. My blue eyes are bright and shiny and I look altogether healthy. The light in the fitting room brings out my blonde highlights just a little too well though and I can see my roots are well overdue a treatment. Just as well I am having a complete overhaul for the wedding. But apart from hanging a little lopsided I think I look rather good for a thirty-two year old.

'Yes, as I thought. You have it on its tightest setting. No wonder you are hanging so badly.'

'Shame on you,' sniggers Georgie.

'Remove it please.'

Justine whips out her tape measure with great flourish and I jump out of my skin. I reluctantly remove the trusted Marks and Spencer bra and wonder if Justine will find fault with my breasts also. This is all becoming very cringe-worthy, so when my mobile bleeps I am quite relieved. I push my hand into my bag and Justine sighs so loudly that I remove it instantly.

'Arms up.'

Georgie sniggers again and I throw her a dirty look.

'Just as I thought, you've been wearing a 34B while you are actually a 36C.'

Georgie gasps.

'Oh no,' she squeals, 'that's all you need on your wedding day.'

'But I've always worn 34B,' I protest. 'My breasts have been cushioned in a 34B for as long as I can remember.'

Justine scowls.

'And look at the state of them.'

I'm starting to feel like a circus freak. She'll be ordering breast surgery next. All I wanted was a bog-standard bra. Justine disappears with a swish of the fitting room curtain to fetch an armful of 36Cs and I hastily retrieve my mobile. I'm about to read the text message when Justine breezes in again, and in one smooth movement whips the phone out of my hand and throws it into my bag and has my arms in the air before I can say *Playtex*.

'There,' she declares, turning me to face the mirror. 'Look how perfect they hang.'

I take the catalogue she hands me and look at myself admiringly in the mirror.

'You look fab,' smiles Georgie. 'Wait till Charlie sees you in your 36C.'

I'm actually quite impressed. It feels ten times more comfortable. However, after a glance at the prices in the catalogue I feel a little giddy.

'I can't possibly pay *that*,' I stammer.

'You would be mad not to pay it,' responds Georgie in her usual nonchalant fashion.

'There is absolutely nowhere else on earth where a woman should buy her bras, and you must buy two. You have to look good in your wedding dress.'

Buckling under the pressure I pull my credit card from my bag and see my phone flashing with the text message from earlier. The card is snatched from my hand and Justine strides to the cash desk. I follow, clicking into the text message as I do so. It is from Charlie.

'*Alice love, I am so sorry ...*'

Justine's voice pulls my attention away.

'That will be one hundred and thirty pounds madam, and may I say you won't regret a penny of it.'

I hate to tell her that I am already regretting *every* penny of it.

'Well, I may not eat for the next month, but at least I won't be hanging lopsided,' I joke.

There is nothing from the stony-faced Justine except for the immortal words *Please enter your pin madam*. I am given a free pair of G-string undies which, gratefully, Justine doesn't insist on measuring me for. I look at my text as Georgie picks up the bag.

I can't go through with the wedding. I should have told you before. I've left the flat and moved in with Geoff ...'

What! What does he mean he has moved in with Geoff? Good God, my fiancé is a closet homosexual. He's left me for another man. This could only happen to me.

'Where do you want to go for lunch?' chirps Georgie, opening the door and setting off a delicate chime.

'Charlie's gay,' I blurt out, dropping the phone and falling onto the chair outside the fitting rooms and grabbing two tissues from the complimentary box that sits on the table.

I stare at the large sign above the till which reads, *put your breasts in our hands*. I've just spent one hundred and thirty pounds on two new bras after well and truly putting my breasts in their hands, and now Charlie tells me he is gay. He could have told me before I spent all that money. Good heavens, what am I thinking? Does it matter about the bras? Charlie has left me for another man. What will my mother say? What will my friends say? What will the vicar say? What about the wedding and the invitations? How can I tell people that Charlie prefers a man to me? Why couldn't he have left me for another woman? In fact, why did he have to leave me at all?

'What, you're surely not serious?'

Georgie takes the phone and studies the text.

'You mad bitch, you didn't read it all ... Here.'

I grab the phone. Oh thank God.

'He isn't leaving me then?' I ask, relief flooding my body.

'Well, I wouldn't say that exactly.'

What does *that* mean? She pulls a face and gestures to Justine for some water.

... just until we get things sorted out. I promise there isn't another woman but I'm not ready to settle with just one, at least not yet. I know I should have told you before. I'm so not ready for marriage. I'm so sorry Alice, please forgive me. This is the worst way to tell you, I know that. Forgive me. I'll phone you in a few days. Of course you can keep the ring, no question.

The assistant hands me a glass of water and the tears I had been struggling to control burst forth.

'He said I can keep the ring,' I sob.

'Oh well,' says Georgie sarcastically, 'that makes everything okay then.'

'It can be an overwhelming experience when you purchase your first perfect fitted bra,' smiles Justine while handing me another tissue.

'Oh do shut up woman,' snaps Georgie. 'Your bras aren't that bloody fantastic. Her fiancé just ditched her.'

Great, thanks a lot Georgie. I grab two more complimentary tissues and hiccup my way out of Hidden Beauty. All I did was buy a bra and now my life has gone tits up.

Chapter Two

It has been three days since Charlie sent his bombshell text. The new bras are still in their shiny pink bags, along with the freebie knickers. The flat feels odd. Charlie has removed half of his things, the CD rack is depleted and what is left I can't play as he has taken the CD player too. There are wide gaps, like missing teeth, between the books on the little bookshelf. There is just a lonely solitary toothbrush in the bathroom and all his shaving stuff has gone. I still can't believe it. I have had only one other text from him, and that was to tell me he has no intention of paying his half of the rent any more because he can't see the point. This morning I had checked my bank balance and realised that, while I can pay the rent this month, there is no way I will be able to pay it after that. Not if I expect to eat as well.

'You'll be able to find somewhere cheaper,' says Mother, pouring a cup of tea and pushing fruit cake in front of me. 'Chelsea is scandalously overpriced anyway. It's probably all for the best, that's what your Aunt Sylvia said.'

Like I could care what Aunt Sylvia said. If I recall, she was the one who told me she would buy her wedding present from Argos, just in case, because they have their sixteen-day money-back guarantee.

'What about Battersea?' suggests Georgie, lifting her head from her P. D. James novel. 'That's cheap isn't it?'

'Do you want my daughter to get mugged? Isn't it enough she's been jilted?' snaps Mother.

I wish there was some vodka I could slosh into this tea.

'I don't think the dogs' home would have me,' I say, attempting a joke.

Mother enfolds me within her bosom and I feel the tears threaten. Casper, decidedly embarrassed, pulls at the kitchen towel holder.

Casper is my second closest friend, successful record producer, queer as a coot and a hypochondriac to boot. Outrageously camp of course. He lives on a houseboat on the Thames and is totally obsessed with his appearance.

'Here you are dear; it sounds like you're going down with something. Did you have your flu jab? You should have, being as it's free in your job and everything. I've some spare antibiotics somewhere if you need them.'

I accept the kitchen towel gratefully.

'Thanks Cas but I'm fine.'

'His head on a platter is what she needs. What man calls off a wedding this late in the day?' says Mum crossly as she snatches the kitchen towel and replaces it with a soft fragranced tissue.

'Perhaps he is sick,' suggests Casper.

'He's sick in the sodding head all right,' says Georgie.

'I'm sure it is just wedding nerves. Charlie wouldn't deliberately hurt me. He's just got into a panic I expect.'

'Your problem is that you are too damn understanding. I swear you'd be able to see the good in Colonel Gaddafi,' scolds Georgie.

'Well, I don't know about that,' I protest.

At that moment my mobile bleeps with a text from Charlie himself. My heart thumps madly. Oh God, has he changed his mind after all? Has he finally realised he really can't live without me? Oh please God let that be it. Please let me stay in my lovely Chelsea flat with my ever so gorgeous fiancé and my ever so lovely bohemian neighbours. I promise never to complain about the smell of their wacky baccy or incense sticks again. Please don't make me move to Battersea or some other godforsaken part of London where my neighbours will be knife-wielding hoody drug dealers.

'It's from Charlie,' I say breathlessly.

There is a sharp intake of breath from my mother.

'You see, he has probably realised how much he misses you. Men always come to their senses. Isn't that right Casper?'

'I wouldn't know lovely. Anyway, he's not a man, he's a wanker.'

'Why don't we leave Alice to her text,' interrupts Georgie.

I click the message icon and feel my heart sing.

Hi, are you okay? I was wondering if you were free to chat. I tried you at work but they said you were off sick.

He does care for me, thank you God, thank you so much.

'He wants to phone me,' I say, my voice trembling.

'We'll leave you to it,' grins Mother, giving me a thumbs up as she pulls Casper and Georgie out of the room.

My finger hovers over the buttons. I don't want to appear too eager but at the same time I don't want to play too hard to get. I don't want him to know that I took the day off because I was too upset to go into work, but at the same time I don't want him to think that I couldn't care less about the break up. If I don't answer soon he will think I am not interested at all.

I'm fine, just a 24 hour bug. Yes, I'm free to chat. It would be nice to.

I study the text for several seconds and then delete the *It would be nice to.* I finally hit the send button and seconds later my phone shrills with an incoming call. I let it ring twice before answering and try to control the tremor in my voice.

'Hi,' I say, trying to sound upbeat but instead sounding like I have just inhaled a lungful of helium.

'How are things?'

What am I saying? Things are bloody awful. He coughs.

'Erm, yup things are fine. How are things your end?'

I want to say *Shittity awful as it happens. It seems the hall we hired for the wedding reception won't refund our deposit. Broken engagements don't entitle you to a refund. But if one of us dies that is different, so I was thinking of hiring a hit man. Are you okay with that?* But instead I say,

'Yes fine, well apart from this twenty-four hour bug.'

He coughs again. Maybe he has the twenty-four hour bug too.

'I erm, managed to get the rings cancelled, so you don't have to worry about paying for mine. Fortunately they hadn't started on them. That was a bit of luck.'

My stomach does a churn and I feel sick.

'Oh,' is all I manage to say.

There is silence and I'm beginning to wonder if he has hung up when he says very quickly,

'The landlord has someone interested in the flat. I think we should go for it while we can. You won't have to worry about the

9

rent and it will be a weight off my mind. Maybe your parents will let you stay with them until you get sorted?'

So, I'm a heavy weight on his mind now am I?

'It seems a bit premature to give up the flat. I thought we could wait a bit, see how we feel and ...'

What am I saying? I know how I feel. He's the one having some kind of breakdown. Maybe it's an early mid-life crisis and he will change his mind and come to his senses after a while.

'I won't change my mind Alice, if that's what you're hoping.'

'But I don't understand Charlie. It isn't like we've had a row.'

Live with my parents? He may as well send me on a suicide mission. I feel my breath catch in my throat and I know if I try to speak I will just start crying. I must have sniffed loudly as he says gently,

'I'm so sorry Ali, but it's better now than five years into our marriage. You surely agree. Like I said, I am happy for you to keep the engagement ring and for you to do whatever you think fit with it.'

I can hear Georgie and my mother whispering the other side of the door. I blow my nose noisily.

'Thank you so much Charlie ...'

'No it's fine, it's the least I can do ...' he begins.

I can hear the relief in his voice.

'What I'd actually like to do with it ...'

'Anything Ali, you don't have to run it by me. It's yours and ...'

'Is ram it up your arse because this is despicable what you're doing Charlie,' I say, my voice breaking as I click off the phone.

I'm thirty-two. I will soon be homeless as well as fiancé less. Not in the least respectable and to make matters worse, I'm still not hanging all that well. Soon all I will have left is two very expensive designer bras and a well-hung bosom. I think I deserve more.

'Shall I pop out and get some Maltesers?' asks Casper as he peeps around the door.

I nod.

'She's on the Maltesers,' he tells Georgie

'It looks like we're on suicide watch then.'

Thank God for friends.

Chapter Three

'I'm not being funny but I could turn around and say to you at the end of the day that I don't really mean that, do you know what I mean? But I do mean it, like. I'm not being funny, but at the end of the day, it just isn't right is it? My mum said it was disgraceful as it happens.'

I have not the vaguest idea what Karen is talking about, but I nod encouragingly just the same.

'I said to my mum I would talk to you, but you know, I'm not being funny but at the end of the day you're not the real thing are you?'

'I'm not?'

'Well like my mum said, talk to the organ player not the monkey.'

'Organ grinder,' I correct.

What am I doing correcting her? She's insulting me and I'm bloody helping her. It's been a hell of a day. There are only thirty-five minutes left of my lunch break and I had hoped to view some flats with Georgie and Cas. We are sitting in my office. Well that is, I'm sitting. Karen, in an attempt to intimidate me, is standing and leaning across the desk. I find myself unwillingly looking at her breasts and thinking how Justine would have a field day with her.

'Well whatever. At the end of the day it isn't right. Why can't she get off her arse and buy her own sandwich?'

I fight back a sigh.

'The GPs are very busy Karen, and if you were going to the shop anyway ...'

'Yeah, well like my mum says, you're not the practice manager exactly are you. I'm not being funny, but at the end of the day I'd prefer to talk to her about this but as she's on holiday, I can't.'

I'm beginning to wonder if I should ask when the end of the day is, and maybe we can come back and do all this then. At least I will then get to view the property. I've got to be out of my flat in two weeks and I still don't have anywhere to go. Not that I haven't been looking, it's more a case of there isn't much to look at, not in my price range anyway. I rub my eyes, sigh, and attempt to explain that the practice manager doesn't deal with this type of problem. Oh no, yours truly deals with this kind of crap, when out of the blue Karen says,

'Are you okay? I'm not being funny but you look like shit if you don't mind me saying.'

I want to tell her that I don't find her in the least bit funny, and that I do mind her saying. Bloody hell, I need Maltesers. I reach into my drawer and see that I have eaten them all. Wonderful. At this rate I will hang beautifully at the top and droop just about everywhere else.

'I broke up with my fiancé actually, and I also need to find somewhere ...'

'Oh, and my mum said I prepare myself for lunchtime. You know, so like at the end of the day, why can't she do the same? That's what my mum says anyway.'

I stand up and knock over my chair.

'Karen, with all due respect your mother doesn't actually work here. The doctor in question cannot plan her time like you can. There are emergencies, or she may run over time. You always have a set lunch break and we should all support each other. It really is not unreasonable for one of our GPs to ask you to fetch her sandwich when you are getting one for yourself ...'

I glance at my watch.

'I'll have a word with the doctor. I'm sure she didn't mean to offend you.'

I watch with a sinking heart as Karen sits down, crosses her legs and leans back in the chair.

'I also want to discuss the uniform with you. Cheryl says she looks awful in navy, and personally I think those tops are a bit *sixties* so I brought you this. This is what they wear in other surgeries.'

She slides a glossy magazine across the table. I stare at her astonished.

'You read *The Lady* magazine?'

She laughs.

'Aww don't be daft, what would I be doing reading that? My mum gets her cleaning jobs from there. Anyway have a look at the bit on receptionist's uniforms. You can keep that.'

A sense of relief envelopes me when she finally stands up.

'You should get some sleep. You look like crap.'

With that final insult she leaves my office and I head out to meet Georgie.

***

I now understand why people use the phrase *flat hunting*. I'm beginning to think even hunting for weapons of mass destruction was a walk in the park compared to this. We must have viewed everything in Chelsea. Those I could afford were either in areas so rough that even the cats wore hoodies, or so small that you couldn't even swing a cat in them. Not that I want a cat of course, but it would be nice to have the option. One flat on the top storey of a high-rise building didn't have a lift and when we finally reached it Georgie nearly had to give me CPR. The flat itself was so small that I could sit on the loo and still reach the front door, and even that one was out of my price range.

'I'll have to move further out,' I say miserably.

'Well, you can't go any further up,' quips Casper, 'or you'll be in heaven and none of us will want to visit you there, at least not yet.'

He slides his hand through my arm.

'Come on love, let's get a doughnut.'

Sighing, I shove *The Lady* magazine into my handbag and follow everyone back downstairs with a growing feeling of desperation. If I eat much more I won't be able to squeeze into my little Beetle. Doughnuts turn into lunch and we all pile into the Veggie Grill. Bess, the owner, greets us with,

'Howdy guys, no Charlie today?'

'She dumped him, turned out to be a bit of a git,' I hear Casper whisper as he takes three menus.

I have never felt more depressed in my life. It looks like I will never find a flat in Chelsea. It seems if I want to stay here I will have to consider a house-share, or even a bedsit. Jane, the practice manager, is away for another two weeks, sunning herself in the

Canaries, which means I'll have to chair the doctor's meeting this afternoon and bring up this stupid sandwich thing of Karen's. Life just doesn't seem the same now that Charlie has gone. I've lain awake at nights trying to think what it was that I could have done to make him change his mind about me. I feel certain he isn't with anyone else and it isn't like I've suddenly ballooned after piling on the weight, or am covered in warts all over my body. I'm not unattractive. I'm no beauty queen, but it would be unreasonable for any man to expect that wouldn't it? My hair is long but well cut and expertly highlighted. I wear nice clothes. I'm not over the top fashion conscious but I know what works and what doesn't. I wear very little make-up as my skin glows naturally. I've tried really hard to be a good vegetarian. Did I mention that Charlie was a devout animal activist? He is forever attending some animal liberation conference or the other. I'm not quite as good at it as he is. He is now actively involved in the *Freedom for Farm Animals Association* also known as the FFFAA. I always forget an 'F', which is easily done isn't it? In fact when I've had a few drinks I tend to forget several 'F's and have called it the FA, which has caused many an upset. Well, it's a silly name. Why not just call it *Save the Cows* or something? The FFFAA sounds like a terrorist group. Charlie takes it all very seriously and once nearly broke up with me when I made a Mary Berry Madeira cake. How was I to know he thinks eggs are living things?

'How would you like someone eating your child?' he asked angrily, making me feel like I had just baked three live babies in my oven.

'It's only a cake,' I had argued.

'Try telling the chicken that.'

I didn't like to say that maybe the chicken wouldn't understand or possibly even care. I'm all for protecting animals from animal cruelty and unnecessary killing, and I hate zoos, but I do feel Charlie goes a bit too far. When someone tells you to let a spider run free around your house it just isn't normal is it? *A life is a life* he would say, *whether it be spider or human*. How am I supposed to sleep with a family of spiders under my bed? I've struggled to remember if I have broken some other animal code of ethics recently. Surely he hasn't left me because I called it the FA instead of the FFFAA. You have to agree there are far too many 'F's.

I'm a nice person. I try to listen to everyone's problems at work and understand their point of view. I should probably speak up for myself more, and I let the practice manager put on me a bit. Charlie is always telling me off for that. *You're doing her job for her. No one will ever realise how much you do until you stop doing it*, he had said once in a moment of anger when I had arrived late for a dinner date. But I know my job isn't the reason he called off the marriage. Georgie said it's just cold feet and in a few weeks he will come running back. I doubt it somehow.

'So what is it with *The Lady* magazine? The flats in there will be ten times pricier than those you've looked at,' asks Georgie, popping a sugar cube into her mouth.

'One of the receptionists wants me to look at uniforms. There is an article in there apparently,' I say.

Bess returns and we all order the sweet potato and pomegranate salad.

'I'll have to move to Battersea,' I say.

'You could take one of these housekeeping jobs. You know how you love cleaning,' laughs Georgie, flicking through the ads.

'Oh, hey look at this. If this isn't you I don't know what is. **Woman needed for help around the house. A bit of cooking, some housework but mostly companionship to professionally retired doctor. Non-smoking**. That's perfect for you, him being a doctor and everything,' she laughs. 'Oh and hey, you get your own little cottage on the estate.'

'Pray, where is this fab estate?' asks Casper, shovelling a forkful of sweet potato into his mouth.

'Ah,' Georgie grins.

'The fly in the ointment,' smiles Casper.

'It's in Yorkshire actually.'

'Ooh I say, Yorkshire. Where men are men and women are wenches. Perhaps I should apply,' laughs Casper.

I push my plate away. How can they think it so funny that I will soon be homeless?

'It's not a joke you know. I may well end up back at my parents, can you imagine that?'

'I've been trying not to.'

Georgie lays her hand on mine.

'We're just trying to cheer you up.'

Georgie slides the magazine across the table to Cas.

'Seriously, you could do worse than look at some of those. At least you get a job and a home all in one. There may be something close to London. We're not a million miles from the country after all. We could come and visit you.'

'Well thanks, but no thanks. I'm just not the domestic goddess type.'

Bess walks towards us with a tray, and Casper pretends to fall off his chair.

'I can feel a piece of heaven coming our way,' he shrieks.

Bess blushes.

'I'll be with you in a sec Mrs Randall. Feel free to bring little Basil in,' acknowledges Bess to a waiting customer.

We all strain to see little Basil.

'It's her dog,' Bess whispers, and then more loudly, 'Here you go, a special treat. Just don't expect this treatment every time. Hot fudge sundaes all round to cheer you up, and I know it's an old cliché Alice, but there are plenty of fish in the sea and when one door closes, another one opens.'

'Like this door for instance. It sounds perfect for you,' says Casper, flicking back a page in the magazine and leaning back to read it aloud. ***Responsible woman required to help on large family estate near Truro, Cornwall,*** you're most certainly responsible. ***Organisational skills an advantage,*** that's right up your street. ***Needed for general maintenance around our large farmhouse***, it sounds grand, what? ***Nothing onerous as other staff will be employed.*** There you go, a practice manager but without the practice. ***Knowledge of farming not necessary. Administration experience essential as this is a working farm.*** This is so you Alice. ***Some light domestic chores to be undertaken. Candidate needs to be flexible with G-S-O-H.*** Up until recently you have always had a G-S-O-H, this is definitely you Alice.'

'Considering my situation, I happen to think I have maintained rather a good sense of humour. Thank you very much.'

'Nice bedsit with all mod-cons for successful candidate, and use of car. UK driving licence essential. It's worth a go isn't it? Like Georgie said, we can come down at weekends.'

'I was thinking more like Chesham, Casper not bloody Cornwall, but still ... P. D. James wrote a brilliant book set in Dorset, you could go there. Just don't go to Cheverell Manor,' she adds gleefully.

I can't believe they are serious.

'Cheverell Manor?' queries Cas.

'Well, in the novel ...' begins Georgie.

'Right, can we perhaps not do murder stories today darling,' Cas sighs.

'They're mysteries actually. Maybe you should read one when you've finished watching re-runs of *Queer as Folk.*

'Ooh bitchy,' he laughs.

'It's a bit extreme don't you think?' I interrupt, 'relocation, change of career, not to mention the farm, I mean come on. All I need is a flat. I don't need to go all the way to Cornwall.'

'This is the best bit; ***Applicants should apply via email to Lady Blanche Fairfax-Mason.*** It's almost bloody royalty. You'll be taking care of the corgis. Just imagine you'll most likely meet Prince Harry or something. There you go, he likes an older woman. It will be like something out of a fairy tale ...'

'Like Princess Diana all over again,' quips Georgie.

'Honestly what are you lot like,' laughs Bess, clearing our plates.

'I'm not applying for a job in Cornwall on a sodding farm. What if Charlie changes his mind? He isn't going to chase me up there is he? How much is the salary anyway?'

'Cornwall is down darling, not up,' Casper grins. 'Are you going to eat that sundae or stir it into a giddy mess? This is aristocracy darling. Money is the last thing to discuss.'

I push the dish towards him.

'It's first and foremost for a non-aristocrat like me.'

'If Charlie wants you back he will chase you up the Swiss Alps,' says Georgie, removing *The Lady* magazine from Casper's sticky fingers.

'See it as something temporary. You can do it for six months, get some money behind you. We'd all get out of London if we could wouldn't we?'

'Speak for yourself darling,' chips in Cas.

'Well, I'm not applying and that's that. I can't believe you're even talking about it,' I say pulling my phone from my bag to check the time.

Shit, it's nearly two-thirty.

'Bugger, I'm late for the practice meeting. Shit.'

'You wouldn't have any of this stress in Cornwall. It would be all sheep dung and cream teas. You wouldn't even have to learn the language.'

'Don't you two have jobs to go to?' I snap, pulling a tenner out of my purse.

'I'm gigging tonight sweetie and she,' says Casper while pointing to Georgie, 'is slumming again, isn't that right sugar lips?'

'I actually rescheduled an important meeting to have lunch with you two pains in the arse,' she responds blowing him a kiss.

'Ooh I love it when you talk dirty.'

I sigh, grab my bag and kiss them both on the cheek.

'I must run. I love you both and I know you mean well. I'm just not ready for Prince Harry yet.'

I turn to the door, trip over Mrs Randall's handbag and step on her dog's tail. There is a yelp from the dog and a scream from me.

'You're not ready for the corgis either it seems,' calls Casper.

Things can only get better, I just need a positive attitude and everything will be all right. That's right isn't it?

Chapter Four

From: Lady Blanche Fairfax-Mason
To: Alice Lane
Subject: Your application

Dear Alice,

Thank you for your application. You are more than qualified for the post. We have had a good response to the advertisement and we have now shortlisted applicants for interviews. Would you be able to meet me at Claridge's for afternoon tea at 3 p.m. on Tuesday?

Kind regards
Lady Fairfax-Mason.

Claridge's, good heavens, is she serious? I hope she's paying because I certainly can't. It will cost her an arm and a leg if she is interviewing all the applicants there. We won't all be there together will we? What was I thinking of applying for a job way out in the sticks? I pick up the phone to call Georgie for advice when my office door is flung open and a tearful Dawn stumbles in followed by Karen and a surge of *Opium* perfume. Oh no, just what I don't need. I hastily close my email programme and drop the phone back onto its cradle.

'I'm not being funny, do you know what I mean, but at the end of the day that Mr Ramsbottom should be struck off or whatever you do with rude patients,' fumes Karen. 'Look at the state of her. I mean, it's not funny is it? She's beside herself aren't you Dawnie?'
I've just about had all I can take of Karen. I know I'm not as tolerant as I could be but I feel like the reception staff are really pushing me

lately. The overpowering smell of Karen's perfume reminds me I need to have a word with her about it. Several other receptionists have complained it gives them headaches.

'I really would appreciate it if you would knock first Karen. I could have been on the phone, patient confidentiality and all that.'
I point to a chair.

'Do you want to tell me what happened Dawn?' I ask gently.
She blows her nose noisily and wipes her eyes, smearing mascara across her cheeks. She perches her petite body onto the chair and attempts a smile.

'Well ...' she begins in a soft voice.

'He's still out there giving it some I tell you,' interrupts Karen. 'I tell you something, if I was the practice manager ...'
Dawn's expression shows she is grateful that Karen isn't the practice manager.

'If you *were* the practice manager,' I correct, 'and you're not are you? I am.'
Dawn gives Karen an astonished look and Karen turns red in the face.

'Well as it happens, you're not either are you? Mrs Francis is and ...'

'While she is not here I deputise, which means I am currently the practice manager.'
Karen lifts her eyes to meet mine.

'Well, you'd better do something then hadn't you, otherwise we're all going on strike and you can't run this place without us,' she says bluntly while nonchalantly studying her manicured nails.

'Hang on Karen ...' interjects Dawn in a pleading voice.

'We're sick of the Ramsbottom types abusing us. I'm not being funny but when all is said and done we're people too. Isn't that right Dawn? It's not our fault Di has gone home is it? We get it all taken out on us. That's the size of it, isn't it Dawn.'

'One of the practice nurses has gone home?' I say, trying not to show my surprise while wondering what it is we are discussing the size of.

'Yeah, she's got an upset stomach or something. Didn't you know?'
Well, obviously not. Is that a smirk on Karen's face? Dawn looks mortified. Her mascara streaked eyes widen and she looks at me

pleadingly. I so wish I had lashes like Dawn. They are so long and full and I imagine a doddle to flutter. I've got those stupid wispy things that one layer of mascara just seems to glue together rather than lengthen. I've tried those eyelash curler things but when you've got zero eyelashes like mine you spend most of your time curling your eyelids. Not something I would recommend.

'I don't want to go on strike or anything Alice. But he said the 'F' word and there is no call for that is there and ...'
She stops at the sound of light tapping. Mark, one of the doctors, pops his head around the door. Karen seductively licks her lips and pushes her chest out and I can't help wondering when she last had a bra fitting. It's amazing how many people seem to be lopsided once you've had your eyes opened. Oblivious to her seductive pose Mark turns straight to me.

'You do know it's manic out there. There is only one receptionist and Marcia has had to go home, one of her kids has gone down with measles. I did email you to reshuffle some of the appointments as James and I can't see everyone, and ...'
He looks at Dawn's tear-streaked face.

'Is everything okay? Only we need someone else out there. Can you reschedule something Alice, and for tomorrow too. Maybe get a locum.'

'No one told me Marcia went home.'

'A patient has been very rude to Dawn,' adds Karen.
Mark rolls his eyes.

'How about if we discuss it after we've got through this crisis? I'll leave it with you Alice.'
Without waiting for a response he leaves my office. Bloody hell is there anything else I can do this afternoon? Alice reschedule, Alice book a locum, Alice hold off a strike, Alice sort out Mr Ramsbottom. I am surprised I was not asked to sort out world peace in my coffee break.

'I'm so sorry that Mr Ramsbottom was rude to you Dawn. Take a little break and have a cup of tea. I will phone him this afternoon. Is that okay? I really should sort out these appointments otherwise we'll have even more irate patients. Karen, would you mind covering while Dawn has a break? I'll sort out these appointments and then I'll come and help.'
Karen pouts.

'I was leaving early today. I did tell you. It's my brother's birthday.'

My phone rings and I answer it eagerly. Anything is better than a confrontation with Karen. It is Mark.

'I'm not being difficult Alice, but can we get this mess sorted, and quickly please?'

'Also ...' continues Karen,

'Of course Mark. I'll just finish slicing myself into pieces and I'll be with you,' I say, barely able to control the anger in my voice.

I slam down the phone. That wasn't it though. That wasn't the straw that broke the camel's back, although it came close. What did break the camel's back was Mark's email which pinged on my screen at exactly five-thirty. In his ten-page missive, which waffled on about the NHS and its strengths and weaknesses, although in my mind finding strengths in this health centre is more difficult than finding Wally in a *Where's Wally?* book. He also gushed quite nauseatingly about how all the wonderful staff at Cranford's health centre made it the success that it was. So successful in fact that he went on to tell us who the partners were laying off and whose hours would be cut. Surprisingly it wasn't the sodding practice manager who, in theory, does more work than me but in practice only does bloody half. So, of course, it is yours truly who gets her hours reduced from forty to thirty. At this rate I'll be lucky if I can even afford a room-share in Battersea. The last thing I wanted was to move down to Cornwall and become some royal household servant, but it was becoming quite clear my nerves and disposition were not up to dealing with the likes of Karen and Mark for much longer, and certainly not on a pittance of a salary. It felt like no one wanted me any more. I'd lost my fiancé and now my job. With a heavy heart I replied to Lady Fairfax-Mason's email.

From: Alice Lane
To: Lady Fairfax-Mason
Subject: Interview

Dear Lady Fairfax-Mason,

Thank you very much. I look forwarding to meeting you at Claridge's on Tuesday, 3 p.m.

Yours sincerely,
Alice Lane.

Chapter Five

'I'm meeting Lady Fairfax-Mason for afternoon tea,' I say grandly, while feeling anything but.

'Follow me madam.'

I am so nervous. In fact I had sat in Casper's car for ten minutes trying to build up my courage to go in. I step through the revolving doors into a world that exudes luxury and am mesmerised by the numerous photographs that adorn the walls portraying the rich and famous that had visited. I wonder if Georgie was right when she had said it will be Princess Diana all over again. I am escorted past the sweeping staircase to a beautifully prepared table adorned with green and white china. I am so intent on looking that I do not notice the elegant immaculately dressed woman who stands to greet me. I do however smell her soft intoxicating fragrance.

'Alice Lane, it is lovely to meet you at last. Thank you so much for coming.'

Her voice is as clear as crystal and as soft as silk. Her perfectly manicured hand clasps mine and then gestures for me to sit down. I look curiously around for the other applicants. Out of nowhere a menu miraculously appears and I lift my eyes over it to get a better look at Lady Fairfax-Mason. I'm no fashion expert but even I know that the simple two-piece floral suit she is wearing isn't off the peg from Debenhams, and that the sparklers in her ears are most certainly the real thing. Her complexion is flawless and expertly made-up.

'I thought it would be much nicer for us to have afternoon tea here rather than in my room. A much nicer ambiance don't you think?' she says casually.

My God, is she staying here? The farmhouse must be enormous and with an army of staff if she can afford this. There is no way I am going to land this job.

'You're staying here?' I ask stupidly.

'I always do when I'm in England. I'll have my usual thank you Chester,' she says to the waiter who seems to materialise from somewhere but I couldn't for the life of me tell you where. It's rather like being a volunteer in a Paul Daniels act. One minute they are there and the next gone. I look at the choice on the menu and wonder what *her usual* is. She smiles indulgently at me.

'The Earl Grey here cannot be matched. Shall I order for you, unless of course ...'

I nod and she quickly and expertly voices our order before relaxing in her seat and studying me.

'I live in Sydney,' she volunteers.

'Sydney Australia?'

'It's the only Sydney I know, unless you know of another.'

I feel myself blush.

'I presumed you lived on the farm ...'

She looks astonished.

'I leave the farm to my son, Edward. It must be very rewarding, working for the NHS,' she says, making it sound like UNICEF. 'Helping people like that. I have great admiration for people like you.'

Christ, she makes me sound like Mother Teresa. And she most certainly hasn't met Mr Ramsbottom. I can tell she has never had to wait in an NHS surgery waiting room.

The tea arrives, along with an assortment of finger sandwiches, scones, Marco Polo jam, cakes and pastries. Already I am thinking I should ask for a doggy bag.

'So when can you start?' she asks.

I choke on my cucumber finger sandwich. What the hell happened to the interview, and what happened to all the other applicants? Did they somehow get spirited away along with the waiters? I listen to the pianist play 'It had to be you,' and wonder if I am in a dream.

'Start?' I hear myself echo.

She wipes her fingers delicately on her serviette and sips from her teacup while eyeing me curiously over the rim.

'Your résumé is impeccable, outstanding in fact. I can't help wondering why the erm ...' she clicks her fingers.

'NHS,' I offer at the same time that a waiter materialises.

'Ah, yes that's it. Oh, we are fine Chester thank you,' she says dismissing him.

'Why these NHS people are letting you go so easily.'
I take a bite of my scone and feel like I have died and gone to heaven. How can anything taste so good? I decide to enjoy this first and then ask about the pay and the corgis and all the rest. She waits patiently as I sip my tea which, by the way, is outstanding indeed.

'The thing is, I return to Sydney in just under forty-eight hours, so if we could sign the contract today ...'

'But don't you have other people to consider?'
She huffs and waves a hand before leaning across to take a sandwich. I have to admit this is doing wonders for my confidence but it all seems a little too unreal to be true. I bet the pay is shocking. That's it, the farmhouse will be like a mansion and my room so huge that they will feel that is payment enough.

'The salary wasn't mentioned in the advertisement. I was wondering ...'

'How much were you earning with the RSPCA?'
Well I know some of our patients are like animals but that is taking things a bit far.

'The NHS,' I correct.
She sighs.

'NSPCC, NHS, they all do good works don't they? So what were you on? A thousand a week?'
A thousand a week, is this woman insane?

'Well, it was more like two thousand a month but I've recently had to take a pay cut ...'
She stares wide-eyed at me.

'We'll pay you a salary of eight hundred pounds a month, with accommodation and food included. Is that enough?'
She looks at me earnestly. I sense another waiter at my side and lean back so he can refill my teapot. Eight hundred a month with no rent, bills or food? Blimey, I'd be quids in.

'What about the corgis?' I ask, returning her earnest look. There is something very suspicious about all this. She squints at me.

'The corgis?'

'Do I have to look after them?'

She looks thoughtful and spoons a little cream onto her scone.

'Do you like corgis? We can certainly get some if that's what you want.'

That's it. I will kill Georgie and Cas. What bastards. I've a good mind to order another tea and tell them to take it to the homeless on the streets. There's a joke and there's a joke.

'So, how much did they pay you? God, they've got more money than sense those two. Where did you hire you from? You're bloody good, I'll give you that. What are you, some out of work actress that Casper hired on the cheap? I don't believe those two. Honestly, like I seriously haven't got enough on my plate with Charlie and everything else. I should have known.'

Her eyes widen.

'I'm sorry Alice, I'm not quite sure I know what we are talking about now.'

'Georgie and Cas, did they put you up to this? It's okay, I know it's not your fault and that you're just doing your job ... I should have known that email was a fake. I mean, nobody would have a ridiculously stupid name like *Lady Fairfax-Mason* would they?'

She smiles. Chester is suddenly standing by our table and she hands him a key card.

'Be a sweetheart and fetch my passport from my room would you please? Miss Lane is under some misapprehension that I am not who I say I am.'

Oh shit. Chester takes the card, his expression impassive. Without another word she finishes her tea and gestures for me to do the same. The pianist has stopped and the uncomfortable silence between us is unbearable. Chester returns with the said passport and hands it to me.

'It would be rather an elaborate joke if we also had a forged passport don't you think?'

I feel my face growing hot and wish the floor would open up and swallow me. I can almost hear Karen's voice saying *Honestly, I'm not being funny but what are you like Alice?* I close my eyes in exasperation.

'Like I said, I would very much like to sign the contract today. I really don't have much time, and as far as I'm concerned you are perfect for the job. If you want corgis, we can get corgis, although

Lynda Renham

there are plenty of animals on the farm if it is animals you like. If you're happy with the salary, which is superior to what the NSPCC are paying you, why don't we sign now?'

If it's animals I like? I'm not David sodding Attenborough. She'll be parachuting in pink elephants if I give the nod. She removes a neat folder from her bag and places it in front of my tea cup.

'The NHS,' I correct quietly. 'But I have no idea what I'll be doing or even where the farm is. When do you need me to start?'

'I'll send you directions to the farm in my confirmation email. You'll be the farm manager in effect. When would you like to start? I imagine it will be similar to whatever you manage now for the N ... Well anyway, much better paid and with more perks and far less sick people ...'

When would I like to start? Blimey, she'll be giving me the farm next.

'But I thought your son ran the farm?'

She beckons for the bill and avoids my eyes.

'Obviously, but he needs help with all the staff and the accounts. There is so much to do when one is a landowner,' she says hurriedly, rummaging in her Mischa Barton handbag.

'How many people will I be managing?' I break in before she has time to conjure up a pen to go with her nice neat folder.

She fiddles with the diamond encrusted bangle that adorns her wrist and shrugs.

'I think about three.'

I raise my eyebrows.

'Although on reflection it could be four maybe even five,' she says quickly, looking at me earnestly and trying to gauge my reaction.

'I imagine that is more than enough for you to cope with anyway. How many do you think you should manage?'

How many do I think? This is ridiculous. Why don't I just email her the job description I fancy, along with some outrageous salary and see if she agrees to it? I so wish Georgie or Cas was here so I could ask their advice. My mobile bleeps and with much flourish Lady Fairfax-Mason produces a Mont Blanc pen and points it at me like an offensive weapon. I pull my mobile from my bag in a bid to play for time. It is a text from Charlie and I've had three missed calls. I couldn't have heard them because of the piano music. I excuse myself to the ladies. I wonder if the loo assistant after opening the door for me and handing me towels is also going to offer to wipe my arse as well. Don't get me wrong, I love luxury as much as the next person, but I'm beginning to feel over cosseted at the moment. With my bum comfortably perched on the most luxurious loo seat of all time I click into Charlie's text.

Are you just being bloody difficult Ali? It's hard for me too you know. Jake has phoned you three times. I made it clear that the inventory had to be done today. We'll lose our bloody deposit. Obviously you can afford to. Can you phone Jake so he knows when to come? We've already wasted his time. God Ali, you're hard work sometimes.

Shit. The inventory. How could I forget? What does he mean *I'm hard work*? How long has he thought that? I must not cry. Christ, not in shitting Claridge's of all places. That's about right. My one and only chance to enjoy afternoon tea at Claridge's and I spend it sobbing in the loo over a man. Well sod that for a game of soldiers. With trembling hands I text back.

I'm busy trying to get a job. Why don't you get your arse over there? You're the one who wants to terminate our tenancy. Talking of deposits, I do believe you paid that, so obviously I can afford to lose what I never had. Maybe that includes you too. Can't stop, having afternoon tea at Claridge's, you know how it is, then again maybe you don't.

I hit the send button without re-reading it. Honestly, don't men have fantastic timing? Lady Fairfax-Mason looks hopefully at me as I return to the table.

'Where do I sign?' I ask.
Her face lights up and her eyes twinkle.

'That's wonderful.'

'Let's hope I'm making the right decision,' I mumble as I scribble my name on the dotted line.

'Oh you are my dear, you are.'

Chapter Six

'Whatever you do don't go getting lost.'

'How can she get lost? She's got the satnav.'

'Huh,' scoffs Cas. 'If I remember, we had the so-called satnav when we went to Sebastian's wedding, and we ended up not only at the wrong church, but the wrong side of town, and all because Georgie cocked up the postcode. I also recall having a terrible attack of psoriasis at the time. God, I was in agony and the stress. It's not set to that mad bitch Serena is it? Because she's mental she is. She tells you to turn left when there is no sodding left to turn into. I swear these things are designed to reduce the number of cars on the road by killing off the motorists.'

'For Christ's sake Casper, don't you know how to take a breath? If you suffer from anything it is most certainly diarrhoea, and that is of the verbal kind,' snaps Georgie.

He grabs my suitcase.

'I hope this farmer is related to bloody Superman. He'll need to be to lift this out of the boot on his own. Give us a hand Georgie love.'

Between the three of us we manage to lift the big suitcase into the boot along with several carrier bags and two smaller bags. Okay, maybe I did go a bit over the top with the suitcase. I had spent over half an hour arguing with Georgie that I did indeed need an iron. Well, you just don't know do you?

'Surely you won't need all these coat-hangers though,' she had persisted, 'and how many sodding towels are you taking, and why the hell are you taking all this soap? They will have towels you know. People live there. You're not going to Outer Mongolia to live with the primitives. But I agree taking a Nigella Lawson cookbook is sensible.'

Finally, I'm all packed and ready to set off in my old little Beetle. I had said my goodbyes to everyone at the surgery at the little bon voyage party they had laid on for me. Charlie had responded to my goodbye text by phoning Georgie to ask what was going on.

'All very weird,' she had commented. 'He didn't seem at all happy about it. Made lots of tutting noises about you working with caged up animals.'

'It's a farm, not a bloody zoo,' says Casper mockingly.

'You know how involved he is in the FFFAA,' I say counting the 'F's on my fingers.

'Oh that little thing that does Fuck Fuck Fuck All, if you ask me,' he laughs.

'Casper!' admonishes Georgie.

'Didn't he sound at all worried about me?' I ask miserably.
She shakes her head.

'I think he was more annoyed at you working on a farm.'
I can't say I am exactly thrilled about it myself. I can't believe I will never see my little flat again or that I will not be going to Pronuptia for my final bridal dress fitting. I'm still having difficulty coming to terms with the fact that I am no longer an engaged woman but a single one, yet again.

'Do I look okay? I'm not overdressed am I? I wanted to get the right balance, you know what I mean, first impressions are important aren't they? I didn't put on my jeans because I don't want the staff to think I'm a pushover, but at the same time I don't want to look hoity-toity and put them off me before we even start. I thought a Marks and Spencer skirt with a nice conservative two-piece outfit would be just right. What do you think?' I ask nervously.

'Great, babe, but I'm not sure about the pearls, love. They scream *I'm royalty*. Do you know what I mean?' remarks Cas while flapping wildly at a wasp.

'It's your aftershave,' says Georgie.

'They're the only things that do bloody chase me,' he cries while running into the road.

'That's because your aftershave kills everyone off before they can reach you,' laughs Georgie, leaning over to kiss me.

I stare at Georgie's hair enviously and sneak another look at mine in the side mirror. Oh God, it looks frightful. What was I thinking of letting a trainee near my hair? I had decided before venturing down to Cornwall the least I could do was get my highlights done. God knows what kind of hair stylists they have down there.

'It's Cornwall Ali, not China. Don't you think you're panicking a bit?' Georgie had tried to reassure me.

'I know but I've always gone to Toni and Guy, and I know Jason. I feel happier. Besides, I want to look good on my first day.'
What was I thinking of letting a trainee within an inch of my roots?

'Alice darling, so lovely to see you again, how are you?' Jason had greeted me warmly and, with a flick of the wrist engulfed me in a black cape.

'Would you be a darling and let Ryan do your highlights? Half price.'
I must have looked sceptical.

'He'll do a grand job. They have to learn don't they?' he whispered.
Blimey, anyone would think he was losing his virginity to me. I smiled at the spotty teenager who handed me a cup of coffee which looked more like dishwater. My intended *I'd prefer you do them actually Jason, and pay the exorbitant fee you charge if that's okay,* came out as,

'No of course, after all everyone has to start somewhere.'
What! Maybe they do but not on my sodding head. Why couldn't he have started on the old woman with the blue rinse sitting opposite me? Why did I even say that? Why is it you can never say no to a hairdresser? My usual blonde highlights I feel sure now have a ginger tinge to them and my once full fringe is now some flimsy thing that is more lopsided than my breasts ever were. When my mother saw it her helpful comment was,

'Well things come in threes. First the broken engagement, then the pay cut and now the arsed-up hair.'
What she meant was the *fucked-up* hair but she can't say the 'F' word so she replaces it with arsed. I let out a sigh and Georgie strokes my fringe playfully.

'The hair is great. You look lovely Alice. Maybe Cas is right about the pearls though.'

'Oh, do you think? I thought it would just add a little something.'

'Yeah, a kind of Princess Anne little something that you could well do without,' offers Cas while fighting off the wasp.

'Sod off you little bugger. Honestly if it pricks me I will swell up.'

'What's new,' Georgie and I say in unison.

I set the satnav to take me to the Cornwall address, and check the ETA.

'So I'll phone you in five hours,' I say hugging them both tightly, 'and you must come down the first possible weekend.'

'Try and stop us darling,' says Cas, squeezing me so hard that I can barely breathe.

It has been just over two weeks since I had signed the contract over my divine tea at Claridge's. I had handed in my notice the next day. There had been a few oohs and ahs but nothing really sincere. Charlie had arranged to go over the inventory at the flat while I was at work so he wouldn't have to see me. In just one month I had called off a wedding, given up my flat, quit my job and was now heading west to begin a whole new life. To say I am nervous would be an understatement. I am shit scared.

'And you must text and phone every day,' I say, shuffling about by the car.

'Oh God, I can't go,' I blurt out and feel the wetness on my cheeks as the tears run from my eyes.

'I'll be as useless as shit in the country, you know I will.'

'You'll be fanbloodytastic, that's what. You'll be talking West Country in no time,' blubbers Cas who cries at weddings, funerals, bar mitzvah's and the opening credits of *Brokeback Mountain*. Georgie squeezes my hand.

'It's the best way to get over farty Charlie,' she smiles.

'Farty farty farty Charlie,' giggles Cas.

A part of me is hoping that absence will make the heart grow fonder, but knowing my kind of luck it will be more a case of out of sight out of mind where Charlie is concerned. I climb into the car. After all, I've signed a contract now so there is no going back. It could be worse. At least I will be working in a stately home. You never know I may well meet Prince Harry, and who knows where that will lead, and then Charlie will be sorry. I watch Casper in the rear-view mirror, dancing and waving his hands like some gay street entertainer. Georgie is waving, although I am not sure if she is waving at me or trying to fan away the smoke from my exhaust. God, I will miss them. I turn the corner and they disappear. Cornwall here I come.

Chapter Seven

'Who's next?'

Thank goodness. I'm starting to feel like I am waiting my turn in a soup kitchen rather than at Costa Coffee. I am about to give my order when an enormous woman pushes in front of me. Or I should say her breasts push in front of me. In fact they practically send me sprawling. Let me tell you, she is only not hanging badly but hanging to the point of scraping her knees and dragging along the floor. I can't imagine what Justine would make of her. Mind you I'm not so sure Justine would be able to get near enough to measure. In fact, I feel quite certain Justine would not want to get near. I've already backed off several feet. I'm not saying she smells bad or anything, but she certainly isn't oozing Issey Miyake if you know what I mean. An equally fat, but shorter and breast-free child pushes in after her.

'What do ya want?' bellows the woman to the child.

'Coke,' responds the child through a mouth full of sweets.

Not diet, obviously.

'One coke, one hot chocolate with lots of cream and ...' She turns to the child and in the process nearly takes my eye out with her left breast. Christ, she could rob a bank with those tits. No one would dare say no to her.

'What cake do-ya-want?'

I let out a sigh and she gives me a dirty look.

'What's your problem?' she asks aggressively.

Shit, I only sighed for goodness sake. I open my mouth to speak.

'We was in front of you and you shoved in. So don't you go giving me all this,' she yells, clicking her thumb and fingers together presumably to imitate me *giving it all this*, whatever *all this* is.

'Well ...' I begin.

But she wallops me again with her breasts and shoves the brat towards a table.

'Sit there Paris, and don't fucking start.'

Paris? Where did that name come from? Not the place of conception surely? But I suppose you can't call a child Wapping can you? Oh dear, this is what service stations do to me. I find myself thinking horrible things about people. Don't you just hate these places? Where there are all those toothless women that you never seem to see anywhere else but always here and the men with their pot bellies pushing though their button-popped shirts. Not to mention the screaming kids. I feel like every child in the country is in this service station. If there were a terrorist attack here the entire generation would be totally wiped out. I only stopped because I needed a coffee to keep me awake. I'm starving, but there is no way I am eating at this place. I swear the food on the streets of Calcutta is safer than the slop that they are dishing up here. As for those Cornish pasties outside, well say no more. Okay, I know I've got to start getting into the feel of everything Cornish, but I really would prefer not to start at the Taunton Deane service station.

'Can I have a latte please?' I ask the assistant, 'to take out.'

'Decaf latte or normal, cream or milk, soya or normal, skimmed or full fat, eat in or take out?'

The assistant licks her lips and quickly applies some salve while I try to decipher her words. Her hair is tied back in one of those perfect messy buns. You know the kind I mean. It looks all messy but you can see it has been expertly done. I can never do that. Within seconds my hair has slipped through the slide and is hanging back down again. She chews at the gum in her mouth and lets out a tired sigh. Didn't I say take out?

'Erm, normal with normal and skimmed,' I say stupidly, feeling that none of that made any sense.

'Oh, and to take out please.'

'You want normal milk, not skimmed, you mean?'

'Erm yes, and to ...'

'Medium or large?'

'Medium and ...'

'Eat in or take out?'

I feel like a contestant on a game show. She'll be telling me I'm the weakest link next.

'Take out please,' I answer pleasantly.

Why is it I can never be rude to people? Not even when they are rude to me. Is this something serious that is lacking in me. I take my coffee and negotiate my way out of the crowds. I am two hours from Truro and getting more nervous by the minute. All kinds of things had occurred to me in the car. The kind of things that I really should have voiced to Lady Fairfax-Mason at my interview but didn't. Even her confirmation email didn't say much to enlighten me. I had hoped she would tell me the exact number of staff I would be managing, and their names. I was just told that everyone was looking forward to meeting me, whoever everybody was, and if there were any problems to email her directly. I constantly tell myself to stop being so anxious; after all, I've been managing people for years haven't I? I find myself stupidly wondering if Charlie is thinking of me and whether he is missing me. Most likely he is not. After all, I've only been gone a few hours. I walk into the loo and it's suddenly like I've entered a surreal dream. In front of me is a row of men with their penises out, and in full flow. Holy shit! What are they doing in the ladies? More importantly what am I doing in the mens'? Oh buggery bollocks. I turn sharply and almost fall over another woman who is following me.

'No don't go in there,' I yell.

'Oh my God, ...why not?'

'It's the gent's loo.'

Her eyes widen so much that I feel sure her pupils will pop out.

'And you went in there?' she squeals.

Crikey, does she have to look quite so appalled. It's the gent's loo, not a live sex show.

'Well, yes ...'

'Oh my God,' she gasps, and quickly heads to the ladies, 'you poor thing.'

Heavens, it wasn't that bad. Just a few more penises than one would normally see at any one time. Some might call me lucky. I push my way into the ladies, and dash into the nearest cubicle which of course has no toilet paper. Sadly I have reached that stage where a woman can wait no longer.

I finally make my way outside, past the Cornish pasty van and the strong smell of fry-ups and cigarette smoke, and head to my little old Beetle. I make a firm decision that any more toilet breaks will be made behind a bush. It can only get better from here on. I find myself thinking of Charlie again and allow myself a quick glance at the photo of him that I had shoved into my purse. After a few seconds I start the engine and reverse out of my parking space leaving my customary cloud of white smoke behind me. I turn left onto the motorway and continue westward.

Chapter Eight

'You have reached your destination.'

I sigh with relief. I have been driving for the past hour in heavy rain and am quite relieved to have finally made it. But I know an estate when I see one and a tiny country church at the end of a lane does not constitute an estate. Already the satnav has misdirected me three times. Once down a no-entry road, another time to turn right which meant demolishing someone's house to do so. It had later told me to take the fourth exit on a roundabout that didn't exist. I strain my neck to see a building that resembles some kind of stately home. I study the map Lady Fairfax-Mason had sent me and realise the bend that she has highlighted, along with the road leading to the house, was the one I had been on five minutes ago. I take a few moments to check my appearance in my compact mirror and climb from the car to straighten my clothes, grateful it has now stopped raining. It has been a long drive. I'm sure the staff will not expect me to emerge looking like royalty but I want to look the best I can.

It had occurred to me, as I was driving, that there may well be situations where I may need to curtsy. What if Lady Fairfax-Mason's son, Edward, has royal visitors? As the estate manager I am bound to be introduced. I'll have to ask the staff how to do it properly. In fact, right at this very minute they are probably worrying where I am. I imagine the kettle has been on and off for the past hour. I really should have asked Lady Fairfax-Mason for the house phone number. My stomach rumbles and I wonder what the cook will have made for dinner. Apart from breakfast I have only had an apple and the coffee at the service station. I turn back and take the bend again only to find the road marked in red is some kind of dirt track. That can't be right, unless the estate is at the end of the track, but surely the road to the house would be better than this. No, this can't be right. After resetting the satnav I find myself, five minutes later, sitting outside the church again. This is ridiculous. There should be *a Brideshead Revisited* drive somewhere. I spot a woman walking her dog and jump from my car as she enters the church gates.

'Excuse me, can you help with directions,' I call, flapping my map in the air.

She gives me a warm friendly smile.

'Where is it you're going to?'

Her dog yawns and paws my leg which I tactfully move away. The last thing I need is paw prints all over my tights.

'Down Rocky!' she snaps.

Rocky, surely that's a name for a bulldog, not a cocker spaniel?

'I'm looking for the Trenowyth estate.'

She raises her eyebrows.

'Trenowyth you say?'

I nod.

'Do you know it?' I ask eagerly.

Rocky wags his tail excitedly and stares up at me.

'Why would you be going there?' she asks curiously and her eyes travel over my two-piece and stop at my feet.

It's not really her business is it but as I can't be rude I reply,

'I'm the new estate manager. I've travelled from London.'

'Ah, London,' she nods, 'Estate manager huh?' like that explains everything.

'Trenowyth estate you say? The same estate as owned by Edward Fairfax?'

So, I am near. I feel my heart flutter with a mixture of nerves and excitement.

'Edward Fairfax-Mason, yes that would be the one.'

She hands back the directions.

'Well, Edward Fairfax is all I've ever known him to be, as has everyone in the village. You'll find Trenowyth at the end of the lane just past the bend. You came round the bend I presume?'

I'm going round the bend it feels more like, and what does she mean she knows him as Edward Fairfax?

'But that's a dirt road isn't it?'

She flaps her hand.

39

'That's the road to Trenowyth dirt or no.'

She yanks Rocky's lead and his paw scrapes my leg, snagging my tights. Bloody brilliant. His eyes have a menacing glare to them and his paw gently taps at my other leg as if to say I haven't finished yet. Oh yes you have. I give him a little kick and smile at the owner.

'You're from the city then,' she inclines her head to my car.

'Driven all the way in that have you?'

What does she mean *in that*? My little Beetle may be a bit old, but not as old as her. She lifts the hood of her jacket to stop the rain from getting to her greying hair.

'You don't see cars that shiny in these parts,' she says shaking her head. 'At least not for long.'

Heavens, it sounds like a threat. Is she planning on sending a local angry mob of villagers with pitchforks in hand to bash it up a bit? Maybe they have initiation ceremonies here. For goodness sake, anyone would think I am a character out of a Stephen King novel. It's only the country, people are different here, weird different if she is anything to go by.

'We'll be seeing you in church then?' she enquires.

Oh crikey.

'Well, I'm ...' I begin, looking down at the hole in my tights and the accompanying ladder that runs down below it.

'We're a God-fearing community,' she says firmly.

Rocky yaps as though confirming this. Christ, are they Amish or something? I'll be wearing special clothes before I know where I am and calling for Cas to be publicly stoned. I know you probably think I'm getting carried away now but you should see this woman.

'Yes, well I'm sure once I'm settled ...'

'Nice to meet you ...' she tails off.

'Alice,' I say warmly and hold out my hand which she ignores.

'Lady Fisher. We'll see you in church.'

Lady Fisher? Blimey they really do have blue blood here. She gives a wave and marches off with Rocky's lead in one hand and her stick in the other. I'm getting a bad feeling about this. I climb back into the Beetle and check my phone. There is a text from Georgie. A small tremor of happiness runs through my body. Just seeing her name on my phone makes me feel a little more secure and takes me back to lovely hectic London. It's much too quiet here, eerily quiet in fact. Surely there should be some noise. In fact another car would be nice, then again maybe not. Knowing my luck it will be the car out of *Jeepers Creepers*. I shiver and open Georgie's text.

So how goes it? You must be there by now. What's his lordship like, and the domestic staff? ☺ *We miss you loads already. X*

'Oh and I so miss you,' I whisper.

Right, this is no good I tell myself. You've got to take the bull by the horns and get on with it. Or, in this particular case, take the cow by the horns. Not that I know anything about cows and bulls you understand. I turn the car around and again head back. After passing Buttercup Farm and Bluebell Lane the dirt road comes into sight and this time I turn into it. After about fifty yards I reach a gate. I strain to see a sign, but there is nothing. Oh honestly, where on earth is this place? It will be dark soon and I will still be driving. I feel like I'm on a Bear Grylls expedition. I get out of the car to open the gate and several birds squawk and flap past my eyes making me jump and shit, and I mean real shit, I have stepped into some sheep crap.

'Bugger it.'

I attempt to scrape it off onto the car tyre. Do I really need all this in my life? Mad countrywomen and sheep dung. Surely there are better jobs than this? Yes Alice, but how many of them offer you a home and better still, get you a long way from Charlie. The thought of Charlie brings tears to my eyes or maybe it's the smell of the sheep dung that does it. Yes, that's most likely what it is. Come on Alice, onwards and upwards.

The gate creaks. It practically hangs off the hinges. I'm beginning to feel like I'm in an Alfred Hitchcock movie ... I'll finally reach the house only to be met by Norman Bates who will, no doubt, murder me in the shower. Jesus Alice, stop thinking such things. My heart is hammering and I need to take a couple of deep breaths to calm myself down. It's the country that's all. Things creak more here. I wince as a splinter digs itself into my finger. I suck at it gently and look down at my tights. Some impression I am going to make. What I wouldn't do for a cup of tea. Stepping carefully around the muddy puddles I get back into the car and drive slowly on. Ahead of me are fields and oh yes, thank goodness, they are full of cows. That must mean a farm is near. From the smell coming through the half open window I feel sure a farm must be near. I certainly hope it is a farm and not sewage works. Oh no, it's neither of those things, it's the bloody sheep shit on my shoe which I now see is all over the car mat. The car will stink for weeks. I look around for any sign of a farmhouse and see some buildings on the left and sigh with relief. My heart beats faster knowing I am getting near to the estate. Feeling tired I do so hope the other staff members are nice and they won't mind me taking a hot bath when I arrive. Passing more fields I turn a corner and the house comes into view. I gasp and brake so sharply that I am thrown forward. I stare wide-eyed and I am sure, wide-mouthed. It is such an astonishing sight that I find myself stepping out of the car in a dream. I don't know what I was expecting. In my wildest imaginings I could never have visualised anything like this. I take a few tentative steps closer and gawp like a mad woman. I close my eyes and open them again and yes the vision is still there. I barely feel the light rain shower or the wind as it whips delicately at my ankles. I can barely think. Well no, that isn't strictly true because I am most certainly thinking of ways I can murder Lady Fairfax-sodding-Mason and let me tell you, they are gruesome thoughts indeed. Norman Bates is a pussycat compared to these thoughts. Grimly and with gritted teeth I venture forward towards the run-down farmhouse where I feel quite certain no dinner awaits me. There are tiles missing on the roof and an upstairs window is broken, the gutter is leaking and water runs down the side of the house and the window frames and door are flaking paint. The house looks as if it has been pebble-dashed with mud. Surely this isn't the house. I'm jumping to conclusions. This is most likely one of the cottages belonging to a farmhand or something. Yes, that would explain it. I breathe a sigh of relief. Most likely the person living here will be able to give me directions to the main house. In fact, they can let the staff know I am on my way. How awful of me to think such terrible things about Lady Fairfax-Mason. I then see the sign on the rickety gate. It clearly says *Trenowyth*. Okay the paint is peeling off the sign, and it is covered in grime, but it definitely says *Trenowyth*. I'm going to kill that bloody bitch, but not until I have tortured her first. What the hell was she playing at? Right, I'm not staying here. I might look silly but I'm not stupid. Well, you know what I mean. God, I'm so angry that I can barely think. I turn to march back to my car and fall over a sheep that bleats like crazy and then starts to eat my skirt. Where did that come from?

'Away, come on away now, you can't eat that,' I say, turning and stepping on it. It lets out a small whimpering sound.

I pull away to the ripping sound of my skirt and the barking of a dog, as a collie comes bounding towards me. Christ almighty, I am going to be eaten alive by a wild dog and a sheep. This could only happen to me. There I was thinking I would be the victim of a psychopath when instead I will be ravaged by wild animals. The collie skids to a halt, looks quizzically at me, lets out a howl and then excitedly sniffs my crotch. I mean, for heaven's sake. The sheep meanwhile has run away, but not without ripping a hole in my skirt first. I've never had so much attention in my life. Oh my goodness, the dog is trying to push my skirt up. I swear if this wasn't a dog I'd be pressing charges.

'I'm so sorry,' I shout to the sheep,

What am I doing, talking to sheep? I'll be three weeks in the country and then they will have to section me if I go on like this. With the dog pawing my thigh and his nose permanently stuck to my crotch I run into the farmhouse and slam the door behind me. The smell of shit is everywhere and I pull my shoe off and throw it outside to a mad scrambling from the dog. I only need birds to start pecking at the windows to feel I am most certainly in an Alfred Hitchcock movie. What have I done? I'm standing in a dark hallway and to the right is the kitchen. There is not a single member of staff to be seen, in fact there is not even a bloody kitchen table to be seen unless you count the four legs. I can't see any more of it because it is covered in engine parts. The kitchen sink is full of dishes, and if anything was cooking for dinner then I'm buggered if I can smell it. With shaking hands I pull the contract from my bag and am about to rip it into pieces when the farmhouse door opens and the dog is at my crotch again.

'Oh, for God's sake, just bugger off you sex-starved animal,' I snap.

'I hope you're not talking to me?'

I spin round at the sound of the voice. The dog determined not to let go seems to spin with me and I wonder if the thing has become surgically attached to my crotch. I come face to face with a remarkably good-looking, if not stiff-necked and very angry, man. His brow is furrowed and he stares at me through grey steel-glinted eyes. I swear if looks could kill I would have dropped dead on the spot. He pulls off the cap he is wearing and runs a hand carelessly through his tousled hair. If this is Edward Fairfax-Mason he is much younger than I had imagined him to be.

'Down Molly,' he says quietly but with a firmness that almost has me obeying. I realise my skirt has risen up over my knees and quickly push it back down. I must look ridiculous with only one shoe on, and wearing a crumpled half-eaten skirt.

'I don't know who you are or what you want. However, what I do know is that you left the gate open and I have sheep running riot down the lane ...' he begins sternly.

How dare he have a go at me? I've been led here under false pretences. I haven't driven I don't know how many miles for him to shout at me.

'Excuse me,' I interrupt, 'I have not driven all the way from London to be told off by you. I don't actually know who you are anyway ...'

'Edward Fairfax, I own this farm, and the sheep you've just let out, and I don't care if you've driven all the way from Moscow, I don't appreciate you walking into my house uninvited.'

He speaks clearly and effortlessly with a well-educated voice that hints of just a tinge of a West Country accent to it. I'm speechless. I've never in my life met someone so rude. Before I can respond another man walks in.

'I've rounded up most but ...'

He stops on seeing me and smiles.

'Oh hello, I'm sorry Ted, I didn't realise you had a visitor.'

'Nor did I until I walked in,' replies Edward while giving me a curious look.

The other man looks uncomfortable.

'I'd better fetch the rest of the sheep. They've gone into Lower End, unfortunately. I'll see you later.'

He nods at me and slaps Edward on the back as he passes. I have never felt so miserable in my life. Everything that could go wrong in my life is going wrong. I hand the contract to Edward as I walk past.

'The door was open actually. Perhaps you should consider locking it if you don't wish people to venture in. Your mother hired me to be the new farm manager, so I was invited. She told me there were other staff here and that ...'

I stop abruptly as I feel my throat constrict. Oh sod it, don't go crying Alice. The thought of the long drive back is unbearable.

'Anyway, it's obviously all a misunderstanding. If you could just direct me to a bed and breakfast, I will get out of your way and return home tomorrow.'

Oh really Alice, and just where is home? The flat will be occupied by the new tenants and unless you intend sleeping at your parents or on Georgie's very uncomfortable sofa bed, there is no home to return to. Could things get any worse? He reads the contract with a serious look on his face before folding it and handing it back.

'My mother, the ever so helpful Lady Blanche Fairfax-Mason no doubt gave you a very far-fetched story. The only staff working here are me and Jed, who you just met. To cut a long story short, and only because I feel someone owes you an explanation of sorts, my mother feels I need a housekeeper. My father died six months ago and I took the farm over. It was a mess and as you can see it's not much better now, but we're getting there. I can't worry about the house while I run the farm. My mother, oh, she remarried a Sir after my parents divorced ten years ago if you're wondering where the title comes from. My mother feels a housekeeper is needed, hence, she goes and hires one ...'

'I was hired as a farm manager,' I correct.

He laughs.

'Well, I assure you there is nothing to manage here except animals, and you need a firmer voice than you have else you'll have a lot more than Molly up your skirt.'

I feel myself blush. He has a half smile on his face and I can tell he is enjoying teasing me. He nods at the contract in my hand.

'You realise you've signed a contract to work here for six months. You could break it admittedly, but knowing my mother, who can be a bit of a tough cow, she'll probably sue you.'

Oh no. He smiles and adds,

'Don't worry, I'll phone her. She's an interfering minx. Frankly though, I could do with a bit of help around the house. I tell you what; I've got to rescue those sheep. Why don't you have a look upstairs? The room at the far end would be yours if you choose to stay. I'll be a couple of hours. My number is on a pad by the phone. If I don't hear from you I'll presume you'll be here when I get back.

I'll bring back extra fish and chips, unless you prefer a Cornish pasty, or were you planning on cooking?'

I shoot him a filthy look. Fish and chips. He cannot possibly be serious.

'I would get you a take-out salad but there's not much call for it in these parts, oh and if you should go out, please don't ever forget the golden rule; *always shut the gate*!'

He smiles and without another word walks out of the farmhouse. Bloody golden rule, this is worse than being back at school.

Chapter Nine

I stare at the door examining every scratch and knock that has been inflicted on it. It's like I am unable to move. I begin to wonder if I am in shock. I look at the contract and drag my heavy legs to one of the chairs at the table. I fall into it and let the tears come. How could I have been so stupid? I should have known the whole farm manager job was too good to be true. Oh what a fool I am. I hate Charlie, I hate him so much. How could he do this to me? I was a good girlfriend, I was never over demanding like some women. Wasn't it enough losing him without losing the flat too? I fumble in my bag for a tissue, slamming it angrily back onto the table when I don't find one. I give the sink a cursory glance in the hope there might be some kitchen towel there, but there is nothing. I've never seen anything like it. Doesn't he have a shed or something? What sort of person piles so much rubbish onto a table? A rude person, that's what. Edward Fairfax is not only rude, he is also a slob. No wonder Lady Fairfax-Mason was desperate to get him a housekeeper, although on reflection, he doesn't need a housekeeper, he needs a sodding skip. The sink is full of dirty dishes and on the floor below is a wash basket full to the brim of dirty washing. I push some engine parts to one side of the table and lay out the contract. He is quite right of course. I had stupidly signed to work here for six months. I angrily yank off my holey laddered tights and with a heavy heart make my way upstairs in the hope of finding some toilet roll in the loo.

The stairs creak under my feet and I pass an oil painting that must be older than my grandmother. The stair carpet doesn't look like it has been vacuumed in months. I mean, who lives like this for Christ's sake? I hear Lloyd Grossman's posh voice echo in my head. *So, who lives in a house like this?* An arrogant untidy slob, that's who.

Honestly, I swear I can see things moving in the stair carpet. One night here and I will no doubt have fleas, not to mention lice. That's if I haven't got them all ready. I so need a bath. It is when I reach the room that is to be mine that I make my decision there and then. I don't give a hoot if Lady Muck takes me to court. Let her, yes let her. I was led here under false pretences. Farm manager my arse. More like farm dogsbody. I can't possibly stay here and eat take away fish and chips and Cornish pasties. I shall become huge like the mother in the movie *What's Eating Gilbert Grape*. Georgie will have to burn the house down as she would be too mortified to have me lifted out of this room. That would teach Edward Fairfax and his mother a lesson. Just the sight of this room is enough to drive me to the Cornish pasties. The floor is covered with a threadbare carpet and the room houses a king-sized bed, a small dresser and a battered bedside cabinet. All are bare, including the bed. I click on the light switch. There is a pop and the light bulb goes out. More tears roll down my cheeks and I walk to the bathroom for toilet roll. I shall tidy myself up and look for a bed and breakfast. There must be one somewhere near here. After all, this is where people come for their holidays isn't it? I push open the bathroom door.

'Oh shittity shit.'

I stumble back and hit the door with my elbow, slamming it shut. There is a gigantic spider in the bath and I mean gigantic. It has the body of a tarantula I am sure. In fact, it probably is a tarantula. I'm in the country after all, and who knows what you get out here. Its legs are the hairiest I have ever seen, well the hairiest I have ever seen on a spider, and what's more the thing has been breeding by the look of it as there are lots of little worm things in the bath too. Christ, I feel sure I will throw up any minute. I'm in some kind of horror movie. What if the thing has been breeding all over the house? It will be like the movie *Arachnophobia,* and I won't get out alive. Oh my God, it's moving. I scream and turn to the door when it suddenly bursts open making me scream even louder. Molly dives in and leaps up at me almost sending me into the bath with the monster. This is awful. I shove her back and rush from the room hurling myself at a large cobweb as I go. I am screaming so much that I am surprised everyone from the local village hasn't rushed round to check I'm not being slashed to death by Norman Bates. In fact, I'm thinking getting slashed in the shower by Norman Bates may well be preferable to getting into the shower with the tarantula. My head is thumping unmercifully. Molly is pushing me backwards into the bedroom. I'm being sexually assaulted by a dog. This could only happen to me. My skirt is now spluttered with mud and my tights look like they have been pecked at by birds. I dread to think what my once well made-up face must now look like. I most certainly fit the part of a heroine for a horror film, that's for sure. I fall onto the bed and sob. Molly has raised herself up and has both paws on my knees and is now licking my face. She is killing me with love and it just makes me cry even more.

'I hate him, I hate him,' I say over and over again. Molly continues to lap at my face, ignoring all my *down girl* instructions.

A bang at the front door makes us both jump and Molly bounds from the room barking madly. God, I don't want anyone to see me like this. I tiptoe to the top of the stairs and look down. There is another thud on the door.

'Hello, anyone here?'

The door creaks open and the face that matches the voice looks up at me.

'Hello there. Is everything okay? Is Ted about?'

A woman of about my age surveys me with piercing blue eyes. She is wearing a boiler suit and wellington boots, and several strands of her blonde hair have escaped her neat bun and she flicks them away with her hand. I stare down at her and admire her beauty. If this is what country living does for you perhaps I should stay. Clarins doesn't seem to be doing very much for me at the moment. Her cheeks are rosy red and her full lips have a natural pinkness to them.

'I was on my way back and I spotted some of Ted's sheep by the church. I've brought them home. I thought I heard screaming. Is everything okay? Edward trying to force you to put a duster round is he?'

I blow my nose and walk downstairs.

'Oh dear, whatever has happened?' she asks on seeing my face. With two quick steps she is standing in front of me and shaking my hand with all the vigour of a man.

'Hello, I'm Sara I live just up the lane. We own Cockspit Farm; well that is my parents do.'

I raise my eyebrows.

'Yes I know. Bloody awful name isn't it?'

49

I smile.

'I'd do anything to change it. I'd sleep with the planner if it came to it,' she laughs. 'Seriously though, are you the new cleaner?'
Cleaner? Do I even look like a cleaner?

'I'm Alice I've come as the new farm ...' I hiccup back a little sob. 'Oh, it's just everything isn't as I thought it would be and Edward is getting fish and chips and I, well I just don't eat fish and chips. In fact I don't remember when I last ate fish, or meat, and my bed hasn't even been made and it will take me hours to get back to London and, I mean just look at everywhere.' I wave my arm around in an effort to encompass all the mess in one sweep.

'Lady Fairfax–Mason told me ...'

'Whoa, you're going too fast. Let's have a cup of tea shall we?'
Well that would be nice if I could even see the kettle let alone fill it with water, and as for cups, I'd be surprised if he has any. Knowing him he probably just swigs from the tea pot. What a disgusting slob. Well, if he thinks I'm eating my chips out of the newspaper he can think again. Who does that these days? To my surprise she lifts a shiny clean kettle from behind a packet of cornflakes and fills it with water. From the Welsh dresser behind the table she retrieves two mugs and rinses them under a tap. I scramble in my bag and take out a foil of Paracetamol. I'd better stock up on these if I'm staying. What am I thinking of? Of course I'm not staying.

'You must think me so stupid,' I say blowing my nose.

'Of course not, I'd have a bloody fit if I walked into this after driving up from London,' she replies in her cheerful sing-song voice.
It occurs to me that she must know Edward very well. Good job I didn't say what a slob he was.

'I hope you don't prefer herbal. There is only builder's tea I'm afraid.'
Well, I'm not surprised. I don't imagine camomile is in Edward Fairfax's vocabulary. She lifts several pieces of engine from the table and dumps them onto the floor. Then with a quick flick of her wrist she flaps a tea towel over it.

'It's a bit of a mess I'm afraid. Ted has tried to get a cleaner but you know how it is?'
Obviously these cleaners haven't met Blanche Fairfax-Mason have they, or they would have been hired before they could say *Brillo Pad.*

'So, you had a run in with madam did you? And if I'm not mistaken you have been led on a bit of a wild goose chase, would I be right?'

I nod miserably. I must seem like a gullible fool.

'She told me there was staff here, that I'd be managing them and would help run the farm. I accepted the position because ... Well, I wanted to get away from London and ... Anyway if you can recommend a decent B and B ...'

She lays her hand on mine. It's the last thing I need. Even the smallest gesture of kindness has me weeping again.

'Look, I tell you what, I can spare an hour. Why don't we get the bed made up in the spare room? Tidy it up a bit. Even if you just stay for tonight, it's better than paying out for a B and B isn't it? I'll text Ted, get him to bring you a vegetable pasty instead of the fish, how about that? Of course if you want to go to a bed and breakfast I can phone around.'

'Oh no, really, the fish will be fine,' I say quickly. The last thing I need is some country farmer ridiculing me because I am vegetarian. Not that I am a strict vegetarian you understand. It's Charlie that is the real vegetarian and animal rights liberator. I only did it to make things easier at meal times. Come to think of it I did a lot of things to make things easier and keep the peace between us. I almost froze to death at some of the animal rights protest movements he took me on. I often used to think animal cruelty came before Alice cruelty. I swear I had mild frostbite once because he snatched my gloves off me. Well, I didn't know they were real leather. My mother had given them to me for Christmas. So, it wasn't strictly my fault was it? My hands were a bluish purple by the time we got home. The truth is I got so tired of going out for a meal and having Charlie ask *is this cheese vegetarian,* or, *was this cooked in the same pan as that meat.* In fact, I'm still riddled with guilt as often I would forget and give him cheese that wasn't vegetarian, or pretend I had made a bolognaise from Quorn when it was in fact real mince. I would lay awake all night waiting for him to have some kind of anaphylactic shock while he snored away happily. I'm still haunted by fears that one day he will spontaneously self-combust because there was gelatine in the trifle or animal fat in the apple pie. It will be something of a relief I suppose to just tuck into some fish and chips without having Charlie say *You do know that is dripping in animal fat don't you?* Plus the fact that I am actually so hungry that I'm seriously beginning to think that if Edward Fairfax slaughtered a cow in front of me I would eat it. After tea I feel a little better and with her help make up the bed with clean sheets and blankets.

'Obviously, if you decide to stay you can buy a duvet in the village shop ...' she trails off.

'Ted is desperate for help around the house. He won't admit it of course, he's a stubborn bugger, if you'll excuse my language,' she smiles and wipes a film of dust from the dressing table.

Excuse her language? Bloody hell, if I can listen to Casper I can listen to anyone.

'This place has gone to the dogs. Poor Ted, I don't think he fully realises what he's taken on. Was he bloody rude?'

I nod.

'He's got a lot on his plate, but I know that's no excuse for rudeness. He's not a farmer, our Ted. He's a brilliant vet but a lousy farmer. So, what made you take a job in Truro of all places?'

I feel tears prick my eyelids again.

'My fiancé chucked me a few weeks before our wedding, and then he gave up the tenancy on our flat and then my hours at work got cut ...' I stop abruptly.

Christ, it sounds even direr than I thought it was when I say it out loud. I've read about people like me. I'm one of those people that cause delays on the Underground. *We're experiencing delays due to person under a train.* I've got nowhere to live, and nothing to live for.

'Crikey. So you've been left without a pot to piss in so to speak?'

That's one way of putting it.

'Charlie did rather leave me in the lurch.'

She nods.

'He sounds a right Charlie if you don't mind me saying.'

I don't as it happens.

'Crikey and now you're lumbered with Edward. Don't get me wrong, I love him to bits but this farming idea is ...' she breaks off, 'Listen to me being the village gossip.'

Heavens, I hope I've not been slagging off my new boss to his girlfriend. She might have said something. What was I thinking of letting Casper and Georgie talk me into taking this job? The thought of Casper reminds me I haven't sent Georgie an *I've arrived here safe* text. Oh my God, knowing those two they will be convinced I've been involved in some multiple pile-up and will be on the phone to the police already.

'I must text my friend to let her know I am safe. Otherwise she'll be worried sick.'

'You won't get a signal here. You'll have to go to End Field to get any. Use Ted's phone, he won't mind.'

Where the hell is *End Field* when it's at home? And what kind of place is this that you can't get a phone signal? The last thing I want to do is phone Georgie where I can be overheard. As this woman will, no doubt, repeat the whole conversation back to Edward Fairfax. I just want to speak to Georgie, eat my fish and chips, and get a good night's sleep before my journey back tomorrow. There is no way, absolutely no way, I am staying. I shall also phone Mark and tell him that the new hours will suit me fine. I'll cope. I can move back in with my parents for a short time until I find a better job. Yes, that's it. I must think positive. In fact, probably after a few months Charlie will come to his senses. Men have these sort of crisis things don't they?

'Actually, I could do with some fresh air,' I say cheerily, 'I'll pop to End Field.'

She looks at me curiously.

'But it's pouring with rain. Wouldn't you rather use the house phone?'

It takes some time to convince her that I would appreciate the walk. She directs me to End Field which, amazingly enough is exactly that, the field at the end of the estate. I mean, how original is that? I mean, who calls the end field *End Field*?' No doubt it was one of Edward Fairfax's great ideas.

'You'll need your wellingtons,' she calls from the bedroom window. 'I'll pop the vacuum over your room and then I'll be off. Tell Ted I'll give him a ring.'

I suppose I could wait until she leaves and then phone Georgie. Of course though, knowing my luck Edward will return and then he will hear my conversation. No best to call her on my mobile. Honestly, what kind of place doesn't have a phone signal these days? It's not darkest Peru for heaven's sake. I don't like to say I've never owned a pair of wellingtons in my life and am not going to start now. I'm about to tell her it is not my room, and it never will be, but bite back the words. After all, she is only being nice, and God knows, being Edward Fairfax's girlfriend can't be easy. I can't help wondering, as his girlfriend, why she doesn't help around the house a bit, but then it's not my business. I shrug and tell myself I will be gone tomorrow.

She wasn't joking when she said it was pouring with rain. It is bucketing down. I retrieve my trainers and rain mac from the car and begin the walk back down the driveway. I don't even want to imagine what I look like in bare legs and trainers, and a chewed up skirt, all barely hidden by a next to useless rain mac. I wave my phone about trying to get a little bit of signal when Molly charges up behind me.

'Come on, just one bar, that's all I ask,' I plead to my Blackberry. Don't they have phone masts here?
Molly is convinced that I am talking to her and wags her tail in gratitude, pawing my bare leg and leaving yet another mud paw print. Sod it. Christ, where did all this rain come from? It's like a bloody monsoon. I've only come to Cornwall for God's sake, not bloody Bangladesh. My trainers squelch as they sink into the mud and I am only half way there. This isn't mud, it's quicksand. I'll be sucked under. They probably call it End Field because that's what it is; it's where you meet your end. I am about to open the gate into End Field when suddenly the cows that had been nibbling contentedly at the grass surge towards me. OH MY GOD, it's a stampede. Molly dives in front of me, barking and dashing from side to side. I slip in an effort to dodge her and my trainer slides on some cow dung and the next thing I know my legs are in the air. I land with a splat in the mud and shit. I feel it splash onto my face and I grimace. I turn wide-eyed and my body freezes. I am going to be crushed to death by stampeding cows and I didn't even make it into End Field. It seems a little unfair that my end should come when I am just a few feet from it. What am I thinking? I can't die here, lying in shit. I can't say my whole life flashed before my eyes. The only thing flashing before my eyes are galloping black and white cows and a fleeting thought that this is so not like Princess Diana. In fact, being crushed by stampeding cows while lying in a heap of cow dung is as far from Princess Diana as one can get I imagine. I close my eyes and clench my teeth and pray it will be over quickly. The pounding of the hooves matches the pounding of my heart. I can barely breathe

when I feel strong arms lifting me. I hear the creaking of a gate as I am being carried to safety. I open my eyes and find myself looking into the hazel eyes of my rescuer. Edward Fairfax's cheek twitches slightly when I fidget to be released and he puts me down abruptly. The stampeding cows stand quietly in a long queue and my mobile is lying in the mud. I look at it forlornly. He leaps over the gate, retrieves it, and hands it to me. I make a pitiful effort at tidying my hair and attempt a smile, but it doesn't work. I notice my phone is flashing. I finally have a signal and realise I am standing in End Field and the rain is absolutely bucketing down.

'What are you doing?

'I was trying to get a phone signal and the cows just …'

'The cows got spooked. They don't often see mad women waving mobile phones around.'

I suddenly feel very shaky.

'Come on, I'll drive you back.'

He holds out his warm soft hand and it seems I have no choice but to take it. My legs turn to jelly and the last thing I remember thinking before I fainted was *no way does he know Prince Harry*.

Chapter Ten

'Oh Ali, thank God. I was all for driving to sodding Cornwall. Why the hell didn't you text me to let me know you had arrived?'

'I'm sorry. Can you believe there is no phone signal here? Honestly it's like the bloody land that time forgot. I almost got trampled to death by a herd of cows. Oh Georgie, it's awful, really awful. I have to go miles into a field to get two bars on my phone. I mean primitive or what ...'

'You're sounding like a snob,' she scolds.

'Sorry, I don't mean to. That's awful. It's just I can't tell you what Edward Fairfax's house is like. It's like that TV programme *How clean is your house?*, except it's not funny.'

'What!'

'Honestly Georgie. I didn't want to touch his house phone but I was desperate to talk to you. Can you believe I actually fainted? His cows charged at me. I mean, seriously they charged. What kind of cows does he have that do that? And then all he did was drop me off at the house and tell me to make myself a cup of tea. He's gone again to fetch his sheep and whatever else farmers do.'

I take a deep breath.

'I've had to wash myself down in the dingy sink downstairs. The bathroom is ghastly. There is a huge spider in the bath.'

'Oh no.'

'Yes, and that's just the house,' I pause and then add, 'No it's worse. There are creatures in the bath. Things are breeding there. It's like one of those films where things crawl out of the woodwork. My head itches too. I swear I've got lice. I actually saw things moving in the carpet. There's this dog Molly. I tell you the thing is possessed. It's either knocking you senseless or killing you with love and the sheep eat your skirt, and as for Edward Fairfax, he's a miserable old bugger, a real laugh-a-minute guy, not. I'm driving home tomorrow. I'll have to stay with Mum for a bit while I cope on the 30 hours ...' I say scratching my head like crazy.

'Hang on Ali I don't think it's as simple as that. The thing is ...'
There is an uncomfortable hesitation and I feel my stomach somersault.

'Your mum has taken a lodger. I wouldn't have known but she phoned this afternoon and asked if Cas and I could pop round and take some of the things you left behind ...'

'What! But she can't do that. I left loads of stuff there ...'
I'm only a few hours out of London and they are removing all trace of me.

'It's okay, they've moved some to the loft and I've got some and Cas ...'

'Oh, share it out why don't you,' I say angrily and instantly regret it.

'I'm sorry Georgie it's just a bit of a shock.'
A bit of a shock, that's an understatement. Where am I supposed to live now? I won't be earning anywhere near enough to rent something. I thought parents were always supposed to be there for you. They've probably written me out of the will already.

'Next you'll be telling me they have someone lined up for my old job,' I say miserably.
There is silence.

'Oh for God's sake,' I moan.

'I never said they had someone, but they are bound to be interviewing, and you can't seriously lower yourself like that and accept shorter hours anyway. What are the other people like at the farm?'
I scoff.

'Oh them, I think Molly must have licked them all to death because I can't find them anywhere. I tell you, it's terrible.'

'Oh come on Ali, you're made of tougher stuff.'
I am? If that is the case why is my mind dwelling on the razor blades I spotted in the bathroom cabinet. Let's face it I couldn't reach a lower ebb if I tried. I've been dumped by my fiancé, pushed out of my job and now disowned by my parents. All that I have left is a crappy job as a housekeeper in the home of Harold Steptoe, and

let's be honest, if that table doesn't resemble the Steptoe home I don't know what does.

'I am coming home even if I have to live in a Travelodge,' I say with my voice breaking.

I have two choices. It is the Steptoe house or the razor blades.

'I'll speak to you tomorrow,' I hiccup, 'I need the loo.'

Edward's loo is one muddle of shaving creams, razors, and more razors. The room smells of him and it's quite comforting in a peculiar way. How on earth anything in this house and that includes Edward Fairfax could be comforting is beyond me. I move gingerly towards the loo and am surprised to find it is clean. With a sigh I lower myself onto it. I look around and feel panic rising within me. What am I doing sitting on this man's loo? Okay, I must keep calm. Make another cup of tea and try to relax. Relax? Who am I kidding? The only thing that would relax me right now is a shot of morphine.

***

Molly's barking tells me that Edward Fairfax has returned. I hear him greeting her warmly and then a loud thumping at the side of the farmhouse. He walks in barefoot carrying a pair of socks which, with a precise aim, he throws into the over-spilling wash basket. I half expect him to cheer himself. The smell of fish and chips precedes him. He gives me a quick glance before throwing my shoe at me.

'I scraped the crap off it,' he says with a sidelong glance. 'Best not to leave shoes like that outside. The sheep are quite partial to a bit of Gucci. There's a farmyard moggy that wanders around too, and frankly, will piss on anything.'

'Seems like no one around her has any manners then,' I retort and feel quite proud of myself for being so sharp.

'You're looking better,' he says, ignoring my comment while lifting bits of engine off the table and placing them on the floor. In a flash he has produced two plates, knife and forks and a tub of salt.

What does he mean *I'm looking better*? What a cheek. He seems to have forgotten that I was almost trampled to death by his cows, and makes no mention of the fact that he scooped me up from the mud and shit, as if that sort of thing happens every day down here.

'Right,' he says as he opens the newspaper and Molly scratches at his muddy jeans.

'I got fish, cod to be precise, but I also got a pie and some sausages in batter seeing as I didn't know what you would like. Can you sort it out? They'll need warming up while I have a shower.'

He stops at the door and turns back.

'I'm presuming as you're still here that you're staying for dinner?'

I nod mutely.

'Great. I'll open some wine.'

Before I can reply he is bounding up the stairs. Molly looks wide-eyed at me and I throw her a chip while popping one in my own mouth. It wouldn't surprise me in the least if this is how Molly gets fed anyway. Aim, throw and catch kind of feeding. He's more of a slob than I first thought. I can't remember the last time I had fish and chips. I've been with Charlie for three years and I certainly never had it with him. I suggested getting some once when we were late home from a holiday and got such a look that anyone would have thought I had suggested a serving of rat poison. The plates are surprisingly clean, and my stomach rumbles at the smell of the food. I cover half of the table the best I can with a checked tablecloth that I find in one of the dresser drawers. After a few minutes Edward bounds down the stairs and into the room. He smells clean and fresh, and is now wearing a beige cashmere jumper over jeans. Without a word he opens the fridge and removes a bottle of Rosé wine. After pouring it into two glasses he turns to me.

'I see you found the sheets and blankets.'

Not even waiting for me to sit down he begins to tuck into the food on his plate. Honestly, no wonder this man does not have a wife.

'Yes, the lady from …' I pause and blush, 'Cock-up Farm came by and she helped me.'

He takes a gulp of wine and I follow suit.

'Cockspit actually, their farm is far from a cock-up.'

He looks at me over the rim of his glass and grins. I give a sour look in return. I'm tempted to ask if she is his girlfriend but refrain. He'd probably tell me to mind my own business. Molly plonks her paw onto my knee and looks up with sorrowful eyes. Either that or it is my sausage she is eyeing up.

'Down Molly, now get out,' he says firmly and opens the door giving her a shove outside but not before I note he gives her a piece of his own sausage. Yes, I was right about the *aim, throw catch* method of feeding.

'I'm sorry about the sheep,' I say while reaching across for the salt pot.

He shrugs.

'They're all back now, that's what matters.'

He cuts the last sausage in half and plonks one half onto my plate before popping the other half into his mouth. I have to admit, it's the best fish and chips I have ever tasted, but then I am starving. I'm trying very hard not to think of the calories. There must be a million in this lot, and that's not counting the wine.

'I'm not a country girl,' I say, trying to make conversation.

'I have noticed.'

He opens a paper bag and grinning says,

'Are you partial to a gherkin?'

I widen my eyes.

'I presume townies eat gherkins?'

I nod and he places one on my plate. He has extraordinarily clean finger nails for a farmer. In fact, overall he is very appealing but without being over the top handsome like Charlie. However, he lacks Charlie's manners. Had he been a little less fiery I may have considered staying for a while, but as it is I have absolutely no idea what to do. As though reading my mind he says.

'I phoned my mother, got her out of bed. She was none too happy but if she will meddle and then bog off back to Sydney. Anyway the upshot of it is that you can tear up that contract. She won't hold you to it.'

Oh, this is good news. What a relief.

'Oh, thank you so much,' I say, nodding eagerly at the extra portion of chips he offers. Stop it Alice, think *Gilbert Grape*. You'll never get into your jeans at this rate.

'Although, I really could do with some help around the place. It's a muddle.'

He pours more wine into my glass. Good heavens he is trying to get me drunk so I won't know what I'm saying. I should be careful. I don't even know this guy and I'm all alone in the house with him. God, have I gone insane? He'll be spiking my drink with rohypnol next. Although the way he's yawning he'll probably be out for the count before I am. No chance of sex tonight then. Not that I was wanting any of course. I can't even believe I am thinking this way. It's not like I'm desperate or anything, although I am missing Charlie desperately. Not that Charlie was a great expert in that area if you know what I mean. Charlie's idea of foreplay was applying a little baby oil over my breasts before kneading them like dough, pulling apart my thighs and asking are you ready? I was never sure if he meant for sex or the oven. He then has this annoying habit when we are halfway through of asking, do you want to come. I mean what sort of question is that? It's like asking if I want a cup of tea. Of course I want to come, I'm not doing it for the bloody exercise am I? I felt terribly pressured and finally did one of those fake things. How the hell men do not realise you are faking an orgasm is beyond me. All that writhing, moaning and face pulling, God, it became my weekly workout, all that thrashing around. No wonder Charlie thought he was good in bed. Perhaps it's best that we have split up after all. I would have become a shrivelled up frustrated old woman if I'd stayed with him. It doesn't bear thinking about.

'When I am here the last thing I've got time for is cleaning up. I don't expect you to stay six months but maybe a couple of weeks to see how you find it. I'll pay you weekly and that way you can leave whenever you want ...'

My mind is pulled back from Charlie and our riveting sex life to Edward Fairfax and our fish and chip dinner. I suppose I could stay for a couple of weeks. I could use that time to look for jobs on the Internet, and I can ask Georgie to look for a flat for me. It would be a perfect opportunity to get to know Edward Fairfax a little better too. Although the chances of him being available or even noticing me are about as likely as getting struck by lightning, but you never know. Edward Fairfax noticing me I mean, obviously I don't want to get struck by lightning. Strangely enough that one isn't on my bucket list. I'm not even sure I want to get noticed by Edward Fairfax as such. I suppose though just getting noticed at all would be nice. That is most certainly on my bucket list.

'Well, I suppose I could give it a couple of weeks and ...'

'Great,' he says while collecting the dishes and putting them in the sink with all the rest.

'You can start with the washing up. Anything you need before I go?'

Go? What does he mean go? Go where for heaven's sake?

'But it's almost eight,' I say stupidly.

He feigns shock.

'Good heavens, so it is. Well as you can see, a farmer's day never ends. I'm going to my study to do the accounts, not to Australia to visit my mother. Is there anything you need to ask before I go?'

Yes, how about what charm school did you attend? And why can't your girlfriend help around the house? She's too busy gossiping to all and sundry no doubt. The country air is bringing out the worst in me I think.

'I need my bags from the car,' I say shortly.

He raises an eyebrow. Oh for goodness sake.

'One is very heavy. I can carry the others. Oh and yes, there's a spider and its offspring in the bathroom. If you could remove that please, then I will be fine thank you.'

I can be hoity-toity too. Two weeks of this, it really doesn't bear thinking about.

'You'll come across a lot worse things than a spider and a few woodlice if you're going to be in the country …' he begins.

Right that's it. I don't have to keep being spoken to like a schoolgirl.

'You could try to be polite.'

Edward reels around and glares at me. Now what have I said?

'You've been here less than five hours. In that time you've managed to shepherd my sheep all over Stantonford, let people you don't know into the house and to top it all you spook my cows. I'm only glad Molly kept the cows under control and I was there, otherwise, no doubt, that would have been another gate left open. What's next on the agenda, a rave in End Field? And you expect me to be polite?'

How was I to know that his cows get easily spooked? They are English cows after all, not some herd from the Wild West.

'Now just a minute,' I say, attempting to be at my most forceful, and believe me my most forceful is pretty pitiful at the best of times.

'Don't worry your highness, I'll fetch your bags,' he barks and slams the door behind him.

Now there was no need for that was there? A few moments later he is back with all my bags, and without even a glance he effortlessly carries them upstairs. I sheepishly follow, although I don't know what I've got to be sheepish about. He deposits the bags in the bedroom and disappears into the bathroom. I wait quietly outside, wishing I had brought the wine up with me. Knowing him, he will probably take it out of my salary at the end of the week if I do. Oh sod it. I run downstairs, pour another glass and survey the washing up. He walks past me and pours the rest of the wine for himself.

'I'll see you in the morning,' he says gruffly and leaves me standing alone staring at a sink full of dirty dishes.

Forty minutes later and with the dishes done and the sink sparkling, and I assure you that sparkling sinks are not my forte, I brave the stairs, and the bathroom, carrying a tin of fly spray. With my heart thumping I open the door and, turning my face away and spray manically at the bath until I'm choking so much that I can barely breathe. I peek through my hands to see if the spray has stunned the spider only to find there is nothing there. No sign of a spider or woodlice. Edward Fairfax had already removed them. Unbloodybelievable. I fortify myself with some wine and begin cleaning my room. Twenty minutes later I step back from the wardrobe and flop onto my cluttered bed. The old chest of drawers stinks of mothballs and there is no way my knickers are going in there. I'll end up smelling like old Lady Haversham from *Great Expectations*. This is awful. The wardrobe is full of dust. I drink the last of my wine and look at my pile of clothes. Okay, the wardrobe can be dusted and the drawers washed, but today the clothes are going back into the case. Of course it will need a lot more to make it look feminine but hopefully I won't be here that long. I run downstairs feeling a little bit more buoyant and make myself a cup of tea and steal a Penguin bar from the cupboard. I stand at the doorway to my room and survey it critically. All that work and the only sign that the room is mine are my Rochas Femme perfume bottle, Body Shop tubs and my Toni and Guy hair products which now sit neatly on the dresser. I just need some candleholders, cushions, and maybe a nice bedspread. That should help. Who am I kidding? The room is as grim as grim can be. Unlike Rebecca who dreamt boringly of Mandalay, I don't think I shall be saying *Last night I dreamt of Trenowyth* unless of course it was a nightmare. A freshly made bed makes all the difference, although I could have done without the loo plunger sitting in the corner. I decide that tomorrow I will move the furniture around and make it cosier. I check the door for a lock and am relieved to see there is one. There is still zilch signal on my Blackberry. I wave it around the room but there is nothing. Honestly, how ridiculous is this? I hang out of the window trying to get some signal until part of the crumbling window frame comes away in my hand and I find myself grabbing at thin air while fighting back a scream. With shaking legs I flop onto the bed before finally climbing into it with a Jackie Collins novel. The bed is a bit springy, but not too bad, and at least the springs aren't poking through the mattress and sticking into my back. I am just starting to relax when I hear a dull thud above me, and then what sounds like manic scratching. Oh my God, what is that? With my body rigid I listen intently for the noise to come again but all is quiet. There is nothing above this room as far as I noticed, except of course a loft. I exhale and slowly relax my muscles. I make a huge effort to concentrate on my book when I hear the noise again. I jump out of the bed and trip over my trainers and stupidly shush myself. I can't even phone for help and even if I could by the time I get my laptop up and running and Skype on the screen *THEY* will already have murdered me. I knew I shouldn't have come. I tiptoe to the door and unlock it as quietly as I can. I open it tentatively with the intention of screaming for Edward but I see all the lights are off. Shit. I quickly pull the door closed before anyone can force themselves in and with trembling hands lock it again. Where is he? What if he is the murderer? This is like something out of *10 Rillington Place*. What is that in the loft? Then a terrible thought occurs to me. What if Edward Fairfax keeps his victims in the attic? Was that why he was so angry when his girlfriend came when he was out? Was he afraid she may have heard something? Oh my God, he isn't going to let me leave alive is he? This really is the house that time forgot. How many bodies are up there? Then a terrible thought occurs to me. What if Lady Muck is an accomplice? Oh, Georgie and Cas, you need to rescue me. Never mind sodding End Field. By the look of it, everything ends here. I run to the bed, grabbing the loo plunger as I go. Clutching it close, I dive under the covers and try to stop my trembling. I must have fallen asleep as in the morning I wake up still clutching it, and for a split second I think it is Charlie. I guess that says a lot about him.

Chapter Eleven

If the sound of cows mooing hadn't woken me I would still be sleeping soundly. Instead I'm all tangled up in the sheets with just a small measure of panic beginning to overwhelm me as I try to work out how an unsightly picture of some strange woman sitting astride a horse got onto my wall. Not to mention how the window managed to move to the left of me when it had always been on the right. Then with a sinking heart I remember the wonderful job I had taken as the new farm manager. My Blackberry says 6 a.m. and I have slept like a baby. Light streams in through the window and for a second I struggle to remember why I took a loo plunger to bed with me. I know I didn't have time to unpack my vibrator but surely I wasn't that desperate last night. I had a couple of glasses of wine but really, that is just plain obscene. I then remember the banging and scratching and my heart begins to pound again. I scramble from the bed and check my door is still locked. From the window I can see Edward Fairfax leading cows into a shed. He's probably going to slaughter them next. He looks up and before I can duck he waves.

'Morning,' he calls, 'there is fresh coffee in the pot. See you in a minute.'

My Blackberry shows zilch signal and waving it around the room like a maniac still achieves nothing. There is only one thing for it. I dress, pack my things, and then armed with a tin of fly killer and the loo plunger I head downstairs. If he tries anything I shall aim the spray straight at his eyes and then while he struggles to see I'll knee him in the balls and bash him over the head with the plunger. Then I'll make my escape. Charlie will be so relieved that I got out alive that he will, no doubt, suggest we start again.

I cautiously enter the kitchen and amazingly, there is no sign of the engine parts. The oak table has not only been cleared but also washed down. A pot of coffee is bubbling away on an Aga which I hadn't noticed yesterday, or more likely, couldn't see because of the mess. Croissants sit temptingly on a plate. Oh, he likes to fatten his victims up first does he? What a bastard. Well, he's picked on the wrong one this time.

'Did you sleep okay? I know it's not the best bed.'

I jump at the sound of his voice. He stands by the back door smiling. I've got one hand behind my back and a loo plunger in the other. I only need rubber gloves and I would pass as Mrs Bouquet. Oh my goodness, is that blood on his shirt and jeans. I attempt to hide the fly spray and accidently hit the spray nozzle. A mist appears from behind me. Shit. He seems not to notice and walks to the Aga. Molly quietly follows and flops onto the flagstone floor. Why is she is so exhausted? No doubt she's been helping to move the bodies. Oh Alice, do stop being so dramatic. You're sounding worse than Cas.

'What's that behind your back?' he asks, his voice gruff and his eyes like steel.

'Nothing,' I say in a high-pitched voice while struggling not to choke on the fly spray.

For a few seconds we stare each other out and I fumble with the nozzle.

'If it's nothing why are you hiding it?'

My mouth is so dry I feel sure my tongue is stuck to the roof of my mouth.

'I know you killed them,' I say, the words choking from my lips.

He gives an evil grin.

'What are you talking about?'

'The blood,' I say pointing to his shirt.

'I had a calving at about five this morning. I've not had time to change yet. I had to milk the cows.'

Calving, milking the cows? Oh no I am making a total prat of myself aren't I? He looks at me oddly.

'Alice, are you on drugs? Is that what's behind your back?' he asks, his mouth tightening.

I hold out the can of fly killer.

'And before you even suggest it, no, I don't sniff fly killer. I heard these noises in the attic and well, I thought, I thought ...'

Oh Christ on a bike, what did I think? He looks down at the blood on his shirt.

'You thought I killed someone up there? As much as I can see that rape and pillage would appeal I just don't think I've got time to fit it into my day. Sorry to disappoint you. That's just my mad wife you heard.'

I gape at him.

'That's a joke. I think there are crows nesting there. Now, I didn't know what to get for breakfast so I bought some croissants while I was in the village. Help yourself. I've got to fix a couple of fences in Meadow Field before I can move the cows. If you can feed the chickens and collect any eggs that would be great. See you later. If you have any problems text me.'

'But I can't get a signal here on my Blackberry, is there any way of fixing that?'

'Fixing the bad signal on your mobile?'

I nod. I know I don't speak West Country yet but my London accent isn't that hard to understand surely?

'Well you could fit a phone mast in the nearest field.'

Very funny.

'By the way, you may need to do a shop. There is a store in the village I'm just about out of everything, and you need a bulb for your room. The one I put in there is actually out of my bedroom, so if you wouldn't mind. I'd better get off. Jed may well come over later. He's got stuff to do in the shop.'

'Jed?' I ask bewildered.

Either I'm totally thick or is he being deliberately vague.

'He works on the farm. You did meet him when you arrived. He rescued most of the sheep you let out. I thought I'd better mention it. What with your imagination and everything you just might think he's the Boston Strangler and bop him one with that toilet plunger.'

He grabs a croissant and has eaten half of it before reaching the door. Under his breath I hear him mumble *crazy woman*. I cringe. Did I really just accuse of him of being a mass murderer? I embarrass myself, I really do. After coffee and croissant and with my Blackberry propped up on the windowsill where I hope there may just be some signal, I decide to explore the house with the brilliant idea of making a detailed list of what needs to be done. After ten minutes I throw the list in the bin. This house doesn't need a clean, it needs demolishing. One look at Edward's bedroom and I'm close to ordering a skip. He has clothes everywhere, and I mean everywhere.

There are jeans slung over the back of chairs, tops and jumpers in a heap on the floor. Shirts are hanging above the windowsill and outside the wardrobe. Obviously he hasn't quite worked out how to open the wardrobe door. The bedside cabinets are piled high with books on veterinary practice and old copies of the *Sunday Times*. The bed is unmade. I turn to leave the room and gasp as I catch sight of myself in an old battered dressing table mirror. I look like Dracula's daughter. I'd completely forgotten about my make-up last night. Edward Fairfax saw me looking like this and didn't say anything. My eyes have black rings under them where my mascara has smudged, and there is one of those big sleep creases down my left cheek making me look like a gangster's moll. Worst of all I've got those crusty bits stuck to the corner of my lips and my eyes. My fringe is pointing upwards like someone glued it together with PVC glue. I wince at the memory of facing Edward Fairfax. How must I have looked and with the stupid fly killer behind my back too? I comfort myself that at least no one else saw me like it, and rush to the bathroom before they can. The bathroom is freezing and I take the quickest shower I have ever had. The familiar smell of my perfume relaxes me and I decide I can do this.

Okay Alice, one step at a time. After all, you're not Superwoman and Edward Fairfax wouldn't expect you to be. On second thoughts, knowing him he probably would. Fancy accusing me of being on drugs? What a cheek. Still, I suppose it's no worse than me accusing him of being a mass murderer. Right, what has the day got in store for me then? Knowing my luck some bloody farm animal will charge at me and by the time Edward gets back I will have been devoured by vultures. The police will have to identify me by my dental records. I really should consider a career as a crime writer; I'm wasted at this farm manager dogsbody stuff.

Okay, feed the chickens and collect the eggs. How hard can that be? Harder than you would imagine seeing as I have no idea where the food is kept but more importantly I have no sodding idea where the chickens are kept either and I have no intention of walking all the way to End Field just to text Edward Fairfax to ask him where they are. They must make some kind of noise. I'll just walk around the farm until I hear them. Even I know a chicken when I see one. The sight on opening the front door is so beautiful it takes my breath away. The view across the fields is magical. There is a mist in the valley and the sun glistens on a rolling patchwork of green and yellow fields for as far as the eye can see. The air is fresh and cool, and it is so peaceful. I walk to the side of the house and in front of me is the chicken coop. Several chickens are running free and pecking at the grass. Well, that was easy enough. There are also dozens of bruised apples on the ground and I look up to see not only one apple tree, but several. I then find myself getting all Mrs Beeton like, and thinking I could bake an apple pie later. Bearing in mind I have never made an apple pie in my life. This is what the country does to you it seems. Further along are the milking sheds, well I presume those things are for milking. Earlier I would have imagined them to be torture chambers. Karen's voice echoes in my head, *Honestly, I'm not being funny but what are you like Alice?*

The chickens are all nestled together and look quite harmless. Lugging the huge bag of feed that I found in the house I gently approach the hens. They look at me intently.

'Nice hens,' I murmur gently bending down to get their feeding bowls, only to get a sharp peck on my hand from the nearest one.

'You bitch. Don't you forget where you are on the food chain missus. I have seen the likes of you in the freezer section at Tesco's, and believe me, it's not a pretty sight.'

She then proceeds to peck at the other hens as they rush towards the food. A trickle of perspiration runs between my breasts and down my arms. This farm lark is harder than I imagined. A Land Rover screeches down the drive and I turn dropping some of the feed near my feet. The next thing I know the hens are pecking away at my ankles and I am hopping from one foot to another. The Land Rover comes to a halt and I attempt to stop my war dance and look dignified as Edward climbs out. Thank goodness I tidied myself up. I'm acutely aware that I may be hanging lopsided however, as I forgot to put on my perfect fitted bra, but at least I'm still not holding the loo plunger.

'I forgot to give you this,' he calls, walking towards me.

I throw the seed into the buckets and step back, kicking the most vicious hen as I do so.

'Dinner,' I hiss at her before turning to greet Edward.

He is holding a small Nokia phone.

'Oh, I ...'

'Is it too basic for you? Sorry, I just didn't think there'd be much call for emails here.'

He has such a manner about him doesn't he?

'No, really it's very kind of you. It would actually be very useful. Thank you so much. What do I owe you?'

He pushes his hands into his jeans pockets.

'It's only a Nokia phone, not a holiday in the Bahamas.'

At that moment that bloody chicken pecks me again and I jump back and am in his arms. I'm not sure if I fell on him, or if he deliberately stepped forward. Whichever way it goes, his arms are around me instantly, warm, comforting and safe. He releases me just as quickly and I step to the side of him away from the hen.

'You need to watch that one; she's taken a liking to you, as did Molly. You obviously have a way with animals,' he says, covering my embarrassment.

'My charm hasn't worked on you then has it?' I mumble.

'Oh God, that was rude I'm sorry.'

The hen pecks me again.

'Suitable punishment,' he smiles.

'That one is going to be dinner tonight,' I say, feeling a blush creep up my face.

'Maybe in a couple of months,' he says with an evil grin, 'she may well be.'

He turns and without another word gets back in the Land Rover and drives off. I am so going to hate it here.

Chapter Twelve

'Hello there, you look lost.'

The breezy voice belongs to a woman with rosy cheeks and short brown hair which has a red streak down the middle. She is wearing long dangling earrings and a multi-coloured shawl. Over her shoulder is an enormous tote bag. Several bunches of dried lavender protrude from the top, and the fragrance drifts on the breeze and caresses my nostrils. I imagine her to be about sixty, but I'm useless with ages. She clasps the handlebars of her bicycle. My mother would have called her *one of those modern women,* which is my mother's term for a lesbian. Any woman with short hair and dangly earrings is a lesbian according to my mother. That's probably why I never ever had my hair short. I probably grew up with the belief that getting your hair shorn turns you into a lesbian. My mother has all kinds of strange ideas. She's convinced that I lost my virginity to a Lil-lets tampon and there's no swaying her.

'Divine isn't it?' she continues, pointing to the lavender.

'Oh yes, it smells lovely. I'm actually looking for the supermarket.'

Oh dear, did that make me sound disinterested? It's just I've been searching for the supermarket for the past fifteen minutes. If I have to circle the village a fourth time and pass the dead pheasants and little rabbits hanging in the butcher's window, I think I will go mad. I'm sure we don't have that in London. I imagine if we had, Charlie would have made an enormous fuss and reported them to the animal protection society. Then there was the baker who I passed just as many times and where the appetising smell of Cornish pasties and fresh bread wafted towards me. I was very tempted the second time around to purchase a pasty there and then, not to mention the lovely doughnuts covered in icing sugar. The only thing that stopped me was the queue. I'd also passed a pub called The Heifer. I ask you, a name like that doesn't encourage you to order an extra portion of chips does it? Then there was the village shop which also seemed to be the local gossip corner with a noticeboard outside which I had quickly studied with a promise to return to later. Then there was a charity shop that smelt musty and a greengrocer's. Opposite the shops is the village green. By the third time I became quite dizzy but amazingly in all that time the only men I saw were the butcher in his lovely striped apron and hat, and the greengrocer in his green overall. Surely they and Edward aren't the only men in the village. It isn't like one of those films is it, where there are only women and the men are used just for sex? Good heavens, they'll be fighting over me. The greengrocer will be in competition with Edward and the butcher as to who will get to me first. Although I have to say Edward isn't trying that hard if fish and chips and Cornish pasty is his best tactic to get a woman into bed, and I could never sleep with a butcher. I watch too many movies that's my problem. I'm beginning to sound like the nymphomaniac city girl who's just ridden into town. Now I'm onto westerns. I should be a novelist. I'm wasted as a housekeeper.

'I'm Lydia,' she says, extending one hand which was supporting the bicycle.

It wobbles and she straightens it with the other hand.

'You must be the lady who has come to work at Trenowyth.'

Blimey, word gets around fast. I take her hand, which is dry and calloused, and almost say *I'm Alice, the famous nymphomaniac from the city,* but fight the impulse and say instead,

'Hello, I'm Alice. I thought I'd do a bit of food shopping ...'

She grabs my hand in a vice-like grip and turns it palm up so viciously that I almost yelp. She takes a step closer and almost stifles me.

'Oh my, I'm getting so much from you,' she cries.

I'm getting far too much from you I think, including the garlic you ate for dinner last night. There's nothing worse is there than those people who cross the imaginary line and then stand boldly in your personal space. If she gets any closer there won't be any personal space left. This is becoming seriously uncomfortable. Maybe it is her that is the nymphomaniac.

'Let me look at your palm.'

Which I have to tell you is quite sweaty at this point.

'Erm,' is all I can mutter.

'Oh my lovely, there is so much here.'

She looks up at me with pitying eyes.

'You've had heartbreak haven't you my lovely, and not too long ago. *Bastards* they are, men, *bastards*.'

Steady on.

'I run an enlightenment group in the village. You must come to our meeting. I read palms, and yours is fascinating. I can see a new love ...' she drops my hand suddenly. 'What am I doing, we've only just met. You must think me so rude. Here, let me give you a leaflet.'

She fumbles in her oversized bag pulling out reams of paper.

'Ah, here we are,' she says, handing me a crumpled leaflet which smells of lavender and bergamot.

'Buddhism on Mondays, you can't beat mindfulness. Yoga on Tuesdays and on Wednesday I do my readings ... Well it's all in the leaflet. They see me as the weird and wonderful one in the village. All crystals and spirit raising you know the sort of thing? Still we can't all live in the dark ages can we?'

I find I'm nodding and shaking my head all at the same time. It wouldn't surprise me if it fell off any minute and it would all be her doing. Some spell or other.

'Thank you, I'm sure once I get settled I'll pop along. I wonder could you direct me to the supermarket.'

'Oh, it's Lidl you'll be wanting, that's a mile and a half out of the village.'

Did she say Lidl? I really don't think I look a Lidl woman. Not that I have a clue what a Lidl shopper looks like of course. I mean, why would I? I don't think I have ever seen a Lidl. I've heard of them, of course and that was enough. One imagines oneself fighting over a trolley before entering the store. You probably need to go tooled up. Oh dear, now I sound such a snob.

'I was thinking more of a Waitrose,' I say hesitantly. After all, she may well be a loyal Lidl customer and have a special card and all sorts for all I know. You know, like knuckledusters and gumshields. I've only been here a day and I don't want to start making enemies.

'Waitrose you're wanting. There's nothing you can't get in the village shop and if they don't have it Martha will order for you. But if it's Waitrose you need ...'

Why do I feel this urgent need to deny any interest in Waitrose?

'No, I'm sure the village store will have everything,' I say pulling out my little list and attempting to look busy and in a hurry.

'Martha still has a few bunches of lavender. Get some for the farmhouse.'

She leans closer and for one terrible moment I think she's going to kiss me.

'So what do you think of Edward? Lovely isn't he,' she says her eyes all glassy.

'Erm ...'

'His father was a bit of a slob. Although one must not talk badly of the dead. They say the rich and royal are filthy don't they?'

They do? And which is Edward Fairfax?

'Anyway, I must get off. You have food shopping to do. So don't forget our little spiritual soirees lovely. I think you'll enjoy them,' she says cheerily while climbing back onto her bicycle.

I open my mouth to speak but she is off again.

'This is what you need, a bicycle. Ted has one I'm sure. Well, see you,' she waves, wobbles and continues.

The next twenty minutes are spent meeting the butcher and deciding what to cook for dinner.

'I've got a lovely bit of rabbit,' he says, proudly holding it up.

I fight the urge to gag.

'Well,' I mumble, swallowing back the bile.

'Edward likes a good rabbit stew,' he grins turning the poor little bugger around and then upside down.

Why am I not surprised that Edward likes a nice bit of rabbit?

'Want me to prepare it?'

Before I can answer he has sliced through it with a cleaver. I wince and half expect blood to splatter everywhere. I presume he means prepare it for the oven, but who knows. After buying two lamb chops and a packet of veggie burgers I head to the greengrocers where Jake the owner fills a bag with onions and carrots for me. Finally, I enter the general store and walk straight into Edward.

'Oh, hello,' I say awkwardly. He looks at the bags in my hand.

'I thought I'd make rabbit stew for dinner.'

He nods and looks impressed.

'Martha has my order, if you could take it back with you. There's chicken feed, dog food and a few other bits. I'll shove it in your boot.'

Now there's an offer I can't refuse. If I had to choose between him, the greengrocer or the butcher I'm bound to be swayed by a line like that now, aren't I?

'Yes, that's fine,' I say sweetly.

'So you're Alice,' squeals a woman behind the counter. 'Well Ted, you never told us she was such an attractive young woman.'

I blush and Edward grunts as he lifts the bags of feed.

'By the way, I won't be home for dinner tonight. I've got the farmers' meeting at the pub. I'll eat there. See you later.'

'But, I've had the rabbit ...'

'I've got to collect some fencing. Jed will be over later to sort out some hiring and get the muck spreading started. See you later Martha. You can give the accounts to Alice.'

He turns at the door and with the late October sun glinting on his hair I can see what Lydia meant. He is rather handsome in a rugged country way and when he smiles it does send your stomach fluttering. It's a pity he has such a manner about him.

'Rabbit stew sounds good though, how about tomorrow?'

I stare at him. How can he be so rude, and in front of Martha too? And he might as well have been talking to me in Swahili for all the sense that made. But the words *muck spreader* do not land well on me. Even I know what muck means, and it sounds very much like he intends spreading it. I cough uncomfortably. The woman smiles and pushes a loose strand of her greying hair back into her bun and pushes in a grip to hold it there. Her watery blue eyes twinkle at me.

'I'm Martha, my son Jed works for Ted. He met you yesterday. Anything you need you just ask. Don't mind Ted, he lost his social skills in the last few months. Isn't that right Ted? Now if you were a gentleman you'd invite this nice young lady to dinner after the meeting. Introduce her to the village ...'

'Oh no,' I interrupt. 'Really, there is no need.'

Edward shrugs.

'I don't think our local is quite what Alice is used to,' he says pushing past me with another bag of seed and practically sending me flying into a tray of fish bait. I shudder at the sight of the maggots and choke back a scream.

75

'But if you want to pop down about eight I'll buy you a plate of sausage and mash.'

Sausage and mash? Talk about the last of the big spenders.

'Oh, I wouldn't want you going to any great expense,' I say sarcastically.

He grins.

'Don't worry I won't. See you later then.'

I turn back to Martha and force a smile.

'Don't mind Edward, it's just his way.'

'Some way,' I huff.

'Don't worry. They do a nice dinner at the local. He was joking about the sausage and mash,' she laughs.

I wouldn't be so sure about that.

Chapter Thirteen

I study my reflection in the mirror and feel that everything is wrong. I have washed and blow-dried my hair twice. Tried it parted on the side, and then in the middle, but no matter what I do my fringe stands on end making me look like an aged punk. My insides are churning with nerves. I hadn't realised just how much the break up with Charlie had affected me. My self-esteem couldn't be any lower. It's just dinner down the pub Alice, not some hot date. It isn't like you'll be necking later down a dark country lane is it? He's just being nice and welcoming you to the village and all that. In fact he isn't even doing that willingly. It's only because Martha bulldozed him into it. All the same he didn't have to offer. Georgie is out. Apparently living it up with the two-timing James. He's taken her to the opera tonight so she won't be available for help.

'I promise to phone during the interval, see how you're getting on,' she had said. 'And we'll be down next weekend.'

I barely know Edward Fairfax. He could be a total nutcase for all I know and here I am living in his house. There must be a reason a handsome man like him doesn't have a wife. That's ridiculous. What's wrong with me, can't a man be handsome and single without being some kind of a weirdo? I give it some thought. No, it isn't possible. He is a weirdo and there is nothing I can do to get out of the dinner date. I only hope he doesn't spike my drink and have his wicked way with me. I take one last look at myself and blow upwards at my fringe. I will kill that bloody trainee. He should never have been let loose with a pair of scissors. I suppose I should be grateful it wasn't my throat. I take another look around the house. The place is spotless, well as spotless as it can be. I had spent all afternoon cleaning, tidying and at one point literally scrubbing. I've never cleaned so much in my life. I rather enjoyed it, in fact.

The engine parts that had so magically disappeared, I had discovered in the lounge, that is if you can call it a lounge. Edward was not wrong when he said the cat will piss just about anywhere. Its favourite place had obviously been the lounge as it stinks of piss, or something like it. Jed had been great and I took to him immediately. As soon as I mentioned the bits in the lounge he had laughed.

'Ted, the poor bugger, is exhausted most days. He's been trying to fix some machinery around here for weeks. I'll tell you what; I'll move it all to the back of the milking shed. If the old codger moans just blame me. I'll drop some stuff into you for the cat pee smell. It should work.'

I also learnt from Jed that the building I had passed on my way to the farmhouse is the warehouse of Fairfax Agricultural Machinery, a business belonging to Edward.

'Edward hires out farm equipment. My mum runs the office from the store and I see to the clients here. You'll get the hang of things as time goes on,' Jed added.

He had kindly stepped around wet floors, shooed out unwanted hens and found me a box that I could use as a bed for the cat. Molly had followed me everywhere and soon she became the perfect companion. Edward didn't return all day and by four that afternoon I had cleaned the whole place, apart from Edward's room which I felt uncomfortable entering. The lounge was cleared and the sofa and chairs vacuumed, the furniture polished and I even tidied the CD collection. The hallway floor was washed thoroughly and the back door scrubbed. Jed gave it a kick and it opened with a loud creak.

'That's not been opened in years,' he laughed.

There was a small room at the end of the hall, which I presumed was Edward's study, and apart from a quick vacuum I left everything as it was. I was exhausted when I'd finished but it felt good, and all the tension I had built up over the past few weeks melted away. By four-thirty I was sitting on a tatty swing just outside the back door reading my book until it got chilly. As the time gets closer to the taxi picking me up, I feel quite shaky. Remembering a bottle of whisky in Edward's study I allow myself a small glass. By the time I'm ready to leave I have allowed myself three small glasses and feel nice and warm inside. You know that feeling, the one where you don't care if your date looks like Count Dracula and the cat peeing on the floor seems romantic in a funny kind of way.

On checking my reflection I see that I resemble a rosy Pink Lady apple. Bugger it. I powder my face so frantically that, when the taxi hoots, I look like a ghost. I run a wet wipe over my face and finally resemble something halfway between a ghost and a Pink Lady apple, which I suppose is something of an improvement. The taxi driver opens the door for me. Heavens, they don't do this in London.

'Where we going love?'

'The Heifer.'

He looks startled.

'You could walk it from here.'

I look down at my shoes and he follows my eyes.

'I don't think so.'

I'm wearing my black ankle strap wedges and if I have any more alcohol I'll go arse over tit in them. It feels like seconds before he pulls into the pub car park and I attempt to manoeuvre my somewhat tipsy body from the car with as much decorum as possible. I make a marvellous effort only to be foiled by the shoulder strap of my handbag. Why do they insist on clipping these bloody things inside the bag? If I'd wanted a shoulder bag I would have bought one. The stupid strap gets tangled in my wedge and I go sprawling forward and where to? Yes, you guessed it, straight into Edward Fairfax's arms.

'I've had some whisky,' I confess. 'I was a bit nervous.'

In my tipsy state he looks rather gorgeous. No, he really is gorgeous. How could I have not noticed this? *Are you mad getting pissed?* I can hear Georgie cry. *Are you asking to be raped?* He slides his hand down my arm and I shiver. Ooh yes, maybe I am. His hair I see has been expertly cut and the style makes him look boyish. His hazel eyes are warm and heavy lidded giving him a sexy sultry look. He smells divine. If I don't eat something soon I will start on him. All I've eaten since breakfast is half a tube of sour cream flavoured Pringles. My breath is a combination of sour cream and whisky. What a turn on, not. I hold onto his arm for support. Good heavens, what is that tingling that's going on down there? I was jilted only a few weeks ago and let's face it I've not had sex for a few weeks. In fact, I've not had decent sex for a few years. Never go on a date with only Pringles and whisky in your stomach. You're likely to do something silly is my experience. There should be a warning on all whisky bottles, *detrimental to your dignity, after three glasses you may screw anything*. Oh, stop it Alice, this is not a date, I repeat, this is not a date.

Wondering if Charlie may have texted me I pull out my Blackberry just to see if, by some freak of nature, I have a signal. His clownish face stares back at me. It was taken at a New Year's Eve party about a year ago. I really should remove it as my wallpaper.

'It seems that whisky has gone straight to your head. Did you leave any for me?'
I tuck the strap safely back into my handbag and follow him into the pub. Even before we enter I can hear raucous laughter and the thump of darts hitting a board. Edward opens the door and the hubbub ebbs away and I find myself staring at a roomful of men. I feel my red apple face grow even redder. I am so conspicuous in my posh frock, wedged heels and make-up. It's the local bloody pub for Christ's sake. I feel like a total idiot. I'd even painted my toenails and popped in my best pearl earrings. It's one extreme to the other. One minute I'm at Claridge's with the rich and famous and the next I'm in a Cornish pub with a load of cow farmers.

'This is Alice,' Edward states flatly.
'I'm so overdressed,' I say self-consciously.
'Just a touch,' he says handing me a pub menu. 'It's the local, not the Savoy.'
Just relax Alice and ignore the laughter from the bar. I peer around the gloomy interior and then study the menu. I feel ravenous. I used to love eating out, but don't think I'll be doing that very often now. I don't imagine Edward will ask me out again. He's more a 'fish and chips out of the newspaper' type.

Edward orders a bottle of wine and no sooner have I taken a sip than my Blackberry seems to go crazy, bleeping and vibrating as if it is having an orgasm. I've got a signal at last. Edward ignores it and studies his menu. There are several messages from Georgie, one from my mother and a load from Vodafone, but nothing from Charlie. I stupidly feel my heart sink. The most recent is from Georgie.

I hope you've got everything. You know, money for a cab should he turn out to be a maniac and condoms should he turn out not to be. You don't want to go catching anything.

Condoms, oh my God, is she nuts? I stand up and feel myself sway. Heavens, has he spiked my drink? Glancing at my glass I see I have drunk half already. Good God, when did that happen?

'I need the ladies,' I say, trying not to sound too dramatic.

Fortunately I do not have to pass his fellow farmer cronies.

'What do you mean condoms? I'm not going to sleep with him. After all, he's my boss,' I hiss down the phone staring at my flushed face in the mirror.

'And why are you texting my Blackberry? You know I have to dangle myself from a window to get any signal.'

'Marie lives near Truro, and she doesn't have this problem. I'm sorry I didn't put your other number in my phone. Hang on let me go somewhere quieter, the bar is packed here.'

I so miss London with its vibrancy and restaurants. I could cry with longing.

'That's better. Like I said, Marie has no problems with her phone and she's with Vodafone like you. There is something suspicious about that village if you ask me. It's a good job we're coming down next weekend. If we leave it much longer I reckon we'll find you strolling around the supermarket in an apron looking like one of those Stepford wives,' she laughs. 'You need rescuing. How is it going with old Edward then?'

'You'll find me walking around with an overall on more like. Can you believe the nearest supermarket is Lidl? I mean, I've never stepped inside a Lidl. I don't think you wear frilly aprons in there, more like body armour I imagine,' I say, slapping my face with a powder puff.

She tuts.

'I never thought you could be such a snob. So, what is he like?'

'He's all right. Reasonably good looking,' I lie, 'but honestly Georgie, condoms? Have you gone mad? I barely know him, and I'm still missing Charlie.'

A thought occurs to me.

'Oh God, Georgie what if you're right?' I say feeling myself go all a tremble and begin looking around the ladies loo for an escape route.

'Right about what?'

'The *Stepford Wife* thing,' I say in a high-pitched whisper.

Georgie laughs.

'Christ, I just swallowed my olive whole. Honestly Ali, your imagination.'

'I bet it's lovely there,' I say with a stab of envy.

'Fabulous and even more fabulous, James told me he is leaving his wife after Christmas. Honestly you could have knocked me down with a feather.'

'I thought he was leaving her at Easter?'

'Well, it was awkward then wasn't it? Easter is a big thing for her apparently.'

And Christmas isn't?

'Look, I have to go, they've rung the bell and you know what the queues are like at the ladies. I'm deadly serious about the condoms. Don't they have any in the loo?'

No they don't and they also don't have any queues outside the ladies either. Oh, I so miss London. Anyway just what kind of woman does she think I am? I've only just split from Charlie for goodness sake.

'Georgie,' I admonish, 'I'm not over Charlie.'

She scoffs.

'Well you should be. He is certainly over you. I saw him in Marco's last night with some brunette with big tits, and he's already marked himself as single on his Facebook profile, not to mention the shopping spree he was having in Marks last week and ...'

'What?'

Oh my God. She'll be after my engagement ring next.

'Got to go, if you can't be good be careful.'

Luckily there wasn't a condom machine in the ladies loo which was just as well, as in my angry and tipsy state I would no doubt have got some. Men honestly.

***

The waitress places the plate of escargot in front of me and I try to look at them nonchalantly. I'm obviously deeply grateful that Edward Fairfax is treating me to more than sausage and mash but escargot? What am I supposed to do with them? She carefully lays tongs at the side of the plate and my stomach churns. What the devil do I do with the tongs, what was I thinking? This is what comes of having too much to drink.

'So just where in London do you hail from?' Edward asks me as he sips his wine.

The smell of garlic drifts up my nostrils. I fiddle with my glass and wait hopefully for him to start on his snails first. Oh no, this is all I need, he is waiting for me. The one time I don't need a gentleman. I so wish I could go back fifteen minutes and order prawn cocktail. I bet he did this on purpose.

'The escargot is very good here. I imagine you eat it all the time in London,' he had said with just the hint of a smile.

'Oh, all the time,' I had replied in a bored tone.

'The chef here used to work in one of the top hotels in London. You really can't beat his escargot.'

'Really, how interesting. Actually though, it would be nice not to have escargot being as we always had it when in London,' I had said trying to impress him although God knows why.

His eyes had widened and he had given me a little bow.

'Wow, a real expert on snails then. In that case you must try Geoff's and tell us what you think.'

Help.

'Well, it would be nice not to have them. You know, for a change.'

What must I have sounded like?

'No I insist.'

And now, here I am, with my first plate of escargot trying to look like a pro and the horrible man is deliberately waiting for me to start. I pick up the tongs casually and twiddle them around in my hand. He does the same, still looking at me. I put them down and drink some more wine.

'You didn't answer my question.'

That's because I'm so focused on the poor dead snails on my plate probably and even more focused on how I can actually get them into my mouth. I feel sick. I need more wine. How much wine can you drink without actually killing yourself?

'I'm a Chelsea girl, born and bred.'

'Ah, I see.'

He nods at the snails.

'Are you going to eat those?'

'I don't like them too hot,' I say.

Maybe if I drink enough wine I will be able to forget those little details that were once my life. You know the kind of thing, fiancé, proper job, a nice flat of one's own. He smiles in that cheeky way that I am already getting to know and carefully places a snail expertly in the tongs. I watch fascinated as he pulls it from the shell and pops it into his mouth so quickly that I don't have time to take notes. I smile and pick one up while trying not to cringe. I attempt to put it expertly in the tongs and slowly lift them up so I can remove the snail. Honestly, it's like one of those intricate operations you see on TV. The slimy little bugger slips and my attempt to re-clasp it results in the shell zooming across the room like a catapulted conker. Oh no. I close my eyes in horror and hear it land with a clatter onto the next table and finally it comes to rest on someone's plate. Classic.

'Whoops, that's the one that got away,' Edward grins and looks over to the table.

'That one is on us Jack,' he calls, 'but we will try not to follow up with the main course.'

The man laughs and waves at me. I blush and gulp my wine.

'Do you want a second go,' he laughs, 'or shall I remove them. You know, just in case the next one lands in Jack's soup.'

'The tong things are different in the country,' I say. 'I never had this problem in London.'

He removes a snail from the shell and holds the fork out to me. I place my hand over his and direct the snail into my mouth with closed eyes. When I open them again he is staring directly at me and my hand is still on his. I drop it quickly and swallow. He looks at me intently. This is a bit intimate.

'Well?' he asks.

'Like a gritty mushroom,' I say pulling my eyes away from his.

'The thing is I've never had escargot before,' I admit and dab at my lips with my serviette.

He roars with laughter.

'You're a good sport. I'll give you that.'

I shake my head. Mad countrymen.

'Seeing as I'm paying, you'll have to eat the rest,' he says seriously.

I look earnestly at him to check he isn't joking and see that twinkle in his eye and before I know what I'm doing I've tossed them all onto his plate. He actually turns out to be good company and isn't as serious as Charlie. It makes a nice change to have dinner without someone continually checking what is in the sauce and if any animal fat has been used and whether the vegetables were cooked near any meat. In fact it feels quite refreshing to just eat what I like.

'Thank you for a lovely evening,' I say genuinely as Edward brings the Land Rover to a halt.

The farmhouse is in darkness. My fuddled brain struggles to think of something else to say when he leans towards me. Oh no, he isn't going to try and kiss me? It wasn't until I stood up to leave the pub that the alcohol practically floored me. I must have got through three large glasses of wine. Every time I thought of Charlie with the brunette I had taken another gulp. It had been a lovely evening, apart from the awkward moment when the bill came. I was about to pay my half when he pulled out a Coutts cheque book. I kid you not. I wanted to grab it off him to see if it was the real McCoy. So this is where the royal connection is. He's probably something like the tenth richest man in England, and I chose the sea bass rather than the lobster because I didn't want to be too extravagant. Bloody fool, I can hear Georgie say. Not because I ordered the sea bass but because I didn't get the condoms. I look down at my crumpled dress to my bright red toenails and take a deep breath to calm my beating heart. What do I do? I'm still on the pill so it isn't like I can't do it with him. I wonder if Charlie is doing it with the brunette. Why do I have to think of Charlie all the time? The chances of him having Aids, or something like that, are unlikely, Edward that is, not Charlie, but then again, if he is one of the richest men in the country he is most likely shooting up with something to overcome the boredom of having it all. I should have that boredom. Then again, if Trenowyth is having it all then I'm a monkey's uncle. You wouldn't see me shooting up, unless it is with Macrolane to sort out these lopsided breasts. I look up and realise he had no intention of kissing me whatsoever but is unlocking my door. I lift my head and before I know it I have headbutted him. My head swims.

'Oh God, I'm so sorry,' I say swaying towards him and thinking how delicious he smells. 'I think I've had too much to drink.'
Well that was sensible Alice. It's like saying *I'm totally out of control, feel free to ravage me as I couldn't possibly fight you off.* He helps me from the car and I look at the farmhouse. It looks really bleak by the light of the moon and I feel like I'm in one of those dreams where every step you take seems to take you backwards rather than forwards.

Edward clicks on the light and I come face to face with my reflection in the hall mirror, and in my drunken state I think I look rather appealing. I can't feel the roof of my mouth mind you, and my head is developing a dull thud, but apart from that I look pretty good. I'm thinking hot bath, a bottle of water and two Paracetamol will make my night complete. Edward has other ideas it seems and before I can focus on the now spotless kitchen he has clicked on the kettle and placed two mugs on the table.

'It looks like you've had a cleaning company in.'
I swell with pride. I must be drunk if I'm flattered by compliments on my cleaning. I'm almost tempted to show him the inside of the oven but instead I pounce on the fridge and devour a bottle of Perrier water.

'You haven't have you?'
What a cheek.

'I did it myself thank you very much and destroyed several fingernails in the process.'

'Right,' he says stirring water into a mug. 'I've got accounts to finish.'
Before I can answer he has disappeared into the hall and I am left with doe-eyed Molly pawing at yet another pair of tights. Make coffee for yourself why don't you? What a selfish man. An urgent need to pee sends me reeling to the loo. A loo which only yesterday I wouldn't have been seen dead in, but now it is a pleasure to pee there. I even take pride in watching the blue toilet cleaner swirl around the toilet bowl. I am sad.

I toddle up the stairs and at some point must have got into bed. I am so relaxed and sleepy that I am asleep in no time.

Chapter Fourteen

My tongue is most certainly stuck to the roof of my mouth and the crowing of the cockerel jars through my head. The memory of Georgie's words hit me like a sledgehammer and I fall back onto the pillows with a groan. What happened to my head? It feels like Satan himself is in there torturing me. Why did I drink so much wine?

I saw him in Marco's last night with some brunette with big tits.

A brunette with big tits, well that clinches it. He's going through some early mid-life crisis. He's a bum man and always has been. Unless of course he really was a tit man all along and I was totally unaware of it. Mine being lopsided and hanging like crap wouldn't have helped at all would it? And he never got to see me in my new bras with everything hanging right way up. This is terrible. How could he do this to me? I reach out to a glass of water that sits on the bedside cabinet, squinting against the small ray of sunlight that is straining to stream into the room as I do so. What a bastard. How dare he live it up in London while I'm doing *Upstairs Downstairs* in the bloody country? He's creating a whole new life while I'm getting housemaid's knee. He's lording it up in Marks and Spencer while I've been reduced to shopping in Lidl. I fight back the tears and dive under the duvet. What have I come to? And why does shopping at Lidl feel like the end of the world? No, If Charlie is shopping at Marks then I'm buggered if I'll shop at Lidl. I don't care if I am a snob. I shall drive around all day if I have to until I find a decent Waitrose, and Edward Fairfax can go to hell. Yes, that's the spirit. Oh God, did I make a total fool of myself last night? I probably talked far too much, and mostly out of my arse I expect. It doesn't bear thinking about, and probably best not to remember. Edward Fairfax was bloody ungrateful. I've a good mind to pack my things and leave. Good plan Alice. Charlie doesn't want you and Mum has rented out your room. I feel like the little orphan Annie. I lean across to check the time on my Blackberry. It's only 6.30. Damn noisy farm animals. Can't a girl have a hangover in peace? I fumble for the foil of Paracetamol, which I know must be in my handbag somewhere, while wondering where I can buy a shotgun. I'll shoot that bloody cockerel first and then I'll move onto the pecking hens. Who knows where my massacre will end? Just let Edward sodding Fairfax start on me this morning and I'll mow him down too. It's not such a bad idea. I don't mean mowing down Edward Fairfax, obviously, but a shotgun. It will be very useful if I do have to go to Lidl. You know, to keep the riffraff at bay. I am such a snob, what on earth is wrong with me? I'm premenstrual that's the problem, and I should never drink when I'm so close to my period. I must stop thinking about shotguns too. They're probably two a penny here in the country. The last thing I should have in my hand five days before my period is a gun, shotgun or otherwise. I can't believe Charlie has already changed his status to *single* on Facebook. I'll unfriend him. That will make him think.

I untangle myself from the bedcovers and remove the earring that is stuck to my bum, check my emails and texts on my Blackberry and then remember there is no signal.

'For goodness sake, how do you people cope in the country?' I mumble while checking the Nokia.

There are two texts. I rub my sore eyes and peer at the first one. It's from Georgie.

What happened? Was he a boring old country fart? Speak later. Love you loads. Xx

The other is from Cas.

Went to the docs this morning and the place is crap without you. They're advertising your job at twenty hours. Tight bastards. Miss and love you. X

That's that then. I can't possibly work for twenty hours. I suppose I'll have to stick it out in the country a little bit longer. I hear Edward crashing around downstairs and feel my premenstrual inner goddess rear her ugly head.

'He's messing up your lovely clean kitchen already. Are you really going to put up with this?' she whispers.

I grab my woollen shawl from the bottom of the bed, and fly down the stairs in my nightie. If I am going to get pissing housemaid's knee then I want some due respect. I storm into the kitchen coming to an abrupt halt when I see my nice shiny kitchen is still nice and shiny, and with a perfectly laid table. Edward is standing at the Aga in his wellington boots and muddy jeans. His hair is tousled where he has removed his cap and his cheeks are ruddy from being outside. What time did he get up? There is toast on the table and coffee bubbling away in the percolator. Before I can turn around and creep back upstairs, he says,

'Good morning.'

I can't even begin to imagine what I look like. I'm in my nightie for goodness sake. I look down fearfully. Yes, and it is the one that has *fondle carefully* in big red letters all over my breasts. Oh piss it and piss it again. I don't know what to do first. Tidy my hair, don some sunglasses or pull my dressing gown around tighter. If I had the shotgun I'd just shoot myself. Stop thinking of shotguns Alice. You're premenstrual, and right now your tongue is more than sufficient to kill at twenty paces.

'There's toast and coffee. I'm making scrambled eggs and there's bacon under the grill. I'm not good at apologies but I make a mean fry up,' he says, turning to face me.

My eyes meet his and there's a little spark which takes me very much by surprise. Don't get me wrong it isn't fireworks or anything. In fact it was probably just the percolator gurgling. Or perhaps it's just something about his rugged appearance. Maybe there is something sexually arousing about farmers and sheep shit, all that rolling in hay and getting back to nature stuff. Or maybe I am so sexually frustrated that I'll copulate with anyone when hungover. But rude, arrogant, Edward Fairfax … what am I thinking of? I'm hungover, not desperate. He strolls towards me. Now what? I shrink back but he pulls out a kitchen chair.

'You look like you need a coffee,' he smiles.

For a second I thought he was going to say *You look like shit*.

'Do you have any Paracetamol?' I ask pleadingly.

'Drugs and coffee? You must be in a bad way.'

'Not really. I just like the celebrity lifestyle. You know, booze drugs coffee, that kind of thing,' I say, fighting the impulse to drop my head onto the table.

He places two white pills and a plate of bacon and eggs in front of me. I pull a face but attempt a forkful of egg followed by a swig of coffee and the two Paracetamol.

'The house looks nice by the way,' he says shyly and covers his face with his mug of coffee.

'You've done a great job. I'm sorry for not seeming more pleased.'

He smells of soap and some other fragrance that I can't quite place. I recognise it from last night. I feel sure it isn't aftershave. He doesn't seem the aftershave type. Just as well. The mixture of eggs, bacon, and aftershave would be the ultimate throwing-up combination.

'Thank you. I have the knees and calloused hands to prove it.'

I feel ravenous and accept an extra bacon rasher.

'The baby calf I delivered yesterday is a bit weak. I was wondering if you could keep an eye on her. Just to make sure she feeds properly. I just don't have the time. Obviously if you can't ...'

As long as he's not expecting me to breastfeed it. I feel my tits are as good as useless after hearing about the brunette with the big ones. I take another gulp of coffee and feel better already. I've even managed to consume the bacon, and the toast is beginning to look rather appetising. As though reading my mind, he pushes the toast rack across the table.

'I don't suppose you've used a teat bucket before have you?'

I look at him over the rim of my cup.

'Is this some country breakfast ritual you're going to introduce me to? Actually no, I haven't, not in the past year anyway. Strangely enough there isn't much call for teat buckets in the city. Although I can't think why not, as I know several people who could use one.'

He laughs. Blimey, it's been years since I made someone laugh. Charlie used to give me strange looks whenever I cracked a joke. Georgie would laugh like a drain, but I always thought she was just being nice.

'After breakfast I'll show you how to use one. To the calf it is just like a teat from her mother's udder, shouldn't be a problem. I'll be in

End Field most of the day. I'm fixing the gates before I move the herd into that field. Regarding money and things ...' He looks embarrassed and places a credit card on the table with a notepad and an envelope.

'That's for food and stuff around the house. The pin number is in the notebook. I thought we'd give it two weeks, see how we go. In the envelope is two weeks' pay in advance. I've rounded it up to four hundred. Make sure you buy everything for the house with the card, even things for your own room, and don't forget to get a receipt.'
He scratches his head and I see flecks of red in his hair in the light from the window.

'I'd better get back,' he smiles, takes a final gulp from his coffee mug and wipes his mouth with a serviette before heading to the door.

'Text me when you're ready and I'll show you the calf. Can you feed the hens this morning and collect the eggs? It is going to rain later so you'll need to put buckets on the landing. The roof leaks. I'll fix it later if I get time but it's not a priority right now. The farm needs a lot of work. I've fed Molly, but she can always eat more if you have time, plus there is a basket of ironing that needs doing ...'
I stare at him. It all started off so well.

'I'll stick a broom up my backside and sweep as I go shall I?'

'That would be useful if you could do that. Of course, there is also the rabbit stew you promised, unless you plan on going out again?'

'Not unless you're planning on asking me?'

'No, I wasn't planning to.'

'That's good, because I would have said no.'

'That's just as well then.'
Well, that's that. God, the rabbit stew. I'd forgotten about that. How the hell do you make a rabbit stew anyway? I'm certainly not going to ask him. I'll look online.

'I'll be cooking dinner later,' I say. That way I haven't committed myself to rabbit stew as such have I?
He dons his cap and grins warmly.

'See you later. Don't forget the buckets or we'll have a flood, and be careful with that broom.'

Well I never, he does have a sense of humour. Thirty minutes later and I am showered, dressed and looking every inch the country girl in my jeans and Aran jumper. Shame about the footwear. I don't think Marks and Spencer riding boots were made for farming. I've already slipped twice in the mud and dung that leads to the cowshed. I arrive at the door, slip again, curse and grab the nearest post, which shakes and shudders under my weight. The place absolutely stinks. I seriously consider going on Ebay and finding a gasmask. These fumes could kill me. The blocked loo at the surgery was child's play compared to this. I've yanked my hair back and clipped it up with a slide and although my headache feels a little better, I'm still not as clear-headed as I'd like to be.

'You'll ruin those boots.'

I turn and feel my feet slip. His arms steady me and then leave my body quicker than greased lightning.

'You'll need wellingtons. There are several pairs in the cupboard under the stairs, I'm sure there will be a pair that will fit you. That jumper is too good for the farm too. It will be ruined in no time, it only needs the tractor to splash through a puddle and you've had it.' Before I can respond he has left my side and is striding ahead into the shed. No wonder he doesn't have a wife. Charm and tact aren't his best qualities.

'Here she is,' he says affectionately, and for a second I think he is introducing me to the cows. I look at the baby calf. She is black and white with a cute little wet nose on her baby cow face, and big brown sad eyes with eyelashes to die for. It comes to something when I start envying the lashes on a cow.

'And here's the teat bucket.'

Heavens, is that what I think it is? A huge red penis stuck to a bucket? What the hell am I supposed to do with that? It looks like an early 19th century vibrator. Very much a do it yourself job. Well, I know where to come when my batteries die. Why is it I can't stop thinking about sex these days. I can't be trusted in the country, all my hormones seem to get stirred up. He shoves it into my hands. Is that a smile on his face? He's mocking me. Just because I'm wearing my Marks and Spencer boots it doesn't mean I can't storm away. I might well storm and then slide into a load of cow dung admittedly, but storm I can. The bloody teat bucket is covered in mud, and now the mud is all over my jumper. Before I know what I'm doing I'm holding it by the penis with my hand wrapped tightly around it no less. What do I look like? Don't even think about it.

'I said that jumper was no good for the farm,' he says, picking up a pail of milk.

'You can go off people you know,' I mumble, pulling the clean part of my jumper out of the calf's mouth. I'll need a whole new wardrobe once the week is out. Next stop Sue Ryder then. Not much call for decent stuff round these parts it seems. The charity shop must be stocked to the brim with torn jeans and boiler suits not to mention second-hand flat caps. The calf pulls at my jumper again and I yank it back, slipping as I do so.

'Wait here,' snaps Edward irritably.

Moments later he returns with wellingtons. Not the height of fashion, but far safer. I reluctantly lean on his shoulder to remove my boots. The warmth from his body is so intense that it quite startles me. He still smells of soap, but there is a strong smell of manliness about him that is quite overpowering.

'I'll leave the milk for you. She needs feeding in the morning and again in the evening. Before dinner is best.'

He takes the bucket from my hand and fills it with milk.

'This bit.' I pull a face as he holds up the teat.

He sighs.

'It's no good if you're not going to take things seriously. I'll do it myself. You just clean and iron and shop. That's what you do best.'

He sloshes through the mud, splattering me with cow dung. I feel it splash onto my jeans and I want to cry. I didn't want to come to the sodding country. I certainly didn't want to be dumped just a few weeks before my wedding or have my home pulled from under my feet by a no good bastard of a man. Now here goes another one thinking he can treat me like shit. I don't think so.

'Now hang on a minute,' I say and feel annoyed that my voice shakes.

'I'm doing the best I can. I didn't want this God-awful job and if your mother had told me you were so sodding objectionable I wouldn't have taken it. The thing is I don't have any other job. In fact, I don't have a home either. I don't have anything. My fiancé dumped me a few weeks before my wedding and now he's seeing a brunette with big tits while all I've got are lopsided ones. And all I'm left with is ...' I wave my arms around angrily, 'this. And an oversized penis in a bucket, and that just about says it all doesn't it?'

I storm past him, slipping and sliding in the mud and dung as I go. It is raining. Wonderful, I shall no doubt get soaked. I feel tears stain my cheeks and wipe my face angrily. Shame on you Alice letting another man make you cry.

'Bollocks to it,' I mumble.

He gently clasps my wrist.

'Alice, I'm sorry. I wasn't aware of the job and fiancé thing. He's obviously a fool. I mean, who goes out with brunettes with big tits these days? It's so last century isn't it? And for what it's worth I don't think you're lopsided in any way.'

I give a half-hearted smile and he hands me the bucket.

'Do you want to try the oversized penis? It might cheer you up.'

I blush and take the bucket without meeting his eyes.

'That's the nicest thing anyone has ever said to me,' I say smiling with my eyes downcast but I can't stop the tears which escape and land onto the teat bucket.

Edward shyly lays an arm on my shoulder.

'Hey, he's not worth crying over.'

'It must be me,' I say self pityingly. 'What woman loses her fiancé a few weeks before her wedding day? A bloody careless one that's what.'

'No, a lucky one. Just think, you could have married the plonker.'

I sniff noisily and he pulls a crumpled tissue from his pocket. The calf looks up at me and sucks hungrily on the teat. Well this is it, I find myself thinking. This is the closest I'll ever come to being a mother.

'I wanted children by the plonker,' I say blowing furiously into the tissue.

'You wanted little plonkers did you?' He smiles and diplomatically removes his arm. 'You've got an oversized penis in a bucket now, what more could you want?'

'Quite right,' I agree while thinking a penis bucket is not quite as good as the real thing is it?

Chapter Fifteen

'Twist that spine. That's it. There's nothing like a good spinal twist to relieve that tension. Now let's do the same on the other side.'

Don't ask how I have managed to get myself into Lydia's yoga class. I only came for a rabbit stew recipe and the next thing I know she has me twisting my limbs this way and that, along with two other women who must be seventy if they're a day, and worst of all, they're wearing leotards. But one of them has a brilliant recipe for rabbit stew, and more importantly, Lydia has the fresh thyme that is the ultimate ingredient. Edward's friend Sara from Cockspit is gyrating herself into a perfect half lotus beside me, and offering side dish advice with every exhalation.

'Baby carrots,' she exhales, 'and baby peas,' another inhalation, 'go so well with rabbit stew.'

I attempt another deep breath.

'Hold it,' instructs Lydia, and begins to count. Jesus, can't she count any faster. 'And ... out.'

I exhale and gasp before I die on the spot.

'Shallow breathing is not good Alice, you need to *feel* the breath, *feel* the breath,' says Lydia, pushing out her chest by way of a demonstration. Right away I can see she is wearing a fitted bra. She hangs so perfectly. I feel myself growing insanely jealous. Anyway, I do *feel* the breath, enough to keep me alive anyway. I breathe my way towards the water dispenser. Georgie is quite right, I am so unfit. Thirty minutes of yoga and I am sweating buckets and feel half dead.

'Let's work those pelvic muscles now shall we. Control the flow,' encourages Lydia, gently pulling me back before pushing me onto the yoga mat. Of course, the minute she mentions the flow I feel an urgent need to go to the loo.

'Contract those muscles Alice, that's it. Now relax. That's the way. One pelvic contraction a day keeps incontinence at bay.'

This may just be the day that I don't keep incontinence at bay. Sara meanwhile is contracting so well I'm beginning to think she is about to give birth. As for the seventy-year-olds, well I'm seriously concerned about them. With every contraction one of them moans so much that I wonder if I should call an ambulance.

'Well done Gloria,' encourages Lydia.

'How are you getting on?' Sara asks without showing a single drop of sweat.

Don't you just hate well-conditioned women? They always manage to make you feel so inadequate don't they? I wonder if Big Tits Brunette is fit. Probably she is. I imagine Charlie is looking for someone who is everything I am not. What I should do is pack in all this pelvic contraction and penis bucket rubbish, and drive back to London to have it out with Charlie. What is wrong with me, letting him go so easily? He was my fiancé for heaven's sake. Am I going to let some big tits brunette steal all that? Yes, I most likely am. After all I can't force Charlie to love me can I?

'Onto your tummies now ladies, we're going into the cobra.'

It sounds and feels like some kind of jungle warfare. I can almost hear an army officer shout *Forward men into the cobra.*

'Are you okay?' Sara asks.

'Fine,' I reply breathlessly, feeling my spine creak under the strain. 'I feel more stretched than an elastic band, but apart from that, things are going okay.'

She laughs huskily.

'Ted is a little stressed at the moment. It's good you're here to help.'

She's got a nerve. Maybe he wouldn't be so stressed if she helped a bit. She obviously likes Edward, although God knows why. If it were Charlie I'd be there like a shot. Thoughts of Charlie remind me of the Brunette with Big Tits again, which in turn reminds me of the penis bucket and Chloe the little calf. I thought it would be nice to give her a name. I wonder what the brunette's name is. I just hope she isn't called Chloe. No, Charlie would never go out with a Chloe. I must ask Edward for the broadband password so I can get online and check my Facebook profile. I hope Charlie hasn't deleted me as a friend. Friend, that's a laugh. I was more than just a friend. I should change my status to single too. I must do a status update, something like: *Held a huge penis in my hands today. They have big ones in the country.* Oh yes, that would make Charlie think.

'I tried helping about the house, but I'm as good as useless,' Sara smiles as though reading my mind. 'I cooked some meals and took them round but half the week I'm in London. Jed's mum tried to get him to go to theirs for dinner but he wouldn't.'

'London?' I say, feeling pangs of homesickness.

'Yes, I'm studying there. I'm a mature student. I've finally decided to go into veterinary practice. I bet you miss London?'
She grasps her feet from behind and stretches backwards. I attempt to reach my own, but my arms must have shrunk. Either that or someone has chopped my feet off.

'Do what you can Alice,' advises Lydia while pulling my arms back.
If I do what I can I'd be doing sod all. I hear a crack and pray it didn't come from my body. I find I can't help liking Sara. I imagine she and Edward would make a lovely couple. I'm tempted to ask why they're not together, but resist. Anyway, once I do that I'll probably end up telling her about Charlie and then I will no doubt get all maudlin. I really must stop thinking about Charlie. Fifteen minutes later I am dragging my sweaty body towards my old Beetle. I feel quite respectfully exercised and am almost proud of the sweaty hair tendrils that stick to my neck. All I need is a paper cup of coffee and a towel around my neck and I would be the image of Princess Diana. I see in the side mirror that my cheeks are warmly flushed. I feel quietly smug, knowing that I must have shed a few pounds. If I go on like this when Charlie does see me again he will no doubt drop the brunette like a hot brick. I'm about to get into the Beetle when I see Sara rushing towards me. My knickers seem to be pushing themselves into the crack of my bum. The nearest pair that I grabbed this morning was the freebie G-string panties that Justine had popped into the bag with the bras. I feel sure they will disappear up my arse any minute. That's all I need. What size did she give me for goodness sake? If only she had studied my backside as well as she did my breasts, I wouldn't be in this uncomfortable state. This is what comes of exercise. I've probably dislodged more than my

underwear. I know women end up at A & E with stuck tampons but not many with a G-string lodged up their arse. Of course, they never believe you at the hospital when you say something has got accidentally lodged, do they? It's always presumed to be the result of some kinky sex game. As if sticking a thong up your backside is pleasurable. I don't recall ever being part of a kinky sex game. In fact, I wouldn't know kinky if I met it. The closest to kinky I've come is receiving an obscene phone call about ten years ago and I've not been called a 'dirty bitch' since, although it would be rather nice to be, I suppose.

'Hey, I nearly missed you. You dropped this in the hall. I hope you don't mind that I looked inside. I didn't know who it belonged to,' she says handing me my purse.

'No, of course not,' I answer while struggling to recall the contents. There was the four hundred quid for a start. No doubt word will get around the village that I'm loaded. Oh yes, and the photo of Charlie. I really should tear that up. God, I hope she didn't see all the store cards, not that I use them mind you. I just can't resist when they offer ten per cent off my first purchase. I even have a Harrods card. Everyone will think I'm a posh snob. The truth is I'm as poor as a church mouse. Although why church mice are considered poorer than any other mice is beyond me. She probably saw all my Waitrose receipts too and now knows I really am a posh snob.

'I should go,' I say. 'I have to get to Lidl.'
I move towards the Beetle and feel the G-string embed itself further into my backside.

'Do have a cream tea first. They do a lovely one in Polly's. Come on. What's the point in sweating buckets if you can't treat yourself afterwards?'
Sara is without doubt a good-looking woman. No matter what she wears, in this case an unflattering tracksuit, she always seems to glow. Her cheeks seem to have a permanent blush. I find myself being gently pulled across the street and away from my little Beetle. Polly's is lovely and the smell of freshly ground coffee immediately halts my protests and I enter the fragrant room and instantly collide with a farmer. I know he is a farmer because he is wearing a flat cap. I'm getting good at this country lark. He bows and apologises.

'Sara,' he acknowledges and then looks to me.

Now this is the kind of man I could go for. Clean cut, good looking, very much in control and extremely well mannered. He has strong features, sultry blue eyes and the most beautiful mouth. When he smiles his nose wrinkles in a cute way. Sara seems to sigh.

'Alice this is Dominic Montfort. He owns Lower End Farm and is a born flirt, and a man to avoid at all costs. He is also unscrupulous in business. This is Alice, Edward's new housekeeper and much too lovely to get involved with you.'

'What a lovely introduction Sara, how can Alice possibly resist me now? Very pleased to meet you Alice. Sorry to hear that you're working for the old grump though ...'

I gasp.

'Dominic!' chides Sara.

'Well, when is he going to give up on that farm and sell it to me? He'll be forever trying to get that milk licence back. It was rather careless to lose it in the first place.'

'Okay Dominic, you've made your point.'

'Let me buy you fine ladies a cream tea. It's the least I can do for being slightly ungracious.'

I go to decline but Sara has nudged me to a table and the next hour is passed laughing while listening to their farm stories. Dominic explains how to properly prepare a cream tea the Cornish way.

'This is the correct order of course. Jam always goes first. They do it all wrong in Devon,' he laughs.

I sip at my third cup of coffee and check the time on my Nokia.

'I should go,' I say hurriedly.

'Already, was it something I said?'

'Alice is making rabbit stew,' reveals Sara.

'I'm sure you'll do marvellous things with that rabbit,' he says laughing.

He makes it sound like I'll be pulling one out of a hat.

'I'm pretty clueless when it comes to animals and farms,' I say.

And teat buckets and hens and calving and crows in the attic. Not to mention Lidl. Oh God, Lidl. I've yet to cook the rabbit stew. And there's the calf to feed as well. At this rate dinner won't be ready until midnight. How long does a rabbit take to cook anyway? They are tender little things aren't they? I feel so cruel. How could I even consider buying a rabbit, let alone cooking one? The thought of pushing it into a casserole dish seems like the final insult to the poor little bunny rabbit. I'll buy some rubber gloves in Lidl so I don't have to touch it. If I tell Edward dinner is late because I spent the morning doing yoga and didn't get to Lidl till lunchtime he may well ask for my pay back. God knows I need it at the moment. I also need to buy some suitable country clothes, although what 'suitable country clothes' are, I have no idea. The butcher waves from his doorway and gives me a saucy wink. Heavens, the country air must be inducing a ferocious release of my pheromones. Either that or I am more sexually appealing than I ever dreamt. Or, most likely, the men in the country are quickly aroused. You know all that earth and back to nature stuff. I bet they're at it like rabbits here. Talking of rabbits, I must get to Lidl.

***

I feel myself hyperventilating. In fact, I feel quite sick and my heart is thumping. On a scale of one to ten on the catastrophe ranking this really isn't that bad. In fact, later I shall, no doubt, look back on this and laugh at myself. But right now as I hit the Lidl car park a sickening feeling of déjà vu hits me and I'm back at the Taunton Deane service station. It feels like all those people must have followed me. A police car zooms into one of the spaces. There must have been a stabbing or something. Knowing my luck it is a crazed gunman who will come running out any minute. Most likely I will get taken hostage. That will make Charlie regret his actions. After all, it is his fault I am here anyway. My body goes rigid as I watch the police climb from the car. Thank goodness I didn't witness anything. I'd have to have given a statement and everything. I feel my stomach clench and my hand reaches for the key in the ignition. Perhaps it would be safer to find a little village store. They emerge from the panda car laughing and talking loudly. One looks over to me and I slink down in my seat. Oh dear, my tyres are okay aren't they? I daren't drive away now, not in my usual cloud of smoke, they'll do me for a faulty exhaust. I can't sit here all day, what about the rabbit stew? I feel like my whole life revolves around a rabbit. What has my life come to? Perhaps I shouldn't slink, it makes me look guilty. I sit up and pretend to rummage through my handbag. One of the policemen shrugs and they walk on into the store. Oh that's good. At least with them inside I should be safe. I attempt a few of the deep breaths that Lydia had shown us in the class and feel my heart rate slow down enough for me to find the courage to get out of the car. I make sure it is locked and, with head held high, walk purposefully towards the store. Crikey, there are a hell of a lot of lopsided women here and I'm not just talking breasts. Okay Alice, you need to get some perspective. It's a supermarket. It may be full of a different class of people than you usually mix with at Waitrose, and no doubt there will not be a nice little green charity chip at the end, but that doesn't mean they are not nice people. You can't judge a supermarket by what it does or doesn't give to charity. You must stop being such a snob. All the same I'd better zip up my bag and hold it close to my chest. I feel like I'm walking into the heart of Harlem instead of the local Lidl. As I reach the trolley park a lady approaches me. I hope she isn't going to ask me for money.

'Do you want this trolley dearie?' she says pleasantly.

That's nice. Now that's what I'm used to at Waitrose. Perhaps I will get a green chip at the end after all.

'Thank you,' I say politely, taking it from her.

She stands looking at me and her smile seems to get stuck on her face.

'Thanks again,' I repeat and begin walking towards the entrance. Surely she doesn't want paying for giving me a trolley.

'I'd like my pound, if you don't mind,' she shouts.

She does? What a cheek. Not a bit like Waitrose then. How stupid am I even thinking that?

'I'm sorry but I'm not paying you a pound just because you gave me your trolley,' I say firmly.

It is like those people who dive on your car and frantically slosh dirty water on your windscreen when you stop at the lights, and then they ask for money for the privilege.

Another woman gasps and gives me a dirty look as she takes a trolley from the park. I watch horrified as she pushes a pound coin into it. Shit and double shit. That's something they don't do at Waitrose. Before I can apologise and fish in my bag for the money the trolley is snatched from my hands.

'Bugger you,' she snaps and waltzes off with it.

'I'm so sorry, I didn't realise about the pound thing ...'

This is awful. Instead of entering the place with as low a profile as possible I have become the centre of attention. I spend an unnecessary amount of time fiddling in my handbag pretending to find a pound coin until all the people who saw the trolley incident have gone inside. Once inside I am astonished. Things are quite cheap here, amazingly cheap actually. In fact I'm only in the third aisle and my trolley is full. They're practically giving away the wine at £3.99 for a box of four. I put two in the trolley, along with three boxes of Coca Cola and by the time I reach the till I can barely push it. Edward will be pleased with my thriftiness. I'm feeling so chuffed with myself that I also throw in a copy of *25 Beautiful Homes.* Maybe I can sort out the farmhouse at Trenowyth. I should have shopped here before. In fact, now I think about it, maybe I could do this in London and then I would have enough money for rent. Of course, I've got to find a job. Still, it gives me hope that I can go home and won't have to stay here too long. I'll get some money behind me and meanwhile Georgie can send me the local rag, and I can apply for jobs. Shopping at Lidl hasn't been so bad after all, and there hasn't been a shooting or anything. I begin putting my things on the conveyor belt ready for the assistant and the next thing I know she is scanning like mad.

'I need bags,' I hear myself pant as I struggle to put the items on as fast as she is scanning.

'Zere is ze bags,' and she points below me.

What did she say?

'The bags are in front of you,' says a woman behind me.

I look down to the mass of carrier bags and grab several feeling the G-string yank itself even further up my backside.

'Could I have help packing?' I ask, banging the trolley into the oversized backside of a woman in front of me. I could park my trolley there, never mind my bike. Oh, dear that was so rude. Why do these places turn me into such a snob?

'Ve don't pack,' says the assistant.

'This isn't bloody Waitrose,' says the lady in front rubbing her ample backside.

You don't say? Blimey if the assistant scans any faster the scanner will blow up. I'm surrounded by half-full carrier bags, and free flowing provisions when she says,

'Vun hundred and tin pence.'

What! She can't possibly be serious.

'But that can't be right, what about the offers? I bought the four bottles of wine for £3.99 for example.'

She shakes her head and points to the card machine.

'You shouldn't look at them love, they're very confusing. It was probably £3.99 a bottle. You have to take them out of the packs,' says the woman rubbing her backside.

Oh, what? This could only happen to me. I stare at the assistant with utter indignation.

'If the signs aren't clear then you really should sell them to me at the price stated.'

There are mutterings behind me but I decide to stand my ground. The assistant looks harassed.

'I take money?' she says looking vacantly around her as if for help.

'You're robbing me.'

Okay, a bit extreme but it feels like I'm being fiddled.

'Look darling, if you don't want to pay for the stuff that's fine but the signs are there, even if a bit obscure. You're holding up the queue,' says the lady behind me.

'I'm so sorry, it's just ...'

'What's the bloody hold up here? I've only got some Hobnobs and Penguins. Hurry up for Christ's sake. Who is she, the bloody queen of England? Come on dolly, get on with it,' snorts a man who looks like he is on a tea-break from a building site.

Honestly, what ignorance. I hand over the credit card and finish packing. Well, I won't come here again. She pulls the card out of the machine and gives me a scathing look before saying loudly,

'No credit card.'

'What? Everyone takes credit cards?' I say appalled.

'Only cash or debit card here darling.'

If she calls me darling one more time I swear I will ...

'But I have to pay on that card,' I say stupidly.

'Don't you have enough money dolly?' calls the man.

If he calls me dolly one time I swear I will ... I scrabble in my purse and pull out a hundred pounds and ten pence while looking around for the policemen.

'It's false advertising,' I tell the assistant.

She hands me a receipt and begins scanning the next person's goods before I have even finished packing. I'm seriously beginning to wish there was a shooting here and that I was the one doing it. I push the trolley outside to find it is now pissing down with rain. Why am I not surprised? I am transforming from domestic goddess to *Miss Totally Inadequate* in one very fast movement. A screaming child pushes past, protesting he doesn't want to go home, while the mother silences his screams with a Snickers bar. I am seriously wishing I was sitting behind some desk, any desk, in an office, any office, with my hand hovering over a mouse while my eyes secretly scan *Vanity Fair*. Surely anything must be better than being a farmer's housekeeper. I spend my usual few seconds struggling with the key in the boot.

'We use crowbars around here dolly,' laughs the builder man as he walks past me.

Well that doesn't surprise me in the least.

Chapter Sixteen

The drive back is nightmarish. Bright sunshine one minute and pounding hailstones the next make driving almost intolerable. I turn into the dirt road to Trenowyth to find it virtually impassable. Now what am I supposed to do? I must be mature about this, after all, how hard can it be? I push on, feeling my tyres slip and slide on the mud until finally I reach the house. It's four o'clock already and I haven't even prepared the rabbit, let alone stuck it in the oven. Obviously that has to be my priority, never mind that I might contract pneumonia from standing in my wet clothes. I throw everything out of the carrier bags. I then realise I forgot to buy rubber gloves. I bought up the whole store but forgot what I needed the most. I can't possibly touch the rabbit. Ten minutes later with my hands wrapped in cling film, and looking like someone in a bio-contamination suit, I tentatively put my hands into the fridge and take out the rabbit, quickly depositing it into a casserole dish along with everything that Sara and Lydia had told me to add. The kitchen clock still says four. That can't be right, what's that ticking then if isn't the clock? Oh shit, the leaky roof. I forgot to put the buckets out. I dash to the living room and open the door. It's like the bloody Titanic in here. The whole of the floor is covered in water. I'll have to swim to the loo if this gets any worse. Okay, stay positive. It's all a matter of perspective. Think, think. What to do first? Well, I badly need the loo but that seems out of the question. Lots of towels. What am I thinking? I'm clearing up a flood not delivering a baby. Buckets first, that's what I need. I fly back to the kitchen trip over the shopping bags and rummage under the sink for buckets. Finally, with them safely in place to catch the leaks I use the dustpan to scoop up the water. Brilliant plan, although I'm not getting rid of much water but I am burning all the calories from my lunchtime cream tea. I seem to have been at it for ages when there is a thud at the door and excited barking from Molly. Oh no, I haven't even fed Chloe. With a bit of luck he will fire me. Oh yes, Edward Fairfax make my day. I hear his footsteps.

'What the …'

I turn to see him running his hands through his already unruly hair.

'I forgot the buckets,' I say, collapsing back against the wall.

'Your clothes are soaked.'

'I didn't have time to change. I went to Lidl and they wouldn't take your card, and they fiddled me. They're crooks that company, I got home and made the stew and then I realised the ticking wasn't the clock but it was the water leaking onto the floor. I came in here and it was like a remake of Titanic with me instead of Kate Winslet, except there was no Jack Dawson to rescue me …'

I exhale. What an embarrassing ramble that was. I must look a sight. My hair is in a tight ponytail and my jeans rolled up. I'm clutching the dustpan for all I'm worth, and the image of four bottles of wine keeps moving across my vision like floaters. Is it too early for a drink?

He takes the dustpan from my hands and I could hug him. He looks weary and I feel quite proud of myself for having prepared the stew even if I haven't unpacked the shopping.

'I'll finish clearing this. You get your clothes off.'

For a second there is a stunned silence and then we both laugh.

'Sorry that came out so badly,' he says rubbing his eyes.

I force myself up with a sigh.

'I'll check on the dinner and then I'll put away the shopping,' I say squeezing past him.

He makes no effort to move and I blush as my breasts brush against his side.

'Ah, I hate to be the bearer of bad news …'

Oh no.

'But there is no dinner. I think you forgot to put it in the oven. But I'm positive you're not alone. In fact I'm convinced when the Titanic was going down I'll lay odds they forgot about dinner too.'

Oh, what! I so want to be in my flat in London, sharing a bag of honey-roasted cashew nuts and a glass of Chardonnay with Charlie. I really so do. I close my eyes in exasperation, mutter fuck under my breath and storm back to the kitchen. I swear I can hear him humming *Nearer My God To Thee*.

'Don't worry. I'll pop out and get some pasties and chips,' he calls cheerfully.

Pasty and chips, fish and chips not to mention fried bacon for breakfast and of course the cream tea. I've probably got furred arteries already. If the pneumonia doesn't kill me the cholesterol will. Molly peers at me through the kitchen window and I throw her a couple of dog treats. I'm packing away the shopping when Edward comes in.

'Sara said she saw you today,' he says casually.

I pull the wine from the box.

'Yes,' I say, equally as casual I hope, 'I had a yoga class with her and then a cream tea.'

He scoffs.

'If I had time for a cream tea in the middle of the day I'd be a happy man.'

I ignore his sarcastic tone and put the last of the shopping in the fridge. The humming from the Aga breaks the silence.

'I'm so sorry about the stew,' I say.

He shrugs.

'Are you expecting us to be snowed in?' he asks while looking in the cupboards. 'Or didn't you believe me when I said I'm not holding prisoners in the attic?'

'I'd never been to Lidl before. I honestly thought everything was really cheap. The way they advertise the goods is so misleading. I had to pay out of my own money as they wouldn't take your card,' I say defensively.

'Don't worry I'll treat you to the pasty,' he says in a deadpan voice.

What a bastard, I can't spare a hundred quid.

'But ...'

'I'm teasing. How much was it?'

Thank goodness.

'A hundred pounds and ten pence. But I don't want the ten pence.'

'That's gracious of you. That helps enormously. I don't think I have ever seriously spent a hundred pounds on food. What did you buy? Caviar?'

Oh, that's it. I've had a hellish day. I bet he has never even been to Lidl.

'Nothing I do is right is it?' I say angrily, shrugging off my wet cardigan revealing my damp shirt.

'I make this big effort to save money by going to Lidl, which was not pleasant by the way, there were police there and everything.'
Well, he doesn't have to know why they were there does he?

'I then drove back in torrential rain, and blinding sunlight, only to find the lane was practically impassable. Then I get here to find the house flooded because *you* didn't fix the roof ...'
I stop when I realise he is not listening to a word I am saying but is staring at my shirt. I look down to see that it is completely transparent and my very expensive, well-fitting bra is clearly visible.

'I'm now going to change,' I blush.

'Right,' he nods and turns to the oven. 'I look forward to that.'
'What?'

'The rabbit stew. I look forward to that tomorrow.'

'Oh,' I mumble and walk out of the room.

'I'll be about twenty minutes,' he calls and the front door slams.
I bet Kate Winslet never had these problems.

***

'Cornish pasties, chips, a couple of gherkins and I also got Cornish ice cream to cheer you up.'
Wonderful. How thoughtful is that? Gherkins and ice cream, well that's the ultimate in cheering up isn't it. Nothing like a good old gherkin to make everything right. Don't men have any conception of weight gain and fat content? How can something that will make me as huge as a house possibly cheer me up? If he really wanted to cheer me up he only had to bring home a pair of rubber gloves. There is enough food here to feed the five thousand. I swear I can feel myself already straining in the new bra. I've never eaten so many chips in my life. Apart from the high calorie intake, this lot will surely bring me out in a raging case of acne. I had intended only eating a small portion of ice cream, you know, just enough to be sociable and to show I am grateful. But then, of course, it looks like you're not grateful when you just peck at it. So, I had a little bit more, so as not to offend, and of course when Edward said we may

as well finish it as there wasn't much room in the freezer, I felt guilty. After all, I was the one who overloaded the place with food. I suppose that's the same reason I drank almost a whole bottle of wine. That and to numb the awfulness of the whole Lidl experience, not to mention the floods. I can't even begin to imagine what Charlie would have said if he had seen so much food, not to mention the rabbit cooking away happily in the oven and smelling quite good, even if I say so myself.

'The stew smells good,' says Edward, as though reading my mind. He holds up his hand to stop me when I go to clear the dishes. I take the solitary chip that sits on my grease-ridden plate, and pop it into my mouth without even a tiny twinge of guilt. I am turning into a slob just like him. Still, it has been a difficult day, and I must have shifted millions of calories mopping up all that water so I don't need to feel guilty.

'Sara told me how to cook it,' I say, merrily swigging back wine and downing the last spoonful of ice cream.

'Sara's a grand cook so you couldn't get better advice.'
He plonks the dishes into the sink and I find myself wondering if Lidl sell cheap dishwashers.

'Is she your girlfriend?' I ask, still basking in my rabbit stew compliment.

'My girlfriend?' He looks puzzled and then his eyes widen, 'Is that what you've been thinking?'
He laughs.

'She's a lovely girl and I adore her, but she'd never look twice at me. If that had been possible I would have snapped her up years ago.'
I gaze into my wine glass and to my surprise find myself feeling jealous of Sara. Okay, he has the manners of a Somali pirate, but for all that I am thinking I would give him a second look. I am so shocked by my own thoughts that for a moment I can't speak. It's the alcohol, that's what it is. The alcohol combined with hormones turns me into some kind of alcohol-fuelled sexual predator. I must be getting desperate if I'm considering jumping on Edward Fairfax, slob of the year. Good heavens, I'm not safe around men any more. I'll be propositioning him next. Obviously I was fine when I was with Charlie because I was getting sex, not great sex admittedly, but sex all the same. This is terrible. Before I know where I am I'll have him

up against the sink making him an offer he probably most certainly would want to refuse. I'm starting to resemble that woman out of *Basic Instinct*. I never realised I had such a high sex drive.

'Besides, the last thing I need right now is another woman in my life. I've got enough to contend with.'

Well, that throws cold water over everything.

'Oh,' is all I say but I swear it is much too breathless as my fertile imagination re-creates the *Fatal Attraction* sink scene. It is suddenly very hot in here.

'She'll make a good vet too.'

Whether Sara would look twice at him or not I don't know, but he has most certainly looked twice at her. There is unmistakable admiration in his voice that I don't recall ever hearing when Charlie talked about me. I suppose at this moment he is sitting in a nice vegetarian restaurant with the big-breasted brunette while *she* gets all breathless. It doesn't bear thinking about. I stand up and feel myself sway. I scrabble for the edge of the table.

'It's terribly hot in here,' I mumble.

I never drank this much at home. I suppose in the country there isn't much else to do is there apart from eat and drink, and have sex of course. I must stop thinking about sex. It's true though isn't it? They don't seem to have anything else to do here. The local cinema must be miles away. I can't imagine these farmers' wives go off on spa weekends. The thought of the spa reminds me of my planned hen weekend. Georgie had bought all the stuff. She had, much to her amusement, given me the 'L' plate in advance. I should be on my honeymoon now, right now. At this very moment I had imagined Charlie and I getting very romantic over tiramisu and a bottle of champagne in a beautiful spot overlooking Lake Maggiore. I never for one minute imagined I would be in some dump of a kitchen, eating pasty and chips, accompanied by Lidl wine. What have I come to? I've reached rock bottom that's what.

'I should have been on my honeymoon now, drinking champagne and eating tiramisu,' I say aloud and swallow hard.

Come on Alice, don't think about that. I'll never snuggle up to Charlie in bed again. Big Tits Brunette has no doubt taken my place. Well, I hope the dodgy spring in our bed shoots up her arse. Oh Alice, that is an awful thing to think. No doubt Charlie and Big Breasts have gone out and bought one of those fancy foam mattresses.

He always talked about those. Edward looks uncomfortable.

'I've got some tiramisu as it happens,' he says thoughtfully. 'It's in the freezer. It's been there some time mind you.'

I stare at him.

'What?'

'If you wanted some. I could thaw it out. I can't help with the champagne though.'

Is he mad?

'I don't like tiramisu,' I say gripping the table as my head spins.

'But you just said …'

'I said I should be on my honeymoon. In Italy you eat that sort of thing, on your honeymoon don't you? Are you going to marry me too?'

'Unlikely. Shall we get some air and feed the calf?'

That was a quick response.

'Are you changing the subject?' I ask boldly.

'Absolutely,' he smiles, taking me gently by the arm. 'Are you sure you can cope with the teat bucket this evening?'

What a cheek. I'm not *that* drunk.

'Good God yes. Lead me to the penis bucket. I've had so much excitement today let's end on a high note.'

Then again, maybe I am *that* drunk. Outside it is lovely and cool. It is also frighteningly dark. I look up at the stars and gasp. I don't think I have ever seen stars in my life. Well, you don't in London do you? What with the smog and the street lights and the constant awareness that it could be a mugger walking behind you rather deflects from gazing into the sky. Chloe greets me by chewing at the sleeve of my jumper.

'She obviously likes you,' smiles Edward while filling the bucket with milk.

'Yes, so it seems. Love is having your sleeve chewed. Charlie never chewed my sleeves, not once. That should have been a clue. Hello Chloe.'

'He sounds like an idiot. Maybe you're better off without him.'

I stroke Chloe's head and she nudges her face against my hand. At least someone appreciates me.

'Your penis bucket ma'am,' he says.

Is that a saucy grin on his face?

'Now there's an offer I don't get every day,' I laugh while taking it from him, and then, with his help, aim the teat at Chloe's mouth. She grabs it urgently and begins sucking.

'Ooh I feel quite maternal,' I say stroking her head.

He laughs and pulls two stools forward. I flop down onto one of them and concentrate on feeding Chloe. Edward's hand touches mine and I feel my pulse quicken and the hairs on the back of my neck rise and I shiver.

'Relax your hands, you're too tense. That's better. Animals pick up on anxiety.'

I hope *he* is not picking up on my nymphomaniacal urges.

'You're the vet, you should know,' I say shakily.

'Indeed.'

He produces a bottle of wine and two glasses.

'Can I tempt you?' he asks with that gleam in his eyes.

Good God, yes you can. When you're not tetchy and irritable you're actually quite likeable. His smooth educated voice seems to be hypnotising me and I accept more wine. Thoughts of Lady Chatterley unwillingly enter my head. Okay, maybe not completely unwillingly. It's just the barn, the stars and the country, and all that. I mean, it's classic Lady Chatterley bonking territory isn't it? I've never had thoughts like these in my life. I need to talk to Georgie or better still Cas, or even better, both of them. For some time we just sit and watch Chloe guzzle the milk. Her big brown eyes look into mine as I hold the bucket. When I shiver with the cold Edward gallantly places a blanket around me. A smelly cow blanket mind you, but a blanket all the same. I can't help feeling grateful even if a little manure covered.

'So what's a milk licence?' I ask innocently.

His sharp intake of breath warns me that may have been the wrong question.

'Why do you ask?' he asks barely able to keep the frost out of his voice.

If he was to breathe over me now I think I would turn to ice.

'It just went through my mind I suppose,' I say, very much wishing it hadn't. 'Dominic Montfort mentioned you'd lost yours and would be forever getting it back, milk licence that is, not your mind,' I say, trying to inject some humour into the conversation.

His shoulders stiffen.

'Without a milk licence the farm can't sell milk, the farm lost its licence and the contract with the dairy. We can only use our milk to feed the calves and sometimes Jed takes some to the pig farm, but we make no money from the milk. This farm is running at a loss.'

'But how did you lose the licence?'

'It was the people my father hired when he was ill, they were careless with hygiene, they broke the golden rule when it comes to milk production.' He stops and bites his lip as though fearing he has said too much.

'But that's terrible.'

I jump as Chloe's mouth wraps itself around my hand. I look down to see the bucket is empty.

'Yes it is. Next time you meet up with Montfort ask him to fill you in a bit more on the situation,' he says crossly, standing up and taking the teat bucket from me.

His hand brushes mine again and heat rushes through my body.

'You're cold, let's go back in. That stew must be well and truly cooked.'

I give Chloe one last pat and unsteadily follow Edward back to the house. The smell of the stew reaches our appreciative nostrils. I'm about to say how good it smells when the cat darts in front of me. It is so dark that I only hear her and the next thing I know there is a screech when I step on her. I jump back, lose my balance and fall straight into Edward Fairfax's arms, sending him wobbling and, would you believe it, we land against the sink. I'm seriously beginning to think they put something in the wine here. I don't recall being this out of control back home. My face is so close to his that I can smell the wine and chips on his breath. If anything should be a turn off that should be, but I'm more aware of his hands. One is on my arm steadying me while the other is tightly around my waist. If I move a fraction closer we could kiss. He mutters something under his breath but I have closed my eyes and can only discern the humming of the cooker, the now purring of the cat and yes, the phone ringing.

'I need to answer that,' he repeats, leaning closer and reaching over for the telephone.

'Hello.'

A pause, and then, 'Well you've got me. I think you should ask Alice that. I'll pass you over.'

Another pause.

'No, why would I? You know my answer.'

He glares at me angrily.

'Montfort for you,' he says with an irritable snarl.

'What?' My head jerks up in surprise.

I hold the phone to my ear while Edward looks on with interest.

'Alice, I hope I didn't interrupt anything. I presumed dinner would be over.'

'It is,' I say licking my lips nervously.

'I hope Edward appreciated your rabbit stew?'

'Mmm yes,' I lie.

Edward begins to crash the plates and cutlery into the sink. He couldn't make more noise if he tried.

'It will be the first time he has appreciated a woman.'

I don't reply.

'Sorry Alice, it's just the thought of you working for the miserable old bugger. It's just, well you're too nice.'

Another crash as cutlery hits a glass. What is Fairfax's problem?

'I'm fine,' I say, which is more than can be said for the china in this place as another plate is thumped onto the drainer.

'We didn't arrange a date to meet again. Are you free on Friday?'

Blimey, he's a bit forward, as my mother would say. I look at Edward whose face is thunderous.

'I'm not really sure if I'm free on Friday,' I say nervously.

Edward's head snaps up.

'Well, let me know if you are. Ted has my number.'

Edward frowns as I replace the phone.

'If you want time off can you check with me first? I am paying you after all.'

I feel tears prickle behind my eyelids. I didn't ask Dominic Montfort to call. I'm not even sure I like him. I can't believe Edward is being so horrible to me. I've cleaned the house thoroughly, attempted to cook rabbit stew when I have never cooked a stew in my life, let alone a rabbit one. I was a vegetarian before I came here and I still cooked it for him. I took my life in my hands going to Lidl, not to mention cleaning up the flood. Okay maybe that was my fault for not putting the buckets out. What am I thinking? It's his house not mine. He should take responsibility for his own roof. Dominic is quite right about him. He is a miserable old bugger and has no idea how to appreciate a woman.

'Dominic Montfort is quite right about you ...'

'What does Montfort know about anything?' he snaps.

'He knows you're an ungrateful bugger for a start,' I say reaching for my glass.

'And that's your opinion too is it?' He looks coldly into my eyes and I turn away as I feel a tear splash onto my cheek.

'I don't know,' I say, looking into the glass.

'You don't know?'

Why is he cross examining me?

'You don't know, but you feel able to say what an ungrateful bugger I am?'

This is terrible. I didn't fight like this with Charlie.

'I didn't say anything about you,' I protest and take a gulp of wine.

'Oh really,' he scoffs. 'That's not how I understand it. Seems to me you talked about everything from my milk licence and how difficult a person I am. You even discussed the rabbit stew didn't you?'

Oh, this is getting so childish.

'Maybe I mentioned the rabbit stew, but ...'

'So you *did* mention it,' he says triumphantly.

My head is thumping and I just want to get away and lock myself in my room.

'For God's sake, you're acting like a child. At least Dominic is polite and knows how to behave around a woman ...'

What am I saying? I barely know Dominic Montfort. He snatches the wine bottle as I reach for it.

'Is this another of my weaknesses that you have discussed with Montfort?'

I feel my eyes smart.

'I'm going to bed,' I say sharply, squeezing past him. He turns abruptly to ensure we don't touch and the next thing I know my wine spills from the glass and lands all over his shirt. Oh bugger.

'Brilliant,' he mumbles.

'Oh God, Edward, I'm so sorry.'

I take a deep breath and grab a J Cloth from under the sink, wiping my eyes as I do so. There is a deafening silence broken only by the hooting of an owl. I turn back and dab gently at the shirt and realise I'm making it a hundred times worse, but if I stop I will burst into tears and he will know how upset I am. His hand stops mine and that odd little jolt rushes through me. He's a slob, Alice, remember? Not to mention a grumpy old bastard who has no interest in women. Well, one woman maybe, but that one isn't you.

'I'm sorry if you think I'm an ungrateful bugger,' he says gently, 'And you're making this ten times worse.'

'I don't think that, not really. I mean maybe sometimes I do ...'
Oh hell, I really am making everything worse aren't I?

'Sorry,' I mutter, 'About the shirt.'
I realise his hand is still on mine and that I'm pressing the wet J Cloth against his skin.

'Not your fault,' he mumbles attempting to avoid my eyes but somehow they lock. 'Charlie was a fool letting you go,' he says quietly.
He steps away from me so abruptly that I stumble and have to grab the table for support.

'I'm not here Friday anyway. Sara and I are going to the *Petplan Veterinary Awards* in London. We won't be back until late Saturday morning.'
He makes it sound like the Oscars.

'Ooh, will you come back with a trophy?' I smile.

'They are very serious awards as it happens. Not that I would expect you to understand.'
Why do I bother?

'Good night Miss Lane, I hope you're in a more agreeable mood tomorrow,' he says tersely, walking past me.
Bloody cheek.

'Ditto Mr Fairfax.'
Before he can respond I have marched to the door. In my room, and with the door locked, I burst into silent tears. Bastard, I hate him and I hate Charlie even more. I can't believe I am here. I'm thirty-two and just been jilted. I should really have checked myself into The Priory or somewhere, like any normal person, and had a mini breakdown like everyone else. For some reason the whole business with Charlie makes me see red. How could he do this to me? We were the perfect couple, everyone said so. It's me isn't it? There is something very wrong with me. Dominic is probably only interested in me

because he thinks as a London woman I'll have sex at the drop of a hat. Well, he can think again. Charm and money won't get me into bed that quickly. And Edward can't stand me it seems. I'm going to end up a shrivelled old spinster. I'd better get ready for that and learn how to knit. After all there is sodding all else to do here in the country. The height of fashion here seems to be boiler suits and wellington boots, both of which do not sit well on me. Talking of sitting that is all I have to do. Stick it out until I have enough money to return home. There's every chance Charlie will come to his senses. Oh stop it Alice, Charlie isn't going to come to his senses because he never lost them in the first place. It seems he prefers Big Tits Brunette to you, and he has probably been seeing her for weeks. I pull the duvet over my head and weep a bit more. Chloe likes me anyway. I have certainly reached rock bottom if my best friend is a cow. I'm pathetic. I can't get a man, and when I have one I can't keep him. I feel my heart flutter and take a deep breath. I'll have a heart attack next, that's all I need. That would be the ultimate embarrassment, being brought out feet first from this dump. No, that would never happen. My mother would be that embarrassed she would do it under the cover of darkness. Deep breath Alice, remember Lydia's relaxation advice and for God's sake, drink less wine. You'll be known as the village lush at this rate, not quite the fame Cas and Georgie had in mind for me. Thank God, they will be here next weekend. With that thought I close my eyes.

Chapter Seventeen

'Darling,' whoops Cas, 'you could have told us you were living across the borders. It's a good job I brought my passport, and that bloody collie sniffed my crotch so much he's passed out from the fumes. I've booked another session for this evening though.'

I am so thrilled to see him that it is all I can do to stop myself from crying. I almost feel like cracking open a bottle of champagne. My legs are trembling from the excitement. I have so much to tell them. I have overwhelming love for Chloe and can't wait to introduce her to Georgie. I know Cas won't appreciate her at all and he certainly won't understand me swelling with pride. He encircles my waist and spins me around before stopping abruptly at the sight of Jed.

'Ooh hello, you must be Edward?'

Jed smiles.

'Where's this bloody bed and breakfast place then?' mumbles Georgie as she stumbles in with the cases. 'Cas wants to change already. It's been a bloody nightmare travelling with him ...'

She stops and looks at Jed in wonder. Heavens, I don't recall Georgie ever looking at a man like that before.

'Oh, you must be Edward,' she repeats like a parrot.

'This is Jed,' I say quickly.

'God, that's a country name if I ever heard one. You can almost see it on the cover of one of those cowboy magazines 'Ride 'em Jed',' says Cas.

'Sounds more like the cover of a porn magazine,' giggles Georgie. Good heavens, is she blushing? That's a Georgie first. Jed throws his head back and roars with laughter.

'I'm so sorry Jed, they are a lame excuse for friends,' I say appalled.

119

'A lame excuse for friends who have just driven five hours to see you. She's an ungrateful bitch. Here you are madam, I bring gifts,' smiles Cas holding up a fabulous pair of pink wellingtons.

'If you must wear wellingtons then at least wear designer darling. These are Hunter's, and from Harrods don't you know.'

I whoop with delight. They are adorable.

'Oh, Cas, they're fantastic.'

'Of course.'

'Are you joining us for lunch Jed?' asks Georgie. 'We promise not to embarrass you too much, do say yes.'

Oh God this is mortifying.

'Where can I change darling?' asks Cas, looking around and pulling at his shirt. 'I feel like I've played three sets with Andy Murray, I'm that sweaty. Not that you can smell it over the stink of this place mind you.'

'Cas,' I admonish.

'The farm darling, I don't mean the house. We can see you have performed wonders and shit miracles here.'

What must Jed think?

'Jed I'm so sorry, there is just no excuse …'

'It's fine. I'm delighted to have been here when they arrived,' he laughs.

'And we're ditto delighted that you were here when we arrived. He is coming to lunch with us isn't he Ali?' asks Georgie without taking her eyes off him.

'Of course he is. How can he possibly refuse such a divine invitation as that?' says Cas.

'Georgie, I'm sure Jed has other things to do and you're putting him on the spot,' my words tumble out. 'You haven't been here five minutes and he doesn't even know you,' I say pushing Cas up the stairs and directing him to my bedroom.

'What better way to get to know us?' Georgie responds.

'I'd love to,' says Jed walking to the door. 'Where are you going?'

'The Heifer.'

'That's a bloody sexist name if I ever heard one,' calls Cas. 'Surely there's a pub called The Gay Farmer, or is it The Jolly Farmer?'

Oh these two, for God's sake. You just don't realise these things are going to happen do you? I love Georgie to bits and I had been thinking that Dominic would be a great catch for her. I hadn't for one moment thought Jed may be an even better one.

'We'll see you later then,' Georgie grins.

As soon as the door closes she grabs me in a tight embrace.

'God, he's lovely, why have you never mentioned him?'

I shrug.

'I guess I never noticed him in that way.'

'Does he have a girlfriend?'

I shake my head and fill the kettle.

'I've no idea. I don't think so. All I know is he works for Edward.'

'Christ on a bike, is this your bedroom?' shouts Cas. 'How old is this Edward? You don't need to excavate this room to find relics. This fireplace is one for a start.'

Georgie leaps up the stairs with me lamely following. We all stand in my bedroom. Me with a sense of pride, Cas with a look of horror and Georgie with a smug smile as she prods at my crumpled dress on the floor.

'Not a room without action though I see,' she comments dryly.

'Nothing happened,' I insist of my evening with Dominic, 'but it was a lovely evening. He lit all these night lights. There must have been about forty in the room. It was so lovely ...'

'Sounds great Alice,' Georgie says, hugging me.

'Sounds a bit crass if you ask me,' snorts Cas.

'Well I don't recall anyone asking you,' retorts Georgie, picking up the dress. 'He sounds really romantic.'

I find myself thinking back to last night and it all seems so surreal. After my first refusal to go out with him he had been relentless in his pursuing of me. I was deeply flattered and after Georgie telling me I was mad not to go, I finally gave in. There were candles everywhere, even in the bathroom and small bottles of champagne. Dominic had cooked the perfect dinner; at least he claimed he had cooked it. He served duck terrine to start, and then wild salmon with beans and buckwheat and finished with a chocolate mousse to die for. But if I'm honest, I much preferred my dinner of Cornish pasty and chips that I had shared with Edward. I almost let Dominic kiss me but thoughts of Charlie stopped me somehow.

'I came close,' I say aloud, turning my back on Cas as he changed clothes.

'To orgasm or actually having sex?' questions Cas.

121

'Oh honestly, is there an old tin mine we can throw him in?' sighs Georgie.

'I'm sure we can find a cesspit. Or we could set Molly the dog onto him for half an hour,' I laugh.

'Now, you're just trying to get me excited,' grins Cas, jumping in front of us. 'How do I look darlings?'

As camp as Christmas but of course we don't say that. But the thought of traipsing into the local with Cas is mildly disturbing to say the least. But we nod in appreciation and fall onto the bed.

'Are you seeing him again?' Georgie whispers into my ear.

'I heard that,' Cas says harshly, studying his reflection in the mirror. 'We don't want you jumping into bed with the first man you meet just because you're on the rebound. Christ, this mirror is awful, no reflection on your cleaning darling, but crikey.'

'Edward says the house isn't priority …'

'So what is? The estate isn't exactly *Tara* darling is it?'

'And this isn't Georgia and she isn't Scarlet O'Hara,' quips Georgie.

'Edward could certainly be Rhett Butler,' I say, and quickly apologise. 'I'm joking, it was just a joke. He is a bit miserable but he has got a lot on his plate.'

I leap off the bed.

'Let's have tea. I've made a cake. I'm entering one of my cakes in the village show,' I say proudly.

'You're what?' cries Georgie in a voice so shocked that you'd think I'd just announced I was having a baby.

'I need a stiff drink,' mumbles Cas. 'Who knows what she'll spring on us next.'

'Oh God, cakes,' Georgie mumbles under her breath. 'She'll be crocheting blankets next.'

I'd better not mention the knitting. The truth is in the past ten days I have acquired a taste for the country life. Okay, a small taste but a taste never the less. Georgie accepts her tea and piece of fruit cake in a bit of a daze. She stares at my Post-it Notes on the fridge and gives Cas a sidelong look.

'God it's like you've been brainwashed by scientologists or something. Post-it Notes? When did you ever use fucking Post-it Notes?'

'We'll be kidnapping her next and getting someone to reboot her,' sighs Cas.

'De-programme,' I correct, 'You reboot computers not people and anyway I don't need de-programming. I'm just making a determined effort to make the best of things until I can save enough money. The villagers are nice, and even you liked Jed. It's also nice to be noticed by someone as charming as Dominic. It makes me feel I haven't lost my pull.'

I sip my tea and my thoughts wander to Dominic, who is charming in every way, which is more than can be said for Edward-chip-on-the-shoulder-Fairfax. Ever since the night of the flood he has only spoken to me in short sentences. Our after dinner chat has gone from *Nice rabbit stew* to simply *Thanks. Good morning* went to *Morning* and now it's just a nod. After finally getting online, and discovering that not only had Charlie updated his relationship status to single but he had also deleted all our joint photos and uploaded a new profile pic of him and Big Tits Brunette, I finally saw the light. Don't panic, I haven't found God, although I did find some knitting needles and wool in the local charity shop, which is perfect for passing the evenings and as close to God as I'll ever come. I am in danger of sounding like my granny. I'm getting to know how the Aga works and am finding cooking very cathartic. I make a mean oxtail soup. Oh yes, I'm buying all kinds from the butcher now. I did consider pheasant the other day but then decided against it, but only because I had enough in the freezer and not on any moral grounds. I decide not to mention all this to Georgie and Cas just yet. Maybe I will after lunch when they have drunk a few glasses of wine. I feel a little glow of pride when Cas asks for another piece of cake.

'I made a lovely ginger one the other day but I gave half to Sara,' I say swelling.

Georgie shakes her head.

'Christ, don't drink the water Cas. I wasn't far wrong about the Stepford Wives thing.'

'Don't worry. I brought crucifixes and holy water.'

'Come on you two. You should be happy that I am not moping over Charlie.'

They look at each other. You know the kind of look, that shared look where you're not involved but somehow it's all about you.

'What?' I ask.

123

Oh God, Charlie hasn't died or something has he? It's like something out of a Nicholas Sparks' novel. Just as everything is going along swimmingly, smash bang wallop and there is a tragedy.

'Has he got leukaemia?'

'What the fuck has leukaemia got to do with anything?' gasps Cas.

'Because they always have it in Nicholas Sparks' novels.'
Georgie sighs.

'What has Nicholas Sparks got to do with it?'
My stomach does a somersault.

'It's bad news about Charlie isn't it? That's why he broke everything off …'

'It depends what you mean by bad news, right Cas?'
He's been shot or something. This is just terrible. Shit, of all the times for this to happen. At that moment the phone rings and I freeze.

'That's them with the news isn't it?' I say, panic rising up and threatening to engulf me.
I rush to the dresser and grab the phone.

'Hello,' I say urgently.
There is a silence for a moment, and then a woman's voice, sharp and clipped.

'Who's that?'

'It's Alice,'

'Who?'

'Alice.'

'Where's Ted?'
Her voice is razor sharp, quick and so abrupt that I feel like I've been slapped across the face. Why is she asking about Ted? What about Charlie?

'He's not here. He went to a veterinary show in Exeter. He'll be back later today. Shall I tell him you called?'
I glance at Cas and Georgie who are staring at me while stuffing themselves with cake.

'Apart from being Alice, just who are you exactly?'
Yes, Alice, just who in the world are you?

'I'm the housekeeper,' I say in a hoity-toity voice. 'And who might you be?'

'Housekeeper, my God, he really is serious about that bloody farm isn't he? Well tell him his fiancée called and all the way from bloody New Zealand. Honestly, he could try and be there.'

Did she say Edward's fiancée?

'Have you tried his mobile?' I suggest helpfully.

'Of course I tried his mobile. The bloody thing's off, just tell him I called.'

The phone goes dead. Edward has never mentioned a fiancée. For some stupid reason I feel my legs go to jelly and I grab the table for support.

'You okay Alice, you've gone all white?' says Georgie, filling a glass with water.

'Edward has a fiancée,' I say stupidly.

Cas slaps his hand to his heart.

'Oh my God, I thought for a minute he had been struck down with a terrible illness.'

'No, that only happens to you Cas and even then it doesn't *really* happen,' sighs Georgie.

'What's so odd about that anyway?'

She hands me the water.

'He's never ever mentioned a woman. I know he doesn't have to, it's just ...'

It's just I really like him and I have no real idea if he likes me. Sometimes I think he does but then I wonder if he is just being kind to me. I know he likes Sara and now I hear he has a fiancée. I never imagined Edward to be such a ladies' man.

'I thought you said this place was a dump,' says Georgie checking out the Aga.

'What are you talking about, it is a dump,' chuckles Cas, 'but a better class of dump than I thought it was going to be.'

'What's wrong with Charlie,' I demand. 'Come on, you can't keep it from me forever?'

There's that look again. The *how do we tell her* look. This is terrible. It's like waiting for that last number at the bingo. He hasn't had a terrible accident has he? Please don't tell me he's had his limbs amputated or something.

Georgie pulls up a chair and pushes me into it. It's worse than I thought.

'You know your honeymoon? The one you never quite went on?' says Georgie grimly.

'The romantic honeymoon of a lifetime in Lake wherever,' adds Cas.

I nod mutely with a mild feeling of distress creeping into my body.

'Well, he didn't cancel it. He's now taking Big Tits instead of you. Honestly, you could have knocked me down with a feather when I heard that,' finishes Georgie.

He's taking Big Tits on my honeymoon? I'm torn between feelings of relief that Charlie hasn't had his legs amputated after a horrific car crash, while at the same wishing I could amputate a certain appendage of his myself. There are moments in life where you feel that if you could just turn the clock back to the point it all went wrong then you may be able to put it right. I so want to go back to that moment with Charlie and put everything right.

'But we spent hours choosing our honeymoon at the lakes,' I say thinly disguising the agony in my voice.

'How can he even consider taking her?'

'Well with a bit of luck they'll drown in one of them,' comforts Georgie.

'What has she got that I haven't? I mean what is she giving him that I couldn't?' I groan.

'Big tits and a permanent erection darling?' offers Cas.

I burst out laughing.

'The only thing that would give Charlie a permanent erection is a little blue pill,' I splutter.

'Enough of Charlie,' declares Cas. 'Lead me to the calf, I've come prepared.'

He whips out a surgical mask.

'I've had my tetanus and hepatitis jabs.'

'Honestly Cas, it just gets worse,' giggles Georgie.

'Well, you were threatening me with the Little Chef remember? No one goes in one of those without protection.'

I eagerly lead them round the back of the house.

'Ooh chickens,' Cas cries excitedly. 'Does Edward have a cock?' Georgie giggles.

'One would certainly hope so.'

I roll my eyes.

'Sorry Ali, it's just us and the country, you know how it is.'

I take them into the milking shed and round the back to Chloe's pen. She runs to me, her eyes wide, hopeful, and I like to think full of love. Cas takes one look inside the shed and backs away.

'She won't charge will she?' he asks nervously.

'It's a calf not a bull,' says Georgie carefully stroking Chloe's head. Chloe responds by chewing Georgie's cashmere cardigan.

'Excuse me sweetie, one doesn't chew a Prada.'

'Unless one has taste,' I laugh, picking up the teat bucket.

'Christ, what's that when it's at home? More importantly, where can I get one? That one certainly makes your eyes water,' exclaims Cas.

'I should have left him in the Little Chef loo. He would have died from the shame of it, and we would have been shot of him,' Georgie sighs.

I place the teat in Chloe's mouth and we sit watching her. The only sounds are Chloe's suckling and the hum of a tractor in a distant field. There's an eerie stillness about everything and Georgie shivers.

'Is this it? Is this all you do all day? Feed her and make cakes. Christ, you must be going insane,' says Cas breaking the silence and scraping cow dung off his shoe. 'How do you stand the smell? You must still have it up your nostrils when you're eating your Cornish pasties.'

Georgie and I ignore him and I show her how to hold the teat bucket.

'It's quite sexual this isn't it? I mean, I could get quite turned on by a teat bucket,' she says in her best Monroe voice.

'Now there's a new use for a teat bucket I've not heard before,' comes a voice from behind us.

Georgie spins round and sprays us in milk.

'You must be Edward,' she says.

Why is it she thinks everyone is Edward? And why is Dominic Montfort here?

'Thankfully no, I'm not Edward. Dominic Montfort. I own the next farm. It's nice to meet you.'

'Oh,' she begins and attempts a sort of curtsy. I say *sort of* because she somehow gets her foot caught up in her skirt and kind of skids towards him. I'm not sure what kind of impression she is trying to make but it's dead embarrassing. She straightens herself up awkwardly and holds out her hand.

'I'm Georgie and this is Cas. We've come from London to visit Alice.'

We watch stunned as Dominic gallantly raises her hand to his lips and kisses it. I feel sure I hear Georgie sigh. Cas gives me a sidelong look and then holds out his hand. I could die from embarrassment.

'You can just shake mine darling, hand that is. Feel free *not* to kiss, germs and all that.'

Oh, the shame of it. What was I thinking inviting Cas to the country? To my relief Dominic smiles and turns his gaze onto me.

'I came to see if you were free for lunch?'

Oh dear.

'We're lunching at The Heifer, why don't you join us?' invites Georgie.

'How lovely. I brought pink champagne. Why don't we all have it as an aperitif before we leave?'

'Ooh pink champagne, how divine,' cries Cas. 'All I've got to do is get past that demonic dog and I'll be in heaven.'

It sounds like Dominic is joining us for lunch. I hope Edward doesn't find out.

Chapter Eighteen

I am concentrating so hard on relaxing that all my muscles have gone rigid. A glass of pink champagne and two glasses of red wine, and I'm still tense. Tipsy but tense. I'm just waiting for some awful disaster to befall our lunch, but so far all is going incredibly well. There was an eerie hush when we walked into the pub, which everyone except Cas was aware of.

'Hello all, we're the city folk here for a visit, just for the weekend, so you don't need to lock up your husbands,' he announced.

I have eaten so much to calm my nerves that I've had to undo the button on my skirt. I know, one is supposed to drink to calm one's nerves. But if I drink much more I'll be paralytic. I wish I could relax. The atmosphere around the table is cheerful, although Jed and Dominic have barely spoken. It doesn't seem to matter as Georgie has practically bulldozed Jed into a corner, and hasn't stopped firing questions at him. He, in turn, seems to be enjoying spending time with my London friends. Cas is his normal self and everyone seems to find him hysterically funny, while I have an uneasy feeling about it all. I wish I was back at the farm sitting with Chloe. I'm worrying about the bill too. I hope Dominic doesn't offer to pay for me. How can I possibly deny him sex if he does? The pink champers must have cost a small fortune. He may be expecting a handjob on the strength of that alone. I must be tipsy. I never have such sordid thoughts normally. I also can't stop thinking about Edward's fiancée. Why has he got a fiancée in New Zealand? If Charlie had buggered off to New Zealand I would have thought he was trying to tell me something. Here I go thinking of Charlie and Big Tits Brunette. What is he doing jetting off on our honeymoon with her? I bet they're having mad passionate sex all over the place and ...

'What are you having for dessert Ali?' asks Georgie in a perky voice.

I feel sick. The mention of dessert in the same breath as thoughts of Charlie and Big Tits having sex is enough to make me throw up my lamb shank. I'm just about to say I'll pass on the dessert when I see Edward walk through the door and, oh no, there is a thunderous look on his face. He looks around, spots us and marches over. I feel an overwhelming urge to dive under the table. He comes to a halt in front of me and then, with a slightly patronising air, nods at everyone. My shoulders lift up even further.

'Alice,' he says firmly, 'can I have a word?'

I have a feeling it's going to be more than one. I'm beginning to feel horribly sick. Why is it I seem to always do something that makes Edward cross?

'Who are you?' asks Georgie in a bold manner that only comes from having too much wine. I roll my eyes. Honestly, the one time she should say *Oh you must be Edward* and she lets me down.

'This is Edward,' I say, alarmed at how slurry my words are. I stand up and sway ungainly. I point my finger at him and he gently lowers it with his hand.

'Alice, the golden rule?' he hisses into my ear.

The golden rule? I didn't know there was a rule about pointing at him. It's getting worse. I frantically scan my befuddled brain for some recognition of the golden rule while fighting the overwhelming urge to throw up.

'What? Do you want a drink Edward?'

'There are buckets of alcohol here,' chuckles Cas. 'What's your poison Edward?'

Edward rubs his eyes tiredly.

'Thank you but not right now.'

The waitress hovers around our table, pen and pad in hand.

'You need to chill Edward, have some fun,' says Dominic dryly.

My stomach churns and I feel the lamb shank and celeriac mash rise up. Please don't let me throw up all over Edward, please God. Edward gives Dominic such a hateful look that I feel sure it sends a hush over the pub.

'I don't need you to tell me how to have fun.'

'Ooh handbags at dawn I think,' I hear Casper whisper.

'Alice, you left the gate open,' snaps Edward. 'It's mayhem. I've got cows everywhere. Why don't you think woman?'

Shit.

'Oh Edward,' I say, and move to take a step towards him when my skirt slides down, landing in a heap around my ankles. Piss it.

'Oh shit,' groans Cas, 'you've just dropped your skirt.'

'Cas states the bloody obvious,' mumbles Georgie.

'Oh well, at least it wasn't your knickers,' he adds.

Cas, please shut up.

'I'll help you, Ted,' says Jed, standing up and pulling some money from his wallet.

'Don't you think you're making a hell of a fuss over nothing Edward? You'll get them all back,' says Dominic irritably. 'Of course if you sold the farm you'd be free of these hassles.'

Georgie helps to pull the skirt up at the back while I struggle with the front. This couldn't be more mortifying. Edward steps menacingly towards Dominic and my lamb shank moves menacingly higher up my oesophagus. Cas jumps from his seat and drapes an arm around Edward's shoulders.

'Buggeration. Sorry Edward, it was me. What do I know? I'm bloody gay and from London. We're a despicable lot, so I'm damned before I start. Let me come and help round them up. I've always wanted to do the *Brokeback Mountain* thing. You lot finish here and we'll see you back at the ranch. Come on Edward, you can show me your cock too. I was asking about it only this afternoon, the cock that goes with the chickens of course.'

Where do I put my face? There is a deathly silence. Edward gives me a piercing stare and walks out. Five minutes later I am throwing up in the loo.

***

I give Georgie a hug and inhale her Chanel perfume, transporting myself back to London.

'God, I so miss you, and London and everything,' I sigh wistfully.

'I know. It's pants, it really is. I bloody hate Charlie,' she says hugging me even tighter. 'We'll be back, and you'll come up to London won't you?'

I nod miserably. We peep round the corner to see Cas fighting Molly off his crotch and dancing away from the pecking hens, while trying to conduct a conversation with Edward.

'Cas has had a good time anyway,' laughs Georgie, 'and so have I. I'm totally taken with these countrymen,' she laughs.

I, however, feel dead depressed. Edward, though perfectly friendly to Georgie and Cas has barely spoken one word to me. I've got the mother of all hangovers to top it all. Now he walks towards us smiling broadly at Georgie. God forbid he might give me one. A smile I mean, obviously, anything else is out of the question. I'm seriously tempted to grab my case and jump in the car with them. I walk past him towards Cas, lifting my head in the most hoity-toity manner I can manage. He might have told me he had a fiancée. I attempt to hug Cas with Molly wedged between us.

'You can't break up a relationship like ours,' he jokes, patting Molly as he kisses me.

'I'm so sorry about the gate thing,' I apologise. 'I don't know what happened.'

'Well I do darling,' he says encircling my waist. 'Mr Montfort left the gate open and ...'

I pull back sharply and glare at him. What is he saying?

'But you said that you ...'

'I know what I said, but that was to stop bloodshed. You know I faint at the sight of blood. He left it open darling. Oh, I'm not saying deliberately, he's just so into himself he probably didn't notice but he was deliberately provocative in the pub.'

He pulls me back into his arms as Edward approaches.

'Edward's all right. I like him. Just be careful sweetie, okay?' he whispers and then says loudly,

'Come up to London soon darling, before you turn into Helen Archer.'

Edward and I watch them climb into the car and wave until it disappears at the end of the lane.

'You've got nice friends,' he comments as he turns to the house.

'Oh I see.'

What does that mean? What do I see exactly? I follow him into the kitchen.

'I'm moving the sheep to another field today so they can graze, and then I'm going to the cattle auction. You're welcome to come, unless you have something else planned,' he says, snapping the ring on a can of coke.

'So I'm pretty awful, but I have nice friends?' I say eventually, grabbing a bottle of water for myself.

'I didn't mention you,' he says abruptly, walking past me.

'You've got nice friends said it all didn't it?'

Do shut up Alice. You're seriously in danger of making a fool of yourself.

'Seeing as that was all I had to say I suppose it did say it all.'

Why does he have to be so bloody logical? He opens the back door and is halfway through when I remember the phone call.

'Your fiancée phoned yesterday. She was quite annoyed that you weren't here and that your mobile was off.'

He stops and seems to struggle for something to say. After what feels like an eternity, he says,

'I'll be leaving in about twenty minutes if you want to come. Although, I don't imagine it's your cup of tea. I need a bull.'

Don't we all? And if that wasn't a red rag to one, what was? Even if I seriously didn't want to go, nothing is going to stop me now is it? Unless of course …

'Doesn't Sara want to go?'

He shrugs.

'I didn't ask her. I'll see you in a bit.'

***

True to his word, twenty minutes later he is back. I have changed into my jeans and the thick Aran jumper I had bought at Sue Ryder. I'm still horribly hungover, and my head feels like someone has just walloped it with a hammer, but otherwise I look okay. I leave my hair loose because I cannot bear the pull of a scrunchie. I rub some cream blusher on my cheeks and pop in some drop-pearl earrings. He takes one look at me and says,

'You'll need wellingtons. It's not a fashion show.'

I blush. How does he always manage to make me feel like a prize prat city girl? I raise my hand in a salute.

'Yes sir.'

He opens his mouth to speak but stops at the sound of a car driving into the yard. There is loud hooting followed by Molly's insistent bark. The door flies open and a flushed and breathless Jed stands in front of us.

'Rob Marcham's just taken a serious tumble on Mabel. They've rushed him to hospital but Mabel's in a bad state and ... well she needs tranquillising and ...'

'We'll come now,' interrupts Edward.

We? What does he mean, we? And who the hell is Mabel? How can someone be in hospital after a tumble?

'I'll just get my gun,' says Edward.

'Alice can you drive the Land Rover? I'll go with Jed and he can fill me in on the way.'

Saints alive, what does he need a gun for? Is Mable a psycho or something? Heavens, she must be if she needs tranquillising. Hold on a minute, I'm not sure I want to go, at least, not unarmed, and I don't see him offering me a gun.

'Well ...' I begin, but the room is empty. Jed has raced back outside and Edward is thumping around upstairs. I should have bought that shotgun after all. My head is pounding. Why did I drink so much? I never drank this much with Charlie. Edward rushes back into the kitchen and throws me the keys. Even in my fragile hungover state I still manage to catch them expertly. It's only ten o'clock. I'm never going to make it through the day at this rate. I grab a bottle of water from the fridge and run after them.

'But ...' I begin and find myself diving into the Land Rover as they shoot off without giving me a second glance.

I drive at breakneck speed, crunching the gears as I try to keep up with them. I pray that the pheasants will stay out of my way, or there will be utter carnage. Although by the sound of it, there is utter carnage at Mabel's place. Christ, what am I doing driving into a dangerous situation. Women are constantly being advised not to do this kind of thing, and what do I do? Jed suddenly turns right and I have to brake sharply and find myself skidding and taking the corner on one wheel. It is like something out of *Top Gear*. The Land Rover, which seriously lacks suspension, bounces back onto the road with a thump, and my head pounds even more. I really can't believe I am doing this while Charlie is on *our* honeymoon with Big Tits. As I am being mowed down by some mad woman, Charlie will be sunning himself at our luxury hotel. What an utter bastard. Jed slows up and indicates left. I follow him through a gateway and down a long driveway. Ahead of us is a farmhouse where a middle-aged woman waves frantically. If this is Mabel then I have to agree that she most certainly needs tranquillising. I'm going to refuse to get out of the Land Rover until she is. She runs and puts her arms around Edward and then points to a field ahead of them. Edward looks over at me and then pushes Mabel into the arms of Jed before beckoning to me to leave the Land Rover. Surely he isn't serious? I shake my head and he approaches with his usual cross look. I wind down the window.

'Alice, I'm sorry to ask you, but I need someone with me. I may have to shoot Mabel and ...'

'What!' I scream. 'But you can't, you just can't. I mean, I can't possibly, I mean, it's monstrous. Oh God, Edward ...'
Tears spring to my eyes.

'Alice, it's how it's done in the country,' he says gently. 'I know you don't understand. I realise these things rarely happen in the city ...'

'Not with this kind of callous calmness they don't. In London it's down a dark alley usually. But this is just horrific. I'm calling the police Edward, I'm sorry,' I say, hiccupping between my tears.
I pull my Nokia from my bag and his hand reaches out roughly to stop me.

'Alice, don't you think you're overreacting. You can't call the police because I'm going to shoot a horse.'

'A horse? You're going to shoot a horse, not her?' I say, pointing to the woman.
He sighs.

'I need Jed to stay with Frances, she's too distressed and she doesn't know you. Look, it doesn't matter, just wait here.'

'No, I'll come,' I say, feeling a sudden surge of courage which I'm sure will wear off as soon as I enter the field. I stupidly can't bear him to think badly of me, although God knows why I should even care. He gives me a grateful smile, and I feel all benevolent and very Princess Diana-ish. Then I see poor Mabel lying in the field. She is struggling to get up but the effort seems to have worn her out, and at the sight of Edward she sighs and flops back down. Edward kneels beside her and whispers softly in her ear. Oh God, this is awful. I can't possibly stay here. I turn to go back but am stopped by Edward's voice. I wonder if he talks to his fiancée in this tone.

'Can you stroke her forehead gently, and talk to her while I give her an injection and check over her leg. Imagine it's Chloe.'

He says it so softly that I have to get closer to him to hear. The grass is damp under me and smells sweet. I don't want to imagine this is Chloe. I don't ever want Edward to give Chloe an injection. I most certainly do not want him to shoot her. I gently stroke Mabel's head.

'Don't show your emotions, she'll pick up on them right away. Be soft and gentle, it's the kindest thing you can do right now.'

He places his hands over her body. Oh sod this. Why can't I be lying by a pool with Charlie? That's where I should be. Covering myself in Ambre Solaire and dripping lovely Italian ice cream onto my well-oiled body while admiring my new wedding ring. I swallow back the tears that threaten to engulf me and stroke Mabel's head in a back and forth rhythmic motion. She twitches slightly as he injects her and Edward's hand touches mine as he also strokes around her ears and around her jaw.

'That's a good girl Mabel, you're doing brilliantly aren't you my beauty.'

I suddenly so want to be Mabel. Not shot in the head obviously, I mean, that goes without saying, but to have Edward talk to me in that way and to touch me with those caressing hands. I shake my head of all thoughts and remind myself he has a fiancée. Mabel looks at him with such doleful eyes that I have to look away. He pulls away from her with a drawn out exhalation and takes the gun from his bag. I feel like I am unable to breathe. I can't do this, but I find I am. I stroke Mabel's back as Edward comes closer with the gun, the whole time he talks so softly and calmly to Mable that I feel tranquilised also. I jump at the sound of the shot and fall back onto the ground in shock. I hear a cry from the farmhouse and feel tears dampen my cheeks.

'Thanks Alice, you really helped,' says Edward, stroking my hand and helping me up. He covers Mable with a blanket. My legs have gone to jelly and I wobble slightly but he seems not to notice. I need a drink and that's not something I thought I'd hear myself say first thing this morning.

Chapter Nineteen

'Wine or something stronger?'

It was Edward's idea to stop at a pub on the way to the auction. I'm having a very quiet mini breakdown. I'm sure there is a time and place for emotional breakdowns and I'm sure mine could have been put on hold until I got to The Priory. I may make it there just before Christmas. I hear The Priory is very nice that time of year. Charlie jilting me, combined with my impending period is enough of a mix as it is, but throw in a shot to the head of a horse and you have a lethal combination that would tip over even Hillary Clinton. Mind you, she turns on the tears at the drop of a hat doesn't she? Let's change that to Margaret Thatcher, The Iron Lady. It's dimly lit for a pub but at least I can whimper on and off without anyone noticing. It's warm too, which is good because for some reason I can't stop shaking. One minute I was fine and normal, that's if I've ever been normal. Georgie claims I am far too nice to be normal and the next I am shaking so much it's like I've been injected with a short sharp burst of Parkinson's disease.

'Something stronger,' I say, thinking a jab with his tranquilliser gun would be helpful. However, he returns with a brandy, which comes close.

I throw it back in one hit.

'Was it that bad?' he asks.

'Worse,' I say knocking back his too.

'The first time I shot a horse I polished off five double whiskies,' he says thoughtfully, before going to the bar for another round.

The first time? How many times have there been? How many poor horses are in horse heaven thanks to Edward Fairfax? He's a serial horse killer.

The brandy warms my insides and my heart slows down and thankfully the shaking ceases. Edward returns with another brandy and a whisky for himself. He pulls his brown woollen jumper over his head, giving me a glimpse of his hairy chest. I stare fascinated. He runs his hand through his ruffled hair and looks at me and I realise I am still staring.

'Charlie waxed his chest,' I hear myself saying and then realise that I have totally given away the fact that I have just seen his.

'Ouch.'

'He wanted me to watch once. You'd think he was being tortured. I hated it then but I think I could enjoy it now, watching Charlie being tortured.'

What am I saying?

'Oh I'm sorry I shouldn't have said that. Sorry I just feel a bit fragile after the Mabel thing.'

He avoids my eyes and downs his whisky.

'I don't usually wish bad things on people,' I say reiterating, just in case he should think I'm Saddam Hussein's evil sister. 'I can't even watch torture scenes in films.'

'It doesn't seem an unreasonable thing to wish considering he jilted you a few weeks before your wedding. What was it like to watch?'

Oh, a fellow sadist.

'This is true. I did consider pulling off his finger nails for the sheer pleasure of it but changed my mind and came to Cornwall instead. He went very red in the face you know that kind of red when you're fighting the scream.'

'Sounds delightful, I can think of a few people I would like to nominate for that.'

He checks his watch and I sip at my brandy.

'You never mentioned you had a fiancée in New Zealand,' I say courageously.

He makes a sucking sound between his teeth.

'Ah well, if we're seriously going to talk fiancés then I'll need some crisps. I can cope without food when we're talking torture but fiancés are a whole other ball game. Or would you prefer pork scratchings?' he adds with a grin.

Pork scratchings? Charlie would have a thousand canary fits if he could see me now.

'Why not,' I smile, 'something else to make Charlie go red in the face.'

'In that case I'll get two bags.'

Well, what a surprise. He has quite a sense of humour.

'So how did you meet Charlie? He asks throwing the pork scratchings at me and avoiding my question.

'In Wetherspoons,' I say cringing at the memory. 'We both went in there to keep warm, I hasten to add, and not for the food. It was New Year's Eve and the queue outside Francine's nightclub was enormous.'

He looks suitably unimpressed.

'I met *Lucy short for Lucinda, but everyone calls me Luce,* that's her little speech by the way, not mine, at a fund-raising dinner for the Arctic Wildlife Conservation campaign.'

Blimey, that rather puts Wetherspoons in the shade. Lucinda? Crikey, that sounds very upmarket. No wonder he has a Coutts cheque book.

'Charlie doesn't have a little speech. I actually think he prefers Charlie to Charles and ...'

God I miss him.

'Why did he break it off?'

If only I knew.

'Why is yours in New Zealand?'

'Ah ...'

'Is not an answer actually,' I say, wagging my finger. 'Charlie said he wasn't ready to settle down with one woman. That was his excuse anyway.'

He tips the bag of pork scratchings upside down and catches the final few in his mouth. God, if Charlie saw this. Oh sod Charlie, what does he care? He's too busy sunning himself on my honeymoon.

'Charlie at this very moment is on our honeymoon with some big-breasted brunette,' I say.

It's out and I feel so much better. Edward coughs slightly and then begins to choke on the pork scratchings. I dive to the bar and return with two lemonades. I hit him forcefully on the back.

'Are you all right?'

'I was until you walloped me.'

He smiles.

'I seriously have to say what a Charlie is Charlie.'

I nod.

'Lucy is in New Zealand because that's what we planned to do. We were both going to work on an animal rescue project for six months. It was our joint dream, and then my father died. I chose to take the farm on and get it back on its feet. Lucy doesn't get it. I'm not sure I get it really. I'm not a farmer but I'm from a farming family. We had the biggest and most prosperous farm in the village. Dad was proud of it, but then he got sick and his mind went and everything went to the dogs. The dementia was so bad and sadly he chose the wrong people to help him at the end. He didn't want me. Sometimes he didn't even know who I was.'

I feel my hand reach out and lay it gently on his arm.

'Edward, I'm so sorry.'

'He was angry with me because I chose the veterinary route. He didn't know what he was doing at the end and some people took advantage of that. Anyway, I didn't want to sell the farm that my dad had worked on all his life for next to nothing, so I chose to stay here and get it back on its feet. Lucy hates it, hates farming, hates this farm and up until last week, wasn't too fond of me either. I think she is coming round now though. Anyway ...'

He stands up.

'To the cattle market. Let's go and have some fun and a few hot dogs.'

Hot dogs? It just gets worse and worse on the food front here doesn't it?

'So that's what farmers do to have fun,' I say smiling.

'Yep. We buy bulls and eat hot dogs. Not necessarily in that order. It's not just city folk who have fun you know.'

Before I can respond he has walked to the door and I find myself thinking isn't Lucy the lucky one, and isn't it just my luck that when I meet someone nice, *that someone* barely notices me and already has a fiancée.

***

'Twenty-five, thirty, fifty-five, one hundred, and over there one sixty and now two hundred, any more?

The man next to me tips his cap.

'Two fifty, yes three hundred.'

It's like a madhouse of people with animals running around just fc good measure. Of course, I realise it's always like this, but to me seems like complete and utter chaos. There are lots of men in oilski jackets walking round with large plastic cups of beer. The smell c baked jacket potatoes makes my stomach rumble.

'Oh look, piglets,' I squeal and point excitedly at the pink bab piglets that are being led to the arena.

Edward lowers my hand gently with his and lays it in my lap with h hand covering it. A jolt of sexual energy charges straight through me There is something about sheep, cows and farmers that seriousl bring out the animal in me.

'You almost made a bid for close on six hundred pounds for cow that, not only do we not need, but don't want. Stay here while fetch the hot dogs and whatever you do don't raise your hand, nc even to scratch your head.'

I've never seen such chaos or smelt so much shit in my life, althoug having said that I must admit to having a whale of time, more than ever remember having with Charlie. But then I suppose in fairness t Charlie it never occurred to him to take me to a cattle auction, and probably would have been appalled had he even suggested it. watch mesmerised at the chaos around me and through the crowd see Edward carrying the hot dogs and drinks. He stops every so ofte to acknowledge someone. He looks so at home and I feel a surge c affection for him. I look at my hot dog like it is some foreign objec to be avoided at all costs.

'The last time I had one of these was when I was sixteen. I was a the funfair with Jimmy Willard. He also bought me a plastic cup o red wine.'

'Why does the red wine not surprise me? But Jimmy Willard? Yo really went out with someone named Jimmy Willard,' he grimaces 'No wonder you ended up with a Charlie.'

'You can scoff. I'll have you know Jimmy and I went steady for a of two weeks.'

He pours mustard onto our hot dogs.

'There you go, the only way to eat a cattle market hot dog Doused in mustard to cover the taste of the rotten frankfurter.'

I stop, with the hot dog halfway to my mouth. He laughs heartil throwing his head back.

'That's a joke. They're actually the best ever.'

A trickle of excitement runs through the crowd as the bull is brought out. There is a moment of quiet and then excited babbling from everyone.

'There he is, what a beauty,' says Edward in an awe-stricken voice. I watch horrified as it charges towards one of the men who jumps behind a screen. Edward is surely not thinking of buying that thing is he? I look to him to see he is laughing along with everyone else. I hope I never manage to spook that beast if I find myself in the same field as him. As the bidding begins I feel nervous but as it gains momentum I am barely able to sit still.

'Stop fidgeting,' Edward whispers, 'I can't concentrate.'
By the time the final bid is made by Edward I am shaking so much with excitement that it really is all I can do to stay in my seat. And then finally Edward is successful and I jump up and shout.

'Yay, well done. We bought him,' only to wet my knickers. Honestly, who would have thought a woman would need Tena pads at a cattle auction? Maybe I won't tell Georgie about this. I excuse myself to the ladies in a place where ladies are few and far between. While there I check my Nokia and see I have had a missed call and, oh no, it is from Dominic Montfort. What on earth possessed me to give him my mobile number? Of course it probably had something to do with the copious amounts of wine I was drinking at the time. Guiltily I ignore it and head back to the auction picking up two plastic cups of Red Bull on the way. The excitement has totally sapped my energy. I see the piglets are now in the arena and they look so cute. I wave to Edward who shakes his head at me. I hope he isn't going to get all moody because he paid a lot for the bull. I rush to my seat and watch as the piglets one by one parade around the arena. I feel so bad eating those pork scratchings, I vow never to eat pork scratchings for the rest of my life. The bidding for the piglets is very quick and finally the last one wanders around looking lost.

'Thirty-five, thirty-eight, forty, forty-five, seventy, any more?'

'Oh look Edward, isn't he just the cutest,' I say forcing his attention from his cheque book.

'Seventy, eighty.'
The man next to me tips his cap.

'He'll make good bacon.'
I snap my head round and stare at the barbarian. Oh no, he can't do that.

'Eighty-five.'

'Ninety,' I shout waving my hand.

Edward quickly grabs it.

'What are you doing?' he hisses in my ear.

'I can't let him be made into bacon.'

His eyes widen in alarm and the man next to me smirks before nodding again.

'Ninety-five.'

Oh no.

'A hundred,' I call.

'You're going to spend your first salary on a pig?' says Edward incredulously.

'Rescuing a pig,' I correct.

'One hundred and fifty,' calls the man who is now glaring at me.

'You're not the sharpest knife out of the drawer are you?' he says nastily.

'How dare you ...'

'Okay Frank, no need for that,' snaps Edward.

Oh, Frank is it. I'll give him Frank.

'Some mothers do 'ave 'em,' I mumble under my breath.

'You can't get emotional over animals Alice, not on a farm,' warns Edward.

I ignore him.

'Two hundred,' I yell.

Edward puts his head into his hands.

'For two hundred pounds lady you're welcome to it. One expensive pig you've got there Edward. You going to buy it a diamond-studded collar?' Frank laughs.

I look at Edward. He shakes his head. What am I doing? I've just bought a pig for two hundred pounds. I didn't spend two hundred pounds on my bras, or even the shopping in Lidl, but I spend it on a pig, have I gone totally nuts?

'Oh, what have I done?'

'You got emotional over a pig,' says Edward flatly.

'It was the pork scratchings,' I say by way of an excuse.

'Remind me never to take you to a cattle auction after a Sunday roast.'

He looks at me seriously for a moment and then we both burst out laughing. I'm laughing so much that I have to cross my legs.

'Come on let's get you out of here before we end up with a herd of sheep. I'll just arrange delivery and meet you at the Land Rover, and you owe me two hundred pounds.'

I hear the Nokia bleep and look to see there is a text from Dominic Montfort.

'Hi Alice, I tried calling you. I've taken the liberty of getting two tickets for the charity concert in Truro tomorrow night. It's for a good cause. It's the last night and I thought you would like it, I'll pick you up at seven.'

Oh, that's nice isn't it, I suppose. Although, I would much rather go to the concert with Edward, but Edward won't ask me because Edward is engaged *to Lucy, short for Lucinda, but everyone calls me Luce*, isn't he? And if he wasn't he would no doubt be going out with Sara. The last thing he is interested in is a townie like me.

'Right,' says Edward joining me. 'Let's go. I thought we'd stop off and get a Chinese takeaway. I'll get you sweet and sour pork.'

He laughs at his own joke and looks at me out of the corner of his eye.

'So what name are you going to give this one? Don't tell me, Babe, right?'

I ignore him and look out of the window.

'Or Miss Piggy,' he laughs, 'or even Princess Piggy, after all you paid enough; she could be a royal pig.'

'Have you finished?' I snap while trying not to smile. 'I'll have chicken chow mein actually, and some chips.'

And some chips? What am I saying? Can't I go a day without chips? This is shameful, shameful but nice.

***

A Chinese takeaway and a bottle and a half of wine later and I am playing gin rummy and sharing all Charlie's weaknesses. We've moved to the living room and Edward has lit the fire. Everything seems romantic and cosy in the firelight glow. Even the room doesn't seem rundown anymore. In fact, thinking about it all the place needs is a lick of paint. A nice cosy log fire, how romantic is that? The only thing missing in my life is a man to share this with.

'I'll take your ace,' I say, leaning across the floor towards Edward who is turning out to be such fun company that I barely recognise him. I haven't laughed so much in years.

'You can't keep taking my cards and not laying down,' he laughs.

'I hope that's not a proposition Mr Fairfax,' I giggle. 'You never said I had to lay down anything.'

'I do believe I have mentioned laying down several times Miss Lane. You obviously just keep ignoring me.'

'Charlie never asked me to lay down, well at least not often,' I say, yawning.

Edward places a tub of ice cream between us and I attack it like a starved animal while he sits back sipping his wine.

'Perhaps that was his big mistake,' he says with a wink.

'He said I could keep the ring,' I say with a snort.

'That was thoughtful of him,' Edward remarks, laying out a fan of cards. 'Still I imagine there's not much he can do with it.'

'I told him to stick it up his arse.'

He nods in agreement.

'It's as good a place as any,' he says laying down his final card.

I gasp and take a gulp of wine.

'You can't do that,' I protest.

'I just did.'

'Does Lucy, short for Lucinda, but everyone calls me Luce play gin rummy?'

He shakes his head.

'She's more a strip poker kind of gal,' he laughs.

I open my mouth in shock.

'No, you're not serious?'

'No, I'm not serious,' he smiles. 'Does Charlie, who prefers Charlie to Charles, play gin rummy?'

I shake my head.

'No, and he wouldn't play strip poker either.'

'He never asked you to lie down and wouldn't play strip poker? He sounds a bit boring to me. He is missing out ...'

He breaks off and meets my eyes and my stomach seems to somersault and my heart skips a beat. Good God, is he coming on to me? No surely not. He is very good looking, fun, and I'm surprised to find that I am deeply attracted to him. He tops up our glasses and

Lynda Renham

looks me straight in the eye. His hazel eyes gleam at me. I feel myself growing hot, and it's not from the heat of the fire. The desire in my body seems to soar out of control and I feel my breath catch in my throat. A strange sensation drifts slowly through my body and my hands begin to tremble. I put a shaky hand out to stop him pouring too much wine into my glass and find myself touching his. I feel an overwhelming desire to kiss him and quickly stand up. What am I doing? He's engaged to be married. How would I have felt if Charlie had done this with other women? I am starting to wonder if he had. Think how devastated Lucy, short for Lucinda, but everyone calls me Luce would feel. I stumble into the kitchen and look in the fridge for some water. I turn and he is standing behind me.

'I need to cool off,' I say shakily. 'We're getting swept along with the moment. Cosy fire, wine, it's the perfect kissing scenario isn't it? I'm engaged ... I mean, you're engaged ... Oh shit.'

What am I saying? He probably has no intention of kissing me. I'm just making a total fool of myself again. His lips are pink and his eyes all sultry. His hand reaches forward and closes the fridge door so I fall back against it.

'I'm wondering why Charlie let you go,' he says huskily.

He leans closer and I rest my hand on his arm.

'Edward, I think that every day. I'm also thinking about Lucy right now.'

The sharp ringing of the phone makes us jump. For some seconds we seem to stand there frozen in time. The phone stops and he sighs. Immediately it rings again. Relieved, I duck under his arm and pick it up. In an unsteady voice I answer it.

'Oh it's you,' says Lucy.

Shit, it is as if she knows what's going on.

'I'll get Edward,' I say, and hand the phone to him. 'Your fiancée,' I say pointedly.

He looks at me with a pained expression before speaking into the mouthpiece.

'Luce, what's the time there?'

He continues looking at me. I turn away and go back to the living room to tidy up suddenly feeling sober. I clear away the playing cards and ice cream. He enters the room and I lower my eyes.

'I'm off to bed,' I say as casually as I can.

'Alice,' he says laying his hand on my arm.

146

'Let's forget it shall we. We've both had too much to drink.'

He nods and drops his arm leaving me bereft of his hand. In that moment I knew with helpless certainty that he is the man I had been waiting for.

'Goodnight,' he says softly.

As I turn from him tears smart my eyes. Oh Edward, why didn't you try and kiss me again? This time maybe I wouldn't have run away. But isn't this just the story of my life? Charlie no longer wants me and when another does he is already engaged to someone else. It couldn't get any more complicated. Some escape to the country this was.

Chapter Twenty

I've never in my life been to a barn dance. I've heard of them, obviously, but attended one? Not on your life. Charlie arranged one some time ago for some animal organisation he was involved with. Fortunately for me I was taken sick that afternoon and couldn't attend. As far as I'm concerned they are a sad combination of checked skirts, jacket potatoes and an excellent opportunity for men to grope women's bums. So when Sara gleefully informed me she had passed the first of her exams and was having a barn dance at her parents' farm to celebrate, I had to fight the grimace from appearing on my face and had reluctantly accepted her invitation. How could I not, especially when she declared,

'Edward is coming. It will be tremendous fun. Do say you'll bake a cake.'

I have no doubt that Dominic will be there also. He is probably many women's dream man and I may have thought that myself if Edward and I hadn't almost kissed. I haven't been able to think of anything else since. The almost kiss, even though it was nearly two weeks ago, haunts my dreams and my waking hours. Things have changed between us since that night. Edward is nice to me but he is so reserved he may as well not be there at all. He stands so rigid when talking to me that Jed thought his shirts had been starched. Dominic on the other hand is there all the time. In fact Dominic is there too much. After the concert date he had bombarded me with texts and phone calls, but each time we met he would steer the conversation to Edward and question me on Edward's plans for the farm. The truth is I have no idea what Edward's plans are about anything. The only thing I do know is that they don't include me and I must not allow myself to think they ever could. The less I think about him the better. I'm actually beginning to love it in the country. It really is so peaceful and best of all, smog free. I never realised how noisy London was until I came here. I'm not sure if I would want to leave now. Both Chloe and Pepper, the piglet, seem to know me and always come when I call them. While my friends have three-year-old toddlers, hanging onto their skirts and screaming mummy, I have a squealing piglet that nibbles at my skirt and a calf that pushes her wet nose onto me. Instead of nappy changing I am cleaning up pig dung and mucking out the cowshed, and quite happily too. Edward's lost milk licence is certainly Pepper's gain. She gets tons of milk. I feed her the scraps each day and even talked Edward into building her a little pig house. Chloe always greets me lovingly by rubbing her head against my hand before feeding. I ask you, what more could a woman want? Love surely is having your own pig and calf. I've begun helping out with the flower arranging in the church and I'm actually finding I can think about Charlie without getting upset. Now that is progress. Lucy short for Lucinda but call me Luce has not phoned Edward again, or at least not when I have been there. I don't even want to think about what will happen when she returns to England. At the moment I have a job, a home, and two little animals depending on me. Not to mention a big decision to make on what to wear for a barn dance. I have no doubt that here in the country they take these things very seriously.

I finally asked Martha for advice who happily supplied me with a Stetson and suggested jeans, checked shirt and boots. Luckily all of which I have.

'Time you've finished do-si-doing you'll be very hot and I have no doubt the men will have you do-si-doing a fair bit,' she had laughed. It's been a long time since any man has do-si-doed me so this should be rather good.

'Come to me for a glass of wine beforehand. Lydia is coming too. We'll all go together. Better than walking in there on your own,' she had suggested.

Edward had shyly asked me this morning over breakfast if I was going.

'I'll grab you for the dishrag dance then. That is always good for a laugh,' he grinned.

'I can't tell you how flattered I am,' I had replied, wiping the sink and pretending to be insulted when I was in fact happy that he was teasing me again. He had tipped his hat.

'I'm taking the bull over to Matt Hardy's and then preparing the sheds so we can bring the cows in for the winter, so I probably won't be back until late.'

'I'm going from Martha's,' I said, making it sound like my wedding day. 'She's invited Lydia as well.'

'I look forward to seeing you there then. Don't forget your dancing shoes.'

Now here I am at Martha's, drinking homemade plum wine on an empty stomach and giggling at Lydia's costume. Georgie had ordered me not to mention a word of it on Facebook.

'Please, I beg you. Don't tell the world you are going to a barn dance not unless you want to lose your reputation as country glamour girl.'

'It's what we do in the country,' I said laughing.

'They also shag behind the barns and press up against the bark of trees, but that doesn't mean you have to.'

'Well if everyone else is doing it I don't see why I shouldn't too.'

'Hussy,' she laughed. 'Give Jed my love and be careful. Remember what happened when Thelma and Louise went dancing.'

I snort.

'No one will get smart with me because if they do I'm gonna splatter their ugly face all over their nice car!'

'Goddam it, Alice, you're disturbed.'

'I sure am,' I laughed.

Lydia has tied her hair in pigtails and overdone the rouge. She looks like a wind-up doll you see in shop windows. I tell her she looks terrific, how could I say anything else? Martha insists I leave my hair down and plops the Stetson on my head. I slip on the only checked shirt I have and complement it with a blue silk scarf that Lydia lends me. I look like I am about to attend the rodeo. We are all slightly merry by the time we leave Martha's and are already doing the soft shoe shuffle to the distant sounds of the band's accordion. Jed passes us in his van and hoots several times.

'Howdy ladies, save a dance for us,' shout the men from the back.

Lydia waves excitedly while turning bright pink. And to think I had her down as an old spinster. As we near Cockspit Farm I feel my stomach flutter. Music blares out of the well-lit barn and the smell of roasted pig reaches our nostrils and I think of Pepper. I vow to stick to salad for the entire evening. Martha opens the door and the music engulfs us. A circle of people are clapping wildly as others spin around the dance floor to cheers and laughter. So this is how they live it up in the country. Martha drags me to the bar.

'Do you want wine Alice, or something else?' she shouts over the music.

Out of the corner of my eye I see Dominic striding purposefully towards us.

'These are on me,' he says kissing me on the cheek.

'You look lovely ladies,' he bows graciously.

Lydia blushes again and looks at him admiringly. The top three buttons of his shirt are undone, I presume deliberately and he is wearing a bolo tie. I almost expect him to leap onto the stage and perform a cowboy striptease. I rather think Lydia would be dribbling in the front row if he did. Before I have time to sip at my drink Martha has pulled me into the circle of dancers and I'm taking the arm of a man I have never set eyes on before. I look back to an irritated Dominic and shrug.

'Matt Hardy, nice to meet you,' says the man spinning me around.

'Five six seven eight,' shouts the caller, 'to the left and spin her around, now to the right.'

'Hello. You've been working with Edward,' I say breathlessly, spinning to the left when it should be to the right.

'Hook arms, and now pass her on,' sings the caller.

'Talk of the devil,' laughs Matt spinning me towards Edward, 'She's all yours Ted.'

How I wish. Goodness I'm dizzy already and I have hardly started. There are an awful lot of men here. In fact, this is the most men I have seen since coming to the village and they've all got lust in their eyes if you ask me.

'Evening,' smiles Edward giving me a sharp head bow. 'Nice outfit.'

'Thank you,' I say as I am propelled to the middle of the room.

'You look very smart yourself.'

He also smells absolutely gorgeous. He is wearing a crisp white shirt tucked into jeans and on his head is a tatty Stetson too. His eyes twinkle from beneath it and his rugged skin is glowing from a recent shower. His hand is warm in mine and the kiss comes rushing back into my mind. Suddenly my hand is wrenched from his and I am being spun around by Jed. I strain my neck to see Edward who is now spinning Sara around. He then lifts her from the ground and gives her a long lingering kiss. I gasp and quickly turn away.

'Congratulations party girl. Well done, we are all so proud of you,' I hear him say.

Jed pulls me to the centre and back again.

'Are you enjoying it?' he asks.

I was. Come on Alice, stop being so stupid. Edward is entitled to kiss whoever he likes.

'Four to the left and four to the right. Now pass that lady over.'

I spin past Sara who giggles happily and am then in Dominic's arms.

'I hate sharing you,' he says and I shudder. I sure hope I don't have to splatter Dominic's brains all over his nice car.

'Last one gents. Spin her to the right, and now the left. Thank her kindly and encircle her waist.'

'Thank you lovely lass,' he whispers before kissing me fully on the lips.

The music stops and I manoeuvre myself out of his arms.

'Phew, I need a drink.'

'I'll catch you for the next dance. That's a promise.'

I head towards the bar where Lydia stands. My heart is thumping and my face burning. I collect the cake I had made and make for the food table in a bid to avoid Dominic, for a short time at least. Sara leaps at me excitedly pulling me towards another woman. I clasp the chocolate cake in my hands and practically throw it on the table in fear of getting it crushed.

'Mum this is Alice. Look at this divine cake she has made for the party,' says Sara, attacking the cake with a knife as soon as it lands on the table.

'How lovely to meet you Alice, of course Sara has told us all about you. You must think us all barbarians down here. It's so different to London.'

'It's lovely though. I really like it in the country.'

'This cake is really amazing Alice,' swoons Sara, offering some to her mother.

'You're so welcome and congratulations on passing your exams, you must be so happy.'

'So this is Alice,' booms a voice.

I turn and come face to face with an exceptionally handsome man. His eyes match Sara's but his nose is slighter longer than hers and his mouth fuller but I immediately see where Sara gets her good looks. His hair is greying at the temples giving him a distinguished mature appearance. His handshake is warm and confident.

'I'm very pleased to hear you're enjoying country life. We in the village are enjoying having you. I'm Sebastian, Sara's father and this is my wife Celia. I hope you're enjoying our little barn dance.'

Edward swings by us with a red-haired woman on his arm and waves encouragingly for us to join them.

'Shall we?' asks Sebastian.

I didn't have to consider my reply as within seconds I am being spun around the dance floor yet again and dancing for all I am worth and loving it. I find myself praying that Luce will never come back. How awful is that? I never thought I of all people would enjoy a barn dance. It feels like I'm in a scene from *Seven Brides and Seven Brothers*. Dominic is standing in the doorway looking very sultry and I remember that he had promised me this dance. Edward twirls the redhead towards us as the caller shouts to change partners. I am in his arms again and he is smiling widely. I am about to speak when I am twirled into Jed's arms. I am beginning to know what it must be like to speed date. I end up back with Sebastian as the music ends. He bows graciously and politely thanks me for the dance. Dominic is eyeing me from the doorway and begins to come towards me when, lo and behold, the greengrocer is standing in front of me. I should sell tickets. I'm beginning to feel like a prize catch.

'If you would be so kind Miss Alice, I do believe the next one is mine. There's a marrow in it for you.'

I tip my Stetson.

'Good heavens Mr Lovell, if it's marrows you're talking then I think I can most certainly squeeze you in,' I laugh.

'Make that two marrow's Ken, this is a long dance. Alice should be paid adequately,' calls Edward.

Good heavens. I wonder if Edward will offer his marrow for the next dance. I wouldn't like to guess what Dominic would offer, a large cucumber I should imagine.

Not so long ago I had been utterly miserable but now I couldn't be happier. An hour and two glasses of wine later and I don't even mind that Charlie took Big Tits on our honeymoon. Martha stands on one of the tables singing an Irish ditty to Sara who is weeping all over the place. Sebastian sits at a table with Edward, Jed and I and is now heartily applauding Martha.

'More, more,' roars Edward, leaning across for the wine. He stops with his face close to mine and winks.

'Having fun?'

'With two free marrows how could I not be?' I say, surprising myself.

Sara sways drunkenly towards me and puts both arms around my neck. Her face is very flushed and her lipstick smudged where she has been kissing everyone. I wonder if I look the same. Not because I have been kissing everyone you understand, but the heat and the dancing, not to mention the wine must have left its mark on me too. It certainly hasn't put Dominic off who has been sending me admiring glances all night.

'Okay, it's ladies' choice. Choose your partners for the do-si-do,' shouts the caller.

'Come on Jed,' Sara says jubilantly.

Oh, that was a surprise. I felt quite certain she would choose Edward. My brain goes into overdrive. If I don't hurry someone will claim him. Goodness, I'm talking about him like he is a lottery win. I could look around all nonchalantly like and give the impression that no one else looks that appealing so it may as well be him. The problem with that is if I take too long someone else will invite him to dance, but if I look too keen he will know how much I fancy him, and fancy him I do. It really is no good denying it. As gorgeous as Dominic is, he is nowhere near as gorgeous as Edward. Oh dear, I can barely stand the tension. I will have to ask him soon. I bite my lip anxiously and taste blood. I see the redhead approaching. He lifts his head to acknowledge her and I pounce on him like a sexual predator and almost land in his lap.

'Come on ladies, grab a man.'

I'm trying. I hover over Edward, all flustered and sweaty and ask,

'How about it?'

I ask you, where did that come from? I was fully intending to say *Edward can I have this dance,* but somehow it came out like an indecent proposal. He smiles, his head cocked to one side. The music begins and for one awful minute I think he is going to say no, but he puts his hand in mine and pretends to allow me to pull him up.

'I'd love to Miss Lane,' he smiles and twirls me onto the dance floor, his hand warm in mine.

The adrenalin levels in my body drop and I feel my legs go weak. My feet feel hot and swollen in my boots, but I couldn't care. Dominic shakes his head and gives me a tight smile. Oh my word, I did it. I actually asked Edward to dance and I got there before anyone else. The dance is a mad spin with the fiddle players seeming to go into complete overdrive. There are lots of shouts and foot stamping and I am actually beginning to feel quite a professional at this. The music slows and Edward pulls me in close.

'Slow waltz now gentlemen, one two three and turn.'

Edward turns me expertly and catches my hand again before joining the other men to make an arch. Breathlessly giggling I follow Sara under the arch and take four side steps before meeting Edward again who glides me around the dance floor in a slow waltz. I pass Martha and Sebastian who are clapping, and then a very happy Lydia who is dancing with Dominic. I smile at him but he gives me a sour look. I have to say that being newly single is finally starting to feel quite liberating. I shiver as Edward's lips gently touch my ear and feel I could stay in his arms like this forever. The waltz comes to an end but the stomping continues. Edward pulls me out of the ring as everyone surges forward.

'Time for some food,' he says pulling me by the hand towards the roasting pig.

'Oh, I couldn't,' I protest.

'Have some cold turkey. You're not nursing one of those are you?' he mocks, ordering drinks.

'Very funny,' I say, struggling to get my breath.

He gives me a heart-stopping smile which isn't very helpful when I am trying to catch my breath. I grab the glass of water from the guy behind the bar and knock the liquid back in one go. They both look at me in amazement. I swallow and shudder.

'That was a vodka and tonic,' says the barman.

'Yes, I know that now.' I splutter.

'For the lady,' he says inclining his head to the redhead. Oh dear. She smiles and drapes her arm through Edward's.

'That's fine. I think Alice needed it more than me. Edward most certainly swept you off your feet,' she laughs.

He most certainly has.

'Alice, this is Mona, believe it or not she owns Orchard Farm. It's the farm at the end of Church Lane and she's doing a grand job,' says Edward with admiration in his voice.

She pushes him playfully in the chest.

'You've helped Ted, along with Jed and Matt. I'm truly grateful too. My husband died a year ago,' she says with a forced smile. 'I've tried to hang onto the farm and the village has been great. I couldn't have asked to be part of a better community. I'm really glad I came tonight. I nearly didn't.'

I feel myself growing hotter and hotter and fan my face with the Stetson.

'I'm so sorry about your husband,' I say before she is dragged away by Lydia.

'It's the all ladies dance, come on Alice,'

I shake my head and fan myself some more.

'Let's get you outside in the fresh air,' offers Edward.

Oh dear, isn't this the kind of trouble Georgie said I must not get into. It looks like it will be Edward's face that will be splattered all over his nice car. Although I don't imagine Edward would make a pass at me. Nevertheless, a woman can hope can't she? The cold air hits me sharply and I clasp his arm for support. It's pitch black and the sky is clear, giving me a view of the stars and I marvel at them, as always. The strains of the accordion reach our ears and a single voice drawls out a country love song.

'In London you can barely see the stars, at least I've never noticed them,' I say dreamily feeling the vodka take effect.

The aroma of the pig roast is overtaken by the smell of burning logs.

'Alice,' he says leaning towards me and just at that moment I get cramp in my toe. I let out a yelp and kick it out and up so high that I practically wallop him in the groin with it. Honestly this could only happen to me.

'I've got cramp in my toe,' I cry.

He looks bewildered.

'What?'

'It must be all the dancing and the heat. Oh God, it's terrible.'
I struggle to pull my boot off so I can stretch the toes. He pushes me back against the barn. Of all the times to get passionate this really is not it. But I see he has no intention of devouring me but instead grabs my foot almost sending me falling to the ground.

'Wrong foot,' I say wincing.
I'm overcome with an ever-growing anxiety that my feet will stink. After all that dancing they are bound to be smelly aren't they? I've always had a tendency to sweaty smelly feet and tonight's no exception. This is just terrible. One whiff of those and he will go right off me or die from the fumes.

'It would be wouldn't it?' he says grabbing the other foot.
This is not quite the pass I had in mind. He pulls the boot off and I cringe, expecting him to pass out from the stench. However, he doesn't, but begins to massage my foot in such a sensual way that I swear if feet could orgasm I would most certainly have a multi.

'Ooh,' is all I can mumble as he removes my sock.
There is silence as we both stare at my deformed toes. Good God, I'm disfigured. My big toe has separated itself so far from my second toe that I look like a crab. Edward laughs, and it's so infectious that I follow suit.

'I've seen horror films that are tame compared to that foot,' he says with mock seriousness.
I stretch the toes upwards with a soft little moan.

'Don't mock the afflicted.'
I shiver slightly and feel his arm goes around my shoulder, and I shiver even more.

'Let's get back inside before your toe gets frostbite,' he smiles, 'that would be the final straw.'
He helps me up and I pull on the sock and boot while leaning on him. In the silence I can hear his steady breathing.

'I've had a lovely evening,' I say.
He kisses me tenderly on the cheek and for a few seconds hovers there before his lips move along it to my mouth. I turn my face slightly to meet his lips. At that moment the music gets louder as the barn door swings open. Edward quickly pulls away as Lydia calls to us,

'Sara is about to make her speech. Hurry.'

Edward gives me an apologetic shrug and taking my hand, escorts me back into the hall to hear the speech that I so much wished could have happened five minutes later.

Georgie

You could have knocked me down with a feather when I saw Charlie standing on the threshold of my flat looking for all the world like a little lost boy.

'I've made such a terrible mistake,' he says looking crestfallen.

I was a bit pissed to see him to be honest. I'd just thrown on my dressing gown after a late Sunday morning shower and was poring over *Cosmopolitan* and completing their *Is your boyfriend being honest with you?* questionnaire, and discovering that, of course, James never had been. I just love the articles in *Cosmo*, especially the sexual ones which frankly have you fumbling about all over the place. So, there I am, stuffing myself full of marshmallow and about to drool over the article *Do you know where your G-spot is?*, when the doorbell rings. Had it been anyone other than Charlie I may not have been so pissed. My feelings for the drivelling little wimp aren't even repeatable. But anyone who interrupts me trying to find my G-spot is never going to be popular now are they?

For a minute I think he means he has made a terrible mistake by knocking on my door and I can't but help agree with him, but of course he doesn't mean that at all.

'I should never have let her go,' he says, his face creasing while I have a mini panic attack at the thought he may actually blubber on my doorstep.

'You'd better come in,' I say in my most unwelcome voice.

He shuffles in and with a sweep of his eyes takes in the *Cosmo* magazine, wine and marshmallows.

'God, I'm sorry, you're in the middle of ...'

I raise my eyebrows. Just what does he think I'm in the middle of?

'Relaxing,' he finishes. 'It's just ... Oh God, I've been utterly bloody stupid, Georgie.'

Well at least he said it.

'I ... I don't know what came over me taking Bianca to Italy. Obviously all I thought about was Alice.'

Obviously.

'It was all so bloody awful,' he says, taking a handful of marshmallows.

'I'm sure.'

'I don't know what I was thinking of.'

'Clearly,' I say, removing the wine.

'It was the sex, I think, that did it.'

'The sex?'

God, I really don't want to go there. I top up my glass while he looks on longingly.

'Somehow it felt lacking with Alice, you know,' he says flopping onto my couch. 'With Bianca it was relentless. I couldn't keep it up to be honest.'

He points to the wine.

'Do you think I could have some of that?'

Not really.

'I guess so,' I say, pouring him half a glass.

'The thing is I can't live without her.'

He takes a long gulp and leans back.

'Alice?' I ask.

'Well of course. I tried with Bianca after Italy. I don't know what I was thinking of, ending it with Alice. I suddenly didn't want to be tied down you know, and then I couldn't find any reason why I shouldn't be tied down to Alice.'

Christ almighty. I'm sure Alice would be dead flattered to hear this.

'The thing is ...' He stops and looks at me urgently, 'Do you think she'll have me back?'

I shrug, shake my head and stammer something.

'I thought I'd go down and see her, what do you think?'

Go down and see her. God, don't ask me for her address.

'Her mum gave me the address. She's on some farm or other. I guess you knew that.'

Holy fuck, I'll kill her mother.

'Erm,' I mumble.

'God Georgie,' he says, grabbing me by my dressing gown cord. 'I can't be without her.'

And I can't be without this cord you wanker. I yank it from his hands and spin away from him.

'It's been over three months Charlie. She's been in Cornwall for seven weeks now.'

'God,' he moans again and sinks into the couch. 'She won't even answer my calls. I made a mistake. I admit that. I was to blame. She is perfect. I was bloody stupid not to see what I had. It's like her Blackberry is permanently off. I don't understand it.'

That's most likely because it is. I'm not giving you the sodding Nokia number. Oh no way Jose.

'Has she met someone else? Is that what you're saying?'

Christ Charlie boy, we're not all fast workers like you. I can't stand the thought of Ali being all shaken up again. The poor cow is just getting on her feet and finally seeing that other men find her attractive. Okay, Dominic Montfort might not be my ideal choice but there are more like him and that's what matters.

'The thing is we're all moving on Charlie. Is it fair to unsettle her?'

He jumps from the couch scaring me half to death.

'Of course it is. She loves me, she's always loved me. I know I've hurt her but I'll make it up to her. You know I will Georgie.'

I try to hide my sigh. I'm not so sure Charlie is the best thing for Ali right now. Country life seems to suit her and what's more I can visit regularly and get to know Jed better. There always has to be a bloody fly in the ointment and here he is.

'What's she doing down there anyway? Is she having some kind of extended holiday?'

I raise my eyebrows.

'Charlie I told you, she got a job there.'

Recognition flits across his face.

'Oh yes I remember. Some farm manager job.'

He shakes his head despairingly.

'She has no real conviction when it comes to her vegetarianism. It's not easy to stick by your principles. The thing is I can't have her doing this if we're getting back together. The president of the FFFAA has just made me chairperson of the London branch,' he says proudly. 'I can't have my fiancée working on a farm.'

I shrug, yawn and pick up my new P. D. James novel. I wish he would bugger off and preferably soon.

'What exactly does a farm manager do anyway?' he asks thoughtfully.

Feeding calves with penis buckets and baking cakes for village fetes I think.

'God knows,' I say heading towards the front door in the hope he gets the hint.

'The thing is,' he says uncertainly, 'I was wondering if you'd put a good word in for me?'

What!

'Charlie, the problem with that is,' I pause for effect, 'I don't have a good word to say for you.'

He pulls angrily on the door handle.

'You were always trying to put her against me,' he says petulantly.

'That's not true Charlie.'

'Just because you can't get a man, you think …'

Oh fuck off Charlie and let me get back to my G-spot. He gives a disgruntled snort of disgust and stomps out. What a turn of events. Bloody Charlie back on the scene is just what we all don't need. I suppose I had better break the news to Alice. Fucking classic this is.

Chapter Twenty-One

'You're a godsend Alice, and that's the truth.'
Martha stands back and surveys my flower arrangement with admiration. I shiver slightly from the chill in the church and rub my hands together. Who would have thought I'd be decorating the church altar?

'It's getting cold. We'll be planning the Christmas services soon. I do hope you'll help with the flowers then Alice?' asks Lydia.
Christmas, that's a bit premature isn't it? Of course, I had planned on going skiing with Charlie. In fact I was the one organising the Christmas party for the health centre staff. I wonder who is doing that now? I suppose Charlie will be taking Big Tits to Austria. Hopefully she'll be so top heavy that she'll go arse over her own tits. I have no idea what I will be doing over Christmas.

'Alice,' booms Reverend Marsh.
I cringe. Don't get me wrong, he isn't one of those creepy priests with his hand stuck up an altar boy's cassock, he's just creepy in a religious fanaticism way. He is always thrusting a bible up my nose and trying to get me to church. Lady Fisher follows him in and I fight the urge to curtsy. She nods at me and takes her seat in the front pew. Rocky cocks his leg, gets a stern look from Reverend Marsh, and lowers it again. Even Rocky can't face the wrath of God it seems. I move towards the door as more people arrive and my hand knocks against some hymn books sending them hurtling to the ground.

'Oh God, I mean, oh bugger. Oh shit. I'm so sorry Reverend.'
Lady Fisher turns to glare at me and I feel obliged to drop my head in shame. Mona who enters at that moment bends with me to pick them up.

'Swearing in church Alice? I say, only you could get three words out in one sentence,' she whispers.

'God, I'm mortified,' I whisper back.

'The flowers look beautiful Alice, just like they did last week,' explodes Reverend Marsh pushing himself between us so we part like the Red Sea.

'Thank you … your,' I quickly stop myself from stupidly calling him *your honour*.

'How can I thank you during my sermon young lady, if you're never here?'

'There is so much to do. Chloe's not been feeding so well and there are the chickens and …'

'Chloe will be fine,' laughs Martha.

'I hope so,' I say worriedly. 'She hasn't been eating properly for days.'

'It's time we enjoyed a little of what Chloe gets every day.'

He can't surely be meaning the penis bucket.

'Ah Dominic Montfort, there you are,' cries the Reverend, rushing towards Dominic with such vigour that he enfolds poor Rocky into the folds of his cassock. There is muffled whimpering as he is swept along.

'Poor little bugger,' mumbles Mona.

'Dominic, how wonderful you could make our little service today,' he crows, almost falling over Rocky as he does so. 'You must talk Alice into staying.'

'Rev, nice to see you,' says Dominic while looking at me.

Oh dear, this is going to be distinctly uncomfortable. I realise there is no escape and squeeze myself into a pew.

'Come and see what has been done to the roof with your kind donation,' chirps Reverend Marsh leading Dominic to the back of the church.

Martha sits beside me and I sigh with relief. I have managed to avoid Dominic all week. As handsome as he may be, he really isn't my type and since the barn dance my dreams and waking moments have been filled with thoughts of Charlie and Edward. Martha breaks into my reverie and hands me a prayer book. The service is about to start and I'm relieved to see that Dominic has been seated next to Lady Fisher, and I fight back a giggle when I see him trying to shake randy Rocky from his leg.

'He certainly likes you,' gushes Lady Fisher placing her hand gently onto his knee.

I stifle a gasp and open the prayer book, and make an attempt to get Edward Fairfax out of my mind by focusing on the flowers and wondering why no man has ever bought me any. Now that's pathetic isn't it? To get to thirty-two and realise that *he doesn't bring me flowers ever*, is just a touch depressing. The only flowers I ever had were from Georgie and Cas when my appendix burst. Even then I think they only bought them to console me. Collapsing in a heap beside the black-peppered mackerel in Waitrose wasn't my best gig of the year. But even then it was only a bunch of white chrysanthemums. Don't get me wrong, I was dead grateful and everything, but it would have been nice to have got something from Charlie. I pull my eyes from the flowers and back to Reverend Marsh who seems to be getting very excited as he delivers his sermon that I'm beginning to fear for the flowers. He is waving his arms around so much that I swear he is whipping up enough energy to take off.

'There will be a second coming,' he cries, 'In the words of Matthew,' he bellows and my Nokia trills along with him.

Shit, I meant to turn it off.

It's a text from Georgie.

Sorry to be the bearer of bad tidings but your mum gave Charlie your address and ...'

'Oh shit.'

Lady Fisher and her pew turn to me in unison and I realise what I thought was a whisper most certainly hadn't been. Reverend Marsh looks at me quizzically and continues.

'And He will send forth His angels with a great trumpet and they will gather together his elect from the four winds, from one end of the sky to the other ...' he yells, causing my knees to quake and the flower petals to flutter.

Rocky cocks his leg to pee on Dominic's trousers. I look back to my text my heart racing.

He's coming to see you. Honestly you could have knocked me down with a feather when he turned up on my doorstep.

Holy crap.

'He's coming here,' I say loudly, 'Oh Jesus!'

Lady Fisher jumps from her seat with an adjoining yelp from Rocky.

'Hallelujah,' she shouts, 'he's coming here.'

She isn't talking about Charlie, that's for sure. Good God, they're all going to go into a religious frenzy. Oh hell, this could only happen to me. Everyone is applauding the second coming of Charlie, except me of course. I begin to explain that I haven't had an epiphany as such, and that Charlie is as far from Christ as anyone can be when I realise all eyes have re-focused on Reverend Marsh who is turning as purple as the veins on his neck which are protruding in a rather sickly way as he bangs on hysterically about the second coming of Christ, of course, not Charlie. I can't believe Charlie is coming to Cornwall. Why does he want to see me? More importantly, do I want to see him? Charlie, the Charlie who represents thousands of pounds lost on caterers, a live band and a half-finished wedding cake. I can't bear to see him. I thought he was having a whale of a time with Bit Tits and shagging for England. He's probably gone and shagged it right off. He always was one to do things to the extreme. He isn't going to bring her too is he? Perhaps he wants to give her my ring. That wouldn't surprise me. After all he took her on my honeymoon. She'll be stealing my identity next. It just gets worse. Actually she can have it. It hasn't done me much good. Maybe I can swap my identity for her abundant tits, and then every man in sight will no doubt want to shag me.

'*When?*' I text back, feeling feverish and light headed.

Does this mean Charlie has changed his mind? Why couldn't he have done this earlier? As in before I packed my whole life into a suitcase and became a cross between Mrs Bouquet and Mrs Herriot. I could have been Mrs Charles Marrow if he hadn't got cold feet. I can't help wondering what Edward will think of Charlie. Charlie will of course take an instant dislike to Edward just because he's a farmer. Farming is breeding animals for murdering he will insist. A feeling of dread clutches at my stomach. I hope Charlie doesn't make a scene. It will be pointless telling him that Edward is a dairy farmer.

No idea, he seemed keen though.

Georgie texts back. Keen! He was far from keen on me the last time I spoke to him. I suppose I should prepare myself for the second coming of Charlie and do all those things that a woman of thirty-two would do when the possibility of re-establishing her engagement stares her in the face. Shave my legs, Immac that little moustache that Charlie always likes to tell me sprouts before a period, and which everyone else says doesn't exist, and pop a few water tablets to squeeze out the excess water so my tummy is flatter. He is worth it, of course he is. I must not burst into tears when I see him. That's the trouble with periods. I've been known to sob hysterically when I can't find a parking space in Waitrose car park. As it is I feel bloated and horrid and know that in a few days a transformation will take place and Alice will turn into a female Damien from the *Omen*, cursing and spitting everywhere.

'Alice shall we get tea?' asks Martha.

I look up and see that everyone is ambling towards the vestry where Martha has prepared tea and cake. Dominic strains to see me but is being pulled along by Lady Fisher. I'm somewhat relieved that the whole second coming debacle is over.

'Mrs Marsh has insisted you join us for dinner this evening Dominic. Come at six for sherry,' Reverend Marsh says as he relieves himself of cassock and dog collar.

Heavens, he looks quite human without them. I check the time on my Nokia and excuse myself.

'I must feed Chloe,' I lie, pulling on my pink wellies.

'Already?' says Dominic, giving Rocky a little kick.

'Yes,' I say with a short embarrassed laugh.

The truth is, I would much rather spend my time at the farm with Edward.

'You're not avoiding me are you?'

'Now why would she want to do that?' Martha snaps. 'She doesn't know you like we do.'

That was below the belt. I think he gave her a mean look, but I can't be sure as his expression softens so quickly that I'm not sure if I imagined it.

'Now don't you go putting her off me Martha.'

Martha gives him a stony look. Oh dear this is so uncomfortable. I thought the yoga class was painful but this is infinitely worse. I am almost wishing I was back inside the church hall doing five cobras, ten spinal twists and a couple of Hail Mary's. In fact, even a spinal tap would be more comfortable than standing here. Before Martha has time to reply Lady Fisher has converged upon us.

'Dominic darling,' she drawls huskily, hooking her arm into his. 'Be a dear and drive us home. I walked here and it's raining cats and dogs now.'

'Well, I ...'

'That's divine of you. Come along Rocky.'

In a flash he is dragged through the vestry and out of the main doors, and I follow only to come to a halt when I see Edward pacing up and down outside the church gates. Oh God, what is it? Surely Charlie isn't here already is he? I tuck the umbrella I was about to open under my arm.

'Edward,' I say as he rushes towards me.

'I thought the service would never end,' he says with a tremble in his voice. 'I need to speak to you and ...'

He frowns for a moment.

'Is everything all right Ted?' asks Martha anxiously.

Edward smiles, ironing out the creases in his forehead.

'I just had to tell you. We've been granted our milk licence. I can't believe it.'

'Oh Edward,' I shrill.

He scoops me up in his arms and laughingly swings me around. I inhale the essence that is so uniquely him and feel that familiar surge of desire. I don't know how I can tell him that Charlie is coming and that I will probably be leaving Trenowyth. His hair is slightly damp from the rain and his shirt feels wet when I place my hands on his shoulders. He places me gently back onto my feet and smiles shyly at me.

'I thought a celebration was in order. I bought champagne and I thought I'd order pizza. You're invited Martha, and of course Jed. Let's have a party,' he laughs.

'You're getting the farm back on its feet Edward. Well done. What time is good Alice?'

Edward looks at me and raises his eyebrows.

'Shall we say seven, it gives us time,' he smiles.

It depends what we need the time for, I think shamefully.

'Seven is fine,' I hear myself say and begin visualising myself as the domestic goddess of the country.

I picture trays of vol-au-vents, dishes of peanuts, plates of olives and hot buttered French bread, tall glasses full of champagne and a celebratory cake. All this by seven would certainly make me a goddess of sorts.

'I'll pop a note in to Cockspit for Sara and her parents,' says Edward.

In that moment I feel my spirits dampen and it has nothing to do with the rain. How stupid of me. I don't imagine for one minute Edward would be outside the church waiting for me if Sara had been at home. Perhaps I should be more responsive to Charlie when he gets here especially if he does want to try again, and after all, someone like Charlie and a life in London is more 'me' than pink wellies and flat caps. Then I remember that Edward had said *we've been granted our milk licence,* and feel a little tingle of happiness.

Chapter Twenty-Two

'This place looks marvellous Alice,' Lydia gushes, folding and refolding the same tea towel as though attempting origami.

I try not to preen like a cat, but it is nice to be complimented on one's domestic prowess. But I do wish she would do something more useful with that tea towel, like, dry up a few glasses. I pull a tub of Philadelphia cream cheese from the fridge and begin spreading it on some crackers. The farmhouse is full of people. I didn't know Edward had so many friends. He is the centre of attention and arguing the rights and wrongs of fox hunting. There are raised voices and much raucous laughter. The champagne is flowing and the atmosphere is jolly.

'Shall I pop these pizzas into the Aga?' asks Sara, strolling in and narrowly avoiding the cat.

'Whoops nearly went a clanger. Fab party isn't it?'

I smile and nod.

'The house is a transformation,' says Lydia.

Okay she's overdoing it now.

'Alice is the best thing to ever happen to Edward,' smiles Sara while hugging me.

I blush and hand her some plates for the pizza.

'You haven't met Luce have you?' asks Lydia, who I'm going off by the minute.

I shake my head and look around for a glass. More champagne I think.

'No. It's a bit difficult as she's in New Zealand.'

'She's so supple, she's like an athlete, isn't that right Sara?'

Sara nods and winks at me.

'And she's got the gift you know?' continues Lydia in hushed tones.

Of the gab?

'Her psychic abilities are amazing,' she adds with a sniff. 'She raised my uncle …'

Blimey, I thought only Jesus could do those sort of things.

'Really,' I say with bated breath.

Ah, that would explain her prescient phone call.

'Yes, Aunt Miriam nearly died on the spot and joined him. It was so real,' she sighs and looks up at the ceiling.

Sara and I look up also, but all I see are yellow stains and damp patches.

'Luce tried to reach Edward's father, but Edward stopped her.'

'Edward doesn't believe in that stuff,' says Sara softly, wiping her hands on a cloth.

'Well,' sniffs Lydia, 'He should come to some of our workshops, especially our spiritual enlightenment one.' She looks curiously at her empty glass and then at me.

'What happened to my champagne?'

'You drank it,' I say, filling her glass.

'I feel so full of positive energy. You've infused this house with beautiful positivity Alice. I feel so light headed and airy when I'm around you.'

You feel drunk, I think, but don't say anything. I fill a glass of champagne for myself and hear Edward laughing above the loudness of the music, but all I can think of is Charlie, and what I will do if he asks me to try again. I jump at a rapping sound on the back door and look in horror. What if this is him? I feel my legs tremble where the sudden surge of adrenalin rushes through my body.

'Oh wonderful,' mumbles Sara, pulling a face.

She opens the door and Dominic pops his head round.

'Do you have room for one more? I hear there is something to be celebrated.'

He smiles at me.

'Of course,' I say apprehensively, and then quickly add, 'I'm sure Edward would have invited you but he thought you were dining with Reverend Marsh.'

He kisses me on the cheek, his lips as cold as ice and I shudder.

'Now you know that's not true Alice. You're just too nice. I'm just on my way back from the old Rev's actually, and Bryce said there was a celebration here, so I thought I'd come and join you.'

'Bryce?' I query.

'The old Rev,' laughs Dominic. 'He told me Edward got the milk licence.'

I hadn't considered the Reverend had a name apart from The Reverend.

Sara brushes past him with a plate of crackers.

'Yes, not bad for a farmer who doesn't know what he's doing,' she says in a sarcastic tone.

'You're looking lovely as always,' Dominic says, ignoring her and lowering his eyes to my breasts.

I had changed into my favourite dress. I bought it a year ago, just after Charlie and I had got engaged. I love the way the plain black sheath dress can look dressed down and transformed with a simple string of pearls. I always feel elegant in this dress. I had pinned up my hair into a neat bun and even I feel I look lovely. In fact, I suppose tonight would be the perfect night for Charlie to come. He would see how well my breasts hang in the new bra. After all, he never did get to see that and he would realise just what he threw away. For goodness sake Alice, don't think of Charlie, not tonight of all nights.

'I'd better go back,' Lydia says nervously, edging her way past Dominic and spilling her drink as she does so.

Dominic is grinning at me in that dangerously handsome way that he has. I turn away feeling embarrassed and fumble at the Aga.

'I should take out the pizzas,' I say, feeling my face grow hot.

His hand bushes my hip.

'Let me do that. I bet you've been slaving over that stove all afternoon. I wish you'd give me the pleasure of slaving over mine for a couple of hours,' he says lowering his voice and stroking my bottom.

Christ on a bike, where is that hand going? I clench my buttocks in a reflex action. They certainly don't need Viagra in the country. No wonder the women down here always have rosy cheeks. They must be having orgasms left right and centre.

'Ooh,' I squeal as his large hand cups my perfect hanging breast.

'So when are you going to slave over my stove?' he whispers in my ear and then hungrily nibbles it.

Before I know where I am his other hand is massaging my breast and he is pushing me against the Aga. This would have been lovely and romantic had the Aga been off. I feel the heat against the back of my thigh and Dominic's hardness at the front. Heavens, I'm not sure which is worse. This certainly isn't the kind of pictures you see in the Aga section of *County Life* magazine, I gently push him back.

'The Aga is hot,' I mumble.

'So are you,' he replies gruffly and spins me around so my back presses against the table.

'When are you going to find time for me Alice? I've so much to offer you.'

Yes I can feel that. I fumble behind knocking off my Nigella Lawson cookbook. At that moment Sara flings open the kitchen door.

'I'll take the pizzas ...' She stops and seems to freeze.

I untangle myself from Dominic and shakily reach for the tea towel that Lydia had left on the table.

'Great timing,' mumbles Dominic under his breath.

I pull a face at Sara and rescue Nigella.

'Too much wine at the Reverend's Dominic?' she says dryly.

'Don't worry Sara, you're safe.'

I gasp. That was a bit mean, but Sara just smiles and responds with,

'Thank God,' before grabbing my arm and pulling me into the living room as Jed taps on his champagne glass.

'I think I can say on behalf of everyone here that this is indeed a special day. Congratulations Ted, and well done.'

Jed looks so handsome and animated. I so wish Georgie was here to see him. Everyone raises their glasses and responds with a raucous *hear! hear!* Edward's eyes meet mine and I feel he is smiling at just me. We lock eyes for a few seconds before Sara bounds into his arms holding a large prettily wrapped parcel.

'It's just an MP3 player and a new pair of boots but Jed and I wanted to get you something,' she grins.

He hugs her tightly lifting her from the ground.

'Put that woman down Ted, how many times do we have to tell you Sara is not your type.'

Everyone laughs heartily and Edward kisses her. Sara blushes and I can see that she really does like him. I turn away. I'm so out of place here. I have no idea about farming. Not in the way that Sara does anyway. I feel very lonely. Perhaps I need to face the truth. Better now than after I make a fool of myself over a man who not only has a fiancée but also a woman who clearly adores him and who he obviously likes. I tiptoe into the kitchen as Edward is dragged to a chair to make a speech. It is chilly outside and I slip back to fetch my shawl before walking to the cowshed. It is a clear night and the stars twinkle in the silvery moonlight. I gaze at them for a while knowing that once I return to London the stars will never look as bright or the air smell so fresh. I open the creaky shed door and gently call for Chloe. The shed has an eerie silence and even after flicking the light on the atmosphere lingers. I look frantically for Chloe with the shawl slipping from my shoulders. I listen for her breathing but all I can hear is the muffled music from the farmhouse.

'Chloe,' I say softly, feeling bile rise up and threaten to choke me. I spin round at a sound behind me and almost slip on some cow dung. It is Edward. He looks drawn and pale in the moonlight.

'Alice … I …'

'Where's Chloe?'

Did I scream that? Oh God where is she? Chloe, the only thing that matters, the only living thing that showed me I was worthwhile. It was the last thing I had left. I feel like I've suddenly lost everything.

'Alice, I started to tell you outside church this morning. That's why I came really and then Martha came out of church and I haven't had a chance to talk to you since … Well …'

I feel overwhelming anger fuelled by the champagne. I cannot control myself.

'What did you do to her?' I cry, tears pouring down my cheeks.

He looks distressed and moves towards me.

'Don't touch me,' I scream.

What has he done?

'Chloe had TB, that's why she wasn't feeding. I had to have her put down,' he says flatly, lowering his head.

'No!' I scream. 'No, no.'

I rush towards him before I know what I am doing, and pound at his chest with inhumane pressure. Damn him, damn Charlie, damn everyone.

'Fuck you Edward Fairfax. You're just a monster. Why didn't you do something? You're supposed to be a vet. It was just the quick option for you wasn't it?'

He grabs my arms, pinning them to my side. Martha and Jed stand at the door with a horror-stricken Sara behind them.

'Alice, I couldn't help her. I had no choice, it would have spread to the whole herd and we would have lost them all, and we've only just got the milk licence. It wasn't easy. I knew what she meant to you.'

'You had no idea what she meant to me. No idea at all. How dare you be so arrogant to say that?'

'Alice, please ...'

I pull myself free by kicking him in the shins.

'Fuck the milk licence and fuck you, you bastard,' I scream, stumbling past him and pushing past Jed and Martha.

'Alice,' calls Sara.

I turn on her angrily.

'Did you know? Did he tell you before me?'

She shakes her head emphatically.

'No, I didn't know Alice. I'm so sorry. I know how much you loved Chloe.'

'Alice please, let's talk about this,' pleads Edward, reaching out to me.

I shrug him off and stride towards my Beetle.

'I don't ever want to talk to you again, and if you touch little Pepper with your murdering hands and turn her into gammon, I'll kill you.'

He lifts his hands in a defeated gesture. I climb into the Beetle and drive off. Tears blur my eyes and I have no idea where I am going. I only know I need a bag of Maltesers and to get as far away from Edward Fairfax as possible.

Chapter Twenty-Three

With tear-streamed eyes blurring my vision, and driving like a maniac, I feel the Beetle start to shudder.

'Damn it,'

My hand is clenched tightly around the gearstick.

'You should never drive when you're angry,' Georgie had once said. 'You practically give the gearstick a handjob when you do.'

I realise I have not only been giving the gearstick the handjob of its life but I've also been driving at almost sixty miles an hour in third gear. My little Beetle must have thought I was trying to throttle it. I've stopped outside an off-licence I didn't even know existed. How fortunate is that? They will certainly sell chocolate. Rain splatters on the windscreen and I throw my shawl over my head and dive into the shop. I must look a sight. My face is, no doubt, blotchy from crying and my hair has come loose from its bun. I try to tuck the loose tendrils behind my ears. The assistant looks at me wide-eyed, and it occurs to me she may think I'm drunk. Next thing she'll be reporting me to the police for drunk driving. I suddenly realise I have been. I'd completely forgotten that I had downed at least half a bottle of champagne, if not more. I am without doubt a drunk driver. They could throw me into prison. I jump back as if she had slapped me and she gives me an even stranger look. I must not let her smell my breath, whatever happens don't breathe Alice.

'Hello,' I say hoarsely pulling my shawl around me to cover my well-hung breasts.

'Can I help you?'

'I only want chocolate. I'm not a drinker, so I don't want alcohol. I hardly ever drink, especially if I'm driving,' I babble. 'In fact, I only came here because I couldn't find a sweet shop.'

I'm beginning to sound incoherent. I lean forward to grab a family size bag of Maltesers and trip over my own feet.

'Are you okay?' she asks kindly.

'Of course, why shouldn't I be?' I reply anxiously and put a packet of mints with the chocolate.

Of course that is probably a clear give away that I have drunk too much. I probably have puffy red eyes from crying, which will make me look even more sloshed. I quickly hand over the money and retreat to my car where I consume a handful of Maltesers before driving off. I think of Chloe and the tears flow again.

'Bastard,' I mumble, popping Maltesers into my mouth.

What will I do without Chloe every day? I can't stay there with him. Bugger the farm, bugger the milk licence and bugger Edward Fairfax. Yes, bugger and bugger him. Poor little Chloe, it doesn't bear thinking about. I hope she didn't feel anything. Don't think about it, that's the best thing. I struggle to think of somewhere to go and realise there isn't anywhere. I would have gone to Sara's, but that's impossible. I bet she is consoling Edward right this minute, no doubt telling him he did the right thing. I can't go back to Trenowyth, I just can't. My phone vibrates but ignoring it I give the gearstick the best handjob ever and crunch the gears before swerving into the next lay-by. I pull the Nokia from my bag; there are three missed calls, all from Edward. He can just piss off. I have never felt so angry since Charlie broke off the engagement. In fact, I'm angrier and certainly more distressed. Turning the car around I head to Dominic's house. Hopefully he will be home by now. I don't think he would have stayed at Trenowyth. Even I won't be staying at Trenowyth. I'll phone Charlie. Tell him I am happy to give us a second chance. The problem is I'm not sure I want to give Charlie and me a second try. I miss Chloe so much already. I turn the Beetle into the driveway of Lower End Farm and feel her judder again. The lights are on thank goodness and he opens the door even before I have left the car, and before I know it he is helping me from the Beetle and drawing me into his arms.

'Poor Alice, it was just too awful. I'm so sorry. I ...'

His breath smells of champagne and his body of Ungaro, a dangerously sexy combination.

'I didn't know where to go.'

This is awful. I'm certain I wouldn't be this distraught if my mother died. Oh dear, that is an awful thing to think isn't it? Of course I would be more upset if it were my mother. She's not a cow. Well, she can be. What am I thinking? I wish there was a magic key that turns my brain off.

'You have come to the right house. Let's get a brandy into you.'
The thought of more alcohol makes me feel slightly sick. Besides, I daren't drink anymore.

'I'm driving,' I say reaching in for the Maltesers.

'Don't be crazy, you can't drive back. Besides you don't want to go back there.'

'Edward may ...' I begin and then immediately forget what I was about to say. I'm more drunk than I thought.

'Don't give that monster a second thought.'
Yes, that's exactly what he is, a monster. Dominic is quite right. He leads me into the cosy sitting room and I flop onto his immaculate cream couch. He pulls my muddy shoes from my feet and I see him wiping some mud off the cream shag pile carpet with a J cloth. Oh dear, did I do that? Of course it wouldn't have mattered in the slob's house. There is always mud there both inside and out. In fact, I was always bringing mud in after feeding Chloe. No, don't think of Chloe, it's too painful.

'Sorry,' I say absently.

'It's nothing,' he says, scrubbing madly at the brown mark.
I look around me at the softly lit room. It's warm and cosy but I feel myself yearning for the messy living room at Trenowyth. Why did Edward have to spoil everything? Dominic carefully drops the J Cloth into a waste-paper basket and gives the carpet a last look before walking to a well-stocked drinks cabinet. I look down and strain to see the muddy patch.

'Here, drink this, it will make you feel better,' he says in a husky voice, pushing a tumbler of brandy into my hand.

'I really can't,' I protest blinking rapidly as the room seems to dim.
Heavens, I most certainly have drunk more than I thought. I then realise Dominic is lowering the lights remotely. Thank God for that. For a second I thought I was going blind with the shock of this evening's events. I'm beginning to wonder if perhaps I overreacted. I know I tend to do that when my hormones are up the creek.

'I'm so glad you came. You're finally seeing Edward in his true colours,' he says leaning closer to me on the couch.

I put the glass to my lips, take a sip and move further along the couch until I realise there isn't actually very far to go. I put my hand onto his chest to push him back. He clasps it and begins sucking on the fingers. I feel a shudder of disgust go through me. Dominic, obviously mistaking it for desire, pushes me urgently back against the cushions. The brandy wobbles in the glass and visions of Dominic on his hands and knees enter my head unwillingly. Brandishing a J cloth that is, to clear up the brandy, and not anything remotely sexual. Good heavens, the last thing I need now is sex. Even a mild grope is likely to have me throwing up all over the cream couch. I try to sit up but he pushes me back down forcefully.

'Dominic, I really don't want ...' I protest, but his hot wet lips silence me.

He is suddenly all over me. His lips travelling wetly over my neck and landing back on my lips again. It's like being waterboarded. I feel like a political prisoner.

'You know you want me. Why else would you come?'

For you to comfort me I think. Perhaps this is Dominic's way of comforting. He pushes his knee between my thighs and I gasp. I push against him in an effort to get him off me but he just waterboards me some more, and pins my arms at my sides. I feel panic rise within me.

'Dominic, please stop,' I cry, struggling to get up.

I feel his hand sliding up my skirt.

'Come on Alice, you know you want to. I'll help you forget the calf. It's not like it was a person. Come on, let's go into the bedroom.'

Oh no, I don't think so. With a big effort I lift my knee and thump into his groin. Okay it was a bit of a reflex reaction. I didn't have that many options did I? The last place I want to end up tonight is in Dominic Montfort's bed.

'Bloody hell Alice,' he yelps falling onto the floor and straight onto his wet patch. 'What did you do that for? That was a bit below the belt.'

I jump up.

'Wasn't it? How dare you force yourself on me.'

He grimaces.

'Running back to Edward are you? He's a ponce, you know that don't you? I offered him a good price for that farm. He and his father are both bloody stubborn. He won't keep that milk licence five minutes with that farm the state it's in. His bloody father should have sold it to me. I gave him the chance. I don't know what you see in that veterinary pleb. He's crazy and so was his father. The old man was rolling in it, and he still wouldn't sell that place. I don't know why I was so soft with him …' he breaks off, stumbles to the drink cabinet and pours a whisky.

'What do you mean?' I ask angrily.

He sighs.

'The old man had dementia. He sold me the farm for a good price. Edward got wind of it and got all legal. I pulled out because felt it was wrong to go through with it, but it's madness Alice. The farm is a mess. It's not about money. The Fairfax's are the most comfortable family in the country. It's sheer bloody-mindedness That land is being wasted. Do you know how many houses can be built on that land?'

'Houses?' I repeat.

What is he talking about?

'Just forget it,' he says dismissively. 'Christ Alice. That was some knee jerk you walloped me with.'

He grimaces and knocks the whisky back in one go. I walk past him and pick up my bag.

'I'm sorry but I am tired of everyone taking advantage of me, or thinking I don't have feelings,' I say angrily.

How dare they all walk over me like this? What is wrong with me for even allowing it?

'First bloody Karen talks to me like she is my boss and not the other way around …'

'Who's bloody Karen?'

'And then Charlie dumps me like a piece of rubbish, and then Edward, well Edward …'

I stop as my breath catches in my throat. Edward is the worst of them all. Edward took away the one thing that had made me feel worthwhile.

'Who's Charlie?'

'The man I should have fought for instead of coming here.'

If I had never come here I wouldn't have met Edward and I wouldn't be feeling as wretched as I am now.

'You can all go to hell,' I say fiercely and walk from the house to the Beetle.

I'm half way down the drive by the time he reaches the front door. He's clutching his groin with one hand and waving me to stop with the other. For a second I feel bad about kneeing him so hard, but that soon passes and the tears come unbidden. Racking sobs make it difficult for me to breathe and I clutch the steering wheel as my vision blurs. Everything was going so well. How could Edward spoil it all? I have no idea where to go. I consider driving all the way home but in my present state that would not be sensible. A sudden fork in the road takes me by surprise and I brake sharply before skidding to the right. The country lane is pitch black. I fumble with the lights and then see a deer. I push my foot on the brake and the Beetle shudders uncontrollably. I swerve and the steering wheel is wrenched out of my hands. I close my eyes and scream as the car spins out of control. It seems to whirl around like water in a whirlpool. There are deafening bangs and the Beetle lurches to its side, and then everything is still. I open my eyes to find myself in total blackness. Christ, I've died, this is awful. I didn't get to marry Charlie. Come to think of it, I didn't get to marry anyone. This could only happen to me. I then see the deer looking in at me through the window and we lock eyes for a moment.

'I'm so sorry,' I whisper and am not sure if I'm talking to the deer or myself.

It runs off into the darkness and I rummage in my bag for my Nokia and pray that I have a signal. Oh thank you God, there are two bars. I try to start the engine but nothing happens, but even if it had started I have no idea how I would get the car back onto the road. Come to think of it, where is the road? A car whizzes past but I don't see it. I'm in someone's field. I open the door and clamber out. I sniffle and hiccup my way through a gap in the hedge, losing my footing twice, scream *fuck it* three times and finally make it to the roadside with muddied hands and knees. I look back to my little Beetle and let out a tiny sob. Falling onto the wet ground I cry silently for five minutes before phoning Edward.

***

Twenty minutes later I hear the sound of the Land Rover. To me it feels like the Batmobile has arrived and I could cry with relief. I have shielded myself from the rain as best I could, but by the time Edward reaches me I am shaking with cold. I burst into tears and cling to him. The fresh smell that is so uniquely him makes me cry even more. He wraps a blanket around me and the familiar smell of Chloe makes me sob.

'It's okay, I'm here now,' he whispers softly into my ear. 'Let's get you into the Land Rover. Are you hurt?'

'I don't think so,' I hiccup.

'The Beetle,' I sob and point to the car.

'I'm going to have a look at it. Let's get you in the warm first.'

He wraps his arm around my waist and leads me to the Land Rover. I watch as he climbs down into the woods and stupidly hope he can get my little Beetle out. I really need my car if I am going home. I study my reflection in the dashboard mirror.

'Shit.'

I look like I have been in the clutches of King Kong. My cheeks are smudged with dirt and my hair is a tangled mess. I certainly feel like I am on Skull Island right now. I shakily take a sip from the bottle of water Edward gave me and wait for him to return. His grim expression does not bode well.

'The Beetle's a write-off I should think,' he says, taking the water from me and guzzling half of the bottle. 'You smashed into a tree. I gave Jed a call; he's coming with a pickup. We'll know more when we see it.'

That's all I need. I must get some perspective on this. It's a little car accident. What am I thinking? It's not a *little* car accident when your car is written off is it? Okay, I must keep calm. It could be worse. It could have been a plane crash and then I most certainly wouldn't have survived, but a write-off, oh dear. Why couldn't I have just dented a wing or scraped the bumper. That's what most women do isn't it? Not me, oh no. I have to drive the thing into the woods and wrap it round a tree.

'How can I get home now?' I whimper.

'Well if you really want to get to London there are trains. It's only Cornwall after all, not the Outer Hebrides.'

He throws the half packet of Maltesers into my lap.

'I rescued these.'

There is silence and I pop three Maltesers into my mouth. Silently he digs into the bag, stroking my knee as he does so. I shudder against my will as that familiar jolt of desire shoots through me. What is the matter with me? It's like being turned on by a murderer. I have no shame. I think back to Dominic and my feelings of revulsion when he had touched me.

'These help,' he says, breaking the silence and reaching for the bag.

'I kneed Dominic in the groin,' I say.

He smiles.

'You did? Well done.'

'He made a pass at me.'

He lowers his eyes.

'I can't altogether blame him,' he says so quietly that I only just hear him.

My heart flutters and I self-consciously pat at my hair.

'Really,' I whisper. 'You don't blame him?'

'No, I rather envy his nerve.'

Double heart flutters. What's happening now? This couldn't be a worse time. I can just discern his face in the darkness of the Land Rover but I can't see the expression there.

'I didn't mean it when I called you a monster,' I say hesitantly and pop a couple of Maltesers into my mouth. Chocolate cures all so they say.

'Chloe didn't feel anything. I want you to know that. It was cowardly of me not to tell you first.'

'You did it? You put Chloe to sleep?'

I feel him nod.

'It did hurt when you called me a monster. Animals are my greatest love. I'd never cause an animal any suffering. I do what is best for them and ...'

I'm such a bitch.

'Edward, I'm so sorry. I really didn't mean it I ...'

Our hands reach in for the Maltesers at the same time and touch. I let out a small gasp and suddenly I am in his arms, and this time it feels far from being waterboarded. It feels like heaven. It actually feels like every chocolate bar you can think of all in one go. It's marshmallow and hot chocolate, and it's divine. I'm drowning in pleasure. His lips are warm and welcoming, his tongue deliciously arousing. I feel my body melt under his touch and yield beneath him when he pushes me back onto the seat. I wasn't prepared for this. I'm overcome by a whirlpool of emotions that I never felt with Charlie, or anybody else for that matter. I'm overwhelmed with a need to hold him so tightly. What is happening to me?

'Just don't knee me in the groin,' he whispers and I can hear the smile in his voice.

'Never,' I say softly.

His lips are on mine again and I groan. I feel myself enveloped in his arms and I feel as if floodgates of love for him have opened. Edward is the man I have waited for all my life, but don't forget he has a fiancée whispers a little voice in my head. Don't forget Lucy short for Lucinda, but everyone calls me Luce. Damn it. I can't do this to her. It's all wrong. I push gently at his chest at the same time that headlights shine into the Land Rover. We both jump guiltily and I hasten to straighten my clothes.

'It's Jed,' says Edward shakily.

'Is Alice okay Ted?'

I'm grateful for the darkness and am relieved to know that Jed can't see my flushed face and trembling hands.

'I'm fine, just a little shook up,' I say.

That's an understatement.

'I'm sorry about Chloe, I really am.'

I nod absently as I strain to see another man walking past the pickup. My stomach lurches. I feel Edward's eyes on me and take a small breath.

'Ali baby, are you okay? God, I was afraid you were injured.'

'Charlie, what are you doing here?'

Even I have to agree it is the worst welcome in the world.

'I've come to tell you that I've been a silly bugger and to beg you to take me back. No one loves you as much as I do.'

I meet Edward's eyes but he turns away.

'Oh,' I say stupidly.

'It's okay old boy,' Charlie says smugly, laying his hand on Edward's shoulder. 'I'll take things from here. Leave it to the city boys.'

I sigh.

'We'll leave you with it then Charlie boy. If you should need a hand to pull out the Beetle don't hesitate to give us country boys a ring,' smirks Edward, climbing into the Land Rover with an uncertain Jed.

Before I have a chance to think I am standing on the road and the Land Rover has driven off.

Charlie snorts.

'Bloody farmers, they don't know anything. I'll phone the AA, they'll have it back on the road in no time. God Ali, I have missed you. Say you forgive me for being a bloody fool.'

I watch the lights from the Land Rover disappear into the darkness and think again of Lucy, short for Lucinda, but everyone calls me Luce.

'I forgive you,' I say.

Charlie

I was cleaning my teeth in the new basement flat in Sloane Square. I'd forgotten to charge up the bloody brush, so I was using the spare that Ali kept for just that very reason. Ali always took care of those things. I hate it when the sodding thing winds down after a few seconds and you still have three minutes left to brush. I don't imagine Bianca has ever charged a toothbrush in the whole of her life. That's probably why she is so good in bed. She saves all her energy for that department and relies on someone else to do the rest. God, she was bloody good in the bed department. I had her coming all over the place. Trouble is she came more than I did. I was bloody exhausted in the end. Alice was never much of a goer in that area but hell I know where I am with her. Thank God she isn't one of those women, you know the type? *I'm responsible for my own life therefore I'm responsible for my own orgasm* type. But that was the moment, that toothbrush moment, when I realised I needed Ali. Not just to charge up the toothbrush but for all those little things that a woman like Alice does. I was a prick to break off the engagement. Alice was everything I needed. The basement flat is the dog's bollocks though, and I can't wait for Alice to move back in here with me. I'm sure she'll love it. I've missed her cute little arse too. Bianca had a nice one, but a bit too wobbly for me. She also had a bit of a bum fetish too, always wanting me to do weird and wonderful things to her anus. I'm not complaining mind you, but backsides aren't really my thing. I still can't believe Alice compromised her beliefs though. There must have been a hundred jobs she could have taken. Why the hell did she take one managing a bloody farm? We'd had so many discussions about that at the FFFAA's debating forum. She's made me look a bit of fool. I could have done without her poncing around on a farm just as I am made chairperson of the *Freedom for Farm Animals Association.* Still, we can put that behind us. It took a bit of persuading to get her mum to give me the address, and bloody Georgie wasn't much help. I don't think Georgie has ever liked me. She's a bloody jealous cow that one. Still, she could have warned me about the farm. What a dump. No worries about Alice wanting to leave this place that's for sure. Christ, what have I put her through? Still, I'll make it up to her. Perhaps I'll take her away for a weekend somewhere. I'll show her my Chanel watch, just casually like, and if that doesn't impress her then nothing will. Not many men get given a watch like that after finishing a contract. A shame I didn't get some Chanel perfume; that would really have impressed her. Hopefully Chanel will ask me to do their next big promotion and then I'll get her some freebies. Looks like I've arrived just as some farmers' get-together is finishing. I'll find Ali and whisk her back to the hotel. Christ, there is muck and shit everywhere. Poor sodding animals, what a life they give them on these places. If it wasn't so dark I'd rescue the poor things right now. At least once things are back to normal I'll get some decent food. Those ready-to-eat Quorn things are bloody shite. Right, where's the front door?

'Shit.'

I skid on the mud as some wanker comes out of the house like some bull in a china shop, and crashes straight into me. He puts his hand out to steady me. I hope his hands are clean. I should have known better than to have worn my Jasper Conran overcoat here.

'Sorry, I didn't see you there. Can I help?' he says in a thick West Country accent.

I straighten myself up and glimpse through the open front door where a young woman is pulling on a Parka.

'I'm coming with you Jed,' she says firmly.

'No, you stay here in the warm Sara. Have the kettle on for when Alice gets back.'

Alice? So I have the right place.

'It's Alice I've come for,' I say stressing my vowels, letting him see I speak the Queen's English even if he can't.

The woman stops in her tracks on seeing me. I don't blame her. I obviously look what I am, successful, enigmatic, and handsome. I really don't think Alice properly appreciated me.

'I'm just going to fetch them,' he says.

'Alice had a car accident,' says the woman named Sara looking me up and down.

Oh God, what kind of car accident? She's not maimed or anything is she? What if she's disfigured? Perhaps I should see her first before asking her to give me a second chance.

'Is she, well, you know?'

'Dead, God no,' he laughs.

'No, I mean, badly injured?'

The woman looks at me closely and then to the other guy.

'Who are you?' she asks abruptly.

What a nerve.

'I'm her fiancé, well ex-fiancé. But I will be her fiancé again once she sees me ...'

'You're Charlie?' she says her tone suddenly clipped.

'Charles actually,' I say proudly, not caring much for her attitude.

Bloody farming philistines who wouldn't know a meat-free burger if it jumped up and bit them. They probably spend their lives around a barbeque. I hate these people. I've spent my whole life trying to rescue animals so these people can't slaughter and eat them at a whim. What the hell was Alice thinking coming here? There must have been hundreds of jobs. Why she didn't get a little flat I do not know.

'Are you the chap she works for?' I say, scraping the shit off my shoe. I'll put him in his place.

'No, that would be Edward. You'll ruin those shoes here. They're not farm shoes are they?' he laughs.

'I'm not a bloody farmer am I,' I snap.

'You got that one right,' snarls the woman and stomps back to the house.

'You'd better follow me if it's Alice you want. Or you can wait here. It's up to you.'

'Alice won't be coming back here,' I say resolutely.

What the fuck is she playing at? The sooner we get back to normal the better. Before I know it she'll be eating sodding lamb shank and T-bone steak. The farmer gives me an odd look and says.

'Right, you'd better follow me then if that's the case.'

He drives so bloody fast that I think the bugger is deliberately trying to lose me. He shoots along the narrow country lanes and takes the bends like Damon Hill. No wonder Alice had an accident if that's how the bastards here drive. Alice is sitting in a Land Rover when we arrive. She looks a bloody mess. I don't remember ever seeing her hair in such a muddle. I dismiss the two village idiots and call the AA. She's totally written off the Beetle. She looks amazed to see me.

'Charlie, what are you doing here?' she says, an element of surprise in her voice. She doesn't seem as pleased as I would have hoped. Still, that's understandable. I imagine she's in a state of shock.

'I've come to tell you that I've been a silly bugger and to beg you to take me back. No one loves you as much as I do.'

It takes her two seconds to forgive me. Bloody Georgie, what does she know about Alice moving on? The only place she is moving onto is my hotel room, and then back to London with me. Life will be hunky-dory and I'll get some decent veggie meals on the table again.

Chapter Twenty-Four

I don't believe this. The one thing I had been praying to happen finally does happen on the one day I really didn't want it to. This could only happen to me. I wish I knew what Edward was feeling right now.

'This is the best hotel I could find,' Charlie says as he pops the little kettle on to boil.

'It's AA accredited, four stars, but the vegetarian menu is crap. What do you expect? They're all bloody philistines in the country when it comes to meat.'

I wonder what Charlie would say if I told him that I had been eating Cornish pasty, not to mention the lamb shank and the rabbit. Best to never mention the rabbit, except maybe on my deathbed, you know as a final confession thing. What am I thinking? I'm not even sure I want to go back to Charlie, and if I do things would have to change. I'd have to change. I actually don't think I'm a real vegetarian, not an honest one anyway. I'd have to tell Charlie. I suppose as it's getting near Christmas we will have to go to Charlie's eco-warrior friends, Myrna and Phil, for their traditional Christmas nut roast with all the veggie trimmings, as always. Bollocks, I really don't think I can face another one of those, and having to listen to Myrna telling me that everything has feelings, including the mother-in-law's tongue plant on the windowsill. Even my parents would know better than that. Okay, so Mum thinks salmon and salad is a good vegetarian dinner and I may have to listen to Mum's running commentary on Dad's haemorrhoids which seem to grow to mammoth proportions at Christmas time. Still, that is preferable to Myrna's endless monologue on seal culling, which is enough to put you off any Christmas dinner. What am I thinking? The truth is I really just want to stay here and go to the farmers' Christmas party.

'It's getting late. Let's go to bed and talk tomorrow,' says Charlie.

'I can't go to bed with you,' I blurt out, looking wildly around the hotel room.

He stares at me.

'I didn't say have sex Alice. I realise it has been a while ...'

'A while,' I repeat.

Why does he keep flashing his watch at me? I feel like I'm being timed or something. Or is there something wrong with his wrist.

'Have you done something to your hand?'

'What?' he looks at his hand as though seeing it for the first time.

'Oh no, just getting used to the new watch, it's Chanel. They gave it to me because they were pleased with how I handled their contract.'

I attempt an impressed nod.

'Yes, well it has been a while and I appreciate we may have to spice things up a bit. We can't go back to the way we were. I know that,' he says, opening a packet of complimentary biscuits that sit on the tea tray.

What is he suggesting? What does spice it up mean? I hope he isn't intending on tying me to the bedposts or something. Knowing Charlie it won't be anything more exciting than getting me to suck on a chocolate penis.

'It's just ...' I begin.

He gently lays his hand on my arm.

'Would you feel happier if you had your engagement ring back on?'

What? Did someone drop you on your head as a baby? In fact, has someone dropped you on your head recently because you seem to be more stupid than before. What am I thinking? That is just plain horrid of me. He falls onto the bed and seems to bounce on the springs. The kettle bubbles away incessantly and the room begins to fill up with steam.

'The thing is Ali,' he says pulling me down beside him as I try to reach the kettle. 'I know I've been a bloody fool. I said as much to Georgie.'

I bet she enjoyed that. It's getting steamier than a sauna in here and it has nothing to do with sexual chemistry. I don't even think a chocolate penis could help us right now. There isn't a single stirring from any of my loins and I don't think much is stirring in Charlie's nether regions either.

'Oh,' I say, because I don't know what else to say.

There is silence, except for the bubbling of the kettle of course.

'Charlie, I think I'll turn the kettle off being as neither of us have croup.'

I jump up, relieved to be off the bed and take a moment to gather myself.

'The thing is Charlie; I can't just go back, not just like that.'

He waves a hand.

'No no, I realise we can't go back to the way things were. To be quite honest Ali, I wasn't totally satisfied with our sex life. I know you were orgasmic every time but for me it was very unsatisfactory and ...'

'Orgasmic?' I echo.

Bloody hell, that will teach me to writhe and convulse all over the place like a pilchard out of water, and what does he mean *unsatisfactory*?

'You've been sleeping with someone else Charlie,' I say, and wonder why I don't get that familiar piercing in my heart.

'That's not strictly fair Ali, after all ...'

'And you took her on *our* honeymoon. She slept in our honeymoon suite. In *my* honeymoon bed and ...'

Oh shut up Alice. She also had your honeymoon champagne and honeymoon hotel chocolates. What a bitch, and no doubt the special honeymoon beauty massage and not to mention the tiramisu.

'I'm sorry I did that Alice. I think I was trying to find myself.'

'A bit careless losing yourself in the first place,' I quip, making tea with what boiled water there is left.

'Whatever. But you must admit you've made a fool out of me with the stupid farming lark. I'm the chairperson of the London branch of *Freedom for Farm Animals Association* now. The president chose me personally and it doesn't look good you getting all involved in farming now, does it?'

I try not to scoff.

'Congratulations on being made chairman. I'm sure the animals of the world salute you.'

'Chairperson, Ali. That's the correct term. You don't have to be demeaning.'

What a night. I've had three men interested in me in a matter of hours. Won't Georgie be impressed and Cas dead jealous. That's all very well but the truth is I don't actually have a proper boyfriend any more do I? The boyfriend I did have has been sleeping with some big-breasted brunette who probably has an all-over bronze tan from my honeymoon in Italy. I don't care if she got it from the sunbed in the hotel spa. The point is it is *my* suntan. All I have are broken nails and chilblains. Okay, maybe not the chilblains. I find myself thinking of little Chloe and tears blur my vision, and I spill some of the hot water onto the cabinet. Poor Edward, if only he had told me I could have been there with him when he put Chloe to sleep. I feel Charlie's arms go around my waist.

'It wasn't that I stopped loving you Ali, I was just scared. I know now that it is you that I want. Only you.'

I sit on the bed nursing my cup of tea. I've no idea what to say to him. All I can think about is Chloe, and the milk licence, and the fruit cake I was making for the village coffee morning. He sits beside me and takes my hand.

'You and I are right for each other. Okay, I made a mistake with Bianca. She didn't understand about animal activism, and she was a bit dumb to tell you the truth.'

He squeezes my hand several times as one would a stress ball.

'Say you'll give me a second chance Ali. I promise to make everything up to you. I won't leave you alone until you do.'

Oh that's just wonderful isn't it?

'I love you Alice. It feels like we've always been together. You can forgive me for getting a bit of cold feet can't you?'

He's quite right I suppose. I've known Charlie for three years. Better the devil you know, another of my mother's sayings, but it sort of makes sense.

'Say yes, Ali.'

Well, how could I say anything else? Charlie is my ex-fiancé after all. In fact, if he hadn't called things off he would be my husband now. I guess he deserves another chance doesn't he? So, like a fool I agree to give him one.

Chapter Twenty-Five

Edward was washing down the milk shed when I arrived back at Trenowyth. I had asked Charlie to stay in the car until I called him. I spend a few minutes with Pepper and fight the desire to scoop him up and take him back to London with me. Although, I really can't picture him in a little pen in the living room of Charlie's flat. I can't really picture me there either, not in a little pen obviously, but in the new flat. It will seem so strange. Edward looks past me to Charlie's car and then back to his hosing. I take a long deep breath of the fresh country air and sigh. I shall miss this all so much. I savour the sights and smells so I can imprint them on my mind forever. I glance at the chicken coop and fight the urge to fetch the feed. I give only a passing look to Chloe's shed. The pain of her loss is still fresh. However, I feel sure I am doing the right thing. Wasn't this what I had wished for, that Charlie would come to his senses and that I would return home to my life in the city?

'I've come for my things,' I say quietly.

'Going back to London are you?' he says abruptly, without looking at me.

'Yes, I am.'

He stops and throws the hose down. Water splashes up my legs but I ignore it.

'You should have your fancy pink wellies on. It's slippery in here,' he continues sharply, and I feel the tears I had been struggling to control prick my eyelids.

'Edward ...' I begin,

He turns steely eyes onto me. His lips are tightly drawn together and his brow is furrowed. I want to run my hands through his hair and hold him close like I did yesterday. I move towards him but his words stop me in my tracks.

'Luce is coming home. She phoned this morning. I told her about the milk licence. She wants me to sell Trenowyth and fly back to New Zealand with her.'

I gape at him.

'But you can't sell Trenowyth. You have the milk licence. You're getting the farm on its feet. That's what Martha said, just like your father wanted ...'

'The plan always was to join her in New Zealand,' he says, cutting me short.

Why is he being so horrid to me? Didn't our kiss mean anything to him?

'But ...'

He picks up the hose roughly.

'Is this why you've come back, to tell me how to run my farm?'

'No, I ...'

'You play at being the country girl for a few weeks and then think you're qualified to give advice.'

'No, of course not, it's just ...'

'You've finished with the country now, is that it?'

'Edward, it isn't like that.'

He strides past and the hose hits my leg. I lose my footing and grab him for support. Suddenly I am pinned against the shed door as Edward holds my arms down with his. My body is on fire. The cows moo and retreat to the back of the shed. Please ask me to stay Edward, please and I will. His eyes bore into mine and his hands grip mine tighter. I find myself transported back to our kiss and my legs go weak.

'Would you give everything up Alice, your cosy life in London and your friends, not to mention your affluent fiancé? Would you really prefer to rough it here where calves die and where the house leaks at the first spots of rain. It's not all coffee mornings and cream teas you know. There is money but it is all ploughed back into the farm. There's no luxury here Alice.'

'I know,' I say and hear my voice shake.

'Do you?'

He doesn't want me. He's trying to get rid of me. He was just using me. He is no better than Dominic Montfort and now he is panicking because he thinks I have fallen in love with him. Damn him, damn him to hell.

'No, you're quite right. There is nothing here worth roughing it for. I'd much rather be in London and with Charlie,' I say spitefully. 'In fact, I wish I had never come here.'

Oh no, I didn't mean that. He releases my hands and turns slowly from me.

'Well I'll always be glad you came,' he says softly, and walks from the shed.

I go to follow him when I see Charlie getting out of his car and Jed and Martha approaching.

'Alice,' Jed calls.

I watch helplessly as Edward strides to the Land Rover and drives away without a second glance. I didn't mean what I had said and bite my lip in regret.

'Everything okay?' asks Jed, turning off the hose. Martha looks at me forlornly.

'You're not really leaving are you?' she asks.

'I'm going back to London,' I say as cheerfully as I can while tears threaten to pour forth.

'We're getting married,' adds Charlie, throwing an arm around me.

'That's a surprise, we didn't realise Alice had a fiancé,' says Martha, narrowing her eyes at Charlie.

'Congratulations,' smiles Jed, but it's a forced smile and his congratulations sound hollow. 'We'll see you again, no doubt.'

'Oh I hope so Jed,' I say, wrapping my arms around him and letting the tears flow.

But I know I will never see Edward again. He will sell the farm and fly out to New Zealand. My last memory of Edward will be him striding stiff backed to the Land Rover and driving away.

'Look after Pepper for me,' I say tearfully.

I cry even more when I feel Molly pawing at my legs.

'We should get going,' says Charlie, pushing Molly away and grimacing at the mud on his shoes. 'You really shouldn't have pigs locked in pens you know,' he says sternly to Jed.

'Charlie,' I admonish, wiping my eyes. 'He's not locked in a pen.'

'Not all pigs are locked in pens Charlie,' quips Martha giving him a scathing look.

'It's cruel, and the same with those chickens. We'll free th animals one day,' he continues, waving his arms and pointing at th cows in the shed.

'Now I am chairperson things will be different.'

'Sorry Jed,' I whisper as I kiss him on the cheek.

'Remind me not to visit him in London,' he whispers. 'We'll mi you.'

I don't ask who the *we* are, but hope he means Edward. Charl helps me pack while lecturing me on the wrongs of livesto farming. I keep my ears cocked for the sound of Edward's Lan Rover and pack as slowly as I can in the hope that he will return an can say goodbye properly. I finally make my tearful exit fro Trenowyth with Molly's doleful eyes following me into Charlie's car

'Thank God for that. The smell is disgusting, I don't know ho you stood it,' sighs Charlie.

I realise that for the first time ever I never even noticed it.

Chapter Twenty-Six

'Alice.'

I turn at the call of my name. Georgie is standing in the middle of the room with her hands on her hips.

'Alice, where are you?'

'What,' I say, coming down to earth.

Georgie has come with me for the final fitting of my wedding dress. I stand looking like a giant ball of cotton wool, while Rita, the dressmaker, pulls frantically at the zip and I feel my face getting redder.

'It's no good,' she puffs, wiping a thin bead of perspiration from her forehead. 'It's stuck.'

Rita flaps her hand at my stomach.

'You've swollen up,' she says accusingly.

'Oh God,' groans Georgie and falls into a chair. 'You're not up the spout are you?'

'It's water probably,' I lie.

It's all those fish and chips more like.

'She's got wedding stress, isn't that right?' sighs Rita.

Although what stress has got to do with water retention I do not know. I shrug and Georgie shakes her head.

'It's all a bloody farce if you ask me,' she grumbles.

I look out of the window.

'What colour is the bouquet going to be?' asks Rita before taking a deep breath and yanking at the zip again.

The mention of flowers pulls my mind back to Cornwall and St Matthew's church and I think of Edward. I did attempt to phone Trenowyth just once. I wanted to apologise for everything but someone else had answered the phone. It could have been Sara. I really wasn't sure. But they had confirmed he was in New Zealand.

'How about peach and cream, we have some lovely collections,' smiles Rita, dazzling me with her sparkling white teeth.

'Is it hot in New Zealand?' I ask. 'You know, at Christmas?'

'Oh, I don't know. I thought you were getting married in St Andrew's,' she replies, the plastic smile disappearing from her face.

'We don't normally dress brides abroad.'

The door is flung open and a flurry of cold air stings my legs.

'Fuck, it's freezing out there,' declares Cas who wafts in swathed in a huge scarf so that I can barely see his face.

'What the hell has New Zealand got to do with anything?' snaps Georgie.

'New Zealand? Who the fuck is going to New Zealand?' asks Cas, draping his scarf around Rita's neck. 'A coffee would be ace darling,' he adds, giving her a squeeze.

He sneezes dramatically and then fumbles in his shoulder bag.

'Is that new?' Georgie points to the leather bag.

He shrugs.

'This old thing? I've had it for days.'

'Is it real leather? Best not let Charlie see it or he'll have your guts for garters,' laughs Georgie, running her hands over it.

Cas laughs.

'I think you may be mistaking me for someone who gives a shit.'

He twirls and accepts the coffee Rita hands him.

'I hope it's *Camp coffee* darling.'

'It's hot actually,' says Rita.

'Yes, thank you darling.'

'In New Zealand I mean. At Christmas,' says Rita, 'it's hot in December. I remember seeing it on a holiday programme.'

That's not right then is it? It should snow at Christmas or at least be cold enough to freeze your bollocks off. Christmas Day huddled around a log fire, a mince pie in one hand and a glass of mulled wine in the other, with the smell of roasted turkey pervading the house is heaven on earth isn't it? It really isn't heaven on earth having Christmas dinner on the patio is it? Besides, the After Eights would melt, and we really can't have that can we?

'Well that's abfab to know darling if any of us were going to New Zealand at Christmas but we're not are we?' Cas looks to Georgie for confirmation.

Georgie in turn looks to me.

'You're going to the Maldives for your honeymoon. Charlie has booked it. You can't change your mind now.'

Cas squeezes my hand.

'You're not changing your mind are you darling?'

There is a silence as all eyes are turned on me. Rita's wide and Georgie's questioning. Cas squeezes my hand a little tighter.

'It's okay if you have you know,' he whispers.

'Of course not, I was simply curious.'

Georgie fans my highlighted hair around my shoulders and surveys me again.

'Yep, it has to be peaches and cream.'

'God you're making me hungry with all this talk of fruit and cream. Shall I pop and get us some doughnuts darlings?' asks Cas, 'or are we onto the cake tasting next?'

It's been six weeks since I returned from Cornwall. Charlie has become the most thoughtful and attentive boyfriend that a woman could wish for. He leaves little presents for me and even writes love notes which he leaves in the bathroom by my toothbrush. Last Friday he took me to the ballet even though he hates it. He secretly booked the honeymoon in the Maldives and went down on one knee and proposed again. The wedding is booked for two days before Christmas. I do love Charlie. He really is trying so hard to make me happy and I am dead grateful.

'A winter wonderland wedding to my very own princess,' he had said, slipping my engagement ring back onto my finger.

Why oh why do things not feel quite right?

My stomach rumbles.

'Doughnuts sound great,' I say.

'It's all the excitement and stress. They say getting married is one of the most stressful things you can do,' says Rita knowingly.

'They say that about divorce too,' adds Cas.

'I'm not even married yet,' I say but everyone ignores me.

'And moving home,' chips in Georgie.

'Starting a new job is also on the list,' chimes Rita.

'Or not being able to find one,' I add.

'And considering you're doing it for the second time,' chips in Cas.

'That's not strictly true is it?' says Georgie, 'Considering the first time never actually happened so in theory this isn't the second time ...'

My sharp look cuts her off.

'But she has moved house and changed jobs and almost married. Frankly I'm surprised she isn't in a loony bin,' contributes Cas, draping his arm around my shoulders.

'I think it is all going to be fabulous. Don't you agree?' asks Rita.

'Yes,' I respond warmly allowing Georgie to drape me in a cream shawl while Rita sticks a small posy in my hand.

It will soon be Christmas and on the twenty-third I will be Mrs Alice Marrow. The wife of Charles Marrow, exceptionally well-paid advertising executive and chairperson of the *Freedom for Farm Animals Association* and vegetarian extraordinaire. But sometimes, just sometimes I so fancy fish and chips.

'It's going to be lovely Alice,' Georgie sighs.

For a split second I think she is talking about fish and chips. Yes, she is right it is going to be lovely. At that moment my Blackberry bleeps and I look down to see it is a message from Charlie.

Thinking of you and can't wait to see you later. Hope everything is going well with the dress fitting.

I look at my engagement ring and again tell myself what a lucky woman I am. I only wish I believed myself.

Chapter Twenty-Seven

Two glasses of wine and a quarter of a meat-feast pizza, and she is sitting on the beach watching the ebb and flow of the sea and listening to the calming sounds of the waves while adding more salt to the sea with her flowing tears. Why does he say things are difficult? It was all supposed to be temporary. Her mouth feels dry and her glass is empty. She looks back to the rowdy crowd and considers joining the barbeque, but knows she will just be the party pooper. A sultry figure approaches and she feels a fluttering in her stomach. It had been a mistake and she really must make that abundantly clear to Jason. It cannot, no it will not, happen again. How stupid to have drunk so much. He walks into the sea waving to her as he does so. She thinks he looks like James Bond. He is incredibly fit and beautifully tanned. He has given her more attention in the past month than any man has ever given her. More tears come unbidden, and she wipes at her face angrily. She shouldn't have phoned while tipsy. She knew they would argue. It felt like everything else mattered except her. How can he not want to be here, where the weather is fantastic, the people are great and more importantly, where she is?

'The water's fabulous. Come on,' Jason shouts before diving into the sea.

She leans back lazily and picks up the wine bottle. One more glass won't matter. She really should eat something though. She steals another glance at the smoky barbeque and feels tempted. Then again, she'll have to be chatty, and she really doesn't feel in the mood for that. Hesitating, with the bottle in her hand she looks at Jason swimming masterfully towards her. If she makes another mistake it will be over. But she didn't make the first mistake, did she? A woman gets lonely. They had discussed their future, it had been what they both wanted and she had been as giving as any woman could be. He shouldn't have left her here for so long. Damn him for letting her down like this. Lifting the glass to her lips, she whispers, *Here's to us, what's left of us that is.* By the time Jason reaches her she is crying tears of anger.

'He's not coming is he?' he says, dripping in front of her.

She shakes her head dumbly.

'Not this week.'

'Need a hug?' he asks the desire evident in his eyes.

What she knew should have been a shaking of her head turns into a teary nod and the next thing she is in his arms and she knows it will happen again and somehow feels entitled.

'Come on Luce, let's take a bottle back to the hotel,' Jason whispers.

She has nothing left to resist him.

Chapter Twenty-Eight

'Oh wow, you came. Groovy,' gushes Myrna on seeing me.
She's wearing a dress that Helena Bonham Carter would be ashamed
to wear. It's black velvet with a huge bow at the waist, and on her
feet are tartan boot slippers. She seriously looks like she is about to
take the lead part in the Christmas panto. She's wearing more Kohl
than Cleopatra and jingles as the beads in her hair clash together
every time she moves her head.

'Philly,' she screeches, 'Alice is here.'
Charlie grins like a Cheshire cat. Talking of cats, the house is full of
them, and if you can't see them you can certainly smell them even
over the sandalwood incense sticks.

'I couldn't stop her,' he laughs, catching me as I go flying over
muddy boots that are blocking the hallway.
Not strictly true. In fact, a complete falsehood but I can't say that
can I? The real truth is that I couldn't possibly let Charlie come for a
celebratory dinner with his best friends without me could I? I had
tried to talk him out of it. Even bribed him with sex, which is really
below the belt I know, but trust me you don't want to have dinner
with Myrna and Phil. We squeeze past the sixties sideboard which is
cluttered with Greenpeace posters and leaflets.

'Charlie said you wouldn't be able to make it because of a dress
fitting,' says Phil as he gives me a welcome hug. His beard scratches
my cheek and I try not to pull away. My eyes widen at the sight of
him. What is he wearing? He looks like the Maharishi Yogi.

'I've been meditating,' he says in way of explanation.

'I managed to change things around,' I say and blush bright red.
I was never very good at lying. Myrna stares at me with her dewy
eyes and over-glossed lips.

'You must be so excited,' she says in a trembling voice, her glossed lips quivering.

'I'm so happy for you guys. Oh Lordy, I'm welling up again,' she tearfully takes the tissue that Phil has at the ready.

I try not to sigh too loudly.

'Let's not stand in the hallway, come through, come through,' bellows Phil as though we are at the end of their drive rather than standing right next to him.

I pass the assortment of china animals that sit on the hall table, step over two cats and enter the lounge.

'Sit down, sit down,' bellows Phil as he points to their flea-infested couch.

'Drinky poos?' asks Myrna, fluffing around an antiquated drinks cabinet.

A double whisky I think.

'We'll both have red wine if you've got it,' says Charlie.

I give him a sidelong glance. Since when did I stop answering for myself? I watch as one of the cats tugs at the hem of Myrna's dress while another jumps up onto the cabinet sending a bottle of brandy flying.

'We've got some special organic wine in the fridge haven't we Philly?'

In the fridge? Oh good God Philly, please say you haven't. The last time I had their special organic wine I was on the loo all night.

'I believe we have,' he replies proudly. 'Do you want wine too Myrnie?'

I carefully remove the cake I had made from a carrier bag.

'I made a carrot cake for you,' I say with a shrug.

She stops in the doorway and puts a hand to her heart. She gives me that dewy-eyed look again and I am reminded of Molly, and I really don't want to be reminded of Molly because that just reminds me of Edward and I go stupidly dewy too.

'Oh Ali,' she says, her eyes filling up, 'you made it for us? You actually made a cake for us? I don't know what to say.'

No, I made it for the cats. Who does she think I made it for?

'Philly, did you hear that?'

'I did.'

I hope he isn't going to well up too but I needn't have worried for he says,

'It hasn't got animal products in it has it?'

That's gratitude for you.

'God no,' replies Charlie.

God yes. I completely forgot.

'Well, I,' I stammer.

The room goes uncomfortably silent with all eyes on me.

'I … I made it especially,' I finish. At least that way I don't admit to using a little butter in the icing do I? Myrna sighs and Phil squeezes me round the waist.

'She is going to make a wonderful wife, Charlie.'

I try not to squeal as his hand glides upwards and strokes the bottom of my breast. Oh my. Myrna hops from one foot to the other excitedly and I fake a yawn, stretching delicately out of Phil's embrace.

'Can I use your loo?' I ask, rushing there before she has time to say yes.

I cannot believe that just a matter of days after being back with Charlie I have cystitis. I sit on the loo studying Myrna's natural birth control chart until I feel dizzy.

'It's all so exciting. I've made a nut roast with roast potatoes and stuffed peppers,' she gushes on my return.

Surprise surprise, and it isn't even Christmas. Ten minutes later we are huddled around the log burner sipping organic wine that tastes like vinegar. What I would do for a glass of Lidl's budget plonk right now. Myrna pops a dish of crisps on the table and I try not to look horrified when two of the cats pounce onto it.

'No Queenie, Mummy said no. She does love crisps,' laughs Myrna.

She certainly does. Her nose is now poking its way into my hand to get a few of mine.

'Ah she likes you. Look Philly, she adores Alice. If I remember she took to you in a big way the last time you came.'

'Yes, I remember.'

How could I forget little Queenie peeing onto my brand new Marks and Spencer boots. Charlie lays his hand onto my knee and strokes it tenderly.

'Lovely fire,' he says.

'So, the big day looms. Is the dress nearly ready?' asks Phil, passing round a dish of salted peanuts.

'We're very excited, aren't we darling?' says Charlie, stroking my leg a bit more and looking at me lovingly.

Meanwhile Queenie is kneading me like a piece of dough and I keep letting out little squeals.

'Queenie what are you doing to your Aunty Alice?' laughs Myrna. Queenie responds by knocking my wine glass over with her tail sending wine all over me. I make another escape to the bathroom where I consider phoning Charlie's mobile and impersonating the police to inform him that our flat is on fire. Of course I don't. Instead I rub at my silk shirt and pray they don't eat the cake while I'm here. I take my time having a pee and finally give my shirt another rub down. The time on my Blackberry tells me I have been in here for close on six minutes. Myrna is laying the table when I come back and the cats are climbing all over it. Phil has a pile of papers on his lap and Charlie is studying them.

'Michael can organise the media coverage,' says Phil.

Oh no, not the animal rights stuff. I reluctantly offer to help Myrna and am grateful when she declines. It isn't that I don't want to help, I just don't want to see what the cats are licking. Ignorance is most certainly bliss in this case. I wander back into the living room where Phil and Charlie are still discussing their next rescue plan.

'We don't want the media on this, at least not until afterwards,' says Charlie.

'I can see the headlines: *Christmas Turkey is History*,' says Phil excitedly.

'Just keep it under wraps until we have the dates, the vans and everything else we need,' says Charlie looking at me and shifting in his seat.

'What are you planning?' I ask suspiciously as Myrna brings in the nut roast and encourages us all to sit at the table.

'Did you put out the chopsticks Philly?' she asks.

Chopsticks? Am I losing the plot altogether? I thought we were having nut roast? She sees my puzzled look and smiles.

'I'm not using cutlery for three months,' she says proudly, 'Isn't that right Philly. You can help too Alice. You give up something for three months. It's for charity.'

I stare at the chopsticks stupidly. But they are cutlery aren't they? Perhaps I could give up visiting them for three months. That sounds like a fabulous idea.

'I'm eating everything with them. It's to help others so I don't mind,' she says in that condescending tone that she has.

Wow such hardship, what can I say?

'Middle-class giving,' I mumble.

'What?' snaps Charlie.

'I said it's good to be giving.'

'You can sponsor me. It's to help gays get the treatment they need so they can be normal.'

OH MY GOD.

'You could give up drinking,' she suggests, pointing to the wine. Good idea Myrna, seeing as there will never be a better day to start than today. Heavens, is she hinting that I am some kind of alcoholic?

'I don't actually feel that gays need treatment. My friend Cas ...'

'Yes, well,' butts in Charlie.

'That nut roast smells marvellous,' interrupts Phil.

'We're going to save lives from the Christmas dinner table,' he adds proudly.

'Rights for farm animals,' shrieks Myrna as she drops the steaming nut roast onto the table.

My God they are raving mad. I then realise what Phil has just said and my stomach churns.

'Where are you rescuing these animals from Charlie?' I ask, feeling my hands tremble.

'Farms, where else Alice?' replies Phil.

I fiddle with my fork and say,

'What farms?'

Charlie stands up.

'Shall I fetch the vegetables Myrna?' he asks, exiting to the kitchen.

Before she can reply I have followed.

'What farms Charlie?' I repeat, taking a dish of carrots with a Simpsons' oven glove.

He picks up a dish of peas and avoids my eyes.

'A few turkey farms, in Cornwall ...'

'What?'

He sighs.

'Not Edward's farm okay, I promise.'

'Why Cornwall?' I ask appalled.

'The president dictates it. He also lives there. It's a fabulous chance for me Alice. He thinks I have what it takes to highlight the organisation. He even mentioned an OBE at one point.'

'People don't get OBEs for raiding farms Charlie. They get them for kicking a football about.'

'You have no idea Alice. The president is an influential man.'

'Why don't you lick his arse while you're there then?'

'For goodness sake Alice.'

'Charlie you can't do this. This is people's livelihood.'

He stops in the doorway.

'God almighty Alice, whose side are you on? I would have hoped that getting attached to animals on that farm would have made you more aware of just how wrong it all is. Besides, this has been organised from high up so please don't shout at me. You should be proud the president trusts me with the operation.'

I wish he would stop making the guy sound like the President of the United States and himself as Superman. The carrot dish burns my hand and I quickly run into the living room with it and drop it heavily onto the table.

'Oh dear,' mumbles Myrna, sawing manically through the nut roast with a chopstick while Phil tops up our wine glasses.

'Charlie, you will cause a lot of damage to these farms if you remove their livestock.'

'That's the general idea,' says Phil handing me another glass of chilled red wine.

'This should be served at room temperature,' I snap and instantly regret it.

'Oh,' he says flustered and studies the bottle intently.

'Shall we partake of this lovely dinner that Myrna and Phil have gone to so much trouble to prepare?' says Charlie.

Myrna and Phil look at each other. I pile roast potatoes onto my plate while glaring at Charlie.

'I love your scarf,' says Myrna finally. 'Where did you buy it?'

'Primark,' I say shamelessly.

She gasps. Charlie dabs at his chin with a kitten patterned serviette.

'Alice always tries her best to shop ethically,' he says, 'but her mother likes Primark. She bought that scarf for you didn't she darling?'

How dare he lie about my mother?

'Actually no, I bought it,' I say angrily knocking back some wine. God, this is awful. Don't drink too much Alice whatever you do. You'll end up saying things you'll regret.

'You're aware that child labour has been condemned by human rights groups,' says Philly condescendingly.

Now I feel dead guilty.

'It's only a scarf,' I say, feeling like I'm on trial and almost adding *your honour*.

'We really feel that consumers need to give a clear message to retailers that this is unacceptable,' says Myrna heatedly, glaring at the scarf while attempting to scoop some nut roast onto her chopsticks.

'This nut roast is the best I've ever had,' I say, trying to change the subject and look to Charlie for help.

'Yes, I agree, and the carrots are cooked to perfection,' adds Charlie.

Myrna's face lights up and the tightness leaves her mouth.

'There isn't too much garlic in it?' she asks shyly.

'Oh no, in fact it's just right, isn't it Charlie?' I lie.

It must be me. There must be something very wrong with me. Myrna and Phil have loads of friends. More friends than I have. I imagine I am the only one who has ever complained about the wine. How can I be so horrid? I stare down into my glass and feel quite despondent, my mind in turmoil. I really want to be a good wife to Charlie and he really does look lovely tonight in his Pierre Cardin shirt. I've always liked Charlie in a white shirt. In fact when we get home I'll ask him to keep it on and make mad passionate love to him. Yes, that's what I'll do and hopefully he'll forget all about Primark and all that slave labour stuff. I may even get him to talk to me about the farm activism he is planning. Myrna leans over with a dish.

'More nut roast Alice,'

I nod pleasantly.

'More wine?' asks Phil.

God, it's so hideous. Still it is nicely numbing everything. A terrible thought suddenly occurs to me and I feel my knees tremble. What if one day Charlie and I are exactly like Myrna and Phil? No, I resolutely forbid myself to ever become like this and I will never ever serve chilled red vinegar flavoured organic wine. Or, God forbid, eat with chopsticks so that Cas can be normal.

'I'll fetch the dessert,' says Phil.

'I've made a rhubarb and cranberry flan.'

'Lovely,' I say.

Let's look on the bright side, at least that should sort out my cystitis.

Chapter Twenty-Nine

'I hope this isn't a bloody bomb. I found it on the pavement and thought it looked like Charlie's.'

I look at the briefcase, let out a scream and cover my mouth with my hand.

'Quick,' I say, pulling her in and looking quickly up the steps to the street.

'Blimey, what's going on?' she asks as I shut and lock the front door.

'We need to get this open.'

'Don't you offer me coffee?' Georgie drops her handbag and strolls into the living room.

'Georgie,' I shriek, 'there's no time for coffee.'

'But you invited me for coffee, remember?'

I clutch the briefcase so tightly that my knuckles turn white. I take a deep breath and push back the clip, but nothing happens.

'It won't open.'

'It's locked,' says Georgie with a yawn. 'Why do you want it open anyway? Can't you just ask Charlie to open it for you?'

I sigh and check the time.

'Damn it. He's bound to come back for it.'

I pull Georgie and the briefcase into the living room.

'You remember I told you that Charlie is planning some kind of farm rescue?'

'Yes,' she says vaguely while glancing through a *Hello* magazine.

'Georgie,' I shout, 'the farms are in Cornwall, and he won't tell me where or when it's happening. I am worried he's going to Edward's farm and I've looked everywhere for his plans, I know there must be some. He left today on a business trip, but I'm sure it's this liberation thing. If the paperwork is not in the flat then it has to be in this case. Which ...'

'Which he'll be back for any minute,' she interrupts.

'Oh my God, it could be Edward's farm.'

By Jove she's got it. Better late than never.

'You need the combination,' she says, studying the case.

Shit.

'I don't have it,' I say miserably.

She stamps her feet in unison with the ringing of my Blackberry.

'That'll be him.'

I stare at my phone.

'Stall him,' she says, sounding like the cop in a badly written crime novel.

'Stall him?' I repeat.

She nods and points to the phone. I grab it and answer in a shaky voice.

'Alice, thank God you're there,' says a relieved Charlie. 'I must have left my briefcase in the street. Can you check? Some stupid woman fell off her bike and I did my Good Samaritan thing, and must have got into the cab without it. I'm at the station now.'

'Oh dear I'll check. Hold on.'

I click the Blackberry onto hold and look at Georgie who is fumbling with the lock.

'What numbers would he use?'

'Try his birthday, 1603.'

She shakes her head.

'How about *my* birthday?'

She shakes her head again.

'Shall we force it open?' I say, surprising myself.

'This is better than a P. D. James novel,' giggles Georgie, pointing to my Blackberry. 'Hadn't you better tell him you've found it?'

Damn.

'I have it Charlie and ...'

'I'm in a cab and on my way now. I'll be fifteen minutes. Can you be there with it? I'll miss my train otherwise.'

Fifteen minutes?

'Okay,' I say in a small voice.

'Think,' says Georgie anxiously. 'Does he do the lottery?'

I shake my head.

'When is his mother's birthday?'

'I don't know.'

'I've got it. It has to be the day you met.'

I shake my head doubtfully and smile knowingly when nothing happens.

'We have to force it,' I say.

She pulls a face.

'That's a bad idea. Won't he know you did it?'

'I'll say that's how I found it. He'll never know.'

She looks uncertainly at the briefcase and pulls her hair into a knot at the nape of her neck, rubs her hands together and says,

'Last try. What's the date of your wedding?'

I sigh.

'He won't use that.'

'He might be more romantic than you think.'

'Twenty-third of December.'

She blows on her hands and deftly changes the numbers. I hold my breath.

'Holy shit,' she yells as there is a click.

'I don't believe it.'

Georgie picks the case up so cautiously that you'd think it was a bomb. She sits it carefully on the couch and we both stand back looking at it.

'They won't fly out by themselves,' she says after a moment of silence.

I jump at her words. I feel so guilty and I haven't actually done anything yet. That's not strictly true. I have opened the case, well that is I got Georgie to open it.

'I don't think I can look inside,' I say while my hands itch to do so. 'It feels like an invasion of privacy.'

'It's not the best way to start a marriage,' agrees Georgie.

Hell, what a dilemma. It is somehow worse now that the case is open. Georgie lowers her head to the opened top.

'What are you doing?' I shout.

She jumps back her hand on her heart.

'Christ Ali. You scared me to death.'

I twist my hands together nervously and glance out of the window.

'You take them out,' I whisper, 'carefully mind you,'

She shakes her head.

'Oh no, no way am I implicating myself,' she says stubbornly, moving further away from the case.

'He won't know …'

'Want to bet? In one of P. D. James's novels …'

I snort impatiently.

'It's not a novel though is it?'

'You wanted to open it so you should take the things out.'

Georgie is quite right of course.

'Okay, keep watch at the door and if you see Charlie coming down the street whistle or something.'

'I can't whistle,' she says bluntly.

I gape at her.

'How can you not whistle?'

She shrugs and lifts her hands irritably.

'I don't know. I just can't.'

'You never told me.'

'You never asked me,' she snaps.

Cagney and Lacey we are not.

'I'll shout *Hi Charlie* as soon as I see him. I'll give the impression I have just arrived. Okay? Christ, I'm beginning to wish I had gone to Starbucks for coffee,' she moans, scooping up her coat. 'It would have been a hell of a lot less hassle.'

I wait until she has pulled the door to and then look longingly at the contents of the case. The question is can I live with myself if I do this? More importantly, can I continue living with Charlie? What is wrong with me, it's not like I'm stealing state secrets and selling them to the Russians is it? I straighten my blue woollen dress over my buttocks and push my breasts out and glance quickly at my reflection in the mirror. I look seductive enough to distract Charlie just in case, not that I seem to be distracting him very much lately. I had done everything under the sun to get information out of him regarding the rescue plan. I had cooked him exotic meals, offered my body left right and centre until he was worn out, and finally had resorted to pleading with him to tell me. Nothing had worked. He wouldn't tell me where, or when, he had just assured me that everything would be fine and that I wasn't to worry. I know he means well. He loves animals and there is nothing wrong with that is there? In fact, if I hadn't gone to Trenowyth I would be supporting

Charlie a hundred per cent. But I did go to Trenowyth and made a lot of friends there. I can't just sit back knowing there could be a raid on their farms. The clock is ticking. I need to make a decision. I hear Georgie's heels clip-clopping on the pavement as she paces back and forth. I take a deep breath and plunge my hand into the case and touch something soft. The next thing I know I am looking at a peanut butter sandwich. A little bead of perspiration has formed on my forehead and I strain my ears for Georgie's heels before pushing my hand in again. This time I fumble around expertly while one ear is cocked for Georgie's warning. I pull out several folders and hastily flick through them. After finding nothing I carefully replace them in the bag and take another wad, praying that there is something there. I somehow feel there won't be time to go back again. I feel myself beginning to shake and tears well up. Why oh why couldn't Charlie have just told me who he planned to target? If he had I wouldn't be doing this. I scan through the folders and am shocked to find between them a copy of *Big Bums* magazine. Heavens, I know Charlie is a bum man, but really, a magazine of bums in his case? It has been well thumbed too. It opens to what is obviously a favourite page and I gasp at the huge bum that is pointing up at me. Talk about in your face. When does he find the time to look at this? Surely he doesn't you know what to these bums. I drop the magazine as the thought enters my head and quickly retrieve it to study the pages for stains. This is terrible. Who thought I would study the photograph of another woman's bum to see if my boyfriend has been wanking over it. My boyfriend is a dirty old man. I'll find condoms next or God forbid, a whip and chain. He said we needed to spice up our sex life. That will teach me to poke around in someone else's things. Hang on. Charlie isn't just someone else, he's my soon-to-be husband and I'm damned if I'll feel guilty because *he* looks at dirty magazines. Anyway it's not hard porn is it? A few bums are nothing to get paranoid about. All the same, I can't help thinking there is nothing wrong with my bum, so why does he need to look at someone else's? Damn it, I can't even confront him without admitting I went through his briefcase. A Crunchie falls out from between the papers and lands at my feet. I am overcome with longing for the smooth creamy milk chocolate coating but I fight off the urge to leap on it and instead remind myself of the Maltesers hidden in my undies drawer. I will most certainly need them later.

Finally, I have found what I have been searching for and a folder titled *Operation Turkey* is in my hands. *Operation Turkey*, I ask you, couldn't he come up with a more original name? There are several copies of the plan, along with diagrams and at the top of the list is Orchard Farm in the village of Stantonford. Oh no, these are people that I know, I can't possibly let them do this to Mona, not after she has worked so hard.

'Why Charlie, hello,' yells Georgie in such a high-pitched anxious voice that he would be bound to guess that something is going on. In my panic I drop the folders, and the bum magazine, and step straight onto the Crunchie.

'Bollocks.'

'Isn't it a beautiful day for December? Do you think that is snow in the sky?' I hear Georgie say.

Charlie grunts.

'Aren't you working today Charlie?'

There seems to be some sort of commotion on the stairs and I take the opportunity to shove a copy of *Operation Turkey* into my handbag. I push the bum magazine and broken Crunchie back into the case before clicking it shut and turning around to greet Charlie. I'm panting as if I've run a marathon. Georgie pushes past him at the front door and runs to hug me.

'Hello darling,' she says loudly, looking at the case. 'Did you change the numbers?' she whispers.

Shit. I shake my head dumbly.

'Great, thanks Ali,' sighs Charlie. 'I thought I'd lost it. Are you okay?' he asks looking at me curiously.

'Yes, shouldn't I be?'

'You seem breathless.'

'I've been doing sit ups,' I say stretching.

'I never knew you did those.'

Georgie studies the briefcase.

'I started today,' I lie and shake my head at Georgie.

'God what a fab case,' she says wide-eyed. 'Is it yours Charlie?'

'My mother bought it for me last Christmas.'

Oh, really? I wonder what she would think of you storing filthy books inside. I bite my lip to stop myself from confronting him.

'I'd better be off. You girls have a good time, and take good care of my car while I'm away Alice.'

As soon as the door closes I flop onto the couch and exhale loudly.

'I can't believe you forgot to change the numbers,' scolds Georgie. 'Did you find it?'

'I found a lot of things,' I say crossly.

'Uh oh.'

'A magazine full of bums,' I say, storming into the kitchen and banging two mugs onto the worktop.

'It could have been worse,' she says, rummaging through a cupboard and pulling out a packet of fig rolls.

'How much worse exactly?' I say, stuffing a fig roll into my mouth.

'Moira Higgs came home early one day after a phone call saying little Thomas was sick. She walked into the house with little Tommy and there was Geoff in her underwear and wearing her make-up.'

'I think that's worse.'

She giggles and carries the tea into the living room.

'The question is, did you find the addresses and was Edward on the list?'

I fish the list from my bag and study it. What disturbs me most is that none of the farms that I know on the list are turkey farms. There is something seriously not right about this whole business. There must be fifty farms targeted for this horrible deed of Charlie's. I feel my legs go to jelly when I read the plan and the name *Operation Turkey* that sounded funny at first doesn't seem so funny any more.

Chapter Thirty

Georgie did her best to talk me out of it. There wasn't a single argument she didn't use. But what the hell was I supposed to do? I couldn't sit back and forget what I had seen could I? I sat nursing a mug of cold coffee for an hour after Georgie left. Eventually I had scooped off the skin and re-heated it in the microwave.

'Shouldn't you at least give Charlie an opportunity to tell you just what is happening?' Georgie had said.

'I gave him that opportunity,' I argued, 'but *Operation Turkey* could be happening right at this very moment.'

'And then again it may not be. There was no date on the plan. Don't you think you're getting things out of proportion? It may never get past the planning stage for all you know.'

I just feel I can't take any chances. I owe it to Mona. I know Edward is in New Zealand with Lucy short for Lucinda, but everyone calls me Luce by now, but I can't leave little Pepper to cope alone. I don't want him going to a little piggy safe house, or wherever they put them. I just hope the farmer who has taken over Trenowyth will understand my feelings and let me take him. I have no idea where I will put Pepper when I rescue him. I think Charlie may spot him if I put him in the bedroom. We don't have a garden, and I can't very well hide him in a car I don't have. As it is, I'll have to bring him back in Charlie's car. I really must look into getting a new car. Best if I make a list of all the things I'll need to take with me. I grab some paper and begin my list …

1)   Overnight bag. It surely won't take longer than one night. Hopefully Charlie will never know I was involved in the rescue operation to foil his rescue operation. I should call it the *Pig*

Operation in Opposition to Turkey Operation. God, I sound demented.

2) Fresh air spray. Mostly for when Pepper has boarded the car. I wonder how often pigs shit? I must ask Jed. Maybe when I stop at the service station she can go then. Obviously not in the service station loo, I'm not that silly.

3) Some kind of defence weapon just in case things get nasty. I'm sure they won't but perhaps I should take a bread knife or something. What am I thinking? I can't possibly take a bread knife. I might well stab Charlie. Obviously I wouldn't stab him deliberately but if it's dark I won't know it's him will I? That would be terrible. I can almost see the headlines *Woman stabs fiancé by mistake*. That would be pretty horrific wouldn't it? No, delete that, better not take the bread knife.

4) Torch. We surely have a torch somewhere. I can't say I have ever seen one. You don't really need a torch that much in the city.

5) Box. I'm not sure what I'll do with a box but it somehow seems a good idea when dealing with animals and the rescue of them. Although of course in theory I'm not doing the rescuing. I actually plan to thwart all rescue attempts, except for Pepper of course. The truth is I'm not actually sure what I plan to do about Pepper after he has been rescued.

6) A plan. Item five brings to mind the fact that I don't have one and I probably should. Right now my only plan is to go rushing down to Cornwall without the faintest idea what I intend to do once I get there.

I flop onto the couch and stare at the blank TV screen as if it will offer an answer. My stomach feels hollow and I realise I haven't eaten since breakfast. I guiltily bite into a mince pie. It is just two weeks before Christmas and two weeks before my wedding day, and I'm nowhere near ready, for Christmas that is, I'm totally ready for my wedding day in the sense that everything is organised. I'm not so sure *I* personally am ready though. I text Georgie to tell her I am leaving for Cornwall.

I consider whether I will need a mask. At least that way I can rescue Pepper without Charlie ever knowing it was me. Although of course it is very unlikely that Charlie will even see me. Nothing ever happens the way you imagine does it? Most likely Charlie and his cronies will get cold feet and not do anything in the end. All the same I ought to go just in case. At least this time I know not to wear Christian Louboutin shoes. I think of my pink wellies and experience a horrible churning in my stomach as memories of Edward and Chloe come rushing back. I consider taking the wellingtons with me but decide not to. I put trainers on and take a look around the basement flat as though I will never see it again. My hands get sweaty when I realise that this could be the end of Charlie and I. If he finds out I tried to thwart his plans especially now that he is chairperson of the FFFAA, he will be livid. There's still time to change my mind, I don't have to go. No, that's not true, I do have to go. I could not live with myself if I didn't. I wrap a pashmina around my neck and throw a shawl around my shoulders. With a determined thrust of my jaw and a straightening of my back I open the door of the basement flat to the snowy cold outside and find myself wondering what Truro looks like in the snow when I walk straight into Georgie.

'I'm coming with you,' she says, shivering and shaking snow off her woollen hat.

'What?'

'I can't let you go all that way on your own.'

'It's Cornwall,' I say smiling, 'not Outer Mongolia.'

'Yes well. You can't cope with a pig on your own and anyway, I need a break. I've taken four days off work and ...' she stops and looks at me tearfully.

'He isn't going to leave her is he?'

I shake my head.

'I'm a stupid bitch,' she mumbles.

I hug her and try not to cry. I've never been happier to see her in my life.

'Come on let's go,' she says sternly, 'before we have to dig Charlie's Jaguar out of the snow.'

Georgie

I'd thought about the bum magazine all the way home. What a bastard. I know it isn't a big deal, and loads of men have bum magazines, or worse, in their briefcase. It wasn't so much that, it's Charlie's attitude that really pisses me off. The way he talks down to Ali, and the smarmy way he slides his hand up her leg in public. Just the thought of him doing his rescue crap behind her back seems all wrong. But that and the bum mag, it is enough to put any woman off. And then there was James. I'd gone to the Veggie Grill in the hope Bess might have some doughnuts. I'd been there only a few minutes and was waiting for Bess to pop the doughnuts into a bag when James had walked in. I was frozen to the spot. On his arm, and laughing loudly, was Maureen. Maureen the wife who, he is fond of telling me, is so depressed most days that she cannot get out of bed. Yes, well I can clearly see that. She is not only happy and blooming but also pregnant. Bugger me. You could have knocked me down with a feather. How could the depressed cow be pregnant when they never have sex? What a bloody amazing recovery she has made. Bess turned me around like some mechanical doll and led me to the back of the café.

'Are you okay dear?' she asked, her cheeks glowing from the heat of the oven matching the bright red of her hair.

I peek through the hatch to check it is a pregnancy bump and not a 'too many doughnuts' one.

'I don't believe it,' I said, too stunned to cry.

'Men are bastards.'

'He told me she was clinically depressed, and that he couldn't leave her in case she killed herself.'

We had peeped through the hatch as James and Maureen had stood laughing and hugging at the counter. Her wispy brown hair looked newly cut and styled.

'She must be on a bloody high dose of Prozac, that's all I can say,' giggles Bess.

I stared mesmerised at the baby bump.

'I agree. She's made a marvellous recovery not to mention the marvellous pregnancy. That was quite a miracle considering he doesn't have sex with her,' I'd scoffed

'Oh really?' remarked Bess.

'Yes. She's always too depressed for that as you can see for yourself,' I said as Maureen roared with laughter at something James said. Her hand instinctively touched her stomach as she rocked back and forth laughing. Bess shook her head.

'One of those Immac conceptions,' she said.

'I don't know that Immac had much to do with it. Immaculate perhaps.'

'That too,' she'd said nodding.

'How much longer are you going to make them wait?' I'd asked.

'Well they seem quite happy.'

'Unfortunately,' I said with a scoff.

'Do you want to go out the back way? I'll throw in an extra doughnut.'

'Bribing me with doughnuts now are you? Is this so I don't make a scene?'

'I don't want the shock to burst her waters.'

'Break her waters. It would be a bit shocking if they burst, unless she's giving birth to Satan or something. Mind you, that wouldn't surprise me.'

'I don't want Damien born in the café. I'll give you two extra doughnuts.'

'Damien has already been born,' I said looking at James and fighting back the tears.

I know it sounds stupid but I never ever considered he had been lying to me. All that talk of leaving her when she was better. That's never going to happen is it, especially considering she isn't even sick? How could I have been so stupid? And how could he have been so cruel? How will I cope now? Who will I have a drink with after work? Who will take me to the opera? I'll be one of those sad single women eating a TV dinner for one and going to bed early with a Mills and Boon novel. Christ, I'd rather slash my wrists than be seen with a Mills and Boon.

'Perhaps I should make a scene,' I'd said angrily, feeling James deserved all he got.

But then James had spotted me and began staring at me like a rabbit caught in headlights. There was a pleading look in his eyes and for a fraction of a second, and only a fraction I assure you, I actually felt sorry for him.

'You can do better girl,' whispered Bess seeing my confusion.

She was absolutely right of course. I didn't need a two-faced prick like James in my life. I had good friends, a brilliant job and I might not be Jennifer Aniston but I'm not far from it.

'You'll regret it,' Bess had warned.

Thankfully I took her advice and left the back way. I hadn't even made it half way home when James phoned my mobile. I ignored the familiar ring tone with a heavy heart. I eventually stopped and sent him a text which simply said *fuck off*. I then turned around and headed back to Ali's. She is my best friend after all, and if anyone will understand what I am going through it will be her.

Chapter Thirty-One

I've always been nervous driving the Jaguar. It's Charlie's pride and joy, a red Jaguar XF Sports. He's had it for over nine months but it still has that new smell which I am dead worried will be overtaken by pig-shit stink. I'll have to get Georgie to spray with a room deodoriser every five minutes. I won't mention it yet. I still haven't found the courage to tell her that I will be bringing Pepper back with us. She's under the impression that we are going to Cornwall to warn everyone, followed by a nice dinner, a few glasses of wine and then we'll come home. It's like a day trip for her. I'm as nervous as a kitten. The nearer we get to Cornwall the more my stomach churns. Georgie moans in her sleep, turns suddenly and hits me in the ribs.

'Christ, it's like a sauna in here,' she groans wiping perspiration from her forehead. 'Can you turn the heating down?'

I shake my head and suggest she opens her window. She squints sleepily at the windscreen.

'It's sleeting out there, why the hell would I want to open a window?'

'Because I can't work out how to turn the heater off,' I snap.

'Bloody hell, keep your hair on.'

Leonard Cohen's *Take This Waltz* plays again for the umpteenth time, and I sigh. Georgie fumbles in her seat and finally sits up.

'I know I said I like Leonard Cohen but this is a bit overkill don't you think? I'll be singing this in my sleep. Are you doing some kind of mind control on me? This is bloody torture.'

'I thought you were sleeping.'

'I was dreaming of James, with Leonard Cohen singing in the background, obviously. I was telling him what a crap fuck he was. I may still text him with that fact actually,' she says angrily pulling her mobile from her bag.

I tilt my head slightly to look at her.

'Bad idea.'

'It's this Leonard Cohen music. It's seriously driving me to slash my wrists.'

'I can't seem to stop it. Nothing seems to work. This car is alive, I swear.'

'Are you seriously telling me that for the entire journey I have to listen to Leonard Cohen while I roast to death?'

I hate to be the bearer of bad news. I raise my eyebrows.

'Oh fuck,' she groans, stroking her head with a stick of *4head*, 'I'll end up with a bloody Leonard Cohen induced migraine.'

A voice butts in with *turn around when possible.*

'Oh piss off,' I say.

'Who the hell is that?' asks Georgie.

'The stupid satnav. I can't turn him off either. He's been telling me *to turn around when possible* for an hour and a half now.'

'Jesus Christ, it's like a bloody Brian Rix farce with you.'

The Jaguar shudders and seems to change gears on its own.

'Christ, what's the bloody thing doing now?' screeches Georgie.

'I'm not sure,' I reply, anxiously checking the temperature gauge.

'The bloody thing needs exorcising. It's possessed.'

There is another shudder and I grasp the steering wheel.

'I'd better pull over onto the hard shoulder,' I say in a panicky voice.

Oh please God don't let there be a problem with the car. I swear Charlie will go mad and he is bound to blame me.

'The services are only two miles away. At least we can get coffee there, and have a pee,' urges Georgie. 'It isn't serious, after all no lights are flashing,' she adds unhelpfully. 'If it's anything serious a light usually comes on, so it must be okay. We'll make it to the services for sure.'

'Maybe this car doesn't give warning lights.'

'Perhaps repeatedly playing Leonard-bloody-Cohen is a warning.'

It shudders again and then begins to splutter and jerk.

'Oh God,' I say anxiously.

'It's having some kind of fit, you'd better pull over. Jesus, I hate peeing in the bushes.'

I slowly move over onto the hard shoulder and bring the car to a halt, along with Leonard Cohen and the heating. Georgie stretches her Pilates-toned arms above her head and groans.

'Now what?'

I open a bottle of coke and drink thirstily from it.

'Phone the AA I suppose,' I say grimly.

'I think it got tired of sodding Leonard Cohen, I mean, who wouldn't? What's Alcoholics Anonymous going to do? My name is Georgie and I haven't had a breakdown since I last played Leonard Cohen,' she laughs.

'It's not funny. This is all I need. Charlie will murder me before he has even married me.'

'As long as you don't call the FFFAA,' she giggles.

I give her a filthy look.

'Cheer up Ali, it could be worse.'

She strains to see her reflection in the mirror while I struggle to find the hazard lights and the number for the AA. The contents of the glove compartment are stacked so neatly that my hand trembles as I search through them for his AA details. Finally, with my heart pounding I abort my mission.

'What do you mean you can't find it?' groans Georgie, wrapping a scarf around her head and shivering.

I pull my shawl tighter around me and tuck my freezing hands inside it.

'Everything is so neat in there,' I say pointing to the glove compartment. 'I'm terrified to touch anything.'

She glares at me.

'How do we get help then?'

'I'm working on it,' I say quietly.

'Oh well, that's okay then,' she retorts sarcastically, 'it will only take them about three hours to get here and by then we will have died from hypothermia, but God forbid you should mess up Charlie's precious glove compartment.'

I suppose she has a point. I'm just about to open the glove compartment once more when a highway recovery van pulls up behind us.

'Yay, the cavalry,' cheers Georgie, who quickly applies lipstick before clambering from the Jaguar.

With the scarf tied neatly around her head she emerges from the car in the manner of Grace Kelly.

'Well hello,' I hear him say in a flirty throaty tone, 'two damsels in distress I see.'

I wouldn't say *in distress* exactly. Mind you, his half-undone flies are distressing me, just a touch. In fact, his whole demeanour distresses me, period. He must be shorter than Ronnie Corbett, with a receding hairline, beer belly and the shiftiest eyes I have ever seen. I really can't believe he is trying to flirt with us.

'We were going to phone the AA but couldn't find their number. Are you going to rescue us?' pouts Georgie acting for all the world like the stereotypical damsel in distress.

He winks in what I imagine he thinks is a seductive manner and saunters towards the Jaguar in the style of James Bond, except he has a slight limp and resembles one of those shifty characters in a horror film. You know the type, the one you stupidly trust even though he looks as suspicious as hell only to have him slash everyone to death. My stomach churns. The last thing I need is for Charlie to find my mutilated body in the Jaguar. He'll never forgive me if he can't get the blood out of the upholstery. The truth is, as desperate as I am to get the Jaguar going again I am terrified of anyone touching Charlie's car, apart from the AA of course, who I know Charlie would trust with his life. I climb from the car, wobble on my wedges, and stroll to the breakdown guy when a huge gust of wind almost knocks me off my feet. I let out a cry as my shawl is whipped from my shoulders and spins around in the air like a kite.

'Oh my God,' cries Georgie, 'that's your cashmere shawl isn't it?'

We stand with mouths open, watching the thing spin round and round in the air like a cashmere tornado. If only I was controlling the strings. The cold icy air stings my face and makes my eyes water. The wind drops and we watch mesmerised as the shawl begins its descent. I look to the right to see an articulated lorry heading towards it and then everything seems to happen in slow motion, and then the shawl is just a few feet from the ground. I try to work out if I can dive into the road and rescue it before the lorry hits it. I must have taken a step forward because Georgie yells *no* and pulls me back so viciously that my wedge slips and I slide backwards, land on my bum, and skid forward into the road all amidst Georgie's frantic screams. This is how I am sitting, with my arse cheeks freezing and my hands over my eyes as the lorry rushes towards the most expensive item of clothing I own, apart from the bras of course. It hits the shawl sending it back into the air before it falls miserably and lands in a crumpled heap. We watch helplessly as two more cars drive unmercifully over it.

'Shit,' mumbles the breakdown man, who looks at us with awe written across his face.

'Don't worry, she's got tons more,' laughs Georgie.

He regains his composure and walks towards her.

'Where are you lovely ladies headed anyway?' he asks cockily while zipping up his flies. For one awful moment I thought he was intending on undoing them even more. That would really have freaked me out.

'Cornwall,' volunteers Georgie before I can stop her.

'Let's get your bonnet up then shall we ladies?' he says with yet another wink. At least I presume he is winking. I'm now beginning to wonder if there is something wrong with his eye. In fact, there doesn't seem to be very much that is right about him. I reluctantly admit to not knowing where the lever is to open the bonnet.

'Leave it to me,' he smiles arrogantly while giving my breasts the once over.

I shudder and grasp my cardigan from the back seat and drape it around me so my perfectly hanging boobs are well hidden.

'I've got a mate in Cornwall.'

Yes, you would have, I think.

'Oh really,' says Georgie feigning interest.

He leans inside the car.

'He lives in Bodmin, you know, well known for the Brown Willy.'

He laughs raucously and hiccups several times.

Good God. Georgie and I exchange looks but remain silent.

'Brown Willy,' he repeats. 'It's a hill.'

I raise my eyebrows and Georgie pretends to laugh.

'You know what your problem is don't you?' he says seriously, poking his head out of the car.

We shake our heads. Oh my God, is this where he produces the garden shears and says *you ran into the wrong guy didn't you* … Slash slash slash. I hold my breath.

'You've run out of fuel. The little indicator tells you that.'

I breathe a sigh of relief. What little bloody indicator would that be?

227

'You are joking?' says Georgie, giving me her most filthy look and hanging onto her scarf for dear life.

'I thought there was a full tank,' I say defensively. 'Charlie normally has a full tank.'

'Well aren't you the lucky little lady,' he winks.

'I'll put a litre in, unless you want me to fill you,' sniggers our rescuer. 'That should get you to the services.'

I glance forlornly at my cashmere shawl, thank him kindly and turn to Georgie who is standing with her hands on her hips.

'If you need to do anything else, I'd do it now. We should really get on our way,' I say as forcefully as I can manage.

'We were on our way until you ran out of petrol,' she snaps.

The breakdown guy slams down the bonnet and shakes his hips at us like some kind of rock god. Frankly it just makes me feel a little nauseous. I only hope he isn't going to break into a performance of Greased Lightning because if he does there is every chance I will throw up. John Travolta he most certainly is not.

'Thank you so much,' Georgie says with a beaming smile and a sidelong look at me.

Good heavens, she surely isn't expecting me to give the guy a tip is she? That isn't to say I can't think of any. I fumble in my bag as they both stand staring at me. I pull out my purse and Georgie grabs it. Before I know what she is doing she is handing him a twenty pound note. I fight back my gasp, watch in horror as he gratefully accepts it and with a final salute walks back to his van. Georgie waves madly as he reverses and I struggle to keep the smile on my face.

'Have you gone mad?' I say, kicking her in the shin.

'It was the only way I could think to get rid of him. I'm dying to have a piss and he'd love to have watched. He was a proper pervert.'

'So we paid him off?'

'Kind of,' she says crossing her legs and hopping towards the bushes. 'I can't bloody hold it.'

'All the same don't you think a tenner would have been sufficient to pay off a pervert? Anyway the services aren't that far, can't you hold it for a bit longer?'

She grimaces.

'I don't hold out much hope for Charlie's Jag then. I may well christen it good and proper, but if you want to get going.'

'You'd better go in the bushes, hurry up though, I'm freezing.'

Two minutes later we are back on the road and I allow Georgie to fiddle with the radio. It is easier than listening to her grumbling.

'Yay, I've found a station,' she squeals, turning up the volume.

'*So Maria, for the Christmas festivities are you going the whole hog,*' laughs the presenter, '*and getting a nice bit of pork?*'

'*Of course John, Christmas isn't the same without a nice bit of gammon. Check our Facebook page for how to cook your pork this Christmas ...*'

'Are you going to Myrna and Phil's?' asks Georgie casually, totally unaware of my inner turmoil.

I nod.

'You won't be getting a bacon butty then,' she laughs.

Oh my goodness. What if the new owners at Trenowyth decide that Pepper will make a nice bit of Christmas pork? No matter what happens I have to rescue him. Edward has probably forgotten all about him by now, in much the same way as he has forgotten about me. I can't bear the thought of him being a bacon butty, Pepper that is, not Edward.

'Talking of which, I'm starving,' continues Georgie. 'I may get one at the services.'

I suddenly feel very sick.

Chapter Thirty-Two

I was perfectly happy to stay in a bed and breakfast close to Stantonford but Georgie has other ideas. After all, this is a short break for her, and she wants to enjoy it. Considering I have every intention of using her as a piglet-sitter on the way home it seems only fair to go along with whatever she wants. The foyer is impressive, housing deep cushioned red-leather armchairs along with a well-stocked bar that boasts the best champagne in the county.

'This is fab isn't it? Just what I'm used to,' she smiles.
My hands are tingling from the cold and my whole body feels weary from driving. I could happily climb straight into bed.

'Dinner is at eight, would you like me to book a table?' asks the receptionist, smiling with a soft welcoming voice.

'Ooh yes,' says Georgie gleefully.
I've never known a woman to eat so much. I really don't know how she isn't twenty stone. I glance around the foyer and my eyes rest on a handsome man who is being tongued to death by a tall blonde. Heavens, it isn't one of *those* hotels is it.

'If you could just sign here, and if we could have your car registration here,' she says pointing to the guestbook.

'Oh good God,' cries Georgie.
I pull my eyes from the sex on fire couple.

'That's okay. I'll just pop out and get it,' I smile at the receptionist.

'Oh no,' says Georgie in a strangled voice.

'What?' I ask.

'Oh my God, what are we doing? We're already booked in at that other hotel,' Georgie says in a slow monotone voice while pulling faces at me.

What the hell is the matter Georgie?

'We are?'

'So sorry,' she mumbles to the confusion of the receptionist. I shrug and take the bag she pushes into my hands.

'Let's go,' she hisses.

'But it's nice here.'

'That's probably why Charlie is staying here.'

I freeze.

'He's here?'

'According to the guestbook he is. What a bastard. I should have known he would pick the best hotel, relegating us to some crap B and B.'

I was right all along. Charlie is in Cornwall and he is planning to rescue the farm animals. I have to warn Jed and all the others. The big question is, when is the big rescue going to happen, and who will be first? I need to study the plans, and soon.

'Come on. We need to get ourselves booked in somewhere quick and go over Charlie's plan. There's no time to lose.'

The cold air hits us as we leave the warm foyer and head back to the car. Georgie unwraps a flapjack and hands me half. I look behind guiltily. It would be just like Charlie to pop his head over my shoulder and say *doesn't that have animal fat in it?*

'I can't believe you're doing this,' says Georgie, yanking the door open with such force that I cringe. 'I bet ten years ago you would never have imagined yourself doing this either.'

She wraps a pashmina around her neck so many times that she begins to look like one of those tribal women with neck rings.

'Doing what?'

'You know, being an activist and fighting ...' she flaps her hand around and looks thoughtful, 'other activists. You know, helping protect the endangered species and all that. Putting your life on the line for the animals ...'

'Well ...' I begin.

'I'm proud of you,' she says getting all teary.

Let's hope she feels this way when Pepper is squealing and shitting in the back of the car all the way home. Mind you, I imagine she will be cursing and moaning so much that we probably won't hear Pepper's oinks. Oh dear, I feel quite sad to think that I had been right about Charlie sneaking up here. Can I really marry a man who isn't honest with me? The thing is if I don't marry Charlie what will I do?

'Oh no, there he is,' shrieks Georgie sliding down in her seat.

Clearly she has forgotten that the car stands out like a sore thumb.

'Go go quick,' she shouts.

I look in the rear-view mirror. Charlie is emerging from the hotel and is busy tapping something into his phone. He looks quite gorgeous in his black overcoat and grey scarf.

'Christ Ali, you don't have time to swoon over your fiancé at this moment in time.'

I wouldn't actually say I was swooning. My Blackberry shrills and Charlie's name flashes up onto the screen.

'He's calling *me*,' I say panicking and struggling to get the Jag into gear.

With my heart in my mouth I watch as Charlie turns and walks away from the car. I push my foot onto the accelerator and zoom around the corner almost knocking a cyclist off his bike. He weaves to the side, wobbles and then thankfully straightens up.

'Shit, shit.'

He gives me the finger while mouthing something unrepeatable. I shakily grab the Blackberry and click it on.

'Oh God, now she's breaking the law and in bloody Cornwall of all places,' sighs Georgie.

'Charlie, hi,' I say, stopping sharply at a red light.

'Bloody hell,' moans Georgie.

'I thought I'd let you know that I've arrived in Leeds,' he says casually. 'Is everything okay with you?'

Leeds, my arse. The little liar.

'Yes, fine, Georgie and I are on the way to the shops,' I say.

Well, we are. It may be the shops in Truro but we are certainly heading towards shops.

'Okay, drive carefully. I'll see you in a few days.'

'I will,' I say, swerving around another cyclist and narrowly missing an oncoming car.

'Bloody bikes. You don't get this in London,' grumbles Georgie giving the cyclist a two-finger salute.

I throw the phone into my bag as the car lurches. This bloody car is driving me insane. I struggle to get into third gear.

'Look out!' screams Georgie.

I look up to see the rear end of a taxi. I jam my foot onto the brake so hard that it sends a pain through my little toe. The car stalls and the next thing I know there is a great deal of honking.

'Where did you learn to drive Mrs?' shouts a bald-headed man as he drives past.

'Christ, this activist lark is all very well but I'm beginning to think I would prefer to be at home, nursing a broken heart and a hangover. In fact, even tea in your mother's conservatory is beginning to seem pleasurable to this,' moans Georgie.

'Tea in Mother's conservatory is never a pleasure, especially when she dishes up her lard-infested mince pies.'

'Driving school for retards was it?' yells the man again as I struggle to start the engine.

'Oh piss off country bumpkin,' yells Georgie, and I die from shame.

'I need Maltesers,' I say. 'Do we have any?'

'I have fig rolls,' says Georgie brightly.

There has to be a good answer to that but right now I can't think of it. The only thing on my mind is how I can hide the Jag. It's not exactly something you can hide under a bush is it? The last thing I need is for Charlie to spot it. We finally book into a tatty B and B on the outskirts of Truro. The nearest eating place is a curry house just up the road where we go to study Charlie's plans.

'So he plans to bombard everyone in one night does he?' says Georgie through a mouthful of chicken biryani. 'After dark, how cowardly is that? I say though, it's terribly exciting. When exactly is this happening?'

I hand her the plans.

'It doesn't say does it?' I mutter, crunching my way through a poppadum while studying the plan.

'Perhaps it's deliberate. Maybe he thought you might find it and purposefully left the date and times off it.'

'Damn it.'

'Do you want any of this mushroom bhaji?'

I shake my head.

'Great,' she says, shovelling it onto her plate. 'How about his emails?' she asks through a mouthful of mushrooms.

I sigh.

'I don't know how to access them.'

Lynda Renham

'Christ Ali, you're a pretty useless sneak. Where else does he keep dates?'

'He duplicates everything in about three diaries. It drives me mad to be honest.'

She chokes on a mouthful of my chicken tikka.

'He wouldn't have a black leather one would he?' she asks, throwing back half a glass of wine.

I nod.

'How did you know that?'

'Because I saw it in the glove compartment, you know, the one you are so afraid to go in.'

'What were you doing in there?'

'That's where I found the fig rolls.'

My eyes widen.

'You stole Charlie's fig rolls?'

Georgie rolls her eyes.

'Forget the fig rolls Ali, just think *diary*. It's in the glove compartment, and you're a fine one to talk, you're the one that raided his briefcase.'

'Okay,' I say sheepishly.

I dash to the car, open the glove compartment with wild abandon and then sit staring at the black book with my heart racing. What am I doing? I should be at home preparing for my wedding, not poking around in my fiancé's things. What's wrong with me? What kind of woman am I who puts a pig before her future husband? No, this is terrible. It couldn't be a worse start to a marriage. I must stop this nonsense once and for all. Edward is in New Zealand and Pepper is most likely at another farm right now, and if not, probably being prepared for someone's Christmas table. Oh God, I mustn't think about it. Charlie is a lovely person and all he wants to do is help the animals, and I should be supporting him not working against him. I push the diary back into the glove compartment and lock the door. That's that. I'll tell Georgie we will drive back tomorrow. As soon as I get back I'll wrap all the presents and put the tree up. That will be a nice surprise for when Charlie returns. I then think of Mona and my stomach somersaults. I tell myself that Charlie is too nice to do anything really awful. All the same, nags my inner goddess, can you really live with yourself if you go home without doing anything? I so

234

hate decisions. Minutes later I am back in the restaurant and handing the diary to Georgie.

'I only hope we're doing the right thing,' I say guiltily.

'Of course you are,' she says handing it back.

'I can't look through his diary. I don't know what I might see.'

She pushes her empty plate to one side, scratches her head and then pulls the diary towards her.

'Would you like the very very nice dessert menu?' asks the waiter with a strong Indian accent.

'Do you have one called *Dutch courage*?' she asks.

'Yes, we have very very nice Dutch courage, I will get for you.'

'What are you expecting to see in here? The dates he has to collect his Viagra?' she scoffs.

I gasp.

'Charlie takes Viagra?'

She shakes her head.

'What do you think?'

'I'm thinking he needs a higher dose.'

She bursts out laughing and pushes the diary over to me.

'It has to be you.'

'No it doesn't. Anyway, I thought you came to help me.'

The waiter returns.

'There is no Dutch courage madam,' he says with a wide smile, 'but we have very very nice saffron rice pudding.'

'Okay,' she agrees pulling the diary back. 'I'll do it on saffron rice pudding.'

I sigh with relief and then hold my breath as she opens the diary and turns the pages to December.

'Ooh, he's bought you a nice Christmas present.'

Guilt washes over me.

'From Ann Summers no less,' she laughs.

I kick her under the table.

'Okay, now I know you're joking. What is in there for today and tomorrow and please don't tell me it's a conference.'

She turns another page and her face blanches and for a second I think she is going to keel over. I'm almost afraid to breathe and begin to think I will pass out if she doesn't speak soon.

'He's not having an affair is he?' I say breathlessly.

She lifts her head and it is as if she has seen a ghost.

'I thought he was playing around,' she says shakily, picking up her glass of wine and pushing the saffron rice pudding to one side.

'I thought us coming here would be a bit of fun. The truth is I didn't really believe it. God Ali, he's even a got a time to collect flares, and I'm not talking trousers. I mean Christ, what does he want them for? What else is he getting, bloody nail bombs?'

'Of course not,' I say grabbing her wine and polishing it off.
Flares? Holy shit.

'I feel like we're dealing with the bloody IRA. They'll be wearing balaclavas.'

'So will we,' I say confidently and beckon to the waiter.

'A whisky, do you want one?'

'Yes, make it a double. What do you mean we will? Bloody Nora, we'll be going tooled up next. I really don't want to be armed and dangerous Ali,' she says downing the whisky in one and then grabbing mine.

'You're driving remember,' she tuts when I go to protest. 'It's tomorrow night. It says here that they will target eight farms. Nine p.m. sharp it says. We have to warn everyone tonight. We must Ali. We should go and see Jed, he knows everyone doesn't he? We can't handle this on our own. Maybe we should phone the police.'

'And show them Charlie's diary? What does that prove?'

'I feel like I'm in a Kimberley Chambers novel. I don't want to wear a balaclava. This is sodding Cornwall not the bloody East End.'

'I don't want Charlie to recognise us and whatever you do don't speak. We'll have to go to a party shop tomorrow.'
She gulps.

'You're not buying flares too are you?'
I shake my head and sigh.

'Balaclavas.'

'Yes madam one very very nice baklava. To share, or one each?' asks the waiter from behind me.
Georgie giggles and stands up.

'I'm going to wet myself if I don't have a pee.'
I watch her walk unsteadily to the loo and wonder what on earth Charlie is planning to do with flares. More importantly, what am I thinking of coming here and attempting to warn everyone. Good heavens, I'm beginning to think I have lost my mind. If Charlie finds out I was the one that sabotaged his operation he would be

embarrassed beyond belief, not to mention hurt. He is my soon-to-be husband after all. Maybe I should just rescue Pepper and not get involved with anything else. *What about Mona?* my inner goddess whispers in my ear. *Don't you care about her?*

'Of course I do,' I say loudly to the odd looks from the waiters and fellow diners. But I have to think of my future, I whisper to myself.

And what about Sara and her parents and of course Jed? How can you just sit back and watch this happen while knowing all about it? Oh, this is just terrible.

'Right,' says Georgie on her return. 'Let's pay and go warn everyone.'

'We can't,' I say bluntly.

'What do you mean we can't? I thought that was why we came all this way.'

The waiter places a plate of baklava in front of her and smiles widely.

'Very very nice baklava to share,' he says.

She pulls the plate towards her and cuts into the sweet.

'I might as well eat this then. It's not like I have a man in my life to stay slim for,' she says stuffing a forkful into her mouth.

'We can't just warn them. I mean, *WE* can't warn them. It's bound to get back to Charlie and they might not believe us and if they do they may phone the police. I'm marrying Charlie in a matter of days don't forget. We have to find a way to do it anonymously,' I say dumbly.

'I've got it,' she says, 'we'll drop leaflets from helicopters. You know, all over the village like confetti.'

I look at her.

'This is not Afghanistan you know,' I remind her. 'Were you thinking of phoning Richard Branson to ask if we could borrow his personal chopper?'

'He owes me a favour for the amount I've paid in train tickets,' she says, pulling a face. 'Okay, well it was an idea.'

'How about coming up with an idea that will actually work?'

'We could photocopy the plan and distribute it all around the village.'

I widen my eyes.

'Okay, that sounds doable.'

'And we could phone everyone on the list and disguise our voices, and wear masks to rescue your pig. That would be okay wouldn't it? Then we pop your pig to the pig sanctuary and drive back home. Charlie will never know and if he is back before you we'll just say we've been Christmas shopping or something.'

Oh dear. It seems now is the time to break the bad news.

'About Pepper,' I begin.

'Yeah,' she says, blissfully unaware of my plan.

'It's just I'm not taking him to a pig sanctuary ...'

Her head snaps up and a small piece of baklava misses her mouth and dribbles down her silk shirt.

'You're surely not taking him back to London?' she asks incredulously, dabbing at the stain.

'Well, where else can I take him?'

She rolls her eyes and exhales loudly before pushing the dessert away.

'Here of course. That's what I thought you were going to do. You know just drop him off at a pig rescue home or somewhere where pigs go. I mean how do I know ...?' she trails off with a groan and puts her head in her hands.

'You can't put him in Charlie's car; it will stink to high heaven.'

'I know. That is why we need to get back before Charlie and get the car valeted.'

'Valeted,' she shrieks. 'Ali, can you hear yourself? If he doesn't smell the pig shit he will smell where it has been valeted. Are you completely out of your mind?'

'I'll tell him I had it valeted as a Christmas gift,' I say defensively.

She shakes her head and signals to the waiter for the bill.

'You cannot put a pig in a car to travel six hours. Christ, we won't be able to open a window it case it jumps out. God Ali, I don't believe you. I'm getting the sodding train home then and ...'

'No,' I shout and quickly lower my voice. 'You have to come back with me. I can't possibly drive and keep a check on Pepper.'

'For fuck's sake,' she moans. 'I hope I get a bloody medal for this, and I'm not talking Blue Peter badge.'

'Thank you,' I say, blowing her a kiss.

'I'm not even going to ask where Pepper is going to live.'

'Well, I ...'

'No, I don't want to know,' she interrupts, 'and before you get any ideas the answer is *no*. No bloody pig is coming to live with me. I know I'm desperate but Christ almighty.'

She stands up abruptly and for one awful moment I think she is leaving me to go home. My heart sinks.

'Come on, I need a good night's sleep or I will never cope with tomorrow's excitement. God help me. Dinner is on you.'

I hug her tightly. I also need a good night's sleep but I somehow have a feeling I won't get a wink.

Edward

I spin Luce around and she twirls expertly before landing pertly back into my arms, her eyes creasing with laughter. She always was good at dancing whereas I am useless.

'Are you enjoying it?' she asks earnestly. 'Malcolm is so thrilled you came. He has been dying to meet you.'

I point to the packed bar.

'Let's get a drink shall we?' I say, deliberately avoiding the question.

'Okay,' she smiles, but I can see the tightness in her mouth.

'Is something wrong Edward?'

I'd been in New Zealand for a week and *everything* is wrong. I'm not surprised; I hadn't expected it to be any other way. Maybe I should have listened to Jed but I like to do things my own way.

'It's a hell of a way to go Ted. I don't mind taking care of everything here but I'm just thinking of you mate.'

And all I can think about is Trenowyth. Maybe Luce was right, I should never have taken on the farm. But I did. Then, of course Alice had come wafting into the farmhouse on a cloud of Femme perfume. Some days I swear I can still smell it in the kitchen. I'm sure it isn't there. It's in my memory in much the same way as Alice got under my skin and in my blood; her perfume has glued itself to my nostrils. I swear I can even smell it here all these miles from England.

I watch Luce as she gets our drinks. She is so comfortable here in New Zealand in a way I will never be. She is fitter than ever and blossoms in a way she never did back home. The life here suits her. Personally, sunshine in December just doesn't seem right. Drinking beer under the stars on a warm muggy night feels alien. Jed said it's freezing back home but he's keeping the place warm so the pipes don't burst.

'The last thing we need is more floods,' he had laughed.

Thinking of floods brings Alice to my mind again. That day I'd come home to find her mopping up the water from the leaky ceiling. Her cheeks had been rosy red from the effort of her shopping trip not to mention the frantic cleaning up. I had desperately wanted to kiss her that afternoon. I push Alice from my mind for the umpteenth time, reminding myself that she is to be married any day now to that toffee-nosed Charlie. Funny the twists and turns that life can take. Just a few months ago I had thought my future was well and truly mapped out. I would get Trenowyth back on its feet and then fly out to join Luce in New Zealand where we would fulfil our dreams and finally marry. I had no idea how much the village would pull me in and how much farm life would fulfil me. Most importantly, I had no idea that my perfect woman would one day waltz into my kitchen and steal my heart. If only I could get her out of my head, but I think that is going to take some time. I have to continually stop myself from rewriting history. That last time I had seen her, what if I had said *don't go Alice, stay here,* what would she have done? Would she have gone back to Charlie? No, I did the right thing. Life on a farm for a city girl would be disastrous no matter what she felt about me. Besides, that Charlie, and he certainly is one, is the kind of guy she ought to marry. He's her type really, not the likes of me.

'Darling, you're miles away aren't you?'

Luce stands beside me with two flutes of champagne. All around dancing under the moonlight are couples happily in love, enjoying the Christmas spirit while all I long for is cold crisp England. I sip the champagne and watch Luce's cheeks turn pink as Malcolm, the chairman of the sanctuary, walks over with his nephew, Jason.

'Edward, it's good to meet you at last. So you're finally joining our little team,' says Malcolm, his ruddy face breaking into a broad grin.

I shake his hand feeling his firm grip in mine. Jason avoids my eyes and holds his hand out awkwardly.

'My nephew Jason, he has been working closely with Luce. We're looking forward to having you on the team. I hear you have been doing wonderful work on your own farm back home in England. You'll be a valuable asset here. How are you enjoying our little party?'

'It's different,' I answer honestly and nod at Jason.

'I hear you've been taking good care of Luce,' I say coldly.

He tries to hide his discomfort by acknowledging a passing guest.

'I've done my best.'

'I'm sure you have.'

Luce squeezes my arm tighter than necessary and gives me an awkward smile.

'So, how's that little farm of yours doing in England?' asks Malcolm, looking at me over the rim of his glass. 'Luce said you've got that out of your system and are ready to do some real work.'

I bristle. Did she indeed?

'Not so little actually, and it's doing very well thank you.'

Lucy blushes.

'In fact, so well that I don't actually think I am going to be able to leave it.'

'Edward, darling, what are you talking about?' Luce asks softly, hooking her arm through mine.

Jason gives me a cold stare and scoffs.

'It sounds like Edward plans on letting you down yet again Luce,' he says cockily.

They exchange glances and Malcolm puts a hand on my shoulder.

'Well when you want to do some serious work Edward, get back to me.'

'When you run a serious organisation, I might well do that,' I snap.

'Edward,' Luce admonishes. 'What's got into you?'

'I could ask you a similar question. Except I'd ask *who* got into you,' I say calmly, meeting Jason's gaze.

Luce gasps and tries to stop Malcolm from walking away.

'I'm so sorry Malcolm, I ...'

He waves a hand.

'We'll see you in the morning Lucy,' he says sternly.

241

'Edward?' she says questioningly.

Jason smiles at me.

'The pleasure was mine,' he says smugly.

Tears roll down Luce's cheeks and I want to hug her, to tell her it really doesn't matter any more.

'You weren't damn well here,' she snaps angrily, wiping roughly at the tears.

'I know,' I say honestly.

'So why have you come at all if you have no intention of staying.'

'Because it's more honest to end it face to face, don't you think?'

'You're trying to make me feel guilty,' she says accusingly.

Jason lays a hand on her shoulder.

'I'll be at the bar if you need me.'

'Truly I'm not trying to make you feel guilty. I wanted to see if you were really happy here, and you are. This life suits you Luce. I thought it would me also, but it doesn't. My life is on the farm ...'

'But there is nothing there,' she cries angrily. 'That village is dead, and they're all old there and it's so cold. I don't understand what you're saying.'

I stroke her hand softly.

'Luce, we want different things ...'

'We didn't always,' she whispers. 'It's not serious with Jason. I just got lonely ...'

'It doesn't matter. I wasn't here, you're right. I don't want to be here Luce and you don't want to be at Trenowyth. You hate it there.'

She averts her eyes confirming the truth in my words.

'Have you met someone else?' she asks softly. 'Or has Sara got something to do with this?'

'Sara has got nothing to do with this. I'm talking about you and me,' I snap.

'There have always been three in this relationship, no wonder it didn't work. I sometimes think that you love Sara more than you love me.'

'You're being ridiculous. You know how things are with Sara ...'

'I don't think either you or Sara knows how it is,' she interrupts. 'You should sort yourselves out for everyone's sake.'

'And you should sort yourself out with that wanker Jason', I say crossly.

She looks at me tearfully.

'Oh Ted. I couldn't do the farming thing, I would go potty, you know that, why don't you just give it a try here?'
I shake my head.

'I know my own mind Luce, that much you know about me surely. I didn't want to end this over the phone, and to be honest this is the most I've seen you since I've arrived, and you've not even tried to make time for me ...'

'The sanctuary is so demanding, and maybe I didn't want to hear what you had to say.'

'My place is on the farm and I can't tell you how much I want to get back.'

'Young Farmers' Christmas bash no doubt,' she smiles through her tears.

'It's not that bad.'

'Neither is Jason,' she smiles, giving him a wave.

'Let's agree to differ,' I frown.
She leans across to kiss me on the cheek.

'I'll always love you, just not in that same way any more.'
I kiss her and hand her my flute.

'I need to book my flight home. This weather in December is driving me nuts.'
Just a few days before Christmas and everyone will be playing happy families and giving presents. It's a time for love. I wonder what Alice will be doing. Cooking up a Christmas storm no doubt with Charlie and planning her winter wonderland wedding, that's if she hasn't already done it. I make my way to the exit and walk slowly to the hotel. After all, there is no reason to rush. I've no one to rush back to.

Chapter Thirty-Three

I decided from the moment we left the restaurant that I was going to be positive about everything. I figured that the slightest bit of negativity could have profound effects on Pepper. Yes, I know he is a pig but right now he is the closest thing to a child I have. Of course I am sure that Charlie and I will go on to have dozens of kids. Well, okay not dozens, but enough. And we'll have one of those huge homes where it takes people all of ten minutes to navigate through the pushchairs, toys, wellingtons, and I suppose a save-the-whale poster in the hall. Okay, maybe not whales as I hope they would have been saved by then but some kind of animal-saving poster. Yes, that will be my life in a few years. At least I hope it will be as I really could not cancel a second wedding. Although I do have reservations about being called Mrs Alice Marrow, and do you blame me? For some reason whenever the name Marrow comes up I think of those marrowfat peas. How awful is that? *Please stand for Mr and Mrs Marrowfat-Pea.* Oh God, I can't bear it. One thing I am determined about is that Charlie will never ever find out that I was the one that thwarted his big operation. So when Georgie and I enter the costume shop the next morning I look for the biggest mask in the shop. The assistant is engrossed in conversation on the phone.

'Hiya,' says Georgie to the spotty-faced assistant in her *you're my best friend* voice, 'how are you today?'

I mime two fingers down my throat.

'What?' Georgie mouths innocently.

I shake my head.

'I'll call you back Max, I've got customers,' says the assistant, making it sound like a couple of stray animals have just wandered in.

'We need masks,' says Georgie, 'for a fancy-dress party.'

I sigh.

'Yeah, that's why most people need them. I didn't imagine you were robbing a bank or hijacking a plane,' responds the assistant with a yawn.

Or gatecrashing an animal rescue attempt.

'What kind of party is it?' she asks.

'Yes, what kind of party is it?' Georgie asks me.

How the hell do I know? I shrug helplessly. I still haven't worked out a plan yet.

'It's a masquerade party is it?' she asks, checking her text messages.

Georgie exhales loudly and says,

'It's a sex orgy actually.'

She finishes typing her text and looks up swinging her long black hair to the side.

'Oh yeah, and my boyfriend is Brad Pitt.'

She leads us to the Venetian masks and I study them with fascination.

'This cat one is fab,' declares Georgie. 'I might get this one.'

I look at her despairingly.

'Georgie, I can clearly see it is you. They have to cover our whole face. The last thing we want is for anyone to recognise you. I thought we agreed balaclavas?'

The girl gives me a funny look.

'Balaclavas at a fancy dress? What you going as, bank robbers?' she giggles. 'What you need are Bauta Masks then. If you don't want anyone to recognise you, they are the best. Everyone is wearing them for the Stantonford Young Farmers' Christmas Ball tonight. Is that the one you're going to? Oh no, I forgot you're going to an orgy aren't you?' she laughs.

'Farmers' Christmas party?' I repeat.

'Yeah, you know as in farmers celebrating Christmas. You do know what a farmer is don't you?' she asks sarcastically.

'We're only the Wurzels' biggest fans,' Georgie grins.

'This is great,' she whispers to me. 'We can go to the party and no one will know it is us.'

The girl pulls open a drawer and produces a dozen colourful, sequinned masks.

'Then,' she adds in a creepy voice, 'the ultimate. This will certainly help you to hide your true identity and have them guessing.'

With a flick of her wrist she produces a cape which she drapes around Georgie's shoulders. I gasp as Georgie suddenly becomes anonymous.

'Cool,' I say staring in awe.

'Drives my boyfriend insane,' laughs the assistant.

Yes, well maybe now we are getting just a little too much information.

'Planning to pull are you?' she asks.

'Only a pig,' responds Georgie, admiring herself in the mirror.

'I know what you mean. Men they're all the same aren't they?' she says, popping a stick of gum into her mouth.

'How about guns?' I say before I realised I have said it.

Georgie gapes at me.

'Crikey,' says the girl, her eyes lighting up. 'You really are robbing a bank. Cool.'

She fidgets excitedly,

'I get it, *Pigs* right?' she adds, contorting her face with an exaggerated wink.

'Oh no,' I stammer.

'You know what you need?' she says, seeming not to hear me.

Our brains tested?

'Smoke bombs.'

'What?' Georgie and I say together.

'Creates a smoke screen or I can get you the ones that just create a hazy atmosphere. What bank are you robbing? I hope it's bloody Barclays, the bastards wouldn't give us a mortgage,' she says with an evil glint in her eye.

Jesus, she will be telling us to do the bank manager's knee caps next. Georgie winks at me.

'It's not a bad idea, as a pre-emptive strike against Charlie's flares, and we can use them if things get out of hand.'

'Out of hand?' I squeal.

If you ask me things are already getting out of hand. There is a little tinkle as the shop door opens and an elderly couple enter.

'My boyfriend has a gadget shop, he can get replica guns and the bombs,' says the assistant. 'His smoke bombs are brill. They look like little grenades.'

'Christ, can you keep your voice down,' I hiss.

'When are you doing it?' she whispers.

'We're not.'

'Yes we are,' Georgie disagrees.

'Not a bank,' I argue.

'A building society,' cries the girl.

'We're not robbing anything,' I hiss louder than I mean to and the elderly couple turn to look at us.

'Why do you need guns then?' asks the assistant.

God, why does everything have to get so complicated?

'Guns,' say the couple in hushed tones backing slowly towards the door.

'I told you Truro was rough,' says the woman pulling her husband from the shop. 'I much prefer Redruth.'

I don't believe this. We came here to be inconspicuous. At this rate we may as well take out an ad in the local rag telling everyone we are here.

'We're actually activists,' explains Georgie. 'Well that is we're kind of secondary activists. The first activists are coming to rescue the animals but we don't think they should, so we're the activists to stop the activists from committing their activist activities.'

I shake my head.

'You what?' asks the girl.

'Yes Georgie. You what?' I mimic.

'So what are the guns for?' the girl asks confused.

'So I can shoot her,' I say pointing angrily at Georgie.

I knew I should have come alone. Twenty minutes later we set off with a box of smoke grenades and a plastic AK47 assault rifle stashed in the boot. I have no idea what we will do with them, if anything at all. Any hopes I had of staying positive had flown straight out of the shop window. I am now consumed by feelings of doom. If we can't buy a couple of masks without problems then how on earth can we thwart the mighty FFFAA? Georgie pushes a Cheryl Cole CD into the Jag's music player and turns the volume up.

'This is all getting dead exciting. I'm going to enjoy tonight. Do you think Jed will be there?'

'I haven't said we're going,' I say, hearing myself sound like a party pooper.

'What do you mean?' she shouts above the music. 'We've got the masks and we can warn them?'

The truth is now that we are here I have no clear idea what to do. I somehow hoped once I arrived a plan would miraculously form in my head.

'I thought we were going to phone everyone?' I argue. 'But it's all getting complicated.'

'So why have we got the masks? It's not fair to say we can't go,' she says, sounding like a petulant child.

'You suggested the masks for rescuing Pepper.'

'I don't think Pepper will squeal on us,' she laughs. 'Anyway they will be wasted on a pig. Come on Ali, let's go. It will be fun. Everyone will be there so it's the perfect opportunity to let them all know. Just because Edward won't be there ...'

'That's not true. Edward has nothing to do with it. He's in New Zealand, and anyway I'm engaged to Charlie.'

'Oh yes, the wonderful Charlie with his perfect company pension plan.'

'Honestly anyone would think I was marrying him for his money, which I can assure you I am not.'

'I never said you were. Keep your Primark drawers on.'

'I'm wearing my freebies for your information.'

'Ooh hark at you, and I seriously think you should slow down.'

'What?' I ask, fumbling in my bag for some Maltesers.

'Slow down,' she repeats, pointing at the speedometer, 'you're doing sixty in a forty speed limit.'

I look with confusion at the speedometer. How can that be? It only feels like we're doing about thirty. In fact, I was just about to put my foot down even more. We screech around a bend and the bag of Maltesers spill over my lap.

'It's my boots,' I say.

'Well, that's the best excuse I've ever heard.'

'Oh, buggeryfuck,' she groans as we zoom past a policeman who happily snaps us with his speed camera.

'Sod it,' I yell pushing my foot down onto the brake but hitting the accelerator instead.

'What in buggeration are you doing? screams Georgie. 'Stop, for God's sake, stop.'

'I'm trying to,' I say as my legs turn to jelly.

'You could have fooled me.'

I bring the car to a hasty halt and we sit in silence. In the rear-view mirror I see the policeman walking towards us. The question is what do I do? I can't possibly tell the policeman the truth, the whole truth and nothing but the truth. The shit will most certainly hit the fan if I do. There will be a raid on the farms and Charlie and his friends will all be arrested and all because of my AllSaints boots. That will teach me to be extravagant. Play it cool, that's the best thing.

'Oh God, what are we going to do? Shit, oh shit,' moans Georgie.

'I'm going to play it cool,' I tell her.

She scoffs.

'You've never played anything cool in your entire life so you can't start now.'

She's quite right of course.

'Step out of the car please madam,' instructs the young policeman and I mean *young*. Heavens, he looks like he has just left school. I'd better not flutter my eyelashes or I'll be arrested for assaulting a minor.

'Hello,' I say in my friendliest voice.

'Were you aware that you were breaking the speed limit?' he asks in a boyish voice.

I point down to my boots.

'I'm so sorry. It's these silly boots. How fast was I going officer?' I say respectfully.

He pulls his shoulders back at the word *officer* and, oh no, did I really just flutter my lashes. Honestly it comes to something when you have no control over your eyelashes.

'According to my colleague, who clocked you five minutes ago, you were doing seventy.'

I hear Georgie gasp. Colleague? What sodding colleague? Seventy, oh my God.

'Colleague?' I say in a strangled voice. 'Seventy, are you sure?'

Oh, what am I saying?

'Are you disputing that?'

Georgie opens her door.

'Officer, if I could ...'

'Stay in the car please madam.'

'He caught you on camera just before the bend. Can I see your licence?'

You know that feeling of doom I was talking about? Well, I feel it is about to become a reality. I fumble shakily in my handbag and finally pull out my purse. I grab the pink photo card and hand it to him. He stares it for several seconds and hands it back to me. I sigh with relief.

'That's a Boots Advantage card. Are you trying to be clever with me?'

Piss it.

'Are there enough points on it to pay the fine, officer?' I joke in a trembling voice.

'I hope you're not trying to bribe me,' he replies seriously, taking a step back.

With Boots Advantage points? He surely cannot be serious. He is probably too young to even need razor blades.

'No, I was just ...'

'Step out of the car madam,' he says angrily to Georgie.

Georgie emerges from the car looking like a terrified rabbit with eyes darting all over the place but unfortunately mostly darting towards the boot. I could gladly have murdered her. I find my licence and hand it to the officer almost curtsying as I do so.

'I'm so sorry. They look so similar.'

Georgie rolls her eyes.

'Is this your vehicle?' he asks suspiciously.

At last, now I can explain why I am so nervous.

'It's my boyfriend's car and, the thing is he doesn't know I have brought it to Cornwall ...'

'Are you saying you have stolen it?'

I never said that did I? I look to Georgie for confirmation. She shakes her head stupidly.

'No, of course not ...'

He cocks his head.

'Obviously I can understand why you would think that ...' I say quickly, not wanting to upset him further. If Georgie rolls her eyes much more they will disappear into the back of her head. That will teach her.

'He has gone to Leeds on business and he said I could use the car, but only around London. We thought we would come to Cornwall for the ... for the ...'

He looks at me expectantly.

'For the sun ...' pipes up Georgie.

For the sun? In bloody December? What is she on?

'... beds,' she adds quickly. 'They have the best sunbeds and spas here. We thought we'd come for a pre-Christmas treat.'

I give her an impressed nod.

'Is that right?' he says with a frown. 'Is there something you need in the boot?'

Georgie sways unsteadily.

'No,' she chokes.

'You can't seem to stop looking at it.'

He clicks a button on his radio and Georgie frowns at me.

'Can you run a check on vehicle registration Charlie-Mike-1-2-Foxtrot-Foxtrot-Alpha, Probably personalised and currently being driven by an Alice Lane.'

He looks at me curiously and I force a smile.

'Open the boot please.'

Oh no.

'Oh,' breathes Georgie guiltily, her face turning white and her eyes as wide as saucers. I feel my stomach turn over.

Okay, I must stay calm. There is absolutely no reason to panic. What am I talking about? There is every reason to panic. My eyes stray unwillingly to the gun that sits innocently in his holster. I really should mention the replica gun and grenades. Oh really Alice, and just how do you plan to do that?

'Before I open the boot officer I should just mention the replica AK47 assault rifle in the boot and oh yes, the replica grenades.'

I don't think so.

'The thing is ...' stutters Georgie.

I glare at her. The police officer's eyes penetrate mine.

'Please open the boot Miss Lane.'

Oh dear, why does he have to be so insistent? I so need a boot full Maltesers right now. Instead I have a boot full of grenades. Classic. The radio crackles and a voice says,

'Can affirm vehicle is registered to a Mr Charles Marrow of Chelsea.'

'Can we just pay the fine?' begs Georgie in a strained voice. 'We really don't want Charlie to find out that we were in Cornwall. He will be *very* cross and will no doubt take it out on Alice.'

I give her a sharp look. What on earth is she saying? The officer's eyes hold mine for a second and he says,

'Do you have reason to fear Mr Marrow?'

'No, of course not, it's just that ...'

Before I have time to reply he has taken the keys and clicked the boot open. The light hits the gun and grenades, and they glint beautifully in the midday sun. The masks seem to smile at us and I suddenly feel very sick. I gasp and Georgie sways unsteadily, mumbling *oh shit* under her breath. For one horrifying moment we all stare at them and the only sound is the crackling of the police radio. Georgie pushes me forward.

'For God's sake don't just stand there, show him the gun,' she yells.

Suddenly there is mayhem. The officer yanks the gun from his holster and points it at us menacingly while yelling,

'Step away from the car. Face down on the ground, both of you, NOW,' he yells.

'Holy shit,' cries Georgie. 'We're not fucking Thelma and Louise you know.'

'On the ground NOW,' he yells again, his voice shaking.

The radio bursts into life as he clicks it back on.

'Requesting back up, repeat requesting back up, have two females, armed and dangerous. Driving vehicle Charlie-Mike-1-2-Foxtrot-Foxtrot-Alpha. Boot full of ammo. Possible terrorist attack. Close all access roads to Truro.'

Isn't he getting just a touch carried away? Two females armed and dangerous? Boot full of ammo. God if I ever needed Maltesers now is the time. I wonder if my mother can bring a crate. Heaven knows how long we'll be banged up for. What am I thinking? I'm sounding like a gangster. I can't go to prison, I can't even be arrested. I need to warn everyone of the turkey attack. I look down at the wet ground and slowly lower myself. This is going to ruin my Fat Face jeans. I could kill Georgie.

'You can't be serious,' argues Georgie. 'Look at the state of the ground. It's been raining all morning.'

'Face down now. Fucking do it.'

Christ this is like something out of *The Sweeney*. I half expect him to say *you're nicked* as he grabs my bag roughly and rummages through it.

'Who are you working for?' he demands.

'I'm not at the moment. I'm actually looking for a job ...'

'What fucking organisation? Don't play games with me.'

Shit.

'Tell him,' screams Georgie.

'The NHS,' I say. 'But not any more ...'

He waves several sheets of paper in my face but all I can focus on is his gun. I am going to die on the A39 to Truro and all because I was going to a fancy dress party. My mother will have to identify my bullet-ridden body. Don't think about it, Ali, just don't.

'Christ, I'm in a Martina Cole novel,' groans Georgie.

Georgie and her damn crime novels.

'Don't piss with me,' he yells again.

'Bloody hell,' gasps Georgie as sirens blast from all directions and helicopters drone above us.

'All this,' she says, wide-eyed, 'for a replica gun. I dread to think what they would have done if we'd had the real thing. Shit, I reckon he would have bloody shot us.'

Three more police vans skid to a halt and dozens of armed police spill out with rifles aimed and decorating us with laser marker dots.

'What the fuck did you say?' asks the officer as he cautiously approaches the gun that sits innocently in the boot.

'Jesus, I don't believe this. Are you two for real?'

'We are but they're not,' she says cheekily above the noise of the sirens.

'I think we're in deep shit Ali, deep shit Truro,' Georgie laughs as the officer fires water into the air from the AK47 rifle.

'You are disturbed,' I laugh back.

Oh well, it was fun while it lasted, but Thelma and Louise we are not.

Chapter Thirty-Four

After a lot of undercover investigations, which Georgie performs with such aplomb that I truly feel she has missed her vocation, we discover the ball is being held at Bradley Hall, a mile out of the village of Stantonford, and is costume or cocktail dress.

'I learnt a lot from P. D. James,' she smiles.

By six-thirty I am ready. I stand in front of Georgie in my new white Tulle sweetheart cocktail dress. A glass of red wine in one hand and shimmering for all I'm worth. She assesses me glumly.

'Do you need that black sash thing?' she asks critically.

'The black sash thing hides my tummy,' I say miserably, knocking back the wine.

'Ah yes, you have got fatter.'

'Fatter,' I say, my voice rising several octaves. 'What do you mean fatter? Surely that means I had to have been fat in the first place.'

She looks at me critically.

'The sash makes you look like one of those Gladiator women.'

I gasp and pour more wine into my glass.

'Gladiator women? This just gets worse Georgie.'

'Well, it's the bloody sequins at the top. They would be okay but with that sash you look like you're about to enter the arena.'

I whip the sash off angrily and her face lights up.

'That's better. Do you have a corset or something?'

I shake my head. She jumps up and rummages through her case while I sip more wine to calm the churning butterflies in my stomach.

'Here,' she says, gleefully holding up what looks like some kind of Lycra torture instrument.

'What's that?' I cry, feeling tears forming in my eyes at the sight of it.

'It will squeeze all the fat in.'

'All the fat? I'm not bloody Lisa Riley you know.'

I snatch it from her and dash to the loo. Five minutes later, red and panting, I return and she claps her hands.

'Perfect, you look fab, even a bit Cheryl Cole like. If you put your hair up you'll look quite sophisticated.'

'But I can't breathe, and how do I pee?'

'There's a little hole in the gusset. You'll cope.'

I check the hole and sigh.

'It will be like peeing through a Polo Mint.'

'You have to suffer for your art,' she says, squeezing into her own dress.

'What art?'

She shrugs.

'I'll think of something.'

'Just as well I have a fiancé. It would take forever for someone to get a grope through this lot,' I say, spraying myself with Femme.

'Trust you to think of sex,' she laughs. 'We're not going there to enjoy ourselves,' she reminds me, 'we're on a mission.'

'It will be a mission impossible in this corset,' I say, attempting to sit only to find I can't cross my legs.

Ten minutes later, somewhat inebriated on red wine and staggering on black snake three-inch stilettos we resemble Charlie's Angels as we march towards the Jag.

'Into the fray,' bellows Georgie as she tumbles into the car and swigs from a bottle of Southern Comfort. 'Let's go slaughter them.' Georgie is obviously on a mission of her own.

***

Fifteen minutes later we are parked on a street corner opposite Bradley Hall, and the place is totally congested with tractors.

'I can't do it,' I say, my throat dry.

'What do you mean you can't do it?' Georgie snaps.

'I can't go through with it. I feel sick,' I say, dropping my head onto my chest.

'Look, we're here now. All we have to do is go in. Put our leaflets onto a few tables; mention it to a couple of people and leave.'
I'm far from convinced.

'What if someone recognises me?' I say anxiously.

'They won't. I don't even recognise you.'
Another tractor arrives and the passengers step off the trailer.

'Don't these people have cars?' asks Georgie, studying her face in the rear-view mirror.

'I think it's tradition. I have a vague memory of Dominic mentioning something about that.'
She licks her lips.

'A lot of talent here lady. Let's go,' she says gleefully swinging back her hair and applying gloss to her lips.

'We're not here to pull,' I remind her checking my own reflection which compared to hers seems very inadequate.

'Speak for yourself, I'm newly single.'

'How can you be newly single when you've always been single?'

'You're so argumentative. Pass the masks and capes.'
I cannot believe how many people are entering the building. We'll never be able to find anyone here. There are so many beautiful and original costumes that Georgie and I seem quite plain by comparison. We watch intrigued as someone climbs from the tractor dressed in a gorilla suit. There's always one isn't there? Another is disguised as a gypsy fortune teller and I recognise her laugh as Sara's. She is wearing green velvet trousers and a colourful jacket. Her head is covered with the most amazing turban but I would know her laugh anywhere.

'I feel underdressed,' Georgie complains, snatching the Southern Comfort from me.
We will be so pissed, we won't be able to see straight at this rate, and God knows I need to see if I am going to piss through a Polo Mint.

'Some are wearing cocktails like us. Put your mask and stuff on and let's go, otherwise I'll lose my nerve. How are yours?' she asks.

'I wouldn't know. I've lost all feeling from the neck down from wearing this Spanx thing of yours.'

'You complain too much. Come on.'
She lifts her hand for a high five.

'Once more into the fray. Into the last good fight I'll ever know.'

'Live and die on this day,' I respond.

I take a final swig of Southern Comfort and open the Jag door. I attempt to take a deep breath which, let me tell you, in this corset is like having my ribs crushed.

'Fuck it's freezing,' cries Georgie.

I tuck my arm into hers and we wobble up the driveway to the entrance, jostling with all the other masked guests. I step into the hall and the sound of Girls Aloud almost bursts my eardrums.

'Hello ladies,' says a burly man, who I recognise as the village butcher. 'How are you this evening?'

'Fab,' smiles Georgie, and I swear I can hear her eyelashes fluttering.

I feel my heart skip.

'Got your tickets have you?'

Shit. Now why didn't I think about that one?

'Oh,' I say stupidly.

Georgie lets out a loud sigh and moves closer to him.

'Did you leave them in the car honey? Please don't make her go back in this cold weather,' she says seductively.

Good heavens, I never knew Georgie had it in her. A raucous group arrives behind us and I can barely hear the doorman's response. There is loud laughter and groans, and an overpowering smell of a cocktail of perfumes. All the men are wearing heavy overcoats and I feel a desperate temptation to steal one as I am shivering so much. I can see into the oak-panelled hall where masked couples are dancing amid tables covered in crystal and shimmering with lit candles. A group of women in backless cocktail dresses push past us, waving their invites as they do so. How could I have been so stupid not to have realised the ball would be by invitation only?

'What's going on? It's cold back here,' shouts a man good-naturedly.

I feel a presence at my side and before I can speak a heavy coat is thrown around my shoulders, and a familiar fragrance takes me so by surprise that I feel my legs weaken.

'What's the problem Mike?'

Oh my God, Edward. It can't possibly be. No of course not, it's just the Spanx is stopping the blood from getting to my brain and I am hallucinating. All the same, I feel myself trembling so much that I seriously may pass out. I'm shaking more with the overcoat on than before I had its warmth. It can't be him. He is in New Zealand, or at least he is supposed to be. Perhaps it's someone with a voice like Edward's. He won't be able to tell it's me, it's too dark in the hallway and my face is closely hidden. Keep your mouth shut Alice. I try not to inhale his familiar smell, but the coat is caressing me with the scent of him, sending a surge of emotion through me that is so powerful I can barely breathe. It's all I can do not to turn around and look at him. A thousand memories assault my brain and I sway towards Georgie and hold onto her arm.

'We left our tickets in the car,' says Georgie without any attempt to disguise her voice. Does she not realise Edward is standing next to me? Is he masked also? I am too afraid to look. His hand rests on my shoulder and I'm sure he can feel me trembling.

'I'll vouch for them Mike,' he says, and the hand is suddenly gone.

I close my eyes and when I open them all I see is Georgie.

'You're quivering all over, are you all right?' she asks.

'Yes,' I mutter, keeping my head down.

'Let's get inside,' she says, taking my hand.

I glance behind me to a mass of people in overcoats and fancy dress.

'Where did he go?' I whisper to Georgie, taking her hand and allowing myself to be led into the noisy ballroom.

'What?' she yells.

I wobble on my heels and grab a drink from a passing tray. Georgie jiggles to an empty table and I follow wobbling as I go, feeling like my legs will give way any second. I look at the men and struggle to see their faces, but everyone is so well hidden behind a mask or a costume that it is impossible to recognise anyone. I down my drink and immediately regret it, and make a quick bolt for the loo. I push my way through the throng of dancers and lock myself in a cubicle. I must calm down, this is ridiculous. I pull the mask off and check my reflection in my mirror. My face is flushed and my lips pink. It couldn't have been Edward, I must pull myself together. You can do this, and Charlie will never know, and you'll have your fairy-tale wedding and all this will be behind you, I assure myself. I'm not quite sure where Pepper will be but I'll worry about that later. Right now the most important thing on my agenda is peeing through this ridiculous hole. I don't mind making sacrifices to look good but when nobody actually knows it's me it rather all seems a bit pointless. The sound of hooting laughter and the banging of the loo door draws me back to the ball.

'I don't believe it,' screams a woman, 'and your parents were fine about it?'

'Yes, absolutely great, especially after they talked it over with Ted.'

I recognise Sara's voice and contract my muscles to stop peeing. Honestly Alice, what's wrong with you? Sara won't recognise the sound of your peeing I whisper to myself, feeling the Lycra roll up and pinch my navel. I stifle back a cry and bite my lip.

'Well, I just know the two of you will be really happy, and I'm thrilled it's finally out in the open,' says the other voice and I fight back my gasp.

'I know, can you believe it? Ted is so great isn't he?' gushes Sara, and I can picture her flushed cheeks and sparkling eyes.

'I'm thrilled for you guys, I really am. Is it going to be a spring wedding?'

Spring wedding? Oh my God. In my distress I miss the hole and splash over the Lycra.

'Bugger,' I say, and quickly bite my lip again to shut myself up.

There is silence and then a giggle before Sara says, 'Come on, let's get back. Frankie will be here soon and I can't wait for you guys to meet.'

There is the sound of a door opening and the loud thumping music from the hall reverberates around me and then all is silent. Looking down at my feet with my heart hammering in my chest I recall her words. Sara and Edward are getting married. He must have gone to New Zealand and broken up with Lucy, short for Lucinda, but everyone calls me Luce and now he's marrying Sara. I'm such a fool. He never fancied me. What was I thinking? Tears fall onto my knees and my vision blurs. How did I get everything so wrong? The happiest times of my life were spent here. I don't love Charlie, at least not enough. I wipe at my tears angrily. I must not cry, after all it's no worse than him being in New Zealand. Why am I kidding myself? It's much worse. I'll always know that the man I love is just a few miles up the motorway, or is it down? Anyway, the point is, being back here has made me realise that it is Edward I love. What a fool I have been. How can I possibly marry Charlie? How can I possibly marry anyone? I shakily dab at the Lycra and curse Georgie for making me wear it. I then repair my tear-streaked face and put my mask back on. The sooner this night is over the better. I enter the noisy ballroom again and look for Georgie. I spot her at the buffet and walk towards her and notice our leaflets on the tables. Blimey, she is a fast worker. I have almost reached her when a hand grabs me and I am spun into someone's arms. Before I know it I am dancing with the Phantom of the Opera. He twirls me around so fast that I barely get a second to look at him. As the music moves to a slower pace he pulls me close and whispers.

'Enjoying the party Alice?'

I gasp. Dominic, but how did he recognise me?

'You look, and smell, gorgeous, as always,' he whispers.

'How did you ...?'

'I have my spies, besides your perfume is a giveaway.'

Oh no, did Edward recognise it too. How could I be so stupid? What does he mean spies? His hand grips mine and I find it difficult to get away. I see Georgie looking at us.

'Dominic, you need to know that there will be a raid on lots of farms tonight. You need to warn everyone ...'

'What are you talking about?' he laughs, pulling me even closer as the tempo changes for a slow dance.

I try to pull away again but he holds me too tightly. He smells of whisky and I turn my face away.

'My fiancé has arranged it. He is part of the FFFAA ...'

Oh dear, I have had far too much to drink and the *FFFAA* sounded more like *fay.* He won't have a clue what I am going on about. His lips brush my neck and I shudder. Something about Dominic makes me uneasy. Now I think about it there has always been something about Dominic that made me uneasy. I think back to the night I went to his house and feel myself stiffen.

'We know all about the FFFAA Alice. You worry too much. Why don't you just enjoy yourself? Your information is all wrong, we know when it's happening and it isn't tonight. Relax.'

He releases me slightly, spins me around and pulls me close again. What does he mean? How do they know? Who told them? I strain to see Georgie but she has gone.

'It must be tonight,' I say insistently and try to pull myself out of his arms but he pulls me roughly back and I can see the perspiration on his neck.

'I just told you it isn't tonight Alice. Anyway, where is your fiancé this evening? Playing away from home are you?' he laughs, his lips brushing my neck again.

I struggle to push him away. My heart races and I feel panicky. The lights dim and then there is darkness. I let out a small cry along with many others.

'Okay guys, time to reach out for a new partner,' shouts the DJ and I feel a hand pull me from Dominic's grasp.

There is laughter and the lights come on again. I find myself looking at a masked man's profile but I know from the fragrance it is Edward, and feel my body weaken.

'Good evening,' he says politely.

He doesn't recognise me.

'Hi,' I mumble, relief enveloping me.

'I'm not a great dancer,' he says, the familiar lilt in his voice making me heady.

He twirls me to the music and my breathing returns to its normal pace. We dance silently and I feel myself relax and begin to enjoy myself. Then the music changes to a slower tempo and, I don't believe it, Leonard Cohen's 'Take This Waltz' drones through the PA system. For a minute I seriously consider getting the gun from the boot and shooting the sodding DJ. I wait for Edward to release me but he pulls me in closer and I inhale sharply.

'Hopefully I won't step on your toes,' he says softly.

He slides his arm around my waist and guides my arms around his neck. I look nervously for Sara. My eyes fall on Georgie who is chatting to someone by the bar and she sees me, rolls her eyes and makes a wrist slashing movement in sympathy with the music. Does she realise I am dancing with Edward?

'Have you had your tongue extracted?' Edward asks suddenly, 'Or have you taken a vow of silence?'

Shit. Can I say both?

'No,' I reply.

He will think I am a retard or something.

'I like your perfume,' he says casually. 'It reminds me of someone.'

'Oh,' I say, laying my head on his shoulder.

His lips gently touch my cheek as I do so. His hand squeezes mine and his finger moves across my engagement ring.

'Is the lucky man here?'

He twirls the ring around my finger and then intertwines his fingers in mine.

'I'm not sure,' I say honestly. I so don't want the music to end and I never thought I would say that about Leonard Cohen. We bump into another couple and they laugh merrily at us.

'Happy Christmas,' they yell in unison.

'You're not sure where you fiancé is?' he questions, seemingly ignoring the couple.

'Where's yours?' I say boldly, trying to disguise my voice and failing miserably. I sound like Lily bloody Savage.

'I don't recall saying I had one,' he whispers into my ear and then gently kisses it.

Oh my God, this is awful. How can he do this with Sara in the same room? I feel like giving him a piece of my mind but I feel a strange tingling in my loins and it has nothing to do with the Spanx.

'But if you really want to know, I left her in New Zealand snuggling up to someone else ...'

I gasp.

'But ...'

I stop as his hand moves from my neck and strokes my back, stopping at the top of my buttocks. He waltzes me to a quieter corner of the room as Leonard Cohen croons *There's a concert hall in Vienna.*

'Have you ever been there?' he asks.

I feel like my breath has got trapped deep inside my body, no doubt in the Spanx somewhere. I lick my dry lips.

'Where?'

'Vienna,' he whispers, his voice husky.

My body is going crazy with desire for him. If this goes on much longer I will drag him outside to tear his clothes off. But he is marrying Sara and I am marrying Charlie. He is acting like a man who doesn't have a fiancée and I'm not behaving much better. I make a feeble effort to pull away but he gently eases me back into his arms.

'Would you like to go,' he whispers breathlessly into my ear, 'to Vienna?'

'Yes,' I whisper back.

'I'd like to take you,' he says so softly I barely hear him. His lips are on my cheeks and moving closer to my lips.

'Yes,' I say again, barely able to breathe as his hot lips meet mine. I close my eyes and spin round and round to Leonard Cohen. I'm on a carousel of love. My arms are wrapped tightly around his neck. My mouth opens to meet his tongue and it is like I had never left him. The music stops, his lips leave mine and I realise he is speaking to me.

'What?' I say shakily.

'I said, what would Charlie say?'

My head snaps up so forcefully that I feel sure I hear a crack. I pull off my mask and stare angrily at him.

'How dare you pretend not to know me,' I say, fighting back tears, 'and with Sara here too.'

He removes his own mask. He smiles and his eyes twinkle.

'How dare I pretend? You should have known your perfume would give you away, and what's Sara got to do with anything?'

I realise he is still holding my hand and against my will I snatch it away. I am shaking with anger and desire, and at that very moment I couldn't hate him more. I open my mouth to speak but the sound of screaming stops me. We turn to the woman who has rushed into the hall whipping off her mask as she does so.

'I've just seen flames and smoke coming from Mona's. Oh God, someone do something.'

Chapter Thirty-Five

'Shit, they've started already,' cries Georgie. 'Of course, it may just be the flares ...' her voice breaks and I see she is crying. 'God Ali, I'm so scared. I never really thought it would happen.'

The hall is in bedlam with people talking on their mobiles. Dominic's voice booms over the loudspeakers and I look up to see him on the stage.

'Keep calm everyone, everything is fine. We've been on the phone to Mona and it was just some Christmas fireworks. No need to worry. Everything is under control.'

He signals to the DJ.

'Let's get this show back on the road folks shall we?'

'What's he doing?' shouts Georgie above the noise.

'I don't know,' I say looking around for Edward but it is impossible to spot him. 'We've got to get to Mona's and warn the others. Chuck leaflets everywhere. Give me some. I'm going to the loo to get out of this Spanx before I explode in it.'

I grab some leaflets and wobble to the loo where I struggle out of the corset, the whole time forcing myself not to think of Edward and Sara and their forthcoming engagement. How could he do that to her? What a bastard. The memory of his hands on me makes me again feel like I am on fire. I can't believe Edward could be so cruel. I fight back tears of frustration. I don't have time for this, I have to rescue Pepper and help the other farmers. Oh Charlie, how could you do such a terrible thing? Leaving leaflets on the sink I dash out of the loo my stilettos clip-clopping in the empty hallway. Turning the corner I walk straight into Dominic's arms.

'There you are,' he says, irritation in his voice.

'Dominic, we have to get back. You have to help us stop this mayhem that Charlie is planning and ...'

Something about his expression stops me dead. I step aside him to walk past.

'I'll have to tell Charlie to keep you on a tighter lease in future,' he says, grabbing me by the wrist.

'What!'

My stomach summersaults and I feel like I am going to throw up. He pulls me back towards the loo.

'I should have known it was you,' he says laughing.

I don't know what he is talking about but I do know he is scaring me.

'I don't know what you mean Dominic but I really think you're not hearing me. Charlie is planning ...'

'Oh for God's sake Alice, stop whining. I know what Charlie is doing.'

He spins me round to face him.

'Dominic Montfort, the president of the FFFAA, very pleased to make your acquaintance.'

His voice echoes in the cold hallway and my head spins. What did he say? No, that can't be right. Just a minute though, didn't Charlie say the president lived in Cornwall?

'But you ate *meat*. You cooked a meat dinner for me. Why are you saying this? You're a farmer ...' I say naively.

He shakes his head impatiently.

'Do grow up Alice. You don't for one minute think I give a shit about the stupid animals do you? It's the land I want. Do I look like a farmer to you? I nearly had Trenowyth but you fucked it up.'

'Me?' I say; my voice hoarse. It's like I'm in some awful nightmare.

'Getting that stupid Edward to fall in love with you. Of course, he wasn't going to bugger off to New Zealand once you came along was he? I can't say I blame him,' he says, running his fingers across my breast like a spider while his other hand tightens around my wrist.

'I could have got Trenowyth for next to nothing. I ran the place into the ground when the old man was ill.'

I gasp.

'Don't look so shocked dear Alice.'

How did I not see this Dominic before?

'I was a help to the old man. You ask the village, I helped at the farm every day but he wouldn't let me do anything. Every two minutes he forgot what he had told me. I ask you, how was I supposed to keep up? It was no surprise they lost the milk licence, the old man changed his mind every second, and he always forgot to clean the milking machines.'

'He had dementia,' I say.

I'm so stunned that all fight has gone out of me.

'I nearly got it Alice and then fucking Fairfax comes along and gets all legal. Do you know how many houses can be built on the land these idiot farmers piss about on? Well, I'll show you. After tonight, they'll all want to sell what's left of their farm's land. There'll be no farms for them to go back to. They'll be begging me to take them off their hands and just think of all those animal lovers I will have pleased in the process.'

'You're sick,' I stutter, punching at his chest feeling fear overwhelm me.

'You bastard.'

I reel around at the sound of voice, although I don't need to look to know it is Edward.

'I knew you were behind the ruin of the farm, I just needed you to admit it. You can expect to receive a summons tomorrow morning.'

'Careful Edward,' I scream. 'He may have a knife.'

A knife? What am I saying? This is Stantonford not Whitechapel, and these are farmers not the bloody Essex Boys. I scream and turn away as Edward throws a punch.

'This is from my father for what you did to his farm ...'

'Fuck you,' yells Dominic as he falls to the floor.

The ballroom door bursts open and Georgie and Jed stand wide-eyed.

'Let's go,' she says grabbing me. I pass Sara and another woman who is talking into her phone.

'Ali,' she says, stopping me. 'What's happening?'

I feel my face grow hot.

'I'm so sorry,' I say, looking down and see that I have a wine stain on my dress. I stupidly try to remember when that happened. She tilts my head up and smiles.

'It's not your fault. We're grateful you have come to warn us.'

Georgie tugs at my arm.

'Come on Ali, Jed is waiting. We have to hurry. The police will be here soon and then Charlie will know it was us,' she says anxiously.

I nod.

'I mean about Edward. I really do hope you'll both be very happy.'

Her face creases and she cocks her head to one side.

'I don't know what you mean?'

I sigh.

'You and Edward getting engaged, I want you to know I am thrilled for you both.'

Like hell I am. God, I am a good liar.

'I'm not getting engaged to Edward,' she laughs. 'Whatever gave you that idea? I love him like a brother and he has been great helping me come out to Mum and Dad. It's Frankie I'm marrying,' she says pointing to the woman on the phone beside her who nods absently to me as she talks animatedly into the mouthpiece.

'Although, if I was into men, Edward would certainly be my choice.'

'Close your mouth,' whispers Georgie. 'The place is full of bugs. Now, come on.'

She pulls me roughly by the hand.

'Oh, and congratulations,' she calls back to Sara.

'She's a lesbian,' I say, gasping as the cold air hits me.

'There are a lot of them about. Shameful isn't it. Now, will you please focus?'

I'm not sure I can take any more surprises. I'll be discovering Charlie is a transvestite next.

Chapter Thirty-Six

I can't take my eyes off the flames from Mona's barn. The smell engulfs me. Mona's screams resonate above the sirens from the fire engines and I hate Charlie more than I have ever hated anyone in my entire life. There are cows mooing and running in panic while Jed and the others struggle to get them under control. Georgie weeps beside me and all I can do is look down at my feet and for some stupid reason think of my trainers in the boot of the Jag and feel a need to go back and get them.

'How did we get the time so badly wrong?' asks Georgie, her tear-streaked face imploring me.

My thoughts drift to an image of the Phantom of the Opera.

'Dominic must have told them to start earlier once he realised we knew.'

Mona stands beside me staring at the remains of her farm buildings, sobs wracking her body.

'Why would they do this?' she asks.

I have no answer to give her. I want to think that Charlie believes what he is doing is good. That he really believes in this cause but I'm starting to see him as an egocentric maniac who got brainwashed by the likes of Dominic. Memories of him praising the president at the FFFAA meetings flood my brain. How could he have been so stupid, so naïve? It doesn't seem possible. Why didn't he see Dominic for what he was? I put my arms around Mona and hold back my tears.

'I'm so sorry Mona. We'll get it back the way it used to be ...'

'We won't,' she sobs.

'We will,' I insist. 'We will Mona, I promise.'

Jed walks towards us, his face red from the heat and perspiration running down his face.

'We've got most of the herd Mona. They've taken the sheep and the cowsheds are ruined, but we'll get the bastards. We will get them.'

He turns to me and shakes his head.

'I swear when I have finished with Dominic he will wish he'd never been born,' he grunts and walks away.

'Jed wait,' Georgie calls. 'Where are you going?'

'Matt Hardy's, his place is a mess apparently. We'll be at this all night. I really don't know how you can even consider marrying that wanker Alice, I really don't.'

'I'm coming with you,' Georgie says and looks earnestly at me.

'I'm sorry,' I say, feeling that everything is my fault.

'Thanks to you we have a list of the farms. That helps. I'm only hoping the police stop them soon. They don't hold out much hope though. Your wonderful fiancé has good intelligence it seems. He is always one step ahead of us,' he says, looking closely at me.

Georgie gasps.

'Jed, what are you saying?'

He shakes his head in confusion.

'I don't know, I'm sorry, it's going to be a long night.'

'Is Edward okay?' I ask quietly.

'I've not heard anything. Strange isn't it, that Edward's farm doesn't get torched?'

'Jed, I ...'

He shrugs and allows Georgie to grab his arm.

'Are you coming with us?' she asks.

There's nothing I can do to help.

'Can you drop me at the Jag? I want to get my trainers and go to see Pepper. I need to talk to Edward too.'

'Like he wants to talk to you,' mumbles Jed.

I ignore him and take Georgie's hand. Ten minutes later and I am standing by the Jag. Georgie kisses me and we agree to meet back at the B and B. Sirens are screaming and all I want to do is plug my ears so I don't have to hear them any more. How can this be the work of my future husband? My engagement ring sparkles at me. I angrily pull it off and chuck it into the glove compartment. The future seems so unknown now. I know that I cannot marry Charlie. I will never be able to forgive him for this. Whatever the future holds I need Edward to know how sorry I am. I start the Jag and glimpse my face in the mirror. I attempt to tidy my messy hair and finally give up. It is hard to remember that we had started the evening looking so good. We had been happy and feeling positive that we could stop the operation. The truth is we never believed it would actually happen, at least not like this. Driving to Trenowyth reminds me of the first time I had driven there. It feels like only yesterday that I had nervously driven down the lane to the farm. I follow the bend and take the turning for the dirt track and feel my pulse quicken. An orange glow lightens the sky and my breath catches in my throat when I smell smoke. It's probably just stuck in my nostrils from earlier I tell myself. However, that doesn't stop my heart from hammering in my chest. Reaching the gate I take a deep breath before stepping out of the car to open it. The burning smell hits me like a smack in the face and for a second it is difficult to breathe. Before I know what I am doing I have jumped back into the car and am pushing my foot hard onto the accelerator. Oh God, please let Edward be okay? Please God, oh please God. Grabbing my Blackberry I see there is no signal.

'Goddam it.'

The car roars down the lane and for one awful second the car seems to lose control as I skid to avoid a stray sheep that stands in the road.

'Fuck,' I bang the Blackberry against the steering wheel.

Trenowyth is ahead of me. I can hear Molly barking and wonder where she is. Please don't let her be trapped anywhere. All the farmhouse lights are on but my eyes are glued to the barns. The smoke from the fire irritates my throat even as I sit in the car and I struggle to open the door. I fall from the Jag as my legs give way and sit in the mud staring at the flames and feeling their heat. Then I am up and hurtling towards the burning buildings as though my life depends on it. The air is thick with smoke and my head thumps. I stop, feeling my body go numb with panic. I don't know what to do. I literally don't know what to do. I dash back to the car, coughing and choking. Mercifully there is a bottle of water on the back seat which I use to soak the Lycra corset and hold it over my mouth before venturing back to the farmhouse. Feeling the Blackberry vibrate in my hand I look to see it is Georgie calling. Frantically I gasp into the mouthpiece. I try to speak but just splutter something incoherent before it cuts out. My eyes are watering so much that I can barely see, but I make out the outline of Edward. He is carrying Pepper in his arms and heading for the house with Molly at his heels.

'Edward,' I scream.

He stops and looks at me before running to me with Pepper under his arm. I stupidly find myself wishing I looked better. I seriously couldn't look any worse now could I? He reaches me and I feel his comforting arms around me and I can't stop crying. His lips are all over me and I cling onto him for dear life.

'Alice, Alice,' he keeps repeating over and over while I keeping saying,

'I'm so sorry, I'm so sorry.'

Molly jumps up at us and barks continuously. Edward pushes me back and hands me Pepper.

'Put him in your car. I've got to get back. The bull is going mad and I need to tranquilise him.'

I grab Pepper and slide my hand reluctantly out of Edward's. As I turn he says quietly,

'They may still be here Alice, be careful.'

Oh God. He takes a gulp of the water from the bottle.

'Keep your face covered. Help should be here soon.'

He disappears along with Molly into the smoke and I'm overcome with panic. My hands tremble again and I stumble back to the car feeling my legs wobble beneath me. I gently place the squealing pig into the back seat.

'There, there. It's okay,' I say reassuringly but think it is actually me I am trying to reassure. As I grab the torch from the glove compartment the sparkling of my ring catches my eye. I give it a cursory glance. The sky is illuminated from the blazing barn and the torch seems redundant. Covering my mouth with the wet Lycra I walk slowly towards the barn feeling the heat becoming more intense as I get closer. The Lycra dries quickly from the heat of the fire and gives little protection. My throat seems to close up and I gulp down some water, only to cough it all up again when my throat refuses it. My head spins as I am overcome from the acrid smoke and feel faint with the heat of the flames. I grab a nearby tree and fall against it, sliding down as I struggle to breathe, feeling a numbness overpower me. The roaring of the flames becomes distant and I willingly allow my heavy lids to close and darkness begins to envelope me. The last thing I remember whispering is,

'Edward I love you and I'm so sorry.'

Chapter Thirty-Seven

'Alice,' cries a familiar voice.

I am yanked up by strong arms and something is being pushed over my face. I struggle to fight and splutter as an oxygen mask is placed over my mouth. Charlie's eyes look into mine and sadness is reflected back at me.

'What the fuck are you doing here?' he yells, removing his own mask.

'We have to get to Edward,' I say hoarsely, pulling away from him.

'We have to get out of here,' he screams, 'Things are way out of hand. They are maniacs. Alice, will you listen to me.'

He pulls me roughly towards the car.

'No, you're going the wrong way,' I say slapping him.

'Christ Alice, what the fuck is wrong with you? These people are nutcases. They're not animal activists, they're thugs. Everything is out of control; even I don't know what's going on. I'm scared Alice. I've tried to contact the president, but ...'

'Get off me. Montfort is a fraud and a monstrous brute,' I scream hysterically, freeing myself and running to the barn.

I watch terrified as Edward struggles to open the doors of the cowshed to free the herd. I shout his name but he cannot hear me above the noise from the cows. The cows pour from the shed like a river between us and I see Edward pick up his tranquiliser rifle and walk to the bull shed. As he opens the door I watch with horror as the adjoining barn collapses, sending burning splinters through the air, igniting the shed like kindling. My heart stops as a burning beam falls across the doorway, trapping Edward and Molly inside, and I can no longer hear the howling flames around me or the cries from the cows. There is just silence. And then my eyes fall upon the rifle and

273

my heart beats again and I hear nothing but the drumming of my heart like a jungle war cry. Edward must have dropped it outside the shed and now he is trapped inside with the bull. I run to the doorway but back away from the heat of the flames. Edward is hemmed between the barn wall and a stack of crates, with the bull snorting and banging like crazy. Molly runs round and round trying to control the bull while backing away from the flames. It then seems like everything is happening in slow motion, Edward's eyes widen when he sees me at the doorway and he shouts, telling me to get away from the shed and for a moment the bull seems to calm down and turn to Edward. To my horror the bull lowers his head, snorts and charges at Edward. I feel sick with fear as the crates scatter and Edward is knocked to the ground. I then see that Charlie is holding the rifle,

'Shoot it,' I scream.

His hands shake. The bull backs up and I see Edward crouching behind a few crates.

'Fucking shoot it Charlie, do it,' I scream.

'I can't take an animal's life,' he sobs.

'It's a *tranquiliser* gun,' yells Edward. 'For pity's sake man, shoot the bull.'

'I don't believe you,' says Charlie, turning the gun on Edward.

My God, what is he doing? The bull lowers his head and scrapes the floor with his foot while Molly stands between him and Edward, barking and snarling at the beast. I close my eyes as I can't bear to look.

'Shoot the damn thing you fucking asshole, or I'm gonna splatter your ugly face all over this nice car.'

I open my eyes to see Georgie pointing the AK47 replica at Charlie's head while Jed looks horrified.

'I thought you would never come Thelma,' I mumble.

I hear a yelp from Molly and the angry snorting from the bull. Charlie drops the rifle and stares shell-shocked as the bull gets ready to charge at Edward. I throw myself forward like my life depends on it and reach for the tranquiliser gun.

'Alice hurry, hurry,' screams Georgie.

My hand slides around the butt of the gun and I aim at the bull's neck.

'No,' screams Charlie.

I squeeze the trigger. Nothing happens.

'Alice,' Georgie screams. 'Hurry.'

I look wildly at Edward.

'Release the safety catch Alice, you can do it,' he says calmly.

I slide the catch up carefully, aim again at the bull and pull the trigger. I am about to fire again when the bull's legs collapse and he totters.

'Enough,' says Edward shakily.

The bull lies limp and I reach out to Edward, and with Georgie and Jed's help we pull him from the barn.

'Goddam it Ali, I think you got a knack for this stuff,' laughs Georgie through her tears.

'I believe I do,' I say, attempting a weak smile.

Charlie leans against his Jaguar.

'Ah, sorry about the dent on your Jag Charlie, but it was blocking our way,' says Jed with a twisted smile.

'You're insane Charlie,' says Georgie, squirting him with water from our replica AK47.

I don't know whether to laugh or cry, and fortunately I don't have to do either as blue lights from the fire engines appear moments later. Thank God for friends like Georgie.

Chapter Thirty-Eight

'The last time anyone saw Dominic was outside the hall,' says Georgie. 'He told someone he was going to his farm. The police called but he had gone and so had his passport they said.'

'So he's got away with it,' I say miserably, allowing the doctor to tend to my swollen ankle.

Trenowyth is surrounded by police cars and fire engines. Through the open doorway I can see Edward talking to a policeman while Molly sits forlornly beside him, licking her injured paw.

'You'll be all right,' says the doctor. 'The ankle is sprained but it will be okay. Take two of these for the pain.'

I take the prescription and thank him.

'What are you going to do?' asks Georgie, inclining her head to the police car where Charlie sits.

'He said he didn't know about the stuff that Dominic had organised,' she says disdainfully.

I look at my feet.

'I believe him,' I say softly.

'Well then you're a fool. If they don't do him for arson they should do him for being an arsehole,' she quips.

She looks at Pepper who is squealing in her arms.

'Here, this is yours,' she wrinkles her nose. 'At least I don't have to travel back with him, although I have to say he is quite cute. I could actually live down here myself and look after the pigs, there is a certain attraction,' she smiles looking at Jed.

Charlie had begged me to forgive him saying he will give up all his animal activism work if I did. He has promised to make me the happiest wife ever. I believe him when he says he knew nothing of Montfort's plans.

'You must think me an utter fool Ali,' he had cried. 'I had only good intentions in rescuing the animals. I couldn't hurt an animal Alice, I ...'

'I know,' I said.

'I don't even know who those people were. I was expecting the Cornish branch of the FFFAA, not a bunch of thugs. Oh God Ali, say you'll forgive me?'

How could I not?

My eyes meet his as the police car pulls away. I jump as a hand strokes my arm. I turn to Martha and give her a weak smile.

'I'm taking these two back to my place. A hot bath and Horlicks is what is needed,' she says.

Jed has wrapped a blanket around Georgie's shoulders and she is snuggled up close to him.

'I like her,' Martha whispers softly with a wink of her eye. 'She's what Jed needs.'

I nod.

'What about you?' she asks.

'I have to speak to Edward.'

'Well, there is plenty of Horlicks if you want to pop over later.'

***

I stand by the door. Edward is at the sink washing his hands.

'Are you okay?' I ask.

He looks at me and my heart reaches out to him when I see his bruised face and bandaged arm.

'It's just a dislocated shoulder, I'll live,' he smiles.

'They've arrested Charlie,' I say dully.

'He said he didn't know anything,' he retorts, slipping his arm into its sling.

'I believe him,' I say softly. 'He was set up by Dominic.'

Neither of us moves and I have no idea what to say next.

'He begged me to forgive him. He wants us to carry on and put this behind us. He promised to make me the happiest wife ever.'

He shrugs and turns back to the sink.

'I'm pleased for you.'

'I said no. I told him I don't love him, not any more.'

His shoulders drop but he says nothing. There is an unbearable silence that seems to last forever.

'Will the farm be okay?' I ask finally.

He exhales.

'It wasn't that great to begin with was it?' he says with a smile, turning to me. 'I was the lucky one. The next few weeks will be hard. We'll all rally round Mona and Matt and get them back on their feet.'

'I'm sorry,' I mumble.

'It isn't your fault.'

We stand in silence until I can't bear it any longer.

'Well, I should go to Martha's. She has Horlicks waiting for me.'

I turn to the door with a heavy heart.

'Of course there will be lots to do. I expect I will need a housekeeper. You don't know of anyone do you? Obviously she will have to get used to having dogs up her skirt,' he says.

'I think I may know someone,' I say.

'Really? I can't pay much, and she may have to cope with spiders in the bath.'

I shrug.

'Oh, she doesn't mind spiders, or animals up her skirt,' I say.

'Is that right?' he grins.

I nod happily.

'She'll need to comfort and cheer me,' he grins, beckoning with his forefinger.

I move into his open arms.

'She refuses to shop at Lidl though,' I say laughing.

'Fine, I'll draw up a contract.'

'Oh Edward,' I cry, covering his face in kisses

'You didn't think I could get this place back on its feet without you did you?'

Molly paws us affectionately and we all fall backwards against the sink and then Edward's lips are on mine, demanding and possessive. Molly howls.

'Get down dog and wait your turn,' he laughs.

I slide my hands over his buttocks and smile.

'It's good to be home,' I whisper.

The Valentine Present
and Other Diabolical Liberties

On arriving home after a friend's posh wedding, launderette worker Harriet, finds her life irrevocably changed when she discovers her flat ransacked and her boyfriend missing. In a matter of hours she is harassed by East End gangsters and upper crust aristocrats. Accepting an offer she can't refuse, Harriet, against her better judgment becomes the fiancée of the wealthy Hamilton Lancaster, with dire consequences. What she had not bargained on was meeting Doctor Brice Edmunds.

The Valentine Present and Other Diabolical Liberties is Lynda Renham's funniest novel so far. A cocktail of misunderstandings, three unlikely gangsters, a monkey and a demented cat make this novel a hysterical read. Follow Harriet's adventure where every attempt to get out of trouble puts her deeper in it.

Coconuts and Wonderbras

A Romantic Comedy Adventure

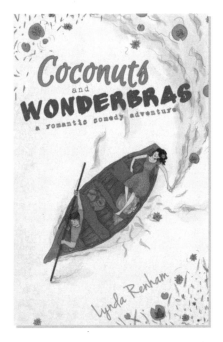

Literary agent Libby Holmes is desperate for her boyfriend, Toby, to propose to her and will do anything for him and if that means dieting for England then she'll have a go. However, when Libby's boss introduces her to her new client, Alex Bryant, her life is turned upside down. Alex Bryant, ex-SAS officer and British hero, insists Libby accompany him to Cambodia for a book fair. What she hadn't bargained for was a country in revolt. Libby finds herself in the middle of an uprising with only Alex Bryant to protect her, that is, until Toby flies out to win back her affections. Come with Libby on her romantic comedy adventure to see if love blossoms in the warm Cambodian sunshine or if, in the heat of the day, emotions get just too hot to handle.

Croissants and Jam
A Romantic Comedy

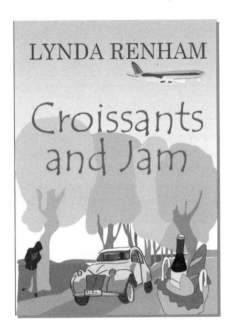

Annabel Lewis (Bels) has two days to get to her wedding in Rome, but her journey is beset with one disaster after another as fate takes its turn. Will the stranger she meets on the way get her to her wedding on time or will he change her life forever? Come with Bels on her humorous romantic journey to see if she marries Mr Right, or if destiny takes her in a different direction.